BOTTICELLI'S MUSE

Botticelli's Muse

Dorah Blume

Illustrated by

D. Bluestein

JUICEBOXARTISTS PRESS
Boston, Massachusetts

Composed in Adobe Garamond Pro at Hobblebush Design,
Brookline, New Hampshire (www.hobblebush.com)

Cover design: Jo Walker
Usage: Flora, detail from the Primavera, c. 1478 (tempera on panel), Botticelli, Sandro (Alessandro di Mariano di Vanni Filipepi) (1444/5–1510) / Galleria degli Uffizi, Florence, Italy / Bridgeman Art Library

Printed in the United States of America

Publisher's Cataloging-In-Publication Data
(Prepared by The Donohue Group, Inc.)

Names: Blume, Dorah. | Bluestein, D. (Deborah), illustrator.
Title: Botticelli's muse / Dorah Blume ; illustrated by D. Bluestein.
Description: Boston, Massachusetts : Juiceboxartists Press, [2017] | Series: [Arno] ; [1]
Identifiers: ISBN 978-0-9981316-0-3 | ISBN 978-0-9981316-1-0 (ebook)
Subjects: LCSH: Botticelli, Sandro, 1444 or 1445-1510--Fiction. | Painters--Italy--Fiction. | Women weavers--Italy--Fiction. | Man-woman relationships--Fiction. | LCGFT: Historical fiction.
Classification: LCC PS3602.L86 B68 2017 (print) | LCC PS3602.L86 (ebook) | DDC 813/.6--dc23

Published by
Juiceboxartists Press
P.O. Box 230553
Boston, MA 02123

Inside us, stories whisper. From the past, the present, and the future. I dedicate this book to those who've left me behind with their sentences unfinished, and to those still with us whose words seek a home. To all late bloomers who dare to take down dictation from the voices within, I say, *"Coraggio!"*

ONCE UPON A TIME . . .

. . . and a very real time it was, there was a land in which Jews and Christians lived in relative friendship. The friars would preach their Lenten sermons and mobs would go into a frenzy. But tempers would cool swiftly and the Jews would repair their broken windows and venture out to meet their Christian friends, and they would carouse in the streets. It was a brief time: the fourteenth to the sixteenth centuries. It was a small land: from Rome to Milan and from Genoa to Venice, a land of rolling hills and rich valleys and a Mediterranean sky . . . In the golden years of Florence, when the Medicis ruled and Botticelli, Donatello, Ghirlandaio, and Leonardo da Vinci were transforming the bare walls of churches and palaces into beauty that forever astonishes, Jews moved with familiar ease through the streets and were part of the everyday scene of that magnificent city. . . .

—Chaim Potok/ *Wanderings*

Italy in 1477

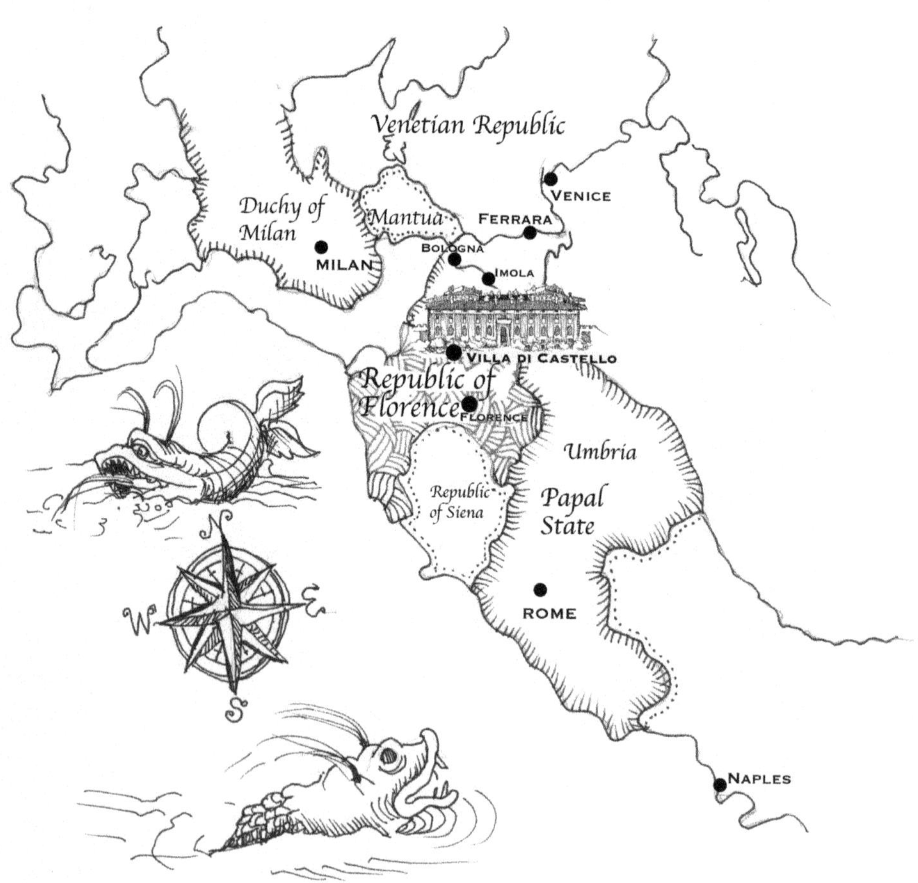

Time and place

Florence, Italy, and around Tuscany, Ferrara, and Imola in 1477 and 1478.

Main characters

Sandro Botticelli, Medici court artist

Floriana, Sandro's muse for his painting *La Primavera*

Gerome (Girolamo) Savonarola, Dominican cleric

Piero de' Medici, Sandro's new, fifteen-year-old patron, an orphan; his full name is Piero di Lorenzo di Piero di Cosimo di Giovanni di Bicci de' Medici

Oslavia, Sandro's sister, a nun

Other characters

Renata, Margarita, Donata, Piero's younger sisters

Poppi, Piero's former nanny and current housekeeper

Lorenzo de' Medici, Sandro's former patron and distant cousin to Piero

Giuliano de' Medici, Lorenzo's younger brother

Claudia, Giuliano's beloved, pregnant by him out of wedlock

Lucrezia Tornabuoni de' Medici, mother of Lorenzo and Giuliano

Bandini, Oslavia's superior

Smeralda and Mariano, Sandro's parents

Marsilio Ficino, clergy, tutor to Piero's sisters, and philosopher and member of the Platonic Academy and translator of the works of Plato and Aristotle

Luigi, a ten-year-old country boy who assists Sandro and lives at the caretaker's cottage on the monastery grounds

Clarice, Lorenzo's wife

Manfredo and Graziella, the moneylender and his unmarried daughter

Piattini and Dono, acolytes and traveling companions of Gerome Savonarola

Bernardino, Franciscan Jew-catcher and converter

Petrarchio, Bandini's assistant

Stella, tarot card reader and midwife

Filippino, Botticelli's assistant and son of artist Filippo Lippi

Contents

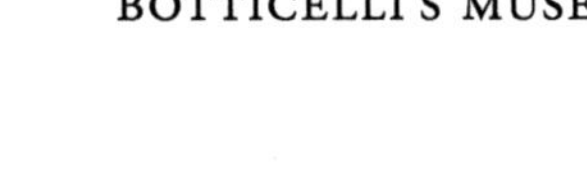

BOTTICELLI'S MUSE

Summer

Florence on a Summer Night in 1477

Above the Arno, pink and lavender skies grow dark
while bat wings flutter high enough so Fear sleeps.

CHAPTER ONE

Somewhere in the Tuscan Hills
July 21, 1477

THE YOUNG WOMAN heard the cry of locusts pulsating in the scorched air. As she floated on her back, her nipples pierced the pond's surface. The sun baked her face. Long strands of hair laced about her head, and a thin chain of gold glittered around her neck. A flock of birds hidden deep in the cypress pines sang to her, and she hummed to them against the chorus of the mating cicadas.

She had walked off through the woods while the others rested. Soon, she knew, they would be searching for her. She quickly rose from the pond and stretched her arms to the sky. As she waded to the shore, her eyes swallowed a sea of yellow—sunflowers cresting over the hill to the water's edge where she had dropped her clothes. She stepped onto the bank. She shook her hair out; then, at the instant she knelt to reach for her dress, a weight fell on her back, the sting of rough cloth against her skin, and the grip of a hand covering her mouth.

CHAPTER TWO

A Monastery in Tuscany
August 21, 1477

NO FACE-TO-FACE CONTACT ALLOWED. No touching. No speaking permitted. Only a knock signaled her daily bread. Once the afternoon prayer bells sounded, the prisoner would listen for the scrape of a basket against the stone walls leading to her tower cell. As soon as the descending footsteps faded, she would slide the tiny door panel open to pull a basket woven of thorny branches inside.

On the first day of her imprisonment, she pierced her lips biting into the bread where thorns lay hidden beneath the crust. She soon learned to tear small pieces from the loaf to remove any thorns before rolling the bread into small pellets she placed in a circle at the bedside table. These she ate slowly to contain her hunger until the next ration appeared.

After several days of confinement, her ankles swelled. The sour scent of her unwashed body sickened her. As the weeks continued, she moved trancelike through a daily drill she had devised to keep her fear and hunger at bay.

She performed the ritual always with the first bread pellet, which she placed under her tongue. She imagined herself no longer in the tower, but lying on the ground under a canopy of thickly woven, thorn-covered branches—the same branches from which her food basket had been made. Thin shafts of light penetrated the vaulted ceiling. Unlike the harsh, dangerous branches of the basket, these imaginary branches held the blessed presence of rosebuds. As she lay beneath this image of flowers among the thorns, she allowed the small pellet to swell with her saliva, then slide down her throat. With the first swallow, she would watch in her mind's eye as the buds burst into full bloom, obliterating the thorns and releasing a sweet perfume.

With the second bread pellet, she would conjure a happy memory to calm herself.

Today, she recalled the path leading to her village outside Ferrara. The cool evening breeze sounded like the roll of the ocean as it rustled through the trees. The moon, an icy sliver, hung in the purple night sky. She imagined herself as a child, weaving together flower stems as she traveled by wagon with her family. Her father had shown her how to double the braid to make it as strong as rope.

"Together," he had said, "we'll climb to the moon and watch the gathering storm clouds. We'll find the lost sheep grazing on the hillside, and discover, at last, where the wolf sleeps."

His fingers were round and thick at the knuckles, like the carrots he grew on their land. She saw them as extensions of his loving embrace as she fell into a peaceful sleep. Dusk descended over the land to mark the end of her thirtieth day of confinement.

Later that night she awoke to the sound of labored breathing as footsteps ascended the stairs. No one had ever come to her cell at this hour. She braced herself in the dark against the straw mattress. Her cheeks burned with an intense heat. A jangle of keys outside her door filled her chest with a dread deeper than her cavernous hunger.

CHAPTER THREE

Our Lady of the Most Holy Rosary

A SECRET TUNNEL joined Oslavia's convent—Our Lady of the Most Holy Rosary—to the monastery where the young woman had been held prisoner for thirty days. The ultimate authority over both houses of God, Father Bandini, had ordered Oslavia to judge if the sinner in his tower had a soul that could be saved.

At midnight of the prisoner's thirtieth day, Oslavia pulled herself off her bed and fell to her knees in a prayer for strength in her encounter with the harlot. She rehearsed her steps to the girl's door: *Light a candle, descend into the cantina, walk to the other side through the damp catacomb-like corridors, announce myself by a bell. Too large and too weak to climb the tower stairs, Father Bandini will have assigned the elderly hunchback Petrarchio to lead me to the tower cell.* After that she could imagine nothing, only feel a sense of dread.

As Oslavia and Petrarchio climbed to the top of the tower, their candles flickered against the stone walls. He stopped every few steps to catch his breath. She kept her distance. The odor from the cracked garlic bulbs he wore around his neck to ward off evil spirits permeated the narrow stairwell.

Oslavia coughed. Soon, another terrible odor overwhelmed the garlic as they reached the final landing. *Perhaps the prisoner has already died and is decomposing.*

Petrarchio pulled out a heavy chain, removed a key and handed it to Oslavia, turned to descend, but stopped.

"Hood yourself!" he said in a gravelly voice to the creature behind the door.

Once Petrarchio was out of sight, Oslavia tried the lock until it turned. Before she pulled open the door, she said, "Tell me that you are covered and then I will enter."

"Covered," a faint voice answered.

As Oslavia entered the cell, the stench of human waste assaulted her. She used the candlelight to approach the young woman's cot, willing herself not to think about what might be lying underfoot in the dark. Beneath the hood of shame, the girl's body shivered in the stifling heat of the tower.

"You were allowed to come here among men?" the young girl whimpered.

"As abbess of the sister convent, I have been ordered to judge if you are a sinner who can be saved or a devil who must be burned."

"I have done nothing. I have been sinned against."

"The young men of the cloth say you offered your body to them, to lure them from God."

"While the others rested, I offered myself to a pond to cleanse myself and one of them pounced on me and defiled me."

"Which one?"

"I could not see his face nor hear his real voice. Only a cruel whisper like the hiss of a snake."

Oslavia waited.

"He told me to say nothing. It was between me and him and God he said. But I do not share your God!"

"Then harlot you are for sure!"

"I have my own God."

"Enough!" Oslavia said. The girl's chest, which had been rising and falling, froze in mid-breath.

"Remove the hood," Oslavia ordered.

When the girl lifted the cloth from her head, Oslavia saw welts on the young woman's face. One look at her, even in this dim light, told her this was no harlot. A tiny Star of David hung from a fine gold chain around the girl's neck reflected the candlelight.

"Tell me what you remember," Oslavia prompted in a gentler tone.

"I remember the taste of earth in my mouth. The crunch of it between my teeth. The smell of it inside my nostrils as he pressed my head to the ground. A musty odor like some crushed herb on his hand and all around him. The scratching of his robes against my naked back. I remember the locusts screaming in the hot air. I remember the stillness of floating on the pond, free and safe and private because no one was watching. I was dressing when he pushed me. The rough cloth. I remember seeing a corner of his robe: Dominican white." She stopped to shiver in the heat of the cell.

By the candlelight Oslavia waited. "What else do you remember? What was his face like?"

The girl said nothing, only sighed deeply.

"Go on."

"He lifted my hips—always keeping my head down in the dirt. I could hardly breathe. The burning as he pushed his snake inside me again and again and again."

"His face?"

"I didn't see his face. He kept my head down. I don't remember when the sound of the locusts stopped but it did. I saw the hair on his arm. Black. I don't remember when the sunflowers started to hate me. And the cypress trees became daggers. I can't remember how long I've been here."

"This is the thirtieth day."

"There were so many of your monks that day bringing us to Florence. It could have been any of them. I don't remember how I got back to the group, only his voice hissing *Zitto!* so I wouldn't make a sound." The girl's shoulders slumped and she collapsed back into her filthy bed, then continued after a few moments. "Then. The hood. I no longer knew if it was day or night. Why have I not been allowed to go to the Florence woolen mills with the others?"

Oslavia did not answer but instead removed the soiled bed linens, and placed the top layer of her habit on the straw mattress for the girl to sleep more comfortably.

The young girl sobbed. "I was so frightened you were that snake returning."

Oslavia wanted to comfort the young woman in an embrace. Instead, she turned her head away to avoid the odor and to hide her own sudden anger.

"I can't bring you any aid until tomorrow. But I will return with a plan. I will find a plan. Trust me."

"I pray to Almighty God that I can trust you, Sister. What can I call you?"

"Mother Oslavia. And you, child?"

"Call me Floriana, the name my father gave me when I was nine years old and had learned to weave flowers together."

"Then be strong, my Floriana. Until tomorrow night."

AS OSLAVIA MADE HER WAY back through the tunnel, the weak flicker of the candle illuminating her way became a symbolic spark to smolder and set her angry heart aflame. Here in her midst was a Jew, not a harlot, and surely not someone begging or even willing to consider the conversion Oslavia knew would be thrust upon her. As she stared at the candle's flame, a boldness overtook her. Who among the men of the cloth she had known over the years would do such a thing? Many. Too many.

Wide rose bushes had been allowed to grow wild as a barrier between the two houses of God. This impenetrable bracken of thorns was intended to prevent any of the novitiates from crossing the border to satisfy carnal appetites. Oslavia had watched others succumb to the impulses of the flesh.

"AND THE HARLOT FROM FERRARA?" Father Bandini asked Oslavia early the next morning.

She had come through the tunnel into one of the two tiny rooms

flanking the pulpit in the nave of the church. From where she knelt in front of Bandini, she could look out into the larger sacred space. Thin shards of light sliced through the church windows and formed distorted patterns along the floor. She took the distortion as a sign for how she was going to stretch the truth to serve some higher good. The word of God was not going to be found in obedience to the most revered Father Bandini, but in obedience to the flame growing inside her. She had prayed for guidance and the courage to follow it, not for the courage to conform or submit.

"Have you examined her? And what are your findings?" Bandini asked.

"The case is typical, Monsignor," Oslavia reported. "No dowry. Parents deceased; relatives have sent her to be part of the weaving pool to keep her out of the beggar's life. And she claims she is no harlot."

"A virgin?"

"No, Your Excellency."

"Repentant?"

"Yes," Oslavia lied.

"And you. Is there room for her in your group?"

"Yes."

"One of the young priests who delivered her here said she was not only a harlot, but she was a Jew. Is this so, Sister Oslavia?"

"Which cleric told you this about her?"

"One of the group that brought her here with the hood of shame," Bandini said. "He suggested that she be silenced, punished, converted, and renewed."

"Sores on her mouth and feet. She was delirious, lying in her own waste. Which one said this? His name?"

"Unimportant! Take her to your side and clean her up," Bandini said. "I give you ninety days to heal her wounds both inside and out. If she has not converted by then we may need to make an example of her. Bernardino will be coming by to collect unrepentant souls. He will be happy to use her for his ends. And it will make us look good to help him. A peace offering between our two orders. The pope will approve."

"Let me take over her tutelage from now on." Oslavia bowed her head.

"I will be watching you." It was a phrase he repeated often and to all over whom he exerted control. She had learned to expect it as peculiar to his speech and never answered, but today she responded. "Monsignor. As you well should."

As for the question of conversion of Jews, she had heard how Franciscan Bernardino called them swine and perpetuated the story they caused the Black Plague, performed ritual murder, and drank sacrificial blood. But what Bandini's monastery had already done to this poor unfortunate was a crime. Oslavia would use her outrage to correct it.

With great difficulty, Bandini lifted his huge body from the chair. A cloud of incense engulfed Oslavia as he moved away from her. The heat of the morning had already seared through his cloak with perspiration stains darkening his robes. His swollen face, his lumbering movements, his heavy wheezing had always frightened her. But on this day, she had only disdain for his predictable lack of compassion for his future convert. Housing a Jew under his auspices was a new matter, one Bandini could work to his advantage. But Oslavia was conjuring a plan to undermine that advantage. It was a plan unknown to her, but her trust in its revelation was strong and unshakable.

CHAPTER FOUR

Oslavia's Brother Sandro in the Medici Palace Courtyard

THE GURGLE OF WATER from the dolphin fountain brought no relief from the sweltering summer day. Only the marble table offered a cool surface to three men who sat there under the portico's shade. With crumbs from their midday meal scattered at their feet, Oslavia's brother, artist Sandro Botticelli, sketched the profile of Lorenzo de' Medici's younger cousin Piero. Lorenzo looked on, sipped his wine, and tossed crumbs to feed the twittering sparrows.

Even though the recently orphaned Piero was one of Sandro's least favorite members of this distinguished family, the boy's foppish and clumsy ways made him one of Sandro's most entertaining subjects. To keep the chubby fifteen-year-old boy's head from its chronic involuntary twitching, Sandro had instructed Piero to lean his elbow against the table and support his head with his hand underneath his chin. Despite the intense heat, Piero, who was prone to overdressing, wore armor trim on his shoulders, elbows, and knees, a flowing cape, red leggings, and a red hat with three long yellow feathers.

Inside his secret sketchbooks, Sandro had often transformed the teenager's head in its silly feathered hats into the head of a bird wearing the full regalia of Medici dress—an enormous plumed hen waddling and pecking above two spindly, spur-covered ankles. Sandro captioned each of his sketches with Piero's pretentious official name: Piero di Lorenzo di Piero di Cosimo di Giovanni di Bicci de' Medici.

Piero's eyes drooped. Three times his chin slipped off his hand, and he let out one fart after another. *The boy needs his nap!* Sandro laughed to himself.

"Move your hand away from your face, Piero!" Sandro said. "I want to get the line of your nose." As Sandro watched Piero struggle to keep his head still, he silently compared him to Lorenzo—the far more elegant of the cousins—who wore no cap, and whose straight, dark hair hung to the edge of his jutting jaw, framing his face. Piero had often been the subject of Lorenzo's jokes and jabs too. Lorenzo was twenty-eight; Sandro, thirty-three.

Piero wrinkled his forehead, ran the palm of his hand across it as he wiped away the perspiration. "I'm getting a cramp in my shoulder. Please hurry!" Breaking the pose, he turned to Lorenzo. "So, Cousin, for the third time today, I'm asking you—"

"Asking me what?" Lorenzo said, sipping his wine and throwing scraps of bread to the birds. Lorenzo knew full well what Piero was talking about—selling one of his country villas to Piero—but Lorenzo enjoyed the tease on one hand yet, on the other, had hoped to keep the news of the transaction from Sandro because it would mean a major change to the artist's life.

"You and your friend here, Sandro, and your Villa di Castello?"

"What's my part?" Sandro stopped sketching.

"I'm buying Villa di Castello from Lorenzo to bring it back to life. After all, before long, I'll be marrying and will need a home of my own. And you, Sandro, are part of the deal. You're going to be working with me instead of Lorenzo."

"Don't rush into the prison of marriage," Lorenzo said, avoiding Sandro's eyes.

"I have no intention of imprisoning myself in any way—unless you think surrounding myself with Beauty is an undesirable confinement," Piero said, looking at Sandro's sketch of him. "My nose! Too long like a trumpet flower. Lorenzo's side of the family has noses like that." Not waiting for the artist's response, he put his arm around Sandro's shoulder. "Without your genius, I can't make Villa di Castello beautiful."

Sandro pulled away, repulsed by Piero's condescending touch and the unexpected news thrust upon him.

"And you're absolutely sure you can finance this villa?" Lorenzo said. "You don't get a *spicciolo* of your inheritance until your eighteenth birthday."

"Imagine you, Lorenzo! Your end of the family doesn't know everything about *our* money," Piero said. "A cash transaction. It's already waiting for you in a special account with no connection to your bank. Let's settle on a price today. Give me Sandro to bring it back from the dead. Not that I meant to imply—with all your traveling—it's gone a bit down, and I do love the country, the country where you no longer go, and my parents' tasteless shack—God rest their souls—is hardly proper for me and my three sisters. What do you say, *Cuginone*?"

"I'd say you're the big cousin—*Cuginone*—not I," Lorenzo said. Turning to Sandro, "Could you work for such a young master?"

Sandro closed his sketchbook, stood, and walked over to a nearby rose bush. He could feel Piero's envious eyes on him, scanning every inch of his body, his straight nose, the deep cleft of his chin, his dark blonde hair, deep-set light eyes. He even imagined Piero's jealousy of the artist's unconfined toes cradled in open leather sandals instead of the high boots Piero wore no matter the season.

Sandro plucked a dead rose from the bush. He pulled the brown petals away one by one and turned to Lorenzo. "God and Beauty are my masters," he said to Lorenzo. "As long as Piero allows me to follow them I will work for him. But what about the other projects you wanted me to do?"

"With all the traveling ahead of me to keep this city safe, I'll postpone them."

Sandro sat next to Lorenzo to pour each of them another glass of wine. He could smell the strong perfume on his friend's body. As it mixed with the sweat of the day, it had taken on a sour edge, but Sandro was used to this and found it comforting, especially when Lorenzo put his arm around Sandro's shoulder.

"And besides, Sandro, the coffers are low. Our banks have lost the pope's account over the Imola mess, and I'm barely getting my name cleared over the alum mines debacle in Volterra. Selling Castello to Piero will give me some cash."

"A daily trip from here would be impossible," Sandro said.

"Exactly!" Piero released a slight burp as his head jerked. "You'll stay with me!"

"Here I'm so close to my mother." Sandro refused to look at Piero and spoke only to Lorenzo. "You know she's not well."

"We'll send food to her daily and give you your own horse so you can visit her when you want," Lorenzo said.

"I have the perfect stallion in mind for you," Piero added. "Dario's fast and gentle."

"In addition to my stipend, I will need my assistant, Filippino, for several days, maybe even a few weeks, to help me build a studio there. And again from time to time as the work progresses."

"All's accounted for," Lorenzo said. He removed his arm from Sandro's shoulder. "You'll find the country comfortable and quiet. You can roam wherever you like."

"It *is* close to my older sister Oslavia's convent," Sandro said, trying to remember the last time he'd seen her, unable to recall her face, and not liking the sound of the word "roam." *What am I, a house pet who can roam and piss wherever he chooses but still is on a leash?*

"Keeping Castello in our extended family appeals to me, Piero," Lorenzo added.

"So?" Piero turned a glowing face toward Sandro.

Sandro stood to gather his sketching materials into a pouch, flung the strap over his head as he secured the bag to his waist. "I'd like to sleep on it."

"Men die in their sleep," Lorenzo said. "I'm off to Naples tomorrow for ten days. Make up your mind."

"It sounds as though you've already decided for me, Lorenzo."

"Go to your mother's. See what she and your father need. Piero and I will work out the financial details without taking up any more of your time. Plan to leave for Villa di Castello in two days' time."

"And what, young master Piero, would you like me to paint?" Sandro looked at the "hen" with shoulder epaulets and feathered hat.

"Whatever you want to paint." Piero beamed, raising his arms out to the side in a wide, open posture suggesting the whole world. "You'll be the one to decide. I'll be at *your* service. We'll bring beautiful girls to pose for you. If you like—"

"I don't like!" Sandro's glare had stopped Piero in mid-sentence. "I choose my own models."

"Come here a moment, Sandro," Lorenzo said.

Lorenzo placed Piero's right hand into Sandro's right hand. "Shake hands, gentlemen, while I make a toast."

"Cheer up, Sandro," Piero said. He squeezed his pudgy fingers around Sandro's hand. "You'll be master of your art with me, I promise you! Whatever you want to do."

"Here's to the continuation of the highest ideals of Beauty for the city of Florence—and for the Medici family." Lorenzo raised his glass.

As he gulped his wine, a sudden pinch of pain, almost a cramp in the center of Sandro's chest, exploded. The intensity of the pinch was like the first loud rip when tightly woven cloth is being torn in two.

CHAPTER FIVE

Sandro's Farewell to Smeralda and Mariano

WITHOUT A WORD OF GREETING, Sandro tossed cuttings from the Medici garden to his parents as they sat in their humble courtyard.

"What's wrong?" his mother, Smeralda, said, but Sandro had already escaped toward the stairs of their small apartment.

"Castello," Sandro said, then fled up the stairs.

"A castor plant! Palma di Cristo!" His father, Mariano, leapt to grab the new plants. "We'll be able to make our own oil!"

When Mariano turned to show his wife the precious plant, Smeralda said, "Something's wrong."

Mariano ignored her. When he turned back to dig a hole in the earth, she reached over her lap, picked up a stone, and threw it at her husband's back.

They both looked toward the sound of Sandro upstairs slamming drawers and doors.

"This place is a Medici cemetery!" Sandro shouted. He threw silk tassels and a dust-encrusted candelabra out the window right onto the courtyard. "We're choking in their hand-me-downs and you don't even know it."

"Don't break anything!" Smeralda said, but it was too late. Thick velvet drapes flew from the window and a vase shattered on the ground.

"Those were valuable!" Smeralda squirmed in her chair to stand, but the pain in her feet forced her to sit back.

"They're worthless if they keep out all the light. The vase was already chipped and water leaked out of it!" Sandro said. He peered at his parents from the window. "And what do you need with those banners, and this lance? Are you going to duel in a pageant, Father?"

"Throw it out," Mariano said. "Throw it all out. It's your mother who hoards. She's afraid someone might see she's spurned a Medici gift."

"Spurn it!" said Sandro. "They've spurned me today. Cast me out just like those moth-eaten drapes. "*Get rid of him!* Get rid of them!"

"Calm down, Son," Mariano said.

Sandro dragged a canvas bag down the steps, sank to the ground at his parents' feet.

"After all these years, can you believe it? Now I'm going to have the fifteen-year-old Piero for a patron. The *puttana*!"

"I told you the day would come," Smeralda told Mariano.

"What day are you talking about?" Sandro said.

"When you are told to move on, to move out."

"Don't make the boy feel worse," Mariano said.

"Who said I feel bad? I couldn't breathe upstairs with all those old, dusty, and broken discards. And you, Mother, for someone who has so much bitterness toward my adoptive mother, Lucrezia, you save every scrap she's given you."

"I pray for her and her family daily," Smeralda said.

"You hate her. Admit it!" Sandro said.

"She's not devout," Smeralda said. "She entertains foreigners as though they're the same blood. Living in that house all these years has robbed you of the joys of a simple life and the comfort of a simple faith. You won't worship God if you only worship what you and those intellectuals call 'Beauty.'"

"And you don't worship these flowers?" Mariano said to his wife.

"And every scrap of cloth the Medicis have given us?" Sandro added.

"You're a servant of God like your sister," Mariano said. "She prays with words. You do it with paint."

"Mother's right. I'm not a servant of God. I'm a servant of Beauty. If they are the same, I serve both. If they are different, I prefer Beauty. The days of painting only Bible stories are over."

"But the truth is," Smeralda said, "you're a servant of the Medici. They ship you from place to place like cattle."

"Don't exaggerate, Mother." Sandro moved closer to her, lifted up her feet into his hands. He removed rags, scraps of more Medici cloth, from around her swollen ankles. He put out his palm as she dug deep into her apron to remove a small vial of oil and placed it in his hand.

"At last they gave us a palma di Cristo plant," she said. "And now you won't be around to put the castor oil on me."

"I took it without asking."

Smeralda had concocted a poor person's substitute salve—a mixture of gardenia-scented olive oil. She used it over the years on all the members of her family except herself. Sandro dripped a few drops of it on the fine white cracks that covered her heels in the pattern of a reptile's hide.

"Press harder, dear, especially around the ankles. I always walk better after you've—are we ever going to see you?" Smeralda asked.

"What about all those years of schooling they offered me and the fun I had with Lorenzo?" Sandro asked her.

"They were paying you to be his companion, to entertain him." The wounded expression on her son's face made her regret her words.

"I had genuine love and affection from them, especially from Lucrezia," Sandro continued.

"You had her gratitude. They used you to train Lorenzo's eyes, to give him the sensibility of an artist. What you were born with."

"Leave the boy alone," Mariano said. "This is what serving the first family of Florence costs."

"This boy is no longer a boy. He's a thirty-three-year-old man." She handed the strips of cloth to Sandro to cover her feet again. "Get yourself a wife before it's too late or this bloated Piero boy will send you off to Rome next."

"You know what I think of marriage," Sandro said. "A few nights ago I dreamed I was married, and it made me so wretched that to avoid falling asleep and having the dream again, I got up. All night I rushed about the streets of Florence as if I were mad! At least you can wish me good luck, Mother."

"I told you Sandro's not the soil you plant a vineyard in," Mariano said.

Smeralda ignored her husband, and she continued lecturing her son. "You know how the pope sees that whole family. His hands are in the Pazzis' pockets now. You could be hired away by the pope and never come back."

"And you, Father?"

"I wish you and your sister passion in your hearts whatever you do."

"How do you know what's in Oslavia's heart?" Smeralda challenged Mariano. "You haven't seen her in five years."

"Because it was you who insisted we send her away!" Mariano glared at his wife. "I know my children's hearts from their first cry. That never changes."

"And I know what my children need from the first moment they suckled at my breast!"

"*Basta!*" groaned Sandro. "You're making me feel worse! I'll judge Oslavia's heart when I see her."

Mariano moved closer to Sandro. "Don't ever forget—your humble beginnings will buy you a place in heaven far greater than any throne of a rich man on earth. You might as easily have been the court barber or a gold-leaf maker like your brother Antonio, rest his soul. Though you have lived with the Medici, you'll always be a tanner's son."

"I might have been better off, Father. Enough talk. Make some tea from the mint plants, Mother, and don't worry about me. Maybe I'll have a home of my own some day to grow the cuttings from *your* garden."

He stood to brush the dirt off his clothing. "I'm leaving for Villa di Castello tomorrow. Whether you like it or not. Whether I like it or not."

CHAPTER SIX

Sandro's Last Night in Florence

ONCE BACK INSIDE the Medici Palace on this final evening there, Sandro was haunted by his mother's words, ". . . from place to place like cattle." Climbing the stairs to his room, he stopped midway and slipped into the tiny palace chapel. Kneeling at the altar, in the dim light of the windowless room, he closed his eyes. After a few moments, he rose to his feet, and as he had done numerous times, he studied the Gozzoli fresco covering all four walls of the chapel. The scene was a procession of the Three Kings on their way to Bethlehem—the biblical theme Lorenzo's grandfather Cosimo had commissioned to portray the Medici household. Discovered by Cosimo during that period, Sandro had been transferred at the age of fifteen from Fra Filippo Lippi's studio to live and work inside the Medici Palace.

Sandro's eyes passed from John Palaeologus, the Emperor of the East, in robes, turbaned crown, and with a melancholy face, to the Patriarch of Constantinople and the bearded Greek scholars from Constantinople. In the procession were Piero de' Medici; Lorenzo's brother, Giuliano, and the elder Cosimo with his personal emblem of three peacock feathers. Though Sandro had been treated as a son by Lorenzo's father, Piero the Elder, Sandro's face was conspicuously absent. *Even the household dogs made it, but not I.*

Lorenzo, who was ten at the time of the portrait, was the most dramatic of the three kings—wearing a jeweled crown and clad in exquisite royal splendor, pale skin, dark blonde hair. Like many artists of the day, Gozzoli had taken license to paint Lorenzo symbolically. With the laurel bush in the background—the word from which Lorenzo's name evolved—and the pattern of five balls—the Medici emblem decorating the horse's saddle—this was surely a depiction of Lorenzo. And yet, this angelic being who personified innocence looked more like Sandro as a young boy. On their rare visits to the Medici Palace to see their son, Sandro's mother and father had always argued over whether Lorenzo's face in Gozzoli's painting was Sandro's. In spite of the figure's skin tone and hair color being the same as their son's, and not Lorenzo's, Sandro had denied it. Today, under the yoke of his dismissal and his mother's words, Sandro allowed himself to not only recognize his likeness there, but to claim it.

All those years he had felt a part of the Medici family, especially when he and Lorenzo lived as brothers roaming through the palace and the city, joking and laughing. Lorenzo idolized his elder adopted brother, but now with the casual tilt of a wine glass, he had relegated Sandro to Villa di Castello. Younger artists would take his place in Florence. Even the devoted Gozzoli, who for months on end had painted the walls by candlelight into the early hours of the morning, had been sent away after Cosimo's death.

Sandro turned to the altar once again. Still, he told himself as he knelt, and this time crossing himself fervently, he *had* been blessed. He had received the privilege of culture and learning while under the Medici roof, gifts he would not have known living under the roof of his father, Mariano, a humble tanner. Noble blood or not, he decided he would forever claim those gifts as his own. After all, he had earned those gifts:

worked for them, painted for them, decorated insipid banners and posters and table settings for them.

But on the climb to his room, Sandro's head burst at the idea of serving the flatulent Piero—a patron half his age. "Give me Sandro," Piero had said. And Lorenzo had released him just as Sandro's mother had said, as though he were a head of cattle.

As Sandro lay on his bed, he lifted his mattress and withdrew a tiny secret sketchbook. He turned to the profile drawing of Piero from the day before. He drew Piero again, only with donkey ears, a trumpet flower nose, and a paintbrush tied to his tail. Sandro drew himself whipping the donkey. He fell asleep with a prayer on his lips: "Help me, dear God, to get through this."

And God answered his request an hour later, waking him with a burst of energy to pack. Soon trunks and sacks covered the floor of his room. Sitting on the edge of the bed, Sandro felt another wave of exhaustion slip over him. "*Alone. Uncared for. A barque in the waters of my life going nowhere*," he wrote in his sketchbook before putting it away. He had walked through a day of obligatory smiles and farewells until his façade had begun to wither. Sleep was too passive an escape, at least for his final night in the city, so he pushed himself off the edge of his bed to his feet. He checked under the bed for forgotten items, then retrieved the tiny sketchbook again, slipped it into his waist pouch, and crept down a back staircase out into the street.

He walked toward the Piazza della Signoria, barely noticing the pink clouds over the Arno. He focused instead on the bats flitting in and out through the last rays of sunset. Chatter filled his head. Questions. Voices yea or nay. Several people who knew him offered an evening greeting, but Sandro heard nothing until a voice, half man and half beast, shook him out of his fog.

As he drew closer to a small crowd, he saw that the voice stuttered out of the mouth of an emaciated monk dressed in Dominican robes, soiled and shredded. When the few bystanders walked away, Sandro remained.

"Re-re-re-repent and sa-sa-sa-save your soul," the monk whispered, causing Sandro to shiver. Although he expected to breathe in the scents of filth, the young man's body instead exuded a warm, spicy, bitter odor, with smoky and musky undertones—a mixture of incense and the medicinal salves he had smelled on the hands of the palace physicians.

Someone from the inner circle of Lorenzo's Platonic Academy as well as his fellow members of Florence's artists' brotherhood, the Company of Saint Luke, had warned its members to avoid Dominicans because of their extreme views. Something in the piercing eyes of this frail, wiry man, barely over twenty, with his hawk-like nose, and strange speech, held Sandro to the spot.

"Let me buy you a drink to soothe your tired throat," Sandro said.

"I've sworn to stay here until twenty bells. God could send me someone at the last moment whose soul I might rescue from this debauched city."

"Debauched?"

"All is vanity here. Madonnas who look like whores painted by artists like you who wear the crest of Saint Luke sewn to your clothing. You have lost your purpose. You paint whatever comes into your heads as though your mission to glorify Christ were a thing of the past. Those talents were given to you by God in order to tell His stories to those who cannot read."

"I'll pay," Sandro said. "We'll talk more about your ideas on art. Perhaps I'll share them with my Saint Luke members at the next meeting if your argument is worthy."

"I should like to show you what you already know to be true. But I won't join you for meat or drink, only, perhaps, a sprig of parsley and some soup."

"Meat will put some flesh on those bones. Your voice will grow more convincing," Sandro said.

On his way to the tavern, Sandro turned around to observe the monk from a distance. With a few strokes of the pencil in his sketchbook, he created the hooded face with a penis nose and pubic beard. On the facing page he wrote the words, "Repent. Repent. Repent," as though they were flowing out of the mouth of the penis nose, its tip with tiny delicate lips. With a laugh he tucked the sketchbook back into his pouch and stepped into the tavern.

Old Faranese hobbled over to give Sandro the usual smothering hug. Born with a clubfoot, Faranese dragged it behind him as he walked, sweeping whatever debris was in his path. Still, "Sweeper," as he was called by most, managed to marry, have a family, and make a life for himself in this tavern in the heart of Florence.

At the moment the bells rang twenty times, Sandro swallowed the first of the roasted sparrows on crusts of bread and Faranese brought him an empty plate with a note on it.

Dear Signor Botticelli,

Excuse me for addressing you directly by your name even though we have only met on the street. Thank you for your offer to feed me tonight, but I have had the good fortune to find a bench inside the Signoria on which to sleep. The bell ringer comes from my home city of Ferrara and insisted on hosting me, but the door will be locked at 9:30.

Food and especially drink are two things I avoid as a matter of faith. The flesh carries more sin than we can slough off in one lifetime. Being a man of the cloth I must prepare myself to receive the word of God at any moment. I leave Florence in the morning. Perhaps on another trip to your fair but ailing city I will sit and talk with you again. May Christ govern us who master nothing, Girolamo (Gerome) Savonarola

Poor monkey. Sandro pulled out his sketchbook. To the penis-faced prelate he added a monkey's tail.

Faranese appeared with steaming sweetbreads smothered in cooked tomatoes and a side of two peacock tongues with a dipping sauce.

"Do you know anything about the monk who sent the note?" Sandro asked.

"A strange incompetent."

"How so?"

"Bologna's bishop sent him here to save our city. Stutters like a frightened child. Talks to himself, and has been laughed off every street corner.

Apparently he's part of a group who brought several weavers into town, most of them young girls. Perhaps being so close to the female sex has rattled his mind. Whatever it is, he's been recalled to Bologna."

"How do you know all this?"

"The other monks who traveled with him came in here, but he was too good to set foot in a common tavern. Wants to keep his flesh pure."

"He has the hand of a rich, well-educated man, not the scrawl of a country priest," said Sandro. "I've seen this script from the pens of intellectuals at Lorenzo's who speak many languages and come from wealth."

"They say he was to be a doctor like his father and his father's father, but fainted at the sight of blood. All the other siblings are in business and finance but this one found his way to the cloth after the woman he wanted spurned him when he was a mere seventeen. After that he renounced the world of flesh."

"And how do you know all this? Surely his fellow clerics didn't share such knowledge with you."

"Oh, paths cross through this tavern. You hear a little, you learn a little. I put it all together. He was the one who sought Niomi, daughter of Titus, the Greek Jew. Titus always came in here to boast about the many suitors who presented themselves to his voluptuous daughter. She finally chose a man of her own faith, another doctor, who keeps her swathed in silks. More and more yards of it are needed as her girth expands after each child."

As the wine helped Sandro dull his melancholy, Savonarola's repulsive, yet hypnotic voice buzzed in the back of his mind, the prelude to the sting of a tiny mosquito, whose poison, at first unnoticed, might soon infect the whole man.

WHILE HIS WINE HELPED SANDRO slip into a mental fog, Savonarola made his way to a tiny side door in the Palazzo Vecchio. He studied the sculpted head on the tip of the doorknocker—the image of a forlorn soul he feared resembled his own contorted face.

Before he could knock it against the door, an old man in rags, and with charcoal streaks across his hands and face, opened the door a crack. He crossed himself and bowed to let in the young friar.

"Your gracious Eminence," he said. "I have prepared a bed for you. An inch of straw as you requested and the roughest woolen blanket I could find."

"Excellent, Maurizio," Savonarola answered, "I am ready to meet the Almighty Father in my dreams."

"But your dinner? I have prepared fried greens Ferrara-style."

"That would cause me homesickness. Pain of the heart, even if it brings pleasure to my belly. A simple cup of the water in which you cooked the greens will suffice."

"But I have already tossed it out into the alley."

"I'll eat something midday tomorrow—after I have prayed for wisdom and communion with God's word."

"Does your family know you walk around in filthy rags, sleep on rocks, and sip only the water in which vegetables have been boiled?"

"I have only one Father, Maurizio. And He is happy when I do His work. What other father could compete with Him?"

"As you say, Girolam*ino*. As you say."

"Please, Maurizio. I am not a child. I'm Savonarola."

"As you say, sir, as you say."

"And please, no sir. I am your humble servant as much as you are offering to be mine."

"As you say. As you say." Maurizio backed away from Gerome.

"One more request, Maurizio," Gerome said. The old man turned to listen but Savonarola said nothing. He knelt on the floor and pulled out of his sack a whip with small pieces of sharp metal beads woven into its strands of rope. This he laid on the cobblestones beside him. He slipped off his robe, revealing raw wounds and scratches on his back, before he curled himself into a ball, tucking his head to his knees with his back rounded like a rabbit.

Maurizio said nothing but did not move.

"If you truly want to serve me, you will do it," Savonarola said. "I'm too exhausted tonight to do it myself. You'll be helping me get closer to Him. I beg you."

Maurizio picked up and unwound the whip. "But I have no experience of these things."

"Have you never whipped an ass?"

"Lightly."

"Use all the strength you have."

"I . . . cannot. I am not God."

"You serve Him if you do it. Now!"

Awkwardly, Maurizio spread his feet apart, and with both hands around the neck of the whip, he flung it into the air and brought it down with all his might. The whip's end snapped against Savonarola's flesh.

"Again! Five times. Again."

Maurizio summoned his strength to crack the whip against the young monk's bony back. A drop of blood splattered onto his own face. The shock of it caused him to release the whip and scamper away into the dark night.

Gerome reached into his sack, removed a small leather purse from which he squeezed a salve of myrrh extract, the same smoky odor that had filled Sandro's nostrils earlier that evening. He spread the burning ointment onto his open wounds, and crawled across the floor onto his makeshift bed to find the most uncomfortable position. Every breath, every action, no matter how seemingly insignificant, was an opportunity for bodily renunciation, and with it came a pleasure of its own. Tonight it was his right shoulder blade that pressed into the cobblestone floor of the Signoria's atrium. Above him he noticed the shadowy flitting of bats.

Sleep was his biggest adventure because it was in his dreams that God often appeared to him, renewing his spirit and offering the next step in his path toward salvation. Visions had appeared to him since he was a young boy. They had ceased during the period of his infatuation with Niomi, but he had crawled out of that dark well with his virginity intact before he took his vows. He had entered the order clean. Unsoiled.

As he ground his shoulder blade into the floor and relished the stinging sensation from the open wounds, that personal member between his legs rose against his will and desire for purity. The moment his prayers would quiet and his breathing go deep within his belly, the beast would rise again, hard, erect, and wagging like some family pet wanting to be taken out for a walk. Not unlike a divining rod for water, this personal member never ceased to badger him, pulling him up and out into a darkness vaster than God's heavens. It was surely the call of the devil.

His life now was about the resistance to that call. Twenty-four-hour vigilance to fight off the demon growing from within his own body, pulling him away from his Father's work. But anyone under such attack by the devil could surely be capable of its extreme opposite and become the object of God's love, he told himself. Saint Augustine's words confirmed that a God so mighty would surely fill him with the grace to defeat the demon.

He bent the stiff member, squeezing it between his thighs, and prayed again for the moment of temptation to pass. Several shadows scurried across the floor. The sight of those rodents of the night put a stab of fear into Gerome's belly, shrinking his rebellious member and allowing him to collapse into sleep as the words on his lips continued, "He has saved me from my filthy self. Jesus be praised."

CHAPTER SEVEN

Filippino and Sandro in the Country

BY NIGHTFALL on their first day outside of Florence, Sandro and his assistant, Filippino, reached Oslavia's compound. Sandro had taken the boy in as an apprentice and the two had worked side by side for years ever since Filippino's father, Fra Filippo Lippi, had died when Filippino was twelve. By now twenty years old, Filippino had gained a few of his own patrons, so his work with Botticelli became intermittent, but his loyalty never wavered. With the classic face of a Greek Adonis and the temperament of a puppy, the young man had no idea how different he was from his philandering father, Sandro's first mentor. Sandro had kept the drama of it all to himself. The boy knew of his father only as a former monk, one who had left the order to marry his nun mother, Lucrezia Buti. He was unaware his father bedded every model and forced the boy Sandro to run across town to tell his wife he couldn't come home for lunch. Lucrezia would turn away with tears in her eyes until one day she simply laughed. That's when she locked the door to her husband. Lippi slept in the studio for a month with paint under his nails and not even a proper home-cooked meal. After thirty days, she let him back into their house and into her bed, resulting in Filippino's conception. Some goddess of gentleness had made their son, Filippino, unaware of his own magnetic gaze, the allure of his full lips, and the beauty and perfection of his physical form.

Arriving at Oslavia's, Sandro made sure young Filippino stayed with the horses at the gatekeeper's quarters, away from the women, who might lose their composure if they saw him. The gatekeeper Federico, a man with tired eyes, brought Sandro to a bench in a tiny room beside the main chapel, and shuffled off to find Oslavia.

A pungent aroma of apples and an herb he didn't recognize filled the room. The faint sound of bells ringing above the chanting of female voices, the cool air of the cloister after long hours under the sun in heavy clothes, lulled Sandro to sleep.

Oslavia's touch on his shoulder awoke him. The cloth binding around her cheeks exaggerated a puffiness in her face he'd never seen. A translucent mask of wrinkles covered her face. Small wire-frame glasses rested on her nose. The lenses magnified her pupils as though they were purple moons in a night sky.

"LET ME LOOK AT MY BABY BROTHER," Oslavia said. She pulled Sandro to his feet from the bench where he dozed.

"Still a baby?" he said, as he towered over her.

"To me. Always." As soon as Oslavia threw her arms around Sandro he began to quiver.

Oslavia tightened her grip, trying to absorb her brother's distress into her own body. The grown man in her arms suddenly shrank to the ten-year-old boy she had rescued from the slimy grasp of a sodomite at the studio where Sandro had been sent to become a goldsmith. The scene flashed back to her in full detail. Rather than scream when she came upon them, she had exited, and rung the outside bell. She reentered noisily and took her brother home. He washed his mouth out in the piazza fountain and held on to her with tears and shaking as he did today. Since she was about to take her vows, she had told him she knew what had happened because she could see through walls. That was the week she made sure Sandro was transferred to Lippi's painting studio.

She assumed Lippi, a former monk, would surely not abuse, or allow anyone under his charge to abuse her baby brother.

Now she held on until Sandro became still enough to release her embrace. They looked at each other face to face.

"I've been cast out of the Medici Palace and drafted to work for a fifteen-year-old *farfalla* who farts and burps and says he knows the mysteries of art," Sandro said.

"And Lorenzo?"

"He thought it was a good idea."

"Perhaps it is. Does this flatulent boy have a name?" Oslavia held one of his hands until he sat back on the bench and looked up at her.

"His name is as long as his body is fat. But they call him Piero though he bears no resemblance to Lorenzo's father, Piero. The boy fancies himself a talented patron of the arts, a copy of his cousin *Il Magnifico*."

"What else?" Oslavia sat beside him.

"What is the herb I smell along with the apple?"

"Rue. It represses lust in all who inhale it."

"Useful for your line of work. Perhaps it brings on weeping too. When I saw you I was suddenly that little boy—"

"I know. I thought that too."

"And here I'm complaining when I haven't even taken the time to come see you in all these years. How are you?"

"I prosper as long as my mind is active. And with these," she said as she removed her glasses and kissed them, "I can continue to learn and read. Yours is a problem of privilege, Sandro. One patron or another. Your talents will always keep you in style and moving among the elite."

"Mother says I'm a slave to them."

"You are a servant of God. Like me you have only one Master and no others."

"You have only one master, Sister. I have many. Each one with his own agenda."

"You are your own master among men. Before God you are a servant."

"Can my assistant, Filippino, and I stay the night?"

"So is that the extent of your soul's work? You change the subject!" Oslavia said. "You can't stay here. Men are not allowed on the grounds."

"I didn't know I would be coming here. There was not enough time to send you a message. Would you have preferred I not come?"

Oslavia ignored the question, rose, and touched Sandro's elbow to get him up too. "Let's see if Federico, the caretaker, will let you sleep on the floor of his cottage."

As brother and sister exited into the still-hot evening air, Sandro tried to put his arm through hers but she pulled it away.

"Now you're angry."

"Not angry, Sandrolino, I'm sad my brothers only seek me out when they need me."

"I'm sorry, Slavia."

"And the last time I came home to visit five years ago you didn't even come by to say hello. The others have their families and their work, but you have had an easier time and no wife or children. I had expected you would keep up the thread."

"I was two when they sent you here."

"I came home often. I spent every waking moment caring for you, teaching you to read."

Sandro opened his mouth to respond, but no words came out.

"Once you went into the Medici Palace you forgot me, and now they've thrown you out—"

"They haven't thrown me out. I've been assigned to another place. And this is the first horse I have officially owned. A gift of my new patron."

They walked side by side in silence toward Federico's cottage.

"I need you, Oslavia. Please don't be harsh. Forgive me if you can find it in your purified heart—"

"Don't attack my sanctity!" she spat back at him. "You, who revel with the whores. I've heard about how you ride with Lorenzo and scour the countryside for innocent lambs for your—"

Just then a small group of nuns passed. Oslavia picked up the pace.

"Who told you this?" whispered Sandro.

"I am not at liberty. Suffice it to say I know a lot more about you than you know about me."

"Why would you speak such a thing without telling me who told you? You sound like a spiteful child." Sandro was silent for a moment. "Why don't we start again as two adults and put aside our mistakes since childhood?"

"One can never put aside the piercing thorns of childhood. You know nothing about me because you have always stayed within your own world. You chose to make it your only world. To forget your roots. You never sought me out, never thought I might be in need of some brotherly affection or some concern for my life."

"You'll have to forgive me. I'm here trying. Why can't you try, too?"

"With the Lord's help anything is possible."

"You'll teach me again. I'll listen. I promise."

By now they had reached the spot where Filippino was asleep on the ground.

"Who's this one?"

"Lippi's baby, Filippino. My assistant since his father died. He came to help me with the transfer of my materials."

"Don't wake him yet," Oslavia said. "I'll be at the caretaker's door at six bells tomorrow morning to bring you both some food and send you on your way."

"I'll be back, I swear it, Sister, on our parents' lives."

"Don't waste your promises in words. Let your actions speak for you."

"You've given me much to think about, Sister."

"This is good, when an elder leads a younger to the righteous path. And if I may offer a word of caution about your next assignment?" she asked.

Sandro's face was open to her every suggestion.

"Do not bite the hand of the one who feeds you next. Be humble now roles are reversed. With Lorenzo you were the master because all knew he worshipped you."

"For one married to the church you seem to know what is happening in the outside world."

"Don't underestimate the cloister, Drolino," she said, a name she hadn't used on him since that day at the fountain.

"For sure, Slavaccia."

At the sound of that name, called only by Sandro, Oslavia embraced him.

"It's bad enough they don't enter poor girls on the birth records. It was as though I never existed for the family once I reached marriageable age. So I made my family here."

He held her tight against him.

"I made my family here," she repeated. "So perhaps it is I who did the neglecting. You who were too young to know better. Forgive my anger."

"It is I who begs forgiveness, Slavaccia. And now you can resume my spiritual tutelage."

"And I reclaim my long lost brother."

"'Do not bite the hand that feeds me,'" he said. "I'll sleep on that tonight as my first lesson from you."

CHAPTER EIGHT

Sandro and Filippino Arrive at Villa di Castello

A DOZEN CHINESE PUG DOGS surrounded Sandro and Filippino seconds after they set foot on Piero's property. *Twelve yapping Pieros!* Sandro laughed out loud at their intense little faces with bulging eyes and their squirming bodies dressed in harnesses of bright colored silk.

The horses reared, emptying a saddlebag of brushes off Sandro's horse and overturning Filippino's cart, catapulting Filippino and the supplies to the ground, where he skinned his knees.

Sandro and a limping Filippino approached the entrance of the villa. They watched men hauling pieces of furniture through open doors and windows onto the lawn. Swarms of moths circled about a cart filled with rolled carpets. The clear air, perfumed by nature, was a welcome change from the narrow Florentine streets with their stench of urine, rotting garbage, and smoldering heat.

Even though this was not the first time Sandro had been to Villa di Castello, its size surprised him. *My painting will match the scale of such a place,* he thought as a bubble of enthusiasm surfaced.

They walked through the front entrance and stood in the inner courtyard. Warm sunlight washed the walls. Stairs and hallways led off in all directions. Sandro shouted Piero's name. A young girl saw Filippino's perfect face and his bloody knees and gasped, then pulled him toward one of the rooms off the atrium.

When Piero did not answer, Sandro mounted the stairs. Respectful of the fact this was not his property, he moved cautiously along the corridor. Most of the rooms were open, several with large sheets thrown over furniture. Sandro's instinct led him to the central door which would correspond to the rooms directly over the entrance—the traditional place for the master of the house to be able to see approaching visitors from a distance.

Sandro placed his ear against the thick wooden door. Scenes from his apprenticeship with Filippo Lippi flashed before him. Once Lippi's eyes had glazed over, the paintbrushes abandoned in solvent, to be followed by the announcement to all that he was taking a nap for "inspiration," Sandro knew he would be ordered across town.

As this memory flashed before him, he was grateful his new master, unlike his ex-patron, Lorenzo, or his former mentor, Filippo Lippi, didn't as yet have a wife he might be cheating on. Then again, perhaps Piero was in the middle of satisfying himself. Sandro knew nothing of the habits of this young man and little of his tastes and sexual inclinations.

He rang the bell that hung on a hook to the side of the door, then knocked loudly. He heard some shuffling around behind the door, followed by muffled voices, and the door opened a crack.

"Ah, Sandro!" Piero's fat face broke into a happy grin as he opened the door wide enough for him to squeeze into the hallway. "Welcome, welcome! Was that you when all the dogs were barking?"

"Yes," Sandro said. He stared at a strange object attached to Piero's neck—a large lizard? A doll? It had a painted clay face, puffed-out cheeks, feathers sticking out of the scalp for hair, and a brilliant purple brocaded suit adorned the doll's torso. Piero adjusted the doll's sword away from his neck, froze, a blush rising in his cheeks. "Imagine you!" Piero said as he tried to remove the doll. "I was unpacking my things from my other home and there was this sweet doll left over from childhood. I made puppets to entertain my family. Meet Babbo, master of ceremonies! I tied him on there and forgot about him."

"I like Babbo."

"Others wouldn't appreciate him." Piero removed the miniature friend, and scurried back to his room to toss it inside with a shout. "Poppi, Please!"

"Poppi?" Sandro asked as soon as Piero returned, a bit out of breath.

"My domestic helper. Since I was a baby. Like a mother. She dresses like a man for convenience of movement and always wears red. Let me show you around." Piero moved to thread his arm through Sandro's then cancelled the action as they walked down the long corridor.

"About Filippino. He had an accident. He'll need to stay a few days longer than expected."

"Please do not be too demanding at first, Sandro."

"I merely want my dear assistant, who has been with me now for eight years, to have a comfortable place to recover from his wounds caused by your yelping dogs."

"*Va bene, va bene*," Piero said as he opened the door to the room at the end of a long corridor. "How about this?"

A huge bed with curtains on all four sides sat against the wall. Sandro could see out through the balcony to the uncluttered hills and the undulating landscape. "For Filippino?"

"No, silly, for you! To inspire you."

As he sat on the bed and looked out on the Tuscan landscape, Sandro's heart shot a burst of energy to every extremity. The space of this one room almost duplicated the entire living space of his parents' apartment. This hand that was about to feed him was surely generous—though highly quirky.

"I'll take it with gratitude. And for tonight Filippino can stay here with me."

"In your same bed?"

"Not as your voice suggests, young master. In the way of two brothers.

I prefer he be housed as my equal. Not to be relegated to the stables like an ass."

Piero's head jerked more than usual after Sandro's demand. Sandro could sense Piero's mind racing ahead to future conflicts. In a softer tone, remembering Oslavia's words of caution, he said, "And is this to be my studio as well, Master Piero?"

"Imagine you! No! I will show you that next."

"You are a man of surprises," Sandro said.

Piero stood taller, pulled in his stomach, and puffed out his chest. With a flourish he waved Sandro through the doorway and they headed downstairs.

When Sandro heard Filippino's scream, he raced through the entrance hall toward the sound, which had turned into a whimper.

He found his young helper on his back on the kitchen table. Compresses covered his forehead. His leggings were rolled to his thighs and the odor of rotten eggs came from his scraped knees. Three young girls bustled around him, with the youngest shouting orders to the others. Filippino looked up at Sandro and winked.

As he opened his mouth to say something, the young girl said, "Silence! Let the poultice work!"

Dressed in simple, tight bodices with the family crest sewn over the left breast, these young girls treated their patient as a large human toy on whom they were performing incantations for instant healing.

"Wipe his wrists with bark serum," ordered the youngest. "Now tap the bottoms of his feet ten times. Look in his ear. But be sure to run your fingers through his hair as you do it!" As the eldest touched his ear, Filippino let out another scream.

"Isn't that a poultice for one whose humor is phlegmatic?" Sandro said.

"Precisely his humor," the youngest said. "You should have seen how he doubted our abilities, so we tied him to the table legs."

"Choleric I'd say," the middle one said.

"Enough, ladies," Filippino said. "The sting tells me the poison is surely out, if not from your brilliant compresses and poultice, for sure from your caring touch."

The girls giggled—a behavior Sandro often saw when young girls found themselves near Filippino.

An older woman not much taller than the youngest girl descended on the scene. She had a slight cast in her left eye, which gave her a wild look. "My kitchen table! What is this nonsense?" she said.

She was dressed in a red tunic and red leggings much like his own. Sandro knew this had to be Poppi.

"My baby sisters," Piero said. "Renata, the youngest—head nurse at age nine. The eldest, Donata, almost fourteen years old. And in the middle, Margarita, twelve."

Poppi waved the girls aside to examine the wounds.

"Excellent," she said. "This is exactly what I would have prescribed."

"I told you so," said Renata, shaking her head back and forth until her braids snapped on her cheeks. She quickly gave Filippino a kiss on his cheek. Donata, with a fully developed chest and wiry hair and lips as full as Filippino's, gasped at Renata's antics and covered her face with her hands to mask her blushing. Margarita, almost as tall as her brother and as thin as he was overweight, snapped her tongue against the roof of her mouth, frowned, and poured water from a pitcher over her hands to wipe off the medicines.

"The only problem," Poppi continued, winking at Filippino as she untied him, "I would have had him eat some as well along with the herb tea, but this is sufficient. Arise, young man! Off my kitchen table!"

As he got back on his feet, he winced with real pain for the first time.

"The final cure will enter your blood system now," Poppi said. "But you ought to be lying down."

In spite of Poppi's advice, Filippino refused to miss the tour to the new studio. Piero led the troupe around the back of the villa. The two eldest girls offered their arms to Filippino to help him walk and Renata skipped in circles around the three of them. Scenes from years ago played in Sandro's mind. He too had skipped and run with Lorenzo through those labyrinthine gardens now overgrown, thrown goose droppings into the fountains, sped through the halls where Cosimo, Lorenzo's grandfather, had walked in slow meditation and prayer before the mighty patriarch had ceased his visits to the villa, choosing instead silent contemplation in his private cell at Santa Maria Novella.

Moments later the group stood before a huge octagonal glass greenhouse with corridors leading to smaller glass chambers on three sides. Vines crept through broken windows onto the roof. Abandoned plants with dried brown leaves crowded the space. A few bright green seedlings shot up among the dead weeds, but there was light everywhere and Sandro could see, in spite of the mess, there was ample space to set up a large painting.

Sandro and Filippino, who had broken free of the dancing nymph nurses, entered the main glass rotunda, leaving Piero behind as he prattled on about its potential and how Poppi was going to make her *profumeria* in one of the smaller chambers. The two artists stood silent in the center, each reading the other's thoughts about how this abandoned, glass elephant could be transformed into workable space. Piero's three sisters followed the artists inside, and tossed dead plants at each other until Poppi intervened, recruiting them instead to drag a large table to the center where Sandro and Filippino stood.

"Lift!" Poppi commanded the three girls. Filippino moved to help but was stopped by a sudden pain in his knees. Sandro watched the girls lift the corner of a long wooden table that lay on its side. Next Poppi slid a large clay pot upside down against the dirt floor of the greenhouse under the bottom edge of the table to hold the weight at that end.

"Now you, Sandro," she ordered, "hold up the opposite edge and I'll put the others underneath."

Within two minutes, ten clay pots elevated the long edge of the table so its top surface leaned back at an angle, supported in the rear by two of the table legs. "You see," Poppi gloated, "the perfect angle for an easel!"

"Now, wood!" Poppi pointed to a pile of rubble from old tables she had demolished to set up her laboratory. The girls placed a long plank across the protruding edge of the pot bottoms. "A shelf on which you can rest your drawing sticks!"

"Excellent," Sandro said, but thought, *This is pathetic!*

"And the curtains?" Poppi asked. "What will you need and where would you like them?"

"One to cover the work at night. I don't want anyone looking at my work in progress, especially early sketches. Bad luck. I'll need two other things: a changing room for the models and one for me to rest and relax as needed."

"Don't we need a theme before we pick the models?" Piero asked.

"Didn't you tell me, Master Piero, I had full artistic freedom?"

"Please don't call me your master. I prefer to think of myself as your collaborator."

"Filippino here has been my collaborator and assistant for years. Are you planning to replace him once I take him back to Florence?"

"Can't he return himself to Florence? Imagine you! You just got here! You are making this hard for me," Piero said. "I'd hoped you would show some sketches before you started. It can be whatever you like. I want to know what it's going to be."

"First, tell me where in the villa you want my first painting to hang and let that space serve as my inspiration. Choose a room with a long wall so I can honor the scale of this villa with a painting that will match its size. When I go back to Florence, I'll hire a woodworker to build the panel, and I'll buy enough gesso to prepare it here. Once I know my subject and not before, I'll go again to the city to buy the colors I'll need. You can help me grind the pigments, crack the eggs, if you like. I don't want to waste your money or my time. Patience, my young Piero, is going to be a necessary ingredient."

"Eggs make me burp," Piero said.

"We don't eat them, we use the yolks to bind the pigments. In the meanwhile, thanks to Poppi and your sisters, I have an easel for sketching. If Poppi agrees to roast charcoal for me in her *profumeria* oven once it's set, I have enough tinted papers with me now to begin."

"Patience," Piero repeated with a twitch of his head. He placed his palm against his forehead. "I will cultivate patience."

"How can I show you something if I myself don't know what I want to create?"

"This is no mere puppet head. This is a Botticelli masterpiece about to be born!" Poppi said.

"And I do not want to stand in your way," Piero added, "but with all this expense: the panel, a woodworker, and now I suppose you're going to tell me you need a stove to cook the gesso too. Why not buy something already prepared?"

"The size, Piero, may not allow it, and I want to prepare the panel myself. Perhaps Poppi will let us heat the gesso and glue on her stove, but those are technical questions you should not even concern yourself with. Let's start with the size and location. Then you must leave the rest to me. Beauty will be my master and I'll paint all I know of the subject if I may." Sandro walked over to the improvised easel and adjusted its angle. With his back to Piero, he said, "And once I begin you must not come to heckle me."

"But I am paying your way. I'm investing in you!"

"In me or in what I can do for you?"

"Stop your quarreling!" Poppi said. "Show Filippino the fountain," she told the girls. They ran to him and pulled him out of the greenhouse and toward a fountain overgrown with vines.

"Now listen to me, both of you," Poppi said, placing herself between the two men. She looked first at Piero, then Sandro, asking him, "How do flowers grow?"

"In sun. In light. With water and food, and without those they die or remain seeds forever," he said. Poppi listened, smiling, with her eyes closed. She turned to Piero. "And you, Piero, what do you say about how a flower grows?"

"The same. Water, sun, weeding so the life is not choked out of it."

"Exactly," she said. "You are each flowers. Don't be weeds. You, my master," she said to Piero, "are barely out of seed and need to tend your own garden. You now have the artist you have longed for under your roof. So let him flower as you know he can. Do not be his weed. Be his food."

"And you, flower of unique beauty, Master Botticelli," she said to Sandro. "Don't make a weed of someone who offers you rain and light. Be companions and friends at best, but allow the other to do his own growing."

Much as Lorenzo, the great diplomat, had done days earlier, Poppi reached out her hands to each man. "Now give a salute of friendship in the name of Beauty—goddess whom you both worship."

Sandro looked into the hopeful eyes of his young patron. *This is no Lorenzo.* Oslavia's words sounded in his head: *Do not bite the hand that feeds you.* He placed an arm around his corpulent young patron and whispered in his ear, "Trust me, Piero. I will make you proud."

"I believe you, Sandro. I'll keep my distance. You can show me as you go or you can show me at the end."

"At the end. But let's go together now into the house to choose the wall to be home for our great masterpiece."

Sandro turned to Poppi. "Filippino and I will organize this space starting tomorrow morning. After we've made it workable, I'll bring him back to Florence. I'll check on my parents, take in a guild meeting, and visit my sister. Maybe you and the girls can hang the curtains, and do what you can to finish." He turned back to Piero. "Then I will begin my finest work. I can feel it. Thank you for your trust, Piero."

"You have it, Master."

"Don't call me master, Master."

CHAPTER NINE

Savonarola in Ferrara

GEROME'S FINGERTIPS felt the smooth threads of the bed sheets. No straw. No stones. Had he died? His mouth opened but no sound came out. Had he spoken? Was this a dream?

He sent a command to his right leg to move, but nothing moved. He willed inside his head, his heart, his belly, Move I say! Carry me! And then a prayer. *God. Beloved spirit, move me out. Waken me from this dream.*

"Gerome? Are you awake?" his father asked. "Gerome. Are you with us?"

Light seeped in through his eyelashes. Blinding. "Babylonian captivity," Gerome said. "Slaves in Egypt. Free the slaves from themselves. Now, I say!"

"Gerome, are you with us?"

"Who is 'us'?"

"Your father. You are in Ferrara. Your sisters. Here. Standing by your bed. We are about to give you the last rites."

"No! Not now. I am . . ." and then he slipped back into a dark room. A dark corridor. Scenes flashed before him. Words. Sounds. He heard his superior from Bologna say, "Ferrara or excommunication for you!"

He saw two boys in clerical robes carrying him. He saw himself with the same two boys sitting in a circle, each one praying and pleasuring himself at the same time. Darkness again. Then bright light, a field of sunflowers. A naked woman floating face down among the reeds. And deafening, incessant screams of cicadas. Though he could not move he struggled to cover his ears. A searing pain in his back demanded his attention and he shouted, "Bring me the whip!"

"No whipping allowed here," a familiar voice said.

"Who are you?"

"Your father."

"I have only one Father in heaven. He shall lead me beside the still waters. My cup runneth—"

"Gerome, Gerome, Gerome," he heard. Then he saw hands place the hood over the young woman from the reeds. Then darkness again.

He heard rustling around the bed. Girls' voices whimpered as his body was being rolled from side to side. Something wet on his forehead. The smell of ginger, the sting in his eye from the liquid, but he could not speak. He had forgotten how to speak. He had chosen not to speak. *Breathe in and out. Chest rising and falling. Alive. I am still breathing. I am alive.*

"Where am I?" he wanted to say. Said it in his mind, then heard an answer. "You are here at home with us. Your family."

"Sleep now, Gerome," his mother said. Yes, his mother's voice. With his head angled on a pillow, tears streamed down his cheeks and no beard caught them. *No beard!* He could not reach his hand to his face to be certain. He could not move. His chest, only, continued to rise and fall, but the repetitive rhythm of his heartbeat seemed to lull him deeper into this dream state. And though he could sense the light filtering through his lashes, he had no strength to open his eyes.

"Sleep," she said. And so he did.

GEROME'S PHYSICIAN FATHER knew his son's illness was no infection for which leeches or bloodletting was the prescription. It was a deeper, darker challenge, one that required a skill for healing beyond his knowledge. Still, he tried to watch and learn. The first few days, Gerome would bring his finger to his mouth, then make a gentle hissing to quiet voices, but his delirium deepened and he lost control of any conscious will for silence. They had removed the rags of voluntary poverty, shorn his beard infested with filth. They had wrapped his torso in white swaddling, hoping for a rebirth, yet preparing for his death.

During the second week, tears streamed from Gerome's eyes. While he began to take nourishment, he wept and the red around his eyes grew brighter. His father led the family in prayer outside the room so the son might not hear, lest they recite some incorrect incantation and trigger Gerome, once more, to starve himself.

One afternoon, when his father had laid yet another compress of ginger on his son's brow, the young monk spoke his first coherent words.

"I am trying to kill the devil in me, but it ceases to die," Gerome said.

"And what precisely does this devil tell you?"

"I am unworthy to lead others because I have not tamed the beast in my own heart. How can I save others if I cannot save myself from sin?"

The father was sitting now beside his son. Grateful the boy's words came out in sentences, in complete thoughts.

"When I was in Florence the first time," Gerome began in a calm voice, "they sent me there because of my writings and they told me to preach. But the people who gathered would laugh and my stuttering grew worse."

"Do you think stuttering is the work of the devil?"

"Who else would cut into my tongue to dishonor my highest intentions? Who else would cause my loins to burn with lust?"

"But you have stuttered since you were a young boy. The force of your sex is not immoral. What you do with it is what matters."

"And there, too, Father, I have sinned in mind and body."

"Desiring is not delighting."

"But I have done unspeakable things not only in my mind, Father."

"Thoughts and dreams are not facts. Actions. Actions are real. And actions interrupted by higher impulses pave the way to reform," the father said.

He did not want to ask what unspeakable things his son was referring to. He did not want to know. When the young boy was rejected by his first love, Niomi, he turned his love toward God. And now, even in this, he had been rejected, sent back to his family in a semi-lunatic state for healing or burial. The boy obviously was not normal, and the parents at this point were praying for his mere survival and his secure and healthy return to the clergy if at all possible.

At least while he was safely stowed behind the granite walls, his fevered ravings would not be directed at his family. After all, with a lunatic brother, his sisters' marriage prospects would say that touch of madness was a touch by the devil and it ran in the blood.

"A saint is a sinner who keeps trying to save himself," the father said.

"Like Saint Augustine?"

"Overcoming temptation builds character. Putting the past behind you and being reborn today offers hope to others and to yourself. If I save a man from choking because he stuffed food down his throat, God is giving him a new chance to put gluttony behind him—if he has the strength of character to do so."

"I think it is the devil tearing out my tongue. It is the sins of the past infecting the present. If I cannot forgive myself, who will forgive me?"

"Precisely." His father wiped a scented cloth across his son's forehead. "Perhaps your stuttering is God himself prompting you to summon more courage."

"Do you think so?" Gerome said dreamily in a faint voice.

"You don't have to live like this. You can help people with medicine. You can take a wife. Have a family. Live a prosperous life."

"I am on a path, Father. I am called to be on it. This I know. But the devil attaches to my back, my loins, my flesh like fire burning deep into my mind, and I become confused."

"First of all, Son, you must build yourself up. If you want to serve your God you've got to hear the messages with a calm heart, otherwise you will not know who is the devil and who is the Christ."

"Can you give me some medicine to kill the devil and leave the man of God in one piece?"

"Perhaps that is your cross. To see the devil in others and share the devil in yourself, together in numbers choosing God's path. With the Bible's words, you can lead all to a higher place."

"But when the very clergy, my brethren, and even the pope himself, is as corrupt and feverish with gluttony, lust, and greed as I, what then, Father?"

Gerome's father sat back. He knew his hysterical son spoke the truth. He had visited the chambers of the highest of the high in the church. And there he had met concubines and their secret children. He had delivered the bastards. In the eyes of the church, these cardinals, popes, and the anointed were celibate because they had never technically entered the bonds of matrimony. Instead, they had married off their illicit lovers to their faithful servants, creating sham families that gave them unobstructed access to their continued sins.

"If you live among us, Gerome, you can take up only your own cause and live your life. But if you take on the world, you must speak to the world with confidence and clarity. Put aside your fearful wavering and put the fire into those who listen to you. To do that, you must be physically strong. Who is going to follow a monk who wears the face of death and whose breath gives off the stench of the grave?"

"And I was doing this?"

"When you got here, you were closer to death than life. You must put away the whip. You must end these vows of silence and mortification. Consider the world to be your congregation." Gerome's father rose to his feet when he saw his son had taken in all he could of his father's guidance.

"Now sleep, Son. Don't prove your strength by how much physical pain you can endure; prove it by how many souls you can touch with your passion."

Gerome was in a deep sleep by the time his father had spoken his last word. He left his son's bedside, relieved Gerome would survive. Once more he had healed someone's body, but this time it had been with words—words of encouragement applied as a salve, not daring to question if they would be words he might someday regret.

CHAPTER TEN

Sandro Visits the Medici Palace

ONCE HE GOT PAST the new guards stationed at the palace entrance, Sandro climbed the long central staircase, lost in worry over his painting. He had calculated the enormity of the expensive wooden panel he was about to order the next day, but he still had no idea what to put on it. Gasps coming from the Platonic Academy room brought him back to the present.

"Don't miss this!" Lorenzo said as he yanked Sandro's arm, pulling him through the doorway and locking him in a tight embrace. Sandro held on with all his strength, smelling Lorenzo's hair thick with scented oil, and feeling the vibration of his warm hello in his own chest. In that moment, they seemed as always. Two close friends. Two equals.

At center stage two dwarfs yanked a wild bear by a chain attached to its nose. They ordered it to sit. Many guests had escaped to the back of the room for safety.

Out of the bear came a voice. "My head, please!"

The dwarfs climbed on tiny ladders to yank the bear's head off. The round, prune-lined face of Marsilio Ficino smiled at the crowd through a long beard. One dwarf toppled to the ground, the other rescued him, and the two scampered to the sides like obedient dogs awaiting the next order. Relieved guests laughed, applauded, and returned to their seats as the famous philosopher, soaked in perspiration, shed the costume and beard to stand before the group.

"Ficino looks better as a bear," Sandro joked, but Lorenzo grimaced at his remark. "Why this elaborate party?" He wanted to ask which new artist was decorating the palace now that he was gone. The scent of jasmine in the hallways, his innovation, had been used again.

"A show of force," Lorenzo said.

"The guards outside? I've only been gone a few weeks, and I had to send up my signature before they let me in. No one recognized me."

"Lucrezia's orders. Like that bear, we were asleep and now we are awakening."

"What does that have to do with the guards?"

"Forget the guards. Sit down and listen to the master."

"Master of what?" Sandro asked. He did not sit.

"Of pulling us out of hibernation."

As Sandro stood beside his friend, strains of music from the ballroom above called to him. Sandro had heard the philosopher expound in his high-pitched voice on everything from food to the afterlife, and not wanting to hear any of it again he refused to sit. When Ficino began, "The human being has been in hibernation like this lazy, lumbering, and clumsy bear . . ." Sandro heard Lorenzo whisper in his ear, "What's wrong with you? Sit down!"

But Sandro had already returned to the mystery of the huge empty surface of his painting. "I'm heading upstairs for the music. Maybe I'll find more inspiration there."

LORENZO'S MOTHER, LUCREZIA TORNABUONI, sat on the edge of her bed in the middle of her private chambers. Above her head hung a blue and gold silk wedding canopy strung from the surrounding bedposts and attached to a central point on the eighteen-foot ceiling. Two ladies used soft sable brushes filled with pale powder to lighten the dark, puffy circles under her eyes and the redness around the lids.

"Enough!" Lucrezia said. She took a huge breath, sighed, and rose to her feet. She wrapped a silk scarf around her shoulders and walked toward the strains of music coming from the doorway.

"I want to dance to forget my sons are blind!" she said, more to herself than her attendants. She swerved around to face them again. "My lips, I almost forgot." She sat back on the bed. "Paint them bright and happy. A mask of color to hide my mood this evening. Say a prayer for me so I might sleep rather than weep tonight."

The ladies waited for Lucrezia's lips to be still, but she spoke again.

"At least I knew what my dear departed Piero was thinking, what he was planning, but these boys of mine run off yelping in every direction, winning hearts the way puppies do."

Her servants giggled, pretended to yelp like puppies, but it did nothing to cheer their mistress.

"A time of reckoning is at hand," Lucrezia said, then pressed her lips together so they could be painted. Her nostrils flared in her long sloping nose—the Tornabuoni trait she had proudly passed down to her two sons, a mark most obvious in Lorenzo.

ONCE SHE REACHED THE ENTRANCE of the ballroom, she saw Sandro at the opposite doorway scribbling in a tiny sketchbook. She cut a path across the room, parting the sea of couples, mostly masked women dancing with women. Lucrezia's skirts, with tiny bells and beads at the bottom, rustled, jingled, and scraped along the marble floor until she reached Sandro.

"Are you drawing the wind?" she said as she looked over Sandro's shoulder at a jumble of swirling lines. When he turned to give her a full embrace, his small sketchbook fell to the floor, opening to his caricature of Savonarola. Sandro broke his hug to rescue it.

"Who's the monk with the strange nose?" Lucrezia said.

"Some of my nonsense."

"You are not capable of nonsense, my Sandro. Your sketches are like notes from God."

"Or maybe the devil." He slid the book under his belt. "Do you think me perverse for having sketched such a creature?"

"I think you have seen some truth and put it into a picture."

"Why this party?"

"Changing the subject, are you?" she said. "To show the Pazzis we are in first position. I have had my sister-in-law Patrizia Pazzi bring all of her siblings."

"The guards? Sending up signatures? All of a sudden, I'm a threatening stranger. I feared I might not be admitted at all."

"Don't be offended, Sandro. We are watching everyone who comes and goes. We should have done it years ago. Downstairs the men talk of world unity, but outside the mercenaries stockpile their coins. There's no end to their assignments. Only you, Sandro, and the artists and musicians and the poets are our true soldiers for peace."

"I never thought of myself as a warrior."

"You are the soldiers. And God is on your side." Lucrezia stood back to look at Sandro from head to toe. "The country does you well. So, will the deputy of Beauty dance with an old hag who has not slept for weeks and whose sons think she is crazy for weeping and worrying about nothing?"

Not waiting for an answer, she opened her arms to invite a dancing partner and grabbed Sandro's hand. She felt the corner of the small sketchbook in her ribs. "And why do you sketch so aggressively tonight?" she said.

"I'm haunted by the aim of my next work. Everything I see, everywhere I go, teases me with a seed of inspiration and so I have no one idea, only countless titillations."

"Even a penis-faced prelate . . . ?" she said, standing still to better hear Sandro's response, but he swept her back into the movement of the dance.

"Not that," he said, moving them toward the flow of the other dancers.

"Absolutely not that. Those sketches are meant for my eyes only and offer me entertainment. You must forget you ever saw it. I beg you."

"And do you think you own what you do? We as your patrons have a right to it," Lucrezia said, pushing her hand against Sandro's to move him outside the other dancers' path.

"Not the scribblings of my imagination." He twirled her away from him, but she refused to turn her head away from his.

"Even those, we own," she said, looking up with a serious expression. "What we don't own is the genius that creates it or the talent that turns that image into magic. That, only God owns, and so you are His soldier."

"And you, Signora Medici, what does that make you? My commander in chief?" He gave her a military salute.

"Your tormentor for your own good. Your gardener to clear the weeds."

"And those might be?"

"Distractions. Cares about these soldiers, concerns about our banks, the exigencies of marriages made and unmade, the politics of wedlock and worth. Do not clutter yourself with those." She pulled him closer.

Sandro said nothing, yet Lucrezia could sense his mind at work—spinning, confused perhaps, vulnerable to her influence.

"I'm old and I can say what I will," she continued, "and I know you're listening. Forget the guards."

"How can I when this place is the home of those I love?"

"You must," she said. She gripped his hand tighter, stood back from him to focus eye to eye. "I command you!"

"But your son has turned me out to his fifteen-year-old cousin."

"It's your greatest opportunity to be away from all this political pestilence!" she said.

"And this young Piero calls me master," Sandro said.

"As he should. As he should. And what is this ghost of a painting that haunts Master Botticelli for the villa in Castello?"

"A large painting for the dining area. For the first time this is not an assignment to fulfill someone else's idea. It's up to me, and I'm swimming with fear, and at the same time I love the freedom."

"Fear?" she said. "Are you not Master Botticelli? A thirty-three-year-old who has chosen to be an artist, not distracted by wife or child?"

"My wife is this city. My child—"

"Your child will be this work you nurture in the country away from the politics and bickering."

"If—just *if*—I were to paint this picture for you, my lady, what would you wish the subject to be?"

They danced side by side now, walking counterclockwise in step with the other couples around the dance floor.

"You are asking me to take away your freedom."

"Merely to suggest. *I* can take it or not. I'm curious."

"Curious! Curious!" she said. "I am suggesting. I am *ordering* you, *commanding* you, to keep painting. I can suggest a topic: the flowering of this city. The flowering of culture and harmony you've heard all those years in the Academy."

"Flowering," Sandro repeated.

"The blood I worry about, Sandro, could wash away the bloom of this city, one family or the next. One pope or the next. One ruling monarch who has decided not to repay his hefty Medici loan. We, the wise ones, have stupidly financed the same people who could wipe us out."

Lucrezia turned her face away to hide her watering eyes. "If commanding you won't work, I beg you to paint the story of the flowering of this city under our family. Paint it however you see it. Use whatever signs and symbols you like from the ancient texts, wherever you find them. Let yourself mix all the beauty together as one whirlwind of joy, one sacred moment. You must. Don't look for direction or approval from me or any other Medici. Only keep God as your guide. Another Virgin Mary we don't need."

"And another Virgin Mary I do not want to paint across ten feet of gesso."

"Exactly," Lucrezia agreed. "Something bigger. Tell a story. You can do it. Do not fear. God will point the way."

"God will point the way," he echoed as the dance music was interrupted by sudden applause.

Lorenzo's younger brother, Giuliano, stepped into the center of the group. Unlike Filippino, whose perfection of form and face attracted, Giuliano's features were compelling in their imperfection. Where

Lorenzo's nose was long and flat, Giuliano's was long with a gentle arch that ran from between his eyes in a soft curve some might call a hook. This dominant feature was paired with a softness in his eyes, his thin brows and lips giving him an innocence that made him look even younger than his twenty-four years. Always aware of his appeal to a crowd, and especially women, he used it modestly, never flaunting or flirting, never taking advantage. With both arms raised, he waited for the crowd to fall quiet.

CLAUDIA SHIVERED behind her disguise in the sweltering ballroom as she watched Giuliano search the crowd for her blue-feathered mask. He waved this frightened bird forward into the light.

Fifty candles burned in the chandelier above. Giuliano stretched his arm out toward his Claudia. As she fluttered toward him through the cloud of summer sweat and the perfume from wilted flowers, she felt as though she might swoon until she attached herself to his side.

"I want you all to meet my betrothed," he said.

At first the crowd applauded tentatively with this unexpected news, then wildly once the musicians released a congratulatory trumpet blare.

Before Giuliano could say another word, a gasp went out among the crowd. People stepped away from the spot where Lucrezia had been standing. She lay unconscious on the floor, surrounded by friends and guests. Giuliano dropped Claudia's hand to rush to his mother's side. He and Sandro scooped the matriarch up and carried her toward a chair.

"Take me to my chambers," Lucrezia said as she came to.

By now Claudia, still masked, had put her fear aside and followed close behind Giuliano as he and Sandro led Lucrezia upstairs.

"Close the curtains, Giuliano," Lucrezia said, "and get Lorenzo!"

Claudia had never seen such a huge bed, nor one surrounded by so many layers of curtains.

"Get Lorenzo," Lucrezia repeated. "Everyone else, please leave. Tell everyone it was the heat and the excitement of the moment."

A white hand barely showed as she parted the curtain. "Forgive me, Signorina," she said to Claudia with icy politeness. "Do not take off your mask. I don't want to meet you under these circumstances. Better you return when I am more composed and we can meet face to face. Come back tomorrow evening, please. Sandro will escort you home."

The curtain closed.

Claudia had not yet been introduced to Sandro, so when the handsome gentleman with the crest of the artists' brotherhood across his chest helped her gather her scarves and shawls, she assumed it was he. In spite of Lucrezia's instructions that he accompany her, she insisted on riding in the carriage to Scandicci by herself.

She did not remove her mask from her tear-filled eyes until she climbed, shivering, into her bed. The cold wind of Lucrezia's false civility had swept her from her true love's side.

OUT OF BREATH from racing up the stairs, Lorenzo dropped his sword and purse the moment he looked into his mother's room. When he saw her heavy winter curtains drawn around her bed on this hot summer's night, he stripped off the layered costume tied around his body. *Not that! Not death for her too!* He kicked away the stepping stool his mother always used to raise herself onto the high bed, pulled the curtain aside, and, already weeping, said, "Mother, I'm here. What is it?"

Lucrezia's pale hand patted the bed for Lorenzo to sit. Giuliano lay next to her, on the other side. She sat up with a great effort.

"Do you know what this boy has done, Lorenzo? He has committed suicide for our entire family!"

"I see no blood," Lorenzo said. "We are all breathing. I had feared far worse."

"He announced his betrothal!"

"To whom?"

"Some mystery woman—"

"Whose party mask was never removed," Giuliano said.

"Because I fainted, thank God."

Giuliano propped himself on an elbow to see his brother better. "It was in the ballroom. I wanted to share the joy of my new love with our friends and family."

"But what about the Pazzi girl?" Lorenzo asked.

"Exactly," Lucrezia said.

"I cannot marry for politics. Isn't it enough Uncle Giovanni married Francesca Pazzi?" Giuliano said. "Lorenzo is the prince. I'm the baby brother. I should be able to do what I want!"

"Patrizia Pazzi was our chance for keeping peace in Florence," Lucrezia said, glaring at him.

"The Pazzis want to take us down the first chance they get, Giuliano." Lorenzo spoke in a gentle tone he rarely used with his younger brother. "You know this. Aunt Francesca died giving birth to Patrizia. This was our only hope to keep the peace and you've upset it. At best they'll pack us up and ship us out of Florence."

"I don't care where I live. I want to have a life of my own. With the woman I love."

"You can't afford it, boy," Lucrezia said. "*We* can't afford it." She grabbed his hair and yanked his head so he would look her in the eye. "When we need alliance, you give me defiance."

Lorenzo saw tears brimming in Giuliano's eyes. He reached over his mother's lap to touch his brother's hand. "It's not fair, Giuli, I know. But we need your cooperation. The banks are weakening. People in high places are defaulting on their loans. We need every alliance we can forge to keep us from drowning."

"It's too late," Giuliano said. "She's pregnant."

The three of them lay silent until the matriarch spoke. "That's only a detail. You'll keep her on the side, have the baby in secret. I won't allow anything else."

Giuliano looked at his brother. "You, Lorenzo the Magnificent, you'll find a way to work around this. I know you can."

"My way is with the mercenaries," Lorenzo said. "To hire them around the clock to preserve at least our lives and the lives of our children. You have never realized the seriousness of our situation. And I have caused your weakness by hoping at least *you* might have a life that was close to normal."

"Now that I've finally found someone, I cannot even show you her face," Giuliano muttered as if to himself.

"Who is she?" Lucrezia asked.

"I will not tell you until you promise me you will forget this Pazzi business. Patrizia is only twelve years old!"

"I cannot forget it. We must at least postpone the betrothal. Please, I beg you, do not announce this to anyone. Do what you must to support your new love, but please, I beg you, do not delude yourself into thinking you are going to marry her."

Lucrezia took several deep breaths. Lorenzo stroked her head, relieved she was not dying.

"Now go, boys. Go out to our guests and act as though all is well. Excuse my fainting spell. And if they ask about Giuliano's announcement, you tell them, Lorenzo, it was another one of Giuliano's practical jokes induced by too much wine and too much melancholy still remaining after Simonetta's death."

"I never loved Simonetta. She was married. The crowds loved it when I chose her at the annual games as the most beautiful woman in all of Florence. I never loved her, not the way I love my Claudia."

"My Claudia," Lucrezia repeated, then turned away from Giuliano to look at Lorenzo. She rolled her eyes as if to say, Can you believe the ignorance of your little brother! She turned back to Giuliano. "And you, my baby," she said, her voice full of affection despite her stern glare, "you must go and sleep off this dream of a normal life. You are in the public eye, and you will be there until your dying day."

"Then I'll die a bachelor, Mother," answered Giuliano.

"God forbid! Now go! Let me sleep. Send in some fans for me and pull back the heavy drapes. Go. But first a hug, my brilliant boys."

She stretched out her arms to pull the two men to her bosom, whispering as she had so many times to them before, "Your only wife is the city of Florence. She is your bride, the one destiny has forced you to place above all others. Now go!"

CHAPTER ELEVEN

Dreaming at Villa di Castello

LOST IN WORRY about the painting, Sandro spent the entire morning upon his return to Villa di Castello pacing back and forth from his studio to his room. "Another Virgin Mary we don't need!" Lucrezia had said to him, and he had laughed out loud with her. The excitement of total freedom seemed to intoxicate him, and yet, her hook was in his side: a hook he both treasured and resented. To be manipulated by one who deserved great respect; to be loyal and devoted and yet, ought he defy? And the "idea" she had proposed—mixing everything he had ever absorbed under her roof—left him reeling. *There is no surface large enough! A jumble, and it will take the rest of my life to paint it.*

When the dogs' yelping brought him back to reality late morning, a sudden dagger of guilt struck. *Oslavia!* He'd forgotten to visit as he had promised her, and now it was too late. He needed to settle this artistic question first. Then, he'd go to his sister.

He rushed to the greenhouse studio, stripping off all the large pieces of paper he had carefully tacked on the improvised easel. In the privacy of his room he would have the time and space to sketch a composition that would inspire him. Then, before the actual painting began, before the large boards he had ordered could arrive from Florence, he would visit Oslavia.

Once in his room he set out the large papers, twenty in number, enough when spread across the floor to equal the size of the painting. Now on his bed, he lay on his belly, head propped in his hand, to contemplate the expanse of the unknown.

The inner dialogue between doubt and hope, action and paralysis, returned. Yes, he had done well, was praised, recognized, even sought after, but maybe Lorenzo had seen his talent was drying up and had sent him off to Piero's to make room for younger, more talented artists. Piero's assignment of no assignment was different. No map to follow, no contract stipulating the number of angels, the buildings to be included, the dignitaries to be painted as saints or sinners or kings. Maybe he was not up to the challenge. Maybe that was why he was so lost, so empty. Or perhaps he could use it as an opportunity to make Lorenzo remorseful for having let him go? This must be a masterpiece of all masterpieces . . . but it was too much. His head grew heavy, and he fell asleep.

THE MEDICI PALACE BALLROOM. *Giuliano's fiancée peels off her mask, revealing the face of a serpent and then a skull exhaling black, noxious smoke fills the room. The people drop away into a deep sleep or death. Only Giuliano is untouched. He holds the creature's hand, which becomes a talon that carries her prey off into the clouds above the roofless building. Sandro is at the water's edge, viewing his reflection in a pond like Narcissus. As he reaches to grasp his own reflected hand, the hand of the same female demon reaches up to pull him into the black water. Down, down the creature leads him, but he breathes effortlessly. Large snails with human heads feed off the bottom of the pond: Cosimo and Piero the Elder, Simonetta and Giuliano. All have swollen cheeks and pale white flesh and elongated tongues that scrape along the bottom. He reaches for Simonetta's shell but the suction of her grasp is beyond his human strength to dislodge. He tries to use both arms to detach her from the bottom, but the she-demon yanks his other arm, and he feels himself splitting down the middle. His intestines float out of his belly toward the current of the black water until they are gobbled by the she-demon.*

Sandro awoke drenched in sweat, heart pounding in his throat. He dragged himself to the window to let the evening air cool his flesh. Picking one of the sheets of paper, he began to sketch the swirling black waters from his dream.

Determined not to leave his room until he had sketched out an idea for his next masterpiece, Sandro locked his door. He slid a note to Poppi under it, requesting she leave food only at one o'clock each day. *"And do not knock!"*

He pushed all the furniture into a corner of the room to create a larger workspace in the center—enough room for him to walk around the sheets of paper and view them from every angle. When he exhausted his supply of paper after two days, he stripped his sheets off the bed to draw on them.

After three days, his leftover food attracted the villa mice, the only company he could tolerate. A beard sprouted on his face, now blackened by charcoal he had rubbed into his skin during his furious effort to settle on a direction for his painting. *Take away all the patrons, the families, the cousins, and the church, and I have no ideas of my own! Years of secret sketches for paintings I had longed to do, my own creations, and now, nothing! My imagination, a desert. A fraud.*

The ugly nightmare of his entrails being consumed by a she-monster from the depths of swirling black waters had been the only new imagery. He rejected it.

As a last search for inspiration, he reached for his sketchbooks. The face of Gerome stared back at him. *The young monk from Ferrara. Art defiling the church! Harlot Madonnas!*

A river of rage boiled in his veins at that boy-priest's dismissal of all those paintings he, the great house artist, had done of Madonna and child—paintings in which he had rendered the religious subjects dictated by a patron, taking only the liberty to alter the posture on one angel or another—but always the Adoration, the same story.

"That's it!" he shouted. "A new story! I'll tell a story not only in images but in layer upon layer of possible meanings no one will understand. The ultimate prank! One hundred years from now, intellects from the Platonic Academy and beyond will still be wondering what it signifies."

Sandro's laugh rose to a loud cackle as he dressed with clothes he had strewn over the floor, then froze at the sound of rustling garments and muffled voices outside his room. He tiptoed to the door and yanked it open.

"We were afraid to knock, but I heard voices and thought you had a guest," Piero said, with Poppi standing behind him holding a plate of food.

"Sometimes I talk to myself while I work," Sandro said.

"The wooden panels you ordered arrived and await you in the greenhouse," Piero said.

The idea of a colossal prank, an intellectual and visual joke, spread a huge smile on Sandro's face—a smile he chose to let Piero interpret however he might.

"I'm finally ready to start," Sandro said. "Give me a few minutes and I'll be down for a proper meal, and then I'll be off to visit my sister. I promised her I would see her regularly, and now that I've finally discovered the theme of the painting, I will see her before I begin."

"Aren't you going to look at the panels? Can't I at least see your sketches?"

Sandro pointed to his head. "They're all up here," he said, "for me to dream and for you to see when I'm finished, remember?"

"Can't I peek at the sketches?"

"Impossible. Even *I* didn't understand them until five minutes ago."

With his creative juices flowing again, Sandro was finally relieved. Humor—not devotion, not a revelation—would be the driving force of the work. Ecstatic with the prize of freedom he was going to exercise over Piero and everyone else, Sandro placed his arm around his new master to shower affection on him, unaware he was soiling Piero's clothes with his charcoal-blackened hands or overwhelming the young patron with the smell of his unwashed body. "No need to see the panels yet. I will begin the moment I return from the convent. Trust me, Piero."

Piero shrank away from the exuberant artist, whose burst of energy and affection had sent him into a fit of coughing that exaggerated the twitching of his head. And once again he repeated his unique, frequent, and involuntary comment, "Imagine you! Imagine you!" as a whisper to himself.

"Imagine me?" asked Sandro. "I'm imagining all I need to. Trust me, Master Piero!"

CHAPTER TWELVE

Our Lady of the Most Holy Rosary September 1, 1477

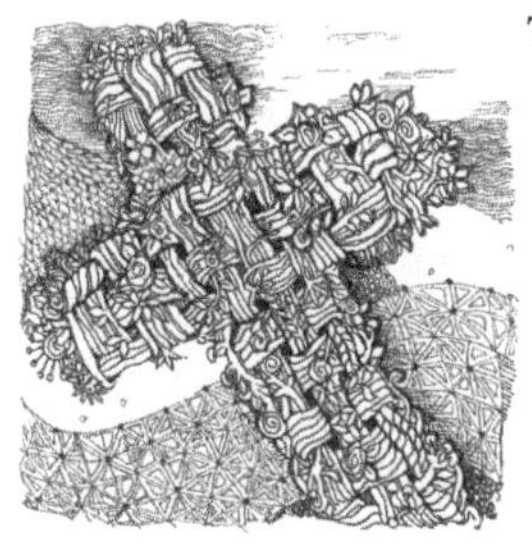

THE BLUE-WASHED WALLS of Floriana's new cell perspired with a film of moisture. Through a high, narrow window at the far end, a shaft of sunlight cut across the floor, burning a hot path along the terra cotta tiles. On the morning of her tenth day in Oslavia's care, Floriana had lain under the sun's rays, bathing in the light and the heat. She passed her hand along the moist wall, then placed her cooled palm against her forehead. Hot and cool at the same moment, she began to hum herself to sleep and felt an inner calm return.

THE SOUND OF SOMETHING SCRAPING along the floor tiles awakened Floriana. She watched Oslavia pull a box from under the bed out into the middle of the room, remove the lid, and lift up a nun's habit, shaking out the fabric and sending a few moths into the air. She motioned for Floriana to stand.

Slowly the girl rose to her feet.

"Put this on. It will save your life," Oslavia said.

"That same cloth!—" Floriana said, shivering.

"Of course it is. We are part of the Dominican order."

"Isn't it enough I was violated by one among you, one who still goes free? That I almost died on your thorns and bread? That my woman's blood—"

"Silence! Do not speak again of that day! Put this on!"

Floriana pressed the coarse garment against her cheek, then threw it back into the box.

Oslavia picked it back up and shoved it against Floriana's chest. "Use your imagination. Make of it whatever you will . . . Now!"

Floriana stepped out of the dress she had managed to clean and repair after her rescue from the tower. It had been her last physical connection to her home. Slowly, after Oslavia turned away to give her privacy, Floriana placed each piece of the novitiate habit onto her naked body.

"Excellent," Oslavia said as she turned back around. "Now you can walk about the yard, even into the sanctuary. You must maintain a vow of silence with all, even me. Can you weave a cross of flowers?"

"I can weave whatever you like, but why the silence?"

"Not speaking will protect you. I'll send in some flowers to your cell and I want you to weave the most beautiful cross you can. Let yourself speak through the flowers and don't think about conversion. Don't think about speaking. Think only about immersion in the beauty of what you are creating. Find your God in the beauty and let Him speak through your hands."

"It is considered a grave sin to renounce our faith. I will never convert."

"I am not talking about conversion. I am talking about saving your life!"

"Let me escape. Tell him you lost me. Why do you hate the Jews so much?"

"It is not I who hates the Jews. It is the others who fear you have some knowledge, some strength that threatens the very center of what we believe. To convert one of you is the highest moment of pride for us. Father Bandini has contacted Bernardino—"

"I have no special knowledge. Only what my uncle the tailor taught me while I traveled with him for three years after my mother died. All I want is to be a weaver. I can sew. I can weave. I can dye cloth and make jewels with my hands."

"You would make such a beautiful nun."

"The only beauty I care about is what I can make. For myself. For others. I will not betray my family, my history. That would be death."

"Every night we die and each morning we are reborn."

"I will weave the garlands and flowers with the children."

"What children?"

"The ones I've heard from the beginning. I see myself laughing and playing with them, teaching them to weave with flowers. I must have something joyful to occupy my mind while you decide my fate."

"It is not I who decides, Floriana. You decide by your unwillingness."

"Send in the flowers and I will show you what I can do," Floriana said as she watched Oslavia gather her dress and take it away.

Floriana threw herself on the mattress. In order to stop a flow of tears, she decided to create a scene in her mind's eye to change her anger or to feed it. She wasn't sure which. She closed her eyes and imagined a pair of large metal shears. She saw herself sitting in a beautiful flowing dress covered in flowers, sitting by a stream. She took the shears and cut the habit into shreds she threw into the water. The habit became sheer and light around her body as she cut and sliced the imaginary cloth. Her anger at Oslavia, at the habit, at her faceless attacker began to lessen. She pulled a small sketchbook from under her pillow and wrote the words "I will be free. I will be free." over and over again until they formed the outline shape of a fish.

HAPPY TO BE WEAVING AGAIN, Floriana passed the days and weeks, her fingers sending energy through her body, carrying her beyond the convent walls.

Flowers separated by a rainbow of colors lay piled against the cool walls of her cell. The honeysuckle's perfume overpowered the wild flowers, while the purple-red of the convent's cultivated roses stood apart, permissive lieutenants to the lilting flower troops.

On one such afternoon, her concentration was interrupted when tiny fists hammered on her door. Two small, giggling girls burst inside, insects from the flowers they had gathered crawling on their arms. Pollen had left orange streaks against their cheeks, and flower buds and nettles tangled in their hair.

The younger girl, not more than five years old, came over to Floriana. The older girl stood behind Floriana—known to the children as the "Flower Nun," who was not supposed to speak. Floriana turned away from a huge cross of branches and twigs through which she had been braiding stems of carnations. She motioned the younger girl closer, gathering small grasses from the floor and spreading them out on her lap. She quickly wove the girl a basket, untangled small buds from the girl's hair, and dropped each one into it. The girl danced around the room holding the grass basket above her head.

Floriana laughed out loud, then put her hand over her mouth to muffle her voice. The older girl approached with eager eyes, so Floriana created a basket for her too. She was placing marigold petals in it when Luigi, the girls' older brother, arrived with armfuls of daisies. He followed Floriana's nods and gestures about where to place his harvest. A sudden sad expression crossed her face when she remembered herself as a child, dancing with her flowers in front of her silent mother, deaf from birth. She hid her gloom with a deep, exaggerated bow to the children, a signal for them to leave in search of more flowers.

When Floriana returned to her weaving, she hummed a prayer from her childhood to dispel the wash of darkness that had descended on her. Surely to hum *Ani Ma Amin*—three Hebrew words that meant "I believe"—with no one listening, was close enough to being silent. Over and over again she repeated her prayer as she added to the cross more lilies of the valley and a surrounding row of roses.

She was grateful her back was to the door when she sensed Oslavia's presence. As she turned to look up from her work, she saw what had become a look of astonishment on Oslavia's face every time she saw Floriana's creations. On a small slate tablet tied around her waist, Oslavia had written in chalk, *Excellent work! Why do you look so sad?*

Floriana reached for the slate, erased Oslavia's words, and wrote. *For my dead parents. May I have such a tablet and chalk?*

Oslavia erased Floriana's beautiful script and perfect grammar to write: *Soon. How did you learn how to read and write so well?*

Floriana wrote, *My uncle. So I could take measurements, and write bills for his wealthy Christian customers.*

Floriana stood, and motioned to Oslavia to sit and look at the woven flowers up close. She stretched her arms and legs to revive them from her concentrated work, and nestled her face into the perfume of the honeysuckle branches propped against the wall.

An unfamiliar knock drew her attention away from the flowers. Without waiting for Oslavia to give her direction, she opened the door and found herself staring into a pair of eyes the exact same color of blue as Oslavia's but in the face of a man. His gaze caused an intense blush to spread across her cheeks. Other than the caretaker, Federico, this was the first man she had seen in three months who did not wear the cloak of a prelate.

Oslavia saw him gaping into the room, taking in not only every detail of the girl's floral weavings, but the girl herself. She shouted, "Sandro," and swept past Floriana to join her brother outside. She closed the door in Floriana's face. Floriana could hear Oslavia scolding the man.

"Baby brother still," Oslavia said. "Has no one taught you the manners of these places? How dare you come upon me unannounced?"

Oslavia spat each phrase in a whisper, but Floriana, her ear to the door, heard every word. She could not see that Oslavia had grabbed the stranger's hand, and squeezed it with a combination of love and punishment, or that he had squeezed back, taking on his sister's challenge.

"First you scold me for abandoning you and then yell at me for coming to see you. Oslavia, dearest, I can't do anything right."

"Your presence as a handsome man without a cleric's garb could be a major distraction to my novitiates."

"Then they should run away!"

"Don't make light of this life."

That was the last Floriana heard except footsteps moving away from her door. She returned to her weaving with a fury, her cheeks throbbing, all sad thoughts of her childhood banished by this Sandro, whose gaze had devoured her and comforted her all at once. She wiped the sweat away with her white habit only to see upon it yellow pollen smudges from the honeysuckles. Had his stare been only one of fascination for the streaks on her face, or was it more? Even in her embarrassment, she smiled. "Sandro," she sounded out his name in a whisper. And again, "Sandro."

CHAPTER THIRTEEN

Savonarola Heads to Bologna

GEROME'S FATHER AND MOTHER had filled saddlebags with ointments, potions, food, wine, and gifts, along with bedding and provisions for their son's solo journey back to Bologna. These they strapped to a donkey, the very one that had been Gerome's favorite while growing up. When the father handed the son the bridle and reins for the animal, Gerome made no motion to receive them. "I prefer to leave as I came," Gerome said.

"You came carried on the backs of those who gave you up for dead." His father placed the bit inside the donkey's mouth, passing the bridle over the animal's head, and handed the reins to his son, who stroked its neck.

"Let this beast serve you so you can serve others," his father said. "If you walk three miles in one day, preaching and talking with people, you will only cover three miles of the world you wish to reach. If you ride ten miles and share your wisdom, and need nothing from others, your message will be more convincing. You must have a plan for yourself, Son."

"God writes my plan and he reads it to me moment by moment."

"Don't separate us from His plan," his father said. "All mortals need nourishment in body and soul, and the family is the place you can count on this. Unlike the last time, when you slipped off in the middle of the night, we send you off today with our blessings."

Feeling a surge of gratitude, Gerome gathered his family into an embrace—mother, sisters, father all together. He bowed his head to deliver his parting words.

"It is one thing to be born a beggar and rise to bring honor to the family. It is another to be born of a respected family like ours and to bring shame upon it and to dirty its name. I am determined to bring honor to this family by my actions and deeds. You will hear of me, and the good works I will do in God's name will be reflected back onto you."

Once on his way, Savonarola preached to the animal, something he had done as a child. Soon all traces of his stutter vanished. Although in the past his custom had been to sleep on the ground with no padding beneath him, on this first night, he pulled from the donkey's baggage a large cloth bedroll his mother had prepared for him. She had droned on in great detail how to use it, but he had hardly listened, so sure he would spread it flat on the ground. But after such a heartfelt departure, Gerome found himself filling the sack with tall grasses, dried hay, and small twigs until it almost burst. He even filled a bag his mother had made him to use as a pillow. He chewed on dried fruit, sipped water, and settled in for the night.

The nearby howl of a wolf sent a shiver through him. He prayed to Saint Francis—clairvoyant to animals—for protection. As he allowed a pleasure of well-being to pass through his body, he thanked his maker that the sexual disruption of earlier abstentions was gone.

He was drifting off to sleep when he smelled smoke and heard the distant crackling of a fire. Men's voices turned from laughter to shouts. An animal let out an anguished cry as though it were being choked to death. Then silence. Gerome stood and reached for a cask of wine his father had packed in the saddlebags. He walked toward the crackling fire. Perhaps someone needed his help.

The men were whispering now, but even these hushed voices fell silent as Gerome approached a clearing. Someone grabbed him from behind. He felt the hardness of an armored chest against his back and a knife at his throat. His captor pushed him into the clearing. Ten men sat around a campfire. Most were soldiers in military body armor, while others seemed of noble birth and two wore Franciscan robes.

"I am a humble priest on the road to Bologna, searching for those in need," Gerome said.

"Of wine, my humble Dominican, we are always in need," said one, who snatched it from Gerome before he could offer.

"It is yours," Gerome said. His captor released his hold. The group rearranged themselves to make room for him.

"I heard shouting, a dog yelping. And now I see this group of friends around the campfire. Did I imagine danger?"

"You're looking at the fire about to cook our dinner. You brought the wine," said the man who grabbed him. His face had a full beard and some of his teeth were blackened, others missing.

"We found no quail and we were fighting over who should kill and skin a victim for the others. Sit and join us," said one of those he took to be noble.

"What brings you here, my gentlemen?" Gerome asked.

"A desire to save our beloved Florence," two said in unison.

"My desire exactly!" Gerome said.

"A worthy cause." A man dressed in peasant clothing stepped forward, holding out a skinned fox dripping blood. He introduced himself as Francesco Salviati. "Lorenzo blocked my appointment as archbishop of Pisa and instead appointed his cousin."

The group grumbled something about fighting and tyranny. Some raised knives in the air.

"Tyranny is inside people who have turned away from God," Gerome said, as he looked to the men in Franciscan robes. Neither one looked up at him. "Killing is not the answer."

"Who said anything about killing?" Francesco said. The fox's blood made a black puddle on the ground. "We who want to give power back to the poor."

"And will you ban the wearing of lascivious clothing, and jewelry, and the making of paintings that show the Madonna as a harlot?" Gerome asked.

"If you join forces with us you can be part of the group to reestablish the church as it should be in that city," one of the clerics said. He was hardly more than a boy, younger than Gerome himself. His deformed left hand held a stick he used to stir the fire. Three fingers seemed fused together, the fingernails forming a point like a talon.

"If you replace one powerful family with another and don't honor the Father who should be Ruler above all else, you are shuffling puppets," Gerome said. "The people's souls will be bankrupt before the banks will be."

"And who says this?" the other cleric asked, raising his hood-covered head for the first time.

Gerome had never heard a member of the clergy speak so rudely to a brother. Perhaps he was a soldier disguised as a cleric.

"I am Gerome Savonarola, from Bologna and Ferrara. And you, Brothers?"

"I am Antonio Maffei," the younger one answered, then pointed with his claw hand to his hooded companion. "This is Brother Stefano da Bagnone. He is a tutor and has been inside the city's houses of plenty and seen much."

"Brothers about to take up arms?" Gerome asked.

The clerics said nothing.

"Many are joining our cause," Francesco Salviati said. "The people of Florence are waiting for a leader to help them overthrow the Medicis. Pope Sixtus condones it, you know. No lay person—I don't care how powerful—has the right to appoint archbishops and to disagree with the pope!"

"Each of us has to save his own soul," Gerome said. "What blessings has the pope offered you?"

No one answered. Two of the men threaded the fox on the spit.

"I have been haunted by visions of the destruction of Florence. All of the families will fade away and our only hope will be a government by God," Savonarola continued.

"You are in *Paradiso* with Dante," the other monk said as he yanked his hood off, revealing a shorn scalp that reflected the firelight. "We have dreams and visions too. But ours will come to pass. What you describe, Brother Gerome, sounds like a Day of Judgment in the clouds. Ours will be a Day of Judgment on earth!"

"I agree it is time for change," Gerome said, "but we must circulate among the people and stir up their souls. We must hold a mirror to their ways so they can change them. When the time is right, they will be ready and eager for a new government ruled by the One and Only Holy Guide."

All the men around the campfire laughed at him. The two clerics laughed the loudest.

Stefano continued, "For four years I tutored Pazzi's illegitimate daughter, Letizzia, who blossomed like a water lily under my care. I was to prepare her for the convent, but she wanted jewels and lace and pompous hats. She found me insufferable except when I accompanied her to see her lover. Environment power is stronger than any will power."

"What do you mean by that?" Gerome asked.

"Being among the wealthy and the privileged, one takes on the tastes of the wealthy and the privileged—tastes that are part of the real world, not the cloisters. Living, praying, and mumbling among the priests and brothers, you become a mumbler. Like them, you pretend to know not only the real world, but also the mind of God. And when the privileged nobles make our religious appointments and the pope turns away to be with his concubines, we must think for ourselves and decide what is holy and what is not."

"We are called by One higher even than the pope to change all that," Gerome said.

"Join with us to bring down the Medici and restore the Pazzis."

"But you just said the Pazzis are like the Medicis . . . that you wanted to give power to the poor."

"Get this fanatic innocent out of here!" said Stefano. Three of the soldiers jumped up and once more a knife was held to Savonarola's throat.

"Let's cut out his preaching tongue right now," one of the soldiers said.

"Another crazy wandering priest," Stefano said. "No one on either side will take him seriously. Don't cut his tongue out quite yet!"

Antonio moved to help Gerome, but Stefano held his fellow

Franciscan back. "Listen to him and you'll return to the monastery and stick your head in the sand. Stay with us and you'll have a real life and know the truth."

Two of the soldiers dragged Gerome into the forest and kicked him to the ground. A searing pain radiated from the base of his spine, sending a burning, tingling ache from his elbows to his fingertips. He pulled himself into a fetal position and prayed silently to Saint Francis.

As he shivered in the chilled night air, Gerome imagined the furry coat of a wolf encircling his shoulders and neck. He smelled the animal's fur and felt its heart beat against his temple. Fear had flown. Instead, he took comfort from the beast as it warmed him into a dreamless sleep.

AS THE SKY LIGHTENED, Gerome awoke with a start. He tried to move but pain from the soldier's attack caused him to close his eyes and pray for a full healing. He fell back to sleep.

Fire. Fire engulfs the city. The alarm bell grows louder and louder. Waves of the Arno rise higher and higher and run through the city. People throw their jewels and paintings and ermine collars into streets that look like canals, as though the city has become another Venice. But the water is not water. It is blood, a river of blood. Flames leap from windows, and the alarm bell grows louder, turning into human screams. A small child drowns in the flood, the liquid gurgling in his tiny throat.

Savonarola woke, sweaty and shivering, in the morning chill. He listened for signs of last night's group. When he heard nothing, he dragged himself back to his camp. Everything was as he had left it. He walked his donkey to a nearby stream, and as the beast drank, Gerome wept, not because of the pain from his beating, but because he believed the horror of his dream had been a glimpse into the future. In the dream he had been shouting from a boat, trying to save the drowning child, but no sound came out of his throat. It was as though he had been held mid-stutter, frozen in time as the city and all the people in it drowned.

CHAPTER FOURTEEN

Playing with Dolls at the Villa di Castello

PIERO SAT ON THE FLOOR of his secret doll-filled closet, attaching a head to the newest addition. It was an effigy of Sandro's assistant, Filippino. Poppi sewed at a worktable a few feet away in the middle of Piero's bedroom. She was creating miniature clothes for the new doll, including the rip in his leggings at the knee, complete with bandages just as Filippino had appeared after his accident on the day of his arrival at the villa.

While caressing the doll, Piero chattered more to himself than to Poppi. "We must make Sandro so comfortable that the work will flow from him like water, like gold, like—"

Yapping dogs interrupted him.

"Must be your master painter, back from his sister's," Poppi said. She put down her work to look out the window. "No, it's no one I know, Master Piero. A young woman and an older man. She's laughing, now playing with the dogs. Oh my God, she's got a mark on her cheek. It looks like a stain of—"

"—red wine on white marble," Piero said in unison with Poppi, not surprised she had used the same words to describe the young woman's mark.

"Imagine you! My private banker, Manfredo, and his daughter Graziella! And no painter painting! This will never do!" Piero tried to pull himself to his feet. The two men had met several months earlier when Piero, having tangled himself in the folds of his cape while on his horse, lost use of his hands and fell off. Manfredo had come along at that moment and helped the injured Piero to his feet, insisting he host the boy to a game of chess at his nearby villa. Once Piero's status as an orphan soon to inherit a Medici fortune became clear to Manfredo, the friendship—at Piero's instigation—blossomed into a secret, gentlemanly business deal.

Always an attentive observer of facial expressions to use for his dolls, Piero had studied Graziella's birthmark when he first met her early that summer. He had tried to imagine the best way to place her distinctive mark on her effigy. He had remarked to himself about her tight lips but when she had made room on her family table to set the chess game between Piero and her father, she had given Piero a faint smile. He changed his mind about her upper lip, which he decided was merely thin and not tense because of any annoyance with him.

Now Piero's descent to the ground floor to meet his guests allowed him enough time to transform his panic into a show of enthusiasm.

He bowed to Graziella as his dogs left her to circle around him.

"As I had expected," Manfredo said. "Our villa has Medici charm. Now that you are in charge, I'm sure you'll bring it back to its original splendor."

"Thanks to you," Piero said with a twitch and a bow. Manfredo's use of the word "our" had sent an ache around Piero's heart and started a loud buzzing in his ears. "Do come in and let me serve you something, Signor Manfredo. I'll have a chess set unpacked by the next time you arrive."

"There won't be a next time," Manfredo said. "As we planned, Graziella will be my ambassador and my accountant. Take me to the first painting. How is it progressing?"

"It is huge," Piero said. He did not move, even though Manfredo had placed his arm in Piero's, ready to be led to the work. Glancing from Manfredo to Graziella, Piero studied their faces once more. What a challenge to create a head to match Manfredo's shiny baldness, his wide jaw covered in a closely cropped beard and that old face with its childlike eyes. Graziella's face was more of a puzzle. He would need to study it more closely. She wore a ring on the third finger of her left hand, but Piero had not seen or heard of any husband. Maybe it was a Jewish tradition for a sole daughter to care for her father and to renounce all else.

"Show me," Manfredo urged him again, snapping Piero back to the present.

"It's a secret. The artist himself is not here now. I can show you the studio, but I cannot show you the painting."

"You are a true man of the times, Piero," Manfredo said, "so I expect you will be ordering paintings of worldly subjects. No virgins and Madonnas, I hope."

"Of course not, of course not."

"And what is the subject of the first work?"

"Subject?"

"What have you and the artist settled upon?"

"As I told you weeks ago, Signor Manfredo, I have left it completely up to the artist himself. It was the trick I used to hook him. He could not refuse."

Manfredo stopped in his tracks, a searching expression on his face made Piero's head twitch more than ever.

"Sandro has been traveling . . . for inspiration," said Piero. "He just got back from Florence, and now he's visiting his sister at a nearby convent."

"The artist is not your house guest. He must produce!"

"He will. He will."

"It's not only for you. It's for me he must produce or your collateral will suffer."

"He locked himself inside his chambers for days. When he emerged he was covered in charcoal so I know he's working. I trust him."

"You trust him?" Manfredo laughed. "He has a reputation for pranks and philandering. He and your magnificent cousin bedded hundreds of women while you crawled around in diapers."

"Please, Manfi, there is no need to insult my family. I believe in Sandro's talent."

"Talent without discipline is like gold rotting in the bottom of a piss pot."

"I beg your pardon?"

"Talent is not enough. Like the land, it must be cultivated, and as his patron it is your duty to him and his talent, and now to me as your financial backer, to put the cage of discipline around him. Show me his studio."

Walking as slowly as possible, Piero led him to the greenhouse. The planks that had arrived that morning from Florence were leaning against the abandoned makeshift easel, unwrapped.

"These pieces will fit together, then hang on the wall of the great room."

"And the cost of this wood?"

"I have not received the bill. I thought you were paying them, not examining every coin, please!" Piero said in a high voice. He twitched once, then lowered his voice. "We will apply metal stays on the back to secure a flat surface, and gesso the front, and then it will be ready."

"We?"

"The surface is not yet ready to receive his genius."

"Who is the master here?"

"Please, Signor Manfi. The money I'll pay you is not the money of a child, so don't treat me as one. Let's allow Sandro to settle in. He wants this to be his finest work, so he is taking his time to let it grow inside him first. My workers will assemble the panel, then gesso it according to Sandro's direction so that he can begin the moment he's ready."

"I am not going to tell you how to run your villa."

"You just did," Piero said. Graziella entered the greenhouse studio with one of the dogs in her arms.

"Where is the painting?" she asked her father.

"Still in the mind of the artist. Gestating," Manfredo said. He turned to Piero. "After today, Graziella will give me reports. She will bring the artist's stipend, and you, Piero, must provide his food and lodging."

"As I have done in a generous style."

"Do not make it too generous, for Sandro will take the comforts and forget the work."

"Signor, how about a game of *bocce*?"

"Absolutely not! My back is hurting me from the trip."

"I will have Poppi put some hot compresses on your bones. You'll be a new man."

Piero opened the door of the greenhouse and stepped outside in hopes Manfredo and Graziella might follow and drop the interrogation.

"Who is Poppi?"

"My former nanny. Now my woman of the house. She has healing hands, healing herbs, and healing remedies," Piero said. As they approached the villa's door, he said, "About Graziella's visits. I think the money should come from me."

"As we laid out in the contract you signed, she will bring the artist's stipend directly to him."

"What if she gives the money to Poppi and Poppi gives it to him?"

"The advantage?"

"Sandro will think it's still coming from this estate, which it truly is since I am going to pay you back."

"If your inheritance is all you expect it to be."

"I am grateful for your participation in the business part of it, but I beg you to leave the details to me."

"Details are a matter of life and death. One inch too close to the heart and an arrow ends a life. One inch away from the skin and it leaves you perfectly preserved."

"The point is, gentle Rebbe Manfredo, *I* own the villa. You own *rights* to it and the paintings *if* I default. That was our agreement. I did not bargain for your interference. The repayment schedule has not even begun, and the paintings to which you will own the title are barely in the mind's eye of the artist."

"And that's where you must, as patron, offer inspiration and structure or else the artist—"

"Enough. I cannot argue with someone more than three times my age. I do not have the vocabulary of experience, but I have the vocabulary of faith. Sandro will produce. You will receive your interest many times over."

"What about those Poppi compresses?"

Perspiration beaded on Piero's forehead as he led Manfredo and Graziella through the villa's entrance toward Poppi's domain. The unshakable confidence he had so many weeks earlier when he had signed away the majority of his inheritance to Manfredo began to crumble along with his faith in Sandro. His steps wavered, throwing him off balance as though he were about to swoon. But in the next moment, some force inside him, perhaps his Medici blood with an obsession to carry on the patron-of-the-arts tradition, would not be punctured, evaporated, belittled by some moneylender. After all, even in spite of the enormity of his financial dealings, Manfredo was still a Jew, one who could be wiped out at any moment by the next fulminating priest who wanted to burn them alive. Piero's head stopped shaking for a second. He passed some wind, twitched his head a few times, straightened his ceremonial waist knife, and strode confidently toward his nanny.

CHAPTER FIFTEEN

While Piero Waits, Sandro's Imagination Ignites

AS SOON AS SANDRO had left his sister's convent, he imagined his horse, Dario, to be a Pegasus, able to fly them above ground back to Villa di Castello without any earthly distraction. This allowed him to forget where he was so he could conjure painting after painting he would make of the flower-weaving novitiate. It was the sweetness of her face, the blotches of color on her cheeks, the childlike splendor she radiated among the flowers. At no point in his imaginary scenes did she wear the habit. Instead, he saw her in a dress covered with blossoms. Springtime personified. His visual prank inspiration was suddenly reduced to ashes. And she, whatever her name was, would be the phoenix rising from those ashes! To find, at last, a being who might inspire him, and to have that being unavailable—confined behind the walls of a convent! The prank had been on him.

Midway between the villa and the convent he came back to earth not only to water his horse but also to quench his own thirst to sketch the girl's face in simple lines. Yes, he was tired of all the nobles memorializing themselves and their betrotheds with the appropriate background symbolism. This woman would be Flora, the goddess of spring, surrounded by others. Who those others might be had no importance to him. He might even throw in a token Madonna, hidden in the form of Venus, but she would not be the subject. He would decorate the painting with an ensemble of supporting players. But she, his Flora, would be the inspiration to carry the work.

His confidence rose with the precision of his vision. When he remounted his horse, instead of continuing back to Villa di Castello, he galloped back toward Oslavia, not knowing how he would secure the girl's release, only that he must. He was not going to allow this first pulse of passion to slip away without a fight.

WHEN SANDRO DID NOT RETURN AS EXPECTED, Piero tried in vain to fall asleep. Obsessed with the fear of being taken as a fool, he rose, lit a candle, and paced back and forth in his room, composing in his head a gentle but stern speech to deliver to Sandro. He sat down to try to write it out, battling his difficulties with the written language, but no sooner had he scribbled and scratched out the first line, "*Mia Carro Sindro*," than his head slipped off his supporting hand onto the desk. He crawled back to bed. Sleep overtook him until a nightmare awakened him: *Locked out of his own villa. His doll creations strewn across the lawn. Vandals ignite his house, and flames shoot out of all the windows. Lorenzo, now a giant as tall as the villa, stands over Piero with a huge sack, into which he collects the dolls and Piero himself—to throw on the fire.* He wakens before he knows what Lorenzo is going to do in the dream, but he carries the fear of domination by his cousin—something he had hoped to dispel by buying the Villa di Castello—into his waking breath.

"DON'T SAY A WORD YET," Oslavia whispered as she pulled her brother through dusk's light away from the caretaker's cottage and into the darkening night of the forest. She kept her index finger to her lips, forcing Sandro into silence. Once they were in a small clearing, she wrapped her arms around the trunk of a silvery tree.

"This is my Peredexion tree," she said. "Its shade is fatal to the forces of evil, so we can speak unharmed and without harming anyone with our words."

Sandro touched the narrow trunk of the tree, its sleek bark hard like stone. The leaves shimmered in the twilight with a celestial glow. Oslavia took both his hands and looked in his eyes.

"What brings you back like this?"

"That cross of flowers. That woman. That girl."

"She came here convicted as a harlot."

"Who is she?"

"Why? Do you know her?"

"I know her in my dreams. I know her for a muse."

"She was left here, separated from a group of virgin weavers from Ferrara. But I, too, am sure she's no harlot, though she's no virgin."

"How old? Seventeen, maybe nineteen at the most?" Sandro asked.

"She is worse than a harlot. She's a Jew."

"A Jew is not a moral offense like harlotry."

"It is *here*. Especially if the Jew refuses to convert."

"But she's making crosses for you!"

"Father Bandini gave me ninety days to convert her and if she doesn't comply he'll give her to Bernardino, the raving anti-Semite who wants them all burned at the stake. What do you want with her?"

"I had decided I was going to paint a joke to send the most intellectual heads of Lorenzo's Platonic Academy spinning for years to come. But then I saw her in her innocence among all of those flowers and she was Flora, goddess of spring and renewal, full of promise and fertility . . . What's her name?"

"You are giving me chills, Sandro. If I tell you her name, I will not be able to say no to you. For her own protection I've imposed a strict vow of silence upon her. If, in some way, I were to enable you to use her as your model, it would be in secret. She must not know where she goes and she must be returned. She would need to be blindfolded. It will be a huge effort for you. There are only sixty days left now before Bandini wants an accounting."

"And you, Oslavia. You're willing to take the risk?"

"My word is beyond question here, except of course to Bandini. But, more importantly, I must move in ways that do not allow my word to be questioned by the larger Him," she said as she clutched the crucifix attached to the rosary around her waist. "Still, I must be discreet. I'll send her to you with the caretaker's children. They can speak for her. If Bandini or anyone else asks to see her when she's with you, I'll say I have given a dispensation to her to assist in the gathering of her own flowers. I cannot bring her to you every day, but maybe we can do this three days a week."

"Why are you helping me?"

"I'm helping her. Beyond that, I have my reasons. Deeper than you know."

"Tell me."

"In time you'll understand, but for now it's enough for you to know I'm joyful to have you back in my life. I don't believe the Jews are Christ-killers, drinkers of blood, and all the rest. Forced conversions are offenses to the Almighty."

"And after the sixty days?"

"We'll deal with that when the time is closer. I'm praying to find a way for her release. But you must swear on your life and on the life of our frail parents you will not speak to her, either about the forced conversion or about my desire to free her, especially if I fail to find a way."

"How can I swear this?"

"You must. Speech attracts evil and deceit. Silence brings protection. Once words permeate the earth, forces hear them and conspire to make them manifest."

"But aren't evil and lustful thoughts as bad as deeds?"

"You're wrong, Sandro. Swear here and now and under the canopy of this Peredexion tree that you will not give her false hopes, or discuss her conversion, and most of all you will not touch her."

"You're asking me to swear against my own nature."

"I need to know you'll put her highest good above your lowest impulses. Right now she might be inspiring you as a muse, but once she's in the flesh beside you, you could—"

"I can be trusted. I can swear to put her highest good above my lowest impulses, but I won't swear to assist you in any conversion. That's your job. I'll keep my art above my crotch. I swear on our parents' lives I will be chaste with her and respect the vow of silence she must keep."

"It is a matter of life and death, Sandro. Enough talking. Send someone, preferably a woman, here to fetch them for the first trip, and bring a wagon you can leave with us. We'll place it under the arbor by the caretaker's house."

"And when do we start?"

"On the new moon. The first days of fall. As soon as I receive the visitor with the wagon, I will send the Jew to you that very day. I will prepare her by telling her this is a special mission and not to speak about it. And that she will not be harmed."

Sandro sank to his knees and kissed his sister's robes, overcome with her generosity and her willingness to grant his wishes.

"Get up, boy! You are helping me, as much as I am helping you. Trust me and keep your promises."

As they walked away from the shade of the Peredexion tree, Sandro stopped short, and pulled his sister back toward the tree.

"One more thing," he said. "You still haven't told me her name."

"Floriana."

"Floriana," he said in a barely audible voice. Then softly again. And again, "Floriana . . ."

Oslavia placed her palm over his mouth to silence him.

"Take this coincidence as a message from on high and paint her in her highest light. Work with her and be with her in your highest self and all will be well."

"In her highest light," Sandro said.

Brother and sister embraced. Oslavia directed him to exit the forest alone. She would stay back for a while. He was not to return to the convent for the sixty-day period. They would stay in touch by letters to be carried by the yet-unnamed assistant.

As the moonlight crept into the forest, Oslavia stayed on under the Peredexion for another half an hour to pray. She was about to thrust off the mantle of the church in her heart even though she would still wear it on her body. She prayed for wisdom, for direction, for answers—not through the psalms, not through the Bible, but through the direct line from her God, so He might infuse her divine soul with courage.

When she was done, she lifted herself from her knees, brushed the leaves and mulch off her habit, and walked through the clearing into the full moon's beam and the unexpected glare of Bandini's gaze.

He stood in a cart clutching both sides of the wagon to keep his balance when Federico, the caretaker, who had been powering the cart with his own legs, almost collided with Oslavia. *Give me the words, Lord,* Oslavia thought.

"So good to see you out and about at this late hour, Monsignor," Oslavia said. "Like old times."

"Yes, I plan to do this every evening as long as I can lift myself into the cart and Federico can pull me. It helps me sleep better to take some night air first. And in the morning too."

"At what hour, Your Eminence?"

"That depends on how I've slept the night before, but today is now the seventh day so it is becoming quite a nice daily practice for me."

Oslavia's heart quickened at the thought that Bandini might have seen her with Sandro—a breach of decorum he would never overlook without an interrogation. She smiled, said nothing, and stood still, praying he might continue along these superficial subjects.

"And the harlot convert, how is she doing?" Bandini said.

"She has embraced our symbolism and has woven implements in flowers for our services. She seems very grateful for her confinement here."

"And the document of conversion?"

"I am working on it, Monsignor."

"I have written Bernardino that we will have a celebration in the spring."

"And that we will, Monsignor, a celebration for sure."

"Good work, Oslavia."

"I choose to serve the Lord and pray for clarity to do so at each moment," Oslavia said.

"Excellent!" Bandini said. "Carry on, Federico. Another time around!"

Fall

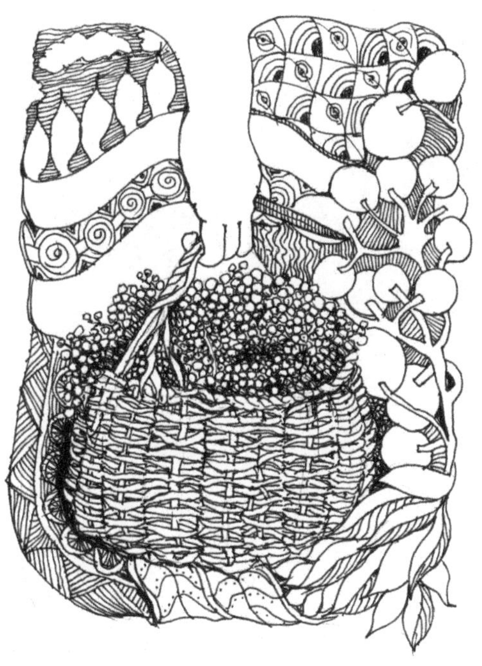

CHAPTER SIXTEEN

Medici Palace

AS THE SOOTHSAYER STOOD at the entrance to the Medici Palace, bats circled above her as the light of the first full moon of the new season illuminated the sky. She brushed thirsty mosquitoes away from her face. After a guard waved her inside, tin ornaments tied to the tassels of her belt tinkled as she walked into the front hall. Two tall vases filled with branches of jasmine sat on the floor, one on each side of a large tapestry with the image of a unicorn. Lucrezia de' Medici entered the space, her arms so overladen with citronella candles that she was unable to extend her hand to welcome her guest, who had never seen such a supply of the rare Asian insect repellent. *The bounty of the rich!*

"Stella Cameo at your service, Signora Medici."

"Did anyone follow you here, Signorina Cameo?"

"No man followed me here, Signora." Stella looked at the cats at her feet. She shook her cape away from them but they jumped toward its tassels with her every movement. "However, as you can see, many creatures are following me as we speak."

"Not that I pander to the pope and his banning of soothsayers," Lucrezia said, shooing away the cats too. "We must be discreet."

"Not that I predict the future," Stella said. "I merely read the signs."

Lucrezia's nostrils quivered as the entryway filled with the perfume and incense that saturated Stella's cape. "Shall we?" Lucrezia motioned a graceful arm toward the inner courtyard.

Stella stopped at the archway. "May I sprinkle a powder of prophecy and power?"

With Lucrezia's nod of approval, Stella scattered a cloud of bronze powder into the air. The cats jumped after it. Lucrezia sneezed so loudly it was almost a scream. Voices from beyond the entryway went silent.

Stella rang a small bell that hung from her wrist and entered the inner courtyard. A blue and yellow parrot stood on a perch in the corner among the bright green mosses bordering the narrow gravel walkways. Four other people stood around the gardens.

As she removed the glove from her right hand, Stella said, "Only one household candle, please, Signora Lucrezia. I'll need the rest of the table for the cards."

A woman with bright red hair and a red silk gown approached. A deep furrow in the center of her forehead punctuated an otherwise round face. "I am Clarice, Lorenzo's wife," she said, running her hand over a protruding belly. It was a proud but silent announcement of her status as the most fertile mother of this important family. This was to be her fourth child, due in the winter months.

Stella held on to Clarice's hand until Clarice's eyes quieted and her heaving milky white breasts settled inside her bodice.

Another woman, not more than twenty years old, wore long braids wrapped around her head. Her close-set eyes and excessively pale skin gave her the look of a glass vessel with a pinched spout. She sat at the table knitting rapidly. She pushed her knitting aside, then rose to curtsy nervously. "Claudia," she said, giving her hand to Stella.

"How nice, Signorina Claudia," Stella said, noticing a baby's cap on the knitting needles, clearly a gift for Clarice's unborn, and yet the heat of something else came off Claudia's touch.

Stella moved her eyes to the next person, Lorenzo. She recognized him from banners she'd seen around the city. *That flattened nose!* She had heard he had no sense of smell. Alas, his excessive use of powders and perfumes. His jutting lower jaw startled her. His gaze undressed her. When he extended his hand, she placed a small, silver amulet into his palm.

"Protection for you and your family and for the city and against any unwelcome spirits who chance to join us through the cards tonight," Stella said while bowing.

When she looked up, Giuliano faced her. Claudia hung on to his arm. Unlike his older brother, he did not look directly into Stella's eyes until she squeezed his hand and held it longer than might seem civilized. Stella read people any way she could. Touch and pulse and gaze told her more than the cards. Although Giuliano's grasp was limp and dutiful, his eyes, clouded by Claudia's charms, shone as a man besotted, yet committed—a rare creature, not to be discounted because of an unresponsive handshake.

"Shall we begin, then?" Stella said.

"I shall fetch that candle you spoke of, Signorina Cameo, and you, ladies," Lucrezia told Claudia and Clarice, "please set the citronella on the benches over there. Giuliano, help me put out the cats." As Lucrezia spilled the load of candles onto Clarice's outstretched arms, Claudia made no move to help but only kept knitting.

Lorenzo stood beside Stella while the others scurried about following his mother's orders.

"I take it, Signor Medici," Stella said, "you do not care for my ilk. We're so far from the intellectual elite of your Academy."

"I'm open. At least my mother and wife have insisted I be so tonight," Lorenzo said, shooting a smile to his Clarice. Like the sharpness of his jaw, his high voice cut into the night air with a masculine edge that defied its pitch.

"And is that a labor for you?" Stella asked.

"You inspire confidence," he said. "May I help you with your cape?"

"Not yet!" The thin veil covering her chin and forehead revealed only her eyes, which she closed as she settled into her chair. The others' voices softened into a quiet rumble as they seated themselves around the table. The candlelight illuminated their faces while the evening continued to darken around them. When the fountain's bubbling and the parrot's babbling were the only audible sounds, Stella removed her other glove and placed her palms upon the table.

Seated between Lucrezia and Lorenzo, she reached out to join hands with each, then nodded to the others to do the same. When all hands were connected and eyes closed by her example, she spoke.

"We are all One. What cards Spirit sends to you are only yours for the moment."

Claudia coughed and Lucrezia shot her an angry glance.

"All One," Stella repeated, turning her head toward Lucrezia. With her eyes still closed, she said, "If you cannot cut the wire, do not judge the stone."

With that impenetrable warning, she squeezed the hands and broke the human chain and opened her eyes.

All looked to her now and waited. "We are all the same underneath our covers," she said, then placed her hands on the edge of her veil at her forehead to slide the fine mesh and hood backward off her head onto her shoulders.

She closed her eyes again as she did this, for she did not want to see if her strangeness frightened or fascinated, she wanted to feel it. She opened her eyes to read their faces.

Lorenzo cast a smile of delight upon her. The other faces, however, flickered at the shock of a woman whose skin was the color of caramel, and who had no hair, not only on her head but also no eyelashes or brows. Her only adornments were a diamond stud in her nose and large golden hoops in her earlobes. And now with her arms naked, they saw tattoos of serpents, amulets, moons, and stars; Greek, Arabic, and Hebrew letters, and Stars of David winding around them.

She unwrapped a stack of circular stiff paper cards. These she spread across the table to shuffle them. The backs were painted in deep shades of red, blue, purple, and yellow. As she moved them about the table, occasionally one would turn over to reveal primitive paintings with strong ink strokes and washes of color together with words and symbols in a language she knew no one at the table would recognize. In addition to the strange words, the cards carried many of the same symbols that adorned her exposed flesh.

Stella dealt out one card in front of each of the players. "Without turning over the card, please slide it to the person on your left."

As soon as Claudia received her new card she said, "Please, I want to go first!" She pushed her card to Stella, then picked up her knitting and clacked the needles while Stella spoke.

"Knight of Cups. This is a very positive sign. You see you have an angel's wings. You are innocent and pure, touched with divinity, yet your body is clad in armor so you will live a long and protected life—"

"Sweet Claudia," Lucrezia interrupted. "Must you carry on knitting everywhere you go?"

Claudia dropped her knitting to the floor. "Everywhere I go, Madame Lucrezia? I go nowhere. Since you've brought me into the palace under the cover of night like some infected lamb, I've forgotten what the streets of Florence look like."

"For your own protection," Lucrezia said, refusing to make eye contact with the girl. Stella heard from Lucrezia's mind: *Scraped off the streets! No wonder she misses them!*

"For *your* protection, Mother!" Giuliano said.

"May I continue?" Stella asked Lucrezia. "Armed against changes, Claudia, you charge against adversity on your mighty steed. See this crab? It means the child you carry will escape the terror of the world by walking sideways away from it—perhaps to the protection of the cloth. Stay close to those of great influence to keep yourself safe. But keep healthy boundaries lest you lose yourself in their greatness."

"How did you know she was with child?" Lucrezia asked. "This is a family secret!"

"I am also a midwife. I felt it in the heat of her hand. The secret will stay with me," Stella said. "As will every detail of this evening." Turning to the group she said, "Who will be next?"

Lucrezia handed her card to Stella. "What does that word say?"

"The word is 'Sorrow,' Signora, but these cards are not to be taken literally. Try not to make your own interpretations here, Signora Medici. Allow me to study it further."

Stella watched Lucrezia take some deep breaths to calm herself, then try to listen. But the image of a sword piercing the center of a flower with two bent swords coming out of it set Lucrezia's body into a shiver. Stella knew what Lucrezia saw in the cards: if not her son's heart, for the card had been the one dealt originally to Giuliano, then it was the heart of her city of Florence with the two bent swords—each of her sons helpless against the violence around her. Stella's explanation that the sorrow was about the death of her husband, Piero, did not stop Lucrezia's shivering.

"Perhaps the mourning is over and the separation you have between yourself and another may be healing," Stella said, even though she had heard Lucrezia's thoughts as though spoken aloud.

And so it went all evening as the cards were pulled and family tensions sizzled in the hot fall night air. Stella learned the truth of what she had suspected from hearsay: Giuliano eschewed his business role, Lorenzo was a frustrated poet under the thumb of his overbearing mother, Clarice was kept continually with child as a distraction from Lorenzo's philandering, and as she saw by the cards, especially the death card that appeared and reappeared, the darkness that lay ahead was speeding toward them. With each appearance of that dreaded symbol, she talked of how the death card merely meant the end of one way of thinking and the beginning of a new era, covering it any way she could with words of affirmation amid the crackle of conflict.

It was as though a dark storm cloud were hovering over this family—each one of them sensing danger, but with a foreboding so constant as to appear normal. Even after Stella agreed to do the second round—"the challenges of the future"—with Lucrezia's own Visconti-Sforza deck, the results were the same: Lucrezia's fear and worry ate through Stella's attempts to calm and heal.

As the cards unfolded, Stella realized that what had at first appeared to be Lucrezia's maternal worry went deeper. This matriarch had her own inner wisdom, her own premonitions, which bound her to Stella in a silence of psychic sisterhood.

After the reading ended and Stella and Lucrezia silently made their way back to the palace entrance, Lucrezia gasped and said, "I almost forgot to pay you, Stella! I was so distracted—that blindfolded matriarch in that Wheel of Fortune card was me!"

Lucrezia pulled out a small silk purse she had set aside for the evening. The person who had arranged the reading had insisted the diviner be paid in florins and not in *spiccioli*, the currency of the poor.

"These florins, not the silk purse, were meant for you. But you have filled us all with such food for deep thought tonight, I want to give you the florins *and* the purse itself, which was given to me by my father-in-law, Cosimo."

"Please do not be offended if I don't touch the purse," Stella said as she turned to the side to open her cloak. Lucrezia stuffed it inside the small leather pouch that hung about Stella's waist. "Tradition says I must not touch payment for twenty-four hours to allow the reading to set into the universe. And thank you."

With a sudden clutch of her hand around Stella's shoulders, Lucrezia stared into the young woman's face. This time it was she, Lucrezia, who wouldn't let go as the two women faced each other. "I know you were covering up the truth. Three death cards!"

Stella said nothing, and waited for Lucrezia to release her grip. As soon as she did, Stella said, "I told you they can mean new beginnings."

"Three death cards!"

"We each are dealt the death card daily when we sleep. The Universe is Change. Every change is the effect of an act of love or an act of hate, which is the inside belly of love. My task is not to say when, but to show the storm clouds and to warn you toward shelter. I do not see the future. Even if I did, you can change it. It is mutable, if you will only look at the signs."

"What did you mean when you started with the words, 'If you cannot cut the wire, do not judge the stone'?"

"Cut the wire of control over your sons, Lucrezia. If you don't they will become stones strung about your neck, and your heart. Instead, make your life today the most joyous you can. Dark clouds are unavoidable and you must travel through them with all your faculties and wisdom and dignity. Build those up instead of your worry. You are strong, but do not strangle. Your grasp is sure, but do not use it to choke. Cut the wire, the knitting yarns, the tongues of others that prattle in your head at night, keeping you awake with fear."

Standing so close to Signora Medici's breath, Stella noticed the pungent aroma of myrrh and incense coming from her own skin—an earthy aroma which had made Lucrezia's nostrils flare at the start of the evening—now seemed to make the matriarch breathe easily for the first time.

"We'll look for you when it's Claudia's time," Lucrezia said, opening her arms and pulling Stella into an embrace.

"I will be honored, Signora Medici. But for tonight, retire soon and release the future by capturing the present with as much joy as you can," Stella said. She folded a small fabric sachet into Lucrezia's fist. "Use this valerian root in a strong tea to keep your nightmares away."

Moments later, when Lucrezia opened her hand to look at what Stella put there, all that remained of the visitor was the cloud of scents, the comfort of being understood, and the tightness in the matriarch's chest of a dark unknown force rumbling its way toward her.

CHAPTER SEVENTEEN

Botticelli Begins

THE DAWN'S RAYS struck Sandro awake. *Today I begin!* Yet with each step that brought him closer to the greenhouse studio, his confidence fell.

The plans for Floriana's transport from the convent had been upset. Bandini had intercepted and interrogated Poppi, who had been the designated person to bring Floriana back to the villa. The caretaker Federico's wife, Nicola, had fallen ill, so their children, Luigi, a young boy of twelve, and his two younger sisters, the same children who had supplied Floriana with all the ingredients for her floral weavings, had been drafted to accompany "the flower nun"—as they named her—to the villa. They would assist Master Botticelli. Seeing Floriana arrive the evening before with a silk scarf tied around her face had upset him, especially when he heard she got sick halfway to Castello.

As Luigi and he set the large board upon some wooden boxes to elevate it to a working height, Sandro looked through the glass panes fogged from the morning mist. Next to the circular fountain at the center of a clearing he saw a large tree with the same silvery bark as Oslavia's Peredexion tree. This one towered above the others with branches forming a canopy. Even if it wasn't a true Peredexion, he would imagine it to be so with all its magical powers.

"We'll set the painting there," he told Luigi. They carried the board to the clearing. The fountain's platform provided easy support for the panel.

"Put the flowers gathered this morning in the fountain. Then bring Floriana to me."

As Luigi turned to run off toward the villa, Sandro grabbed his shoulders and spun the boy around to face him.

"Can you whistle?"

Luigi looked at Sandro as though he had no idea what the word "whistle" meant.

Sandro cupped his left hand inside his right one, then brought his thumbs together and blew through them to make a long, low sound much like the call of a mourning dove. He changed the pitch of the sound by moving his fingers as though playing a flute.

"When I need you, I'll whistle, and you must stop whatever you are doing and whistle back to me."

Luigi tried to roll his fists together, but no sound came out of his small hands until Sandro corrected his grip; the boy made the secret sound.

"Only to be used between you and me. Not a game to be played. Now, practice to make sure."

Luigi cupped one hand in the other and blew through the opening of his thumbs, his cheeks filling with air, to make a sweet, long cooing sound.

"Excellent! When you have the Signorina Floriana with you, you must make that sound so I know you are almost here."

Even though he'd been raised in rags in the shadows of his father's caretaker country life, Luigi, with his thick black curls, long eyelashes, and intense gaze, would surely be as bright and helpful as any city apprentice. While Sandro waited for Luigi's return with Floriana, he read Oslavia's letter a second time:

Bandini saw the cart. You must keep Floriana and the children over two nights and send them back on Wednesday, past noon, after Bandini has done his rounds. We'll need a new plan unless your master agrees to give a different cart and a donkey—or better yet, a horse—as homage to Bandini. We can use it once he finishes his morning rounds.

As he folded the letter, relieved to have Floriana for three whole days, he heard Luigi's little sisters running toward him. Their arms spilled over with flowers. The sight of Puzzi in her peasant rags and soiled face made Sandro want to draw. He welcomed a chance to warm up. It would bolster his confidence to sketch one of his specialties: cherubs.

"You, Puzzi—" he said, motioning her to sit.

"That's not her real name," Mirabella said. "We call her Puzzi because she messes her bed at night. Her real name is Elizabetta."

"Come here, Elizabetta and Mirabella. Let me draw your faces in my secret book while we wait for Luigi to bring Signorina Floriana."

Sandro set the two girls across from him on the rim of the fountain. He pulled the sketchbook from his waistband.

Both girls hopped off and rushed over to look into his book, but Sandro pulled it to his chest, saying, "How can this be secret if I show you? Go sit back on the fountain. Pretend to be angels resting your wings. For angels you are and will be to help bring a beautiful work of art from heaven into this world. Now polish your wings!"

The girls giggled as they climbed back onto the fountain's rim.

"Don't you know how to polish angel wings?" he asked. "I'm polishing my own wings this very moment. Polishing angel wings happens when you sit still and trust that all will be perfectly right even though you want to run around screaming and crying. You have to sit and wait. So we're all polishing our wings together."

"And the donkey, and your horse too?" the elder girl asked.

"Hmm," Sandro said, looking only into his sketchbook.

After a few moments, Sandro had ceased to bring his head up from the pages of his sketchbook. The girls climbed down and tiptoed behind him to look over his shoulders. When a tiny hand reached across the surface to touch one of the paper wings, Sandro snapped the book closed as though trapping a fly. Mirabella squealed.

"What kind of secret is it now that you've seen it?" he said. His stern expression brought tears to Mirabella's eyes. Her little sister held her hand. She, too, began to cry.

"I'm only joking," he said, "but now you've seen it before I was ready to show it to you, and this you must never do to an artist! Do you understand?"

The girls hung their heads, pouting.

"Go sit," he said more gently.

Sandro continued to sketch them, directing their movements with his face, wrinkling his brow, sticking his tongue out, crossing his eyes, all the while waiting to hear Luigi's whistle.

"Now," he said, "I invite you both to come and see your angel wings."

He turned the book to show them their beautiful curls and strong, detailed wings with layers of short scalloped feathers.

"Don't angels live only in heaven?" Mirabella said.

"They're everywhere. We can't see their wings. But if you look hard enough into someone's eyes, you can tell if she has invisible wings. All children have them, but sometimes they lose them when they turn twelve."

"Has Luigi lost his?"

"I hope not. We're going to need his wings a lot to help with this giant painting."

"How giant is it?" both girls asked.

Sandro opened his arms and scooped the two girls up, surprising them both. He had hugged his brother's children before and held Lorenzo's also, but he could not remember having felt the same love in his heart as in this moment.

The sound of their squeals couldn't drown out the low warble of Luigi's whistle. Sandro shut his sketchbook and slipped it into his belt.

"Does the flower nun still have her wings?" asked Mirabella.

"She's coming right now. If you try hard you'll be able to see them. They're strong and wide—big enough to carry all of us."

Sandro turned to face the blank board. The fear of the first stroke hovered—a stubborn ghost—but vanished the moment Floriana appeared.

This was the first time he had seen her out of her religious habit. She wore the same dress, complete with Medici emblem, he had seen on Piero's eldest sister. She had gathered her golden hair together, and tied it away from her face with flower stems. Long strands of it framed her cheeks and forehead. As soon as Floriana gazed at him, her face turned red. He looked at her for a full minute as the color rose in her cheeks.

Under the shade of the mock Peredexion tree, Sandro had placed a soft, white muslin garment he had found in a trunk in the villa. The bottom hem was threadbare in places, but the muslin was of a natural hue and the softness of the cloth would surely conform itself to the young woman's body.

He had placed a modesty curtain from one branch of the tree to the other. Honoring Oslavia's wishes that he not speak directly to Floriana, he approached her and gently led her by the elbow behind the curtain. He motioned to the garment on the ground and clasped his hands together as though to beg her to change. As he exited, he motioned to the young girls to go in and help her.

Sandro took his place in front of the panel. He pulled out a small compass from his belt, spun himself around, and stretched his arm out toward the huge board. Wherever the needle pointed, there he would begin. The needle's force pulled him to a section slightly right of center, and there he froze. In the past the composition would have been worked out ahead of time and he would proceed from the center and paint toward the edges, but this time he followed his instincts without question. Three feet in from the right-hand side was where he would start. He spread his colors out on a nearby table and made a blackish-brown mark directly on the board. This would be the trunk of a Peredexion tree, which he would paint for good luck and fortune and to ensure the truth and beauty of every stroke. The paint flowed on the surface with a smooth consistency, bringing him an instant internal calm. At last he was doing his beloved work again.

The voices of the children grew louder as Floriana emerged, draped in her simple gown. Her bosom was much less full than he had expected, and her abdomen had a slight soft curve to it. Her neck was long, her limbs long and flowing. She had removed her shoes and stockings and placed some of the woven flowers about her neck.

"Hold her skirt, Mirabella, and you, Luigi and Elizabetta, gather flowers from the fountain and pile them into the apron of her skirt," Sandro said.

Floriana smiled openly at him. The redness of her face had not diminished and he noticed beads of perspiration on her brow.

"Give our flower lady some water, please, Mirabella," he said, and he filled a cup for her. She gulped it down. Poppi stood by watching all of this.

"Don't we have something to cool her, Poppi?"

Poppi whipped out a rag from under her shirt, wet it in the fountain's water, and placed it on Floriana's forehead. The young woman took a deep breath, let out a sigh, and fainted to the ground.

"She's so frail!" Sandro said as he ran to her. "A chair, Luigi, go get one from the house."

The dogs yelped at Luigi's feet as he ran back toward the villa.

"In the front courtyard, boy, run!" Poppi yelled after him.

Floriana opened her eyes and raised herself on one elbow. "I'm so sorry," she said, despite Oslavia's orders to maintain silence even when she was away from the convent. "I must be hungry. And I didn't sleep at all last night. I could only think of my uncle and how frantic he must be with no word and no *spiccioli* from me in all these weeks."

"Ask her where her mother is," Sandro directed Poppi.

"She was deaf from birth and died when I was fifteen. My father died three years later while I was an apprentice to my uncle, a traveling tailor. I was to send money to him from my weaving at the Medici Palace. He taught me all I know about weaving and sewing. And how to read and write."

"Tell her there are no weavers at the Medici Palace," Sandro said. "Only bankers. Medici woolen mills and a silk mill are in another part of town. I have never seen a loom in the palace." He abandoned the charade of silence and looked directly at Floriana. His vow to Oslavia now seemed unimportant since Floriana spoke to him first. "Who told you you'd be working in the palace?"

"The priests who told my uncle. It was the end of my three years apprenticing with him, which is why he let me go. On the way they threw me into a tower in the monastery until your sister got me out. Now I'm like a lump of clay being tossed here and there with no shape and no future, and no tongue!"

Sandro wanted to run to her, to comfort her, especially because her body seemed to shake as though with sobbing. But remembering his vow to Oslavia, he reverted to the vow of silence and looked at Poppi. "Tell her she will have a future for centuries to come in my painting. Tell her I can pay her. I'll send money to her uncle."

"But he'll know something bad has happened to me," Floriana said, looking with red eyes at Sandro. "I know I'm supposed to be silent. But I grew up in silence with a mother who could not speak. And sometimes I speak too much for the joy of hearing my words come back to me in the response of others. And all those days in the tower in Oslavia's compound with no one speaking to me, no one looking at me. God bless your sister for saving my life, but this silence she wants me to follow is another torture!"

"And she has sworn me, too, to not speak to you for fear of what? I'm not even sure but I am grateful she has allowed you to come here, so please do not be angry if I try to honor my promise to her by speaking my words to you through others."

Floriana put her hand over her mouth and nodded in agreement.

"But first, my sweet—" he said, speaking to Floriana, but directing his gaze to Poppi.

"Your sweet, am I?" said Poppi. "I like this. Yes," she joked.

"What next?"

"I must put the first strokes of color and form onto the board to place Floriana in the picture."

"I can stand now," Floriana said, just as Luigi dragged a heavy chair to the clearing. The upholstered seat was dark red velvet with gold threads in a fleur-de-lis pattern running through it.

Here, my Beauty, Sandro thought, as he placed the chair so Floriana could lean against it from behind. The blush had gone out of her cheeks and her skin wore a soft white pallor.

"Now I insist everyone but the children leave us in peace," Sandro said.

"I'm the everyone," said Poppi.

"I mean no one is allowed to come here to watch. I will need the children to assist me."

"I'll bring her some food first," Poppi said.

"Please do. But don't bring Piero back here with you. I want it to be a surprise for him."

As Sandro watched Poppi stride off, a wave of affection for her came over him. Her knowledge of flowers and perfume, her experience of worldly and domestic concerns, would make her one of the midwives in the birth of the largest painting he had ever attempted.

"Please remember where you are standing, Floriana, and your pose. Sit whenever you need to." Sandro repeated these instructions to Luigi and asked him to tell them to Floriana again in hopes of fulfilling his promise to Oslavia. "And bring a table to her for the flowers."

Sandro resumed his place in front of the painting. For a time he threw off these little interruptions as though they were innocuous summer gnats until Poppi returned with a tray of food and he put his brushes down.

"Mirabella, take the tray to Floriana," Sandro said.

When it was placed before her, Floriana gave Sandro a pleading look. He nodded and she began to eat. First the slices of orange she ate whole, including the skins. More tears came to her eyes. Perhaps the sweet taste triggered memories of home. Sandro came over to her and motioned her to sit.

To Luigi, he said, "Tell her I can wait. She must eat first."

Floriana perspired as she ate. She finished the oranges and some grapes, then reached for the loaf of bread. Sandro had never seen anyone eat bread the way she did. She brought it close to her eyes to examine it before she tore it into little pieces, like pellets, before she placed them in her mouth. Breadcrumbs fell onto her gown. She shook them onto the ground; tiny sparrows instantly descended to attack them.

Sandro prepared his brushes as he waited for her to finish her meal. After she swallowed every drop of apricot nectar, she looked at him.

He motioned for her to stand and lean against the chair. He walked to the fountain, scooped handfuls of flower buds, and approached her.

"Can you weave a crown of flowers for yourself while I pin these to your gown?" he asked.

Mirabella ran to him. She placed a finger over her lips to remind him to be silent, then repeated to Floriana.

"Can you weave a crown of flowers for yourself while he pins the buds to your gown?" she asked, then giggled.

"I would love to weave whatever you want me to. Bring me those daisies and carnations," she said. Mirabella ran over to a nearby patch of the flowers. She yanked them up in bunches and ran back with them to Floriana, whose hands tied the flowers together.

Standing so close to her, Sandro inhaled her body's perfume as he pinned the blossoms on her dress. He took care not to jab her with the pins, touching her as little as possible and avoiding her direct gaze.

"I'm not a harlot," she whispered. He stared at her and said nothing. She could say whatever she wanted to and he could not and would not answer her, even though behaving as an obedient novitiate seemed the furthest thing from her mind. She whispered again, "I am no harlot!"

Sandro came closer.

"You must help me escape the convent. One of the young acolytes who brought me and several other women from Ferrara to Tuscany attacked me. Like some evil wind, he changed my life forever. He climbed onto my back so I did not see who it was. The next thing I knew, all the other women were brought to the city. Only I, with this Star of David, was brought to a monastery and your sister's convent, where I have been held against my will ever since."

Sandro sighed. He looked at her for a long while, one finger on his lips. He hoped his compassionate gaze would tell her he had listened.

She smiled, placed two fingers over her lips. She would not say any more. She had told him of the dark well into which she had fallen, and who had pushed her in.

Sandro motioned to Mirabella to take away the food tray. He kept his mouth closed, breathing only through his nostrils as he had learned from the Indian yogis at the Medici Palace to calm his spirit and his heart. It did not quell his rage at the lascivious boy in a cleric's robe who had defiled her, yet at the same time a titillating string of images flashed through his imagination—a dark tempest entering her as she ran from it. He would paint her now as she appeared to him in all her flower-decked splendor—full of the blush of youth and spring, and right next to her image, he would paint the darkness. To follow custom of the day, he would exaggerate the fullness in her abdomen as though there were a child growing within.

He must give his full attention to the task, to caress with his eyes and brushes each strand of her hair, each detail of her face, each curve of her body. How he would create such emotion equal to her image across the rest of his picture plane was not a care to explore at the moment.

With a few quick flourishes of the brush, he rendered her face. She seemed more at ease now. She had told him her story. He would help her.

He rapidly mixed skin tones, painted the slightly parted lips as though she wished to whisper more to him. That chin with the gentle cleft and her pale, translucent eyes—the color of an afternoon's last light. No longer would he obediently paint symbols to signify family crests and veiled political postures. This time, with his newly won freedom—thanks to Piero, the boy he had cursed weeks ago—every symbol, every flower Sandro painted would have its special meaning and secret. *Carnations, yes! More and more carnations on the dress!* He would make a pattern out of them, but later when she wouldn't be available, when he would have to work on her from memory. Today, this moment, it was her face he must capture. The Star of David she wore about her neck he would omit for now. Perhaps he would find a way to include it and show it to her someday, but for the moment he would do the face only.

After several hours, her eyelids began to droop. He set her in the chair, placed more flowers on her lap.

Talking to Floriana's face on the picture plane, he said, "A little bit longer. Without looking down, weave something, anything with the flowers on your lap."

To the children he said, "Tell Signorina Floriana when I want to speak to her I will speak to her picture which is breathing in paint!" To Luigi, he said, "Tell the Signorina Floriana what I said, please."

"The master says when he wants to speak to you, he will address your likeness on the panel."

She smiled. "And when I want to speak to him, to whom shall I speak?"

"To me, or the girls, of course, as you have been doing," Luigi said.

"But if you are off collecting flowers, or playing with the dogs, to whom shall I speak?"

"Tell her to speak into the palms of her hands," Sandro said. "Tell her she holds my heart in the palms of her hands. If she closes her eyes and imagines it, she will feel it beating there. I will hear it with my heart."

She blushed again and her eyes grew moist.

"Go pat the cheeks of Signorina Floriana, Mirabella," Sandro said, "and kiss her forehead and tell her to lie down on the blanket and rest."

CHAPTER EIGHTEEN

Conversion of the Prelates

ONCE REUNITED WITH HIS SUPERIOR at the great cathedral in Bologna, Gerome Savonarola had his first assignment, to place himself inside the curtained confessional booth as a faceless priest.

The monsignor accompanied Gerome into the church, and then exited to round up two young aspiring priests, the very ones who left Savonarola in Ferrara on what they had assumed was his deathbed. Gerome listened from behind his curtain as they followed their superior back into the great hall.

"Since you missed the daily rituals this week," the monsignor told them, "I want you to take your confession with a traveling priest. We are fortunate to have him for you today."

"Sit here in the pews. Quiet yourselves with prayer. Then you," he said to the first one, "go share your cares with him who waits for you. When you are finished, you," he said to the second, "go and visit him as well."

The monsignor pretended to leave the chapel, but when the two prelates sank to their knees in the ritual prayer posture, he tiptoed back inside and crouched on the floor a couple of rows behind.

He heard them mutter in low voices.

"Are you going to tell the truth?" asked the first.

"Absolutely not!" said the other.

"I would be locked in my cell repenting for the next six months just from the thoughts that crossed my mind this morning."

The second pushed the first out of the pew. "Go," he said to his friend, who stood, straightened his robes, and walked toward two elaborately hand-carved confessional booths. The acolyte slid into the one on the right and knelt on a low bench, his face even with the screen. He could vaguely see the brother who would absolve him. The man's head was bowed and his face hidden. The young confessor was relieved. The priest would not see his insincere facial expressions of remorse. And so they began.

"*Allora*," Gerome said in the deepest voice he could summon.

"Bless me, Father, for I have sinned."

"And in what ways, my son?"

"I have eaten sweetmeats meant for the children when the hunger attacked me."

"And . . ."

"I have missed my family for the warmth I knew there and the special treatment I received on my last visit."

"And?"

"My old girlfriend. She has visited me in my dreams and caused me to awaken engorged, which I tried to suppress. Only when I was able to relieve myself did it return to normal size so I could kneel for my prayers."

"And?"

"There is nothing else."

"And?"

"Well . . . I did take a piece of bread without paying. The storekeeper said since I am a man of God, it was always fine to help myself—"

"And?"

"The fruit cakes. I took those as well."

"And?"

"I still have some of them on me now."

"Place them on the altar as an offering and return."

The acolyte exited from the confessional and walked toward the altar, shaking his head at the other, who had begun to rise. He placed the stolen cakes and disappeared inside the booth again.

The brother confessor resumed. "As you have cleaved those stolen sweetmeats to your body, so your lusting thoughts and actions will sour your soul. Blood will run from your eyes and face; your ears will no longer hear and they will leak of the blood of vanity and possession unless you repent now for the larger lust I hear in your voice. I have seen your kind, I have *been* your kind: covered by the sanctity of the cloth, you trap a trusting woman under it and spill your seed." Gerome waited for a reply, but there was only silence.

"Admit you have never acted in lust," he continued. "If you lie, your blood will join that of all who lust after body and possessions, who place jewels and ruffles and bows over themselves to hide their sinful lives. Say the truth, repent, and save yourself this moment, this day, or lie and risk a flood that will choke not only the city streets but your homes, your family, and the purity of your own sisters."

Shocked by the priest's words, the young acolyte felt his mouth go dry and tears ran down his face. He touched his eyes, then looked at his hands to see if they were stained with blood.

"Confess now and save yourself. Change your ways, or soon those tears will fill the streets with blood and your betrayals of the Lord will mark you as one who leads the citizens away from their own salvation. Tell the truth now!"

The young man whimpered. "It was a young peasant girl. She tempted me and I followed her into the woods," he confessed.

"Bow your head, Son, and pray with me.

"I, your humble subject, do swear . . . repeat after me."

"I, your humble subject, do swear . . ."

"To suspend my lustful life from this moment forward . . . say it!"

"To suspend my lustful life from this moment forward . . ."

"To live a life of service, replacing my baser instincts with acts of zeal."

"To live a life of service, replacing my baser instincts with acts of zeal."

"To praise God through Jesus Christ as the sole rescuer and protector of my soul."

"To praise God . . . but I am only a young man."

"And it is especially because of your youth others will listen to and watch you!" Gerome said.

"To praise God through Jesus Christ as the sole rescuer and protector of my soul," the boy repeated.

"That He might appoint me guardian to all those I see and meet or strike me dead."

"That He might appoint me guardian to all those I see and meet or may He strike me dead . . . but, Your Excellency. I have not taken my vows . . . I have six months before I do so."

"And in those six months do you intend to behave as you have or are you serious as a priest? This is the vow you must take every morning of your life. Your mission is a serious one: it is to save the world. How can you do this if you are led astray by the seduction of the world?"

The boy continued to whimper, but said nothing.

"Sit with this in your cell for one week. Take only enough food to keep you strong, and search yourself to learn if you are with the army of the Lord or with the sheep doomed to slaughter by their own weakness. Now go. I will pray for you."

The young man wept as he walked, trancelike, past his friend. He saw nothing now but his own sinful ways. He would surely be destroyed, as the cleric predicted. His life had been altered by the priest's questioning, by the hammering of the word "and" the priest had relentlessly thrown at him. Suddenly, he turned and walked toward the altar, fell on his knees, and sobbed before his Lord.

The second man, alarmed by his friend's behavior, approached the confessional booth with great fear, his heart pounding. As he sat inside the tiny space, he, too, began to weep.

"And why are you weeping, young man?" Gerome asked with a gentle tone.

"I do not know except my friend has melted into tears and taken himself before the altar in a way I have never seen in all our months at the monastery."

"Why does this make you weep?"

"Because I fear what he has seen and felt, and I want to feel it too, but there is a part of me that wants to run away."

"Then go. Please leave this instant," Gerome said.

"But what about the confession? What about my sins?"

"The sins you were about to recite or the sins you keep hidden even from yourself?"

"Is there a difference?"

"If you must ask, you must learn the hard way."

"What do you mean? Tell me."

"*You* are here to tell *me*," Gerome said, his voice going deeper and more serious.

"Bless me, Father, for I have sinned."

"How so?"

"I have harbored lustful thoughts not only toward women but also toward young boys and even sometimes toward the dogs I pet. Everything I touch sets my member astir and the only way I can quiet it is to . . ."

"And are you relieved?"

"Only for moments. The more I avoid it and try to prevent it, the more it happens."

"And are these thoughts or actions?"

"Both."

By now the young man had long forgotten the standard list of mild offenses he had been rehearsing. He could still hear his companion sobbing.

"Do not tell me any more," said Gerome. "Confess to yourself all those things you have done that are cause for shame. Write them down and set the paper aflame to burn them out of you. Use them from this day forth as a source of compassion as you go out in the world to save souls, to save the world from its continuous river of lust. For if you fail to do this today, right now, this instant, you will help create the flood of destruction heading our way. It will be a wave so tall and huge, a wave of blood and disaster that will wash away the vanity of the world, and you along with it. Row yourself out of the flood of blood and sacrifice. Go forth and rescue all you can from the river of our endless desires. Let this be your only desire: to serve and to save. You are forgiven."

Gerome repeated to the second acolyte the austerities he had given the first. Shocked at his own direct admissions of the things that afflicted him the most, the boy tearfully joined his friend at the altar.

Now the monsignor rose from his hidden place and walked over to them.

"My sons," he said with a great smile. "How were your confessions?"

They looked at him, their eyes red and swollen.

"And would you care to meet him face to face?"

They both nodded.

"Brother Gerome," he said. "Please step out and meet your charges now."

"Brother Gerome! How is that possible?" one said.

They looked at Gerome, who bestowed a sudden look of such sublime loving kindness on these two repenting souls they melted once again into tears.

The other one said, "Brother Gerome, we thought you had died in Ferrara, and here you are so strong and so—"

"So persuasive?" asked the monsignor. "He, my sons, has had a visitation and it has healed not only his body but his mind. It has seared into his soul his mission with the power of a thunderbolt, and you have felt a tiny part of its power. Do not ever give up on any soul, especially your own. Now you've seen how words can turn you inside out and change your life in an instant. I charge you both to be his servants and companions as he travels through the Tuscan hills."

The young men kissed Gerome's feet and babbled words of gratitude.

"Stop it," Gerome said. "This is exactly what I do not need. I need soldiers strong and steadfast in the truths that come to me from on high. We are facing the end of the world, the end of Florence, for certain unless we carry this warning to the core of each listener. Now stand!"

Both young men brought themselves to their feet. In place of tears they now wore a look of pride as though they had been singled out for excellence.

"Remember, you have not been chosen for your merits, which, to me, are sadly few," Gerome said and watched the pride fade from their faces. "You have been chosen for your sins and your desire to turn away from them. Pride is not a weapon to carry. It will be your Achilles' heel, if you remember your classical studies. Your power is in your knowledge of your mistaken ways. Do not ever place yourself above the souls you preach to. We are of them, have tasted their hunger and lusts. We have stepped into the mud of their vanity but we have changed direction and with the help of the Almighty we can help them do the same. This is a holy war against human craving. We must be vigilant and not proud, because human craving takes many forms, and we can slip back into our own sea of sin if we do not save ourselves first from drowning."

The four men slowly walked the length of the cathedral, following the nave as they made their way toward the main entrance. "On my way here," said Gerome, "I passed other men of the cloth who are plotting to overthrow the Medicis, to place yet another family at the helm of Florence, when in fact, the only family fit to govern is God's, with the Lord as Prince and King and all God's laws serving as man's laws. When that happens, we will have a chance to save the world. And that, my young men, is our task."

CHAPTER NINETEEN

Floriana Returns to Oslavia

FLORIANA WAS FAR FROM THE IMAGE of an acolyte readying for conversion as she stumbled laughing out of a new cart while holding hands with Luigi, Mirabella, and Elizabetta. She was covered in brambles, her wilted necklace of flowers hung on top of her habit, her Star of David wound around her neck with its tiny marcasites sparkling against the dusty white cloth.

Oslavia gave the sign of silence to Floriana, yanked the new carriage's whip out of Luigi's hand, and snapped it in the air. All three children as well as Floriana jumped at the sound.

Oslavia sent one of her more piercing gazes at the children. "Don't speak of where you've been or what you've done. Do you understand? And the scarf?" she asked Luigi. "Why does the Signorina Floriana not have a scarf over her eyes?"

"She vomited when she wore it when we drove there. We were afraid she would do that again so we left it off," Luigi said.

Oslavia motioned to Floriana to step back inside the cart. She grabbed the whip, got into the cart, and shooed the children away as if they were flies, then drove toward the forest. At the edge of the convent grounds,

Oslavia hid the cart behind tall bushes and led Floriana through the forest toward the Peredexion tree.

Once they were seated across from each other under the tree, Oslavia made the sign of the cross. Floriana held on to her Star of David. Oslavia reached toward Floriana and took the young woman's two hands in her own. They sat in silence for a moment.

"We are in the shade of the Peredexion tree and only the truth is to be spoken here. It is for the protection of all who come to this spot. You can speak now," Oslavia said.

"Master Sandro placed me under a tree like this when he began the painting. He did not explain its powers."

"How often have you vomited?"

"I have not been well since that beast of the cloth climbed on my back as though I were a dog." Floriana's eyes filled. Her cheeks grew red. "My mother had a sickly stomach and fits of vomiting before my sister was born."

"When you were in the tower, did you bleed?"

"Only because of the thorns baked into the bread. I learned to remove them, to chew the bread into a liquid, and pretended it was my mother's milk to keep my strength." Her breathing became shallow.

"We must speak honestly. And since you've been with me on the convent side, have you had any blood?"

"None."

"And the rape. I must call it that. When did it happen?"

"July the twenty-first."

Oslavia calculated in her head. "You will give birth late in the month of April or early May."

Floriana pulled her hands out of Oslavia's to wipe the tears from her eyes.

"If you convert and take your vows you will be protected."

"And the baby?"

"Not the baby. The baby, if she is a girl, will—" Oslavia stopped herself. "If I allow you to leave the convent now, Floriana, I'm sure to lose the standing I have worked my whole life to achieve. A tiny corner of independence in a world where women's names are not even recorded on the birth records—a white bean, at best, thrown into the city's counting pot—Stop crying! Listen to me!" Oslavia ordered. "What we decide in this spot is secret and beyond the power of the church. It is heart to heart."

"My heart is with your brother. This I can tell you already after two days with him."

"Has he broken his vow of silence to you?"

"I have watched him with those children. He is honorable."

"He is not a Jew."

"Is he married?"

"To his world of art," Oslavia said. "To his city of Florence. To his patron family, the Medici."

"Now he's married to me."

"What!"

"I see his devotion to the painting and I am in it, so I feel he is devoted to me."

"But what about when he's finished? What then?"

Floriana began to sob.

"*Basta! Forza!*" Oslavia commanded. "If you are going to get out of this alive, you must be strong. We must be strong. No one here at the convent must know of your condition. You must continue to wear the habit at all times."

"But Sandro will see it growing."

"We will deal with that when the time comes. Right now you are not showing. We can hide it. Now, about conversion."

"I won't."

"If you pretend to convert. If you go through the motions, I will not be thrown out or excommunicated for my failure to follow orders. After the conversion ceremony we'll have a plan ready to protect you."

Floriana took long, deep breaths, put her hands to her face, and cried silently into her palms.

"You must write nothing on paper and speak nothing about this. Decide this moment while we are under the protection of this spot."

"Why are you risking so much to help me?"

Floriana squeezed Oslavia's hands.

"When I was your age—actually a few years younger—there was a sister nun who found herself in your condition. She was already behind the walls, so she was protected on one hand. Her family never knew."

"The man?"

"A boy. A young novitiate. He convinced her that allowing him to mount her before he took his final vows would prevent him from having to do it later when he would risk excommunication. When she became with child he ran away."

"And the child?"

Now Oslavia's eyes filled.

"The child is here in the convent."

"She is a sister?"

"Her body is here."

"In the cemetery?"

"In the walls. Along with the other babies who came from unions of sin, as they are called."

"How old?"

"One day. Taken from the mother's breast," Oslavia said.

Both women sat in silence for a long time.

"And the mother? Where is she now?"

"Here. But sworn to silence forever on this event. And I will never name her to you either. Now you know why I cannot condone this again. If you convert I will be saved, my place here protected, and you can escape. I'm sure Sandro will help you. You'll have your child in safety."

"Did the child have a name?"

"We called her Empiria—Greek for experience."

"Empiria, how beautiful."

"Beautiful she was. Her vision still appears before me when I least expect it."

"If I convert," Floriana said, "my child will be owned by the church. Will I be forced to take vows?"

"If you convert we can hide the sign of your child under the robes and you can be released as a normal lay person unless Bernardino decides to take you with him to show you off. Even as I tell you this, I can't be sure which plan is best. But now you know my help is sincere, and you will regain your freedom and the freedom of your child."

"And how can my child be free if he doesn't know who his father is?"

"We all have the same Father. Jews and Christians share the same father of God in heaven. Think of Mary and Joseph."

"I'd rather not think of them." Floriana's hand was wrapped around her Star of David. "The Zohar, the most important words from the Kabbalah, says we are all light. To take in more heavenly light we must cast out the darkness. If this act of impregnating me was an act of darkness, I will pray to cast it out with the beauty and freedom of my child, boy or girl, who will defy the darkness with the light of the love I will shower on her. Please forgive me, Oslavia, for saying this, and I pray you will not take offense from my words, but I could never allow this child to be soiled by the belief of original sin Christians say we are all born with. It is a curse to work off every day of your life. I must pray now to find the truth for me and my child. That is what I will follow."

"Pray all you like, but do not do it out loud because what you have uttered is blasphemy, enough to keep you locked here forever, conversion or not!" Oslavia said. In spite of a twinge of annoyance from Floriana's attack on Christianity, she took a deep breath, and chose the way of tolerance and acceptance for this young woman's beliefs, and continued, "All of your talk of the Zohar, and your beliefs, must stay here in these dark woods and never be uttered, especially in the convent or in the presence of Bandini when—and if—you ever meet him face to face."

"Will I be released again to the Villa di Castello?"

"The plan is for you and the children to be dispatched at least two days a week until my brother has finished your part in the painting."

"I am so grateful for what you are doing, Sister Oslavia. For what you are risking."

"Don't speak of it again. Your way to safety is secured even if I can't see its path. You must trust my brother and me. I am praying for your highest good, Floriana."

CHAPTER TWENTY

Sandro Meets Graziella

A FEW DAYS BEFORE Floriana's expected return to Villa di Castello, Sandro and Poppi met in the greenhouse to conjure a flower strategy.

"Every blossom," Sandro said, "must tell its own story. Educate me so I'll be able to continue to choose the perfect ones to paint, especially around Floriana's face and body."

In perpetual motion, Poppi pinched wilting blossoms, pruned and watered plants as she spoke. "Carnations," she said. "Surround your Floriana with as many carnations as you can find. They will lift her homesickness. I found a huge secret crop of them on the hill above the villa. You can take her there yourself. I've left a red ribbon tied to the branches so you can find them. You'll have to squeeze through some narrow fissures in the stone, but when you get to the other side, you'll be glad I kept the spot secret for you. Not a word about it to Master Piero!"

Yelping dogs interrupted their conversation; Piero and a young woman approached the perfumery. Large yellow circles, the sign of a Jew, normally only one worn over the left breast, were sewn into the design of her clothing. As she drew closer, Sandro noticed a stain, like red wine spilled on white marble, marked the right side of her face. She stretched out her hand toward Sandro's.

"Graziella, daughter of Nannino Manfredo Abramo," Piero said.

When she gripped Sandro's hand he noticed a loose red string encircling her right wrist. The open, direct stare she gave him was riveting. Her black hair with a few random gray strands was tightly braided and a small cluster of dried lilac tucked into her bodice gave off a sweet scent. A large leather pouch like the ones he had seen on the officials from the Medici banks was slung over her shoulder.

"She's part of my banking team," Piero said. "Here to arrange payments to you, Sandro. But as you know, the payments will be tied to satisfactory progress on the work."

"Which is well under way, as *you* know," Sandro said to Piero, but his attention was on Graziella, who cradled one of Piero's dogs in her arms.

"The only problem, Sandro," Piero said, "is she needs to see the stages of the work."

When Sandro's face grew tense, Piero continued, "I know. I know . . . Imagine you! I won't look at it, but Graziella must. It's a matter of record and business. She'll not comment on it in favor or disfavor."

"Very well," Sandro said.

"Roses of course," Poppi said, trying to finish her conversation with Sandro and insert herself into the group. Poppi nodded a hello to Graziella.

"Shall we go to the painting, Master Sandro?" Graziella said.

As soon as Sandro and Graziella were outside of the greenhouse, Piero's dog leapt out of Graziella's arms. He pushed his pug face against her legs, tripping her.

She pulled herself to her feet before Sandro had a chance to offer her his hand. "Fierce little soldier, isn't he?" she said.

"Those dogs push and shove, but then run away. Just like their master Piero," Sandro said.

Graziella gave Sandro a surprised look, said nothing, and continued to walk alongside him.

"And the red string?" Sandro asked.

"To ward off evil spirits."

"Jewish tradition?"

"Hardly a tradition. Frowned upon by some of us and followed with great zeal by others," she said.

"And are you a zealot?"

"I believe a little bit in everything."

As they approached the clearing under the large tree, Sandro pulled a curtain aside for Graziella to enter.

She walked to Floriana's image.

"I feel as though she is about to speak to me!"

"If you look long enough, you'll see a secret message from her directly to you."

"You have a reputation for playing tricks. Am I to be your next victim?"

"Look closely and tell me if you can read something only one of your kind might recognize."

"One of my kind. *One of my kind?*"

"It's in the flowers."

She stared but said nothing.

"Look harder."

"These four small white blossoms surrounding her face?"

"What do you see?"

"If in reality those flowers have six petals, then it is less likely to be the clue. But if, in fact, they have the usual number of five as you've already painted them in other locations, I would suspect she might be a Jew. Others may not say this or see it, but Jews might take it to be a code for the sign of the Star of David."

"Excellent! How many do you see?" Without waiting for an answer, he went on to say there would be many of them hidden throughout the work.

"Why do you hide it, Master Botticelli? Is this not a painting you are free to do with as you please?"

The question stunned him. He could feel the blood—and with it, the ability to see color—drain out of his head. Suddenly everything appeared to him in black and white.

With all his "freedom," he had not dared to openly paint the Star of David. Jews were curious and intelligent. If it weren't for their translations of Greek and Arabic, Plato and the others, they might never have been included as members of the Academy. Her question had pierced his pride and made a joke of his secret symbolism.

"Is she from your imagination?" Graziella asked.

"Yes and no." Sandro felt unease with Graziella's probing.

The sting of her question, "Why do you hide it?" had been like the venom of a bee—unexpected and sharp.

"And the rest of this?" Graziella asked, as she ran her hand across the untouched surfaces of the painting's ten-foot expanse.

"A whole world is about to unfold here. But at least you can see, Signorina Graziella, I have made a strong start."

Graziella opened the mouth of her purse under Sandro's nose. "Seven payments will be earmarked for you. Today I give you the first. Show me your planned drawing and we can use it to schedule the other six."

"I have no sketch, no drawing."

"No plan?"

"There's a plan for sure, just not on paper."

"I'm listening."

Explaining to himself as well as Graziella, Sandro walked to the panel and described what he saw in his mind's eye: three figures on the right corner of the painting, all manifestations of this Flora character. He added, he had intentionally not wanted to show any religious content, Christian or Jewish.

But Graziella's stinger had entered him—a bite of her rage on behalf of her people. He passed his hand across the board, indicating "something" in the center and "perhaps" a couple of more images on the left. "The foreground, background and top area, the sky area. That's six items," he said, content for the first time he had a plan after all. Content, also, that she had dropped the questions about her religion.

"When you're done with the figures on the right, I want you to release the first of six pigeons I've brought with me today. Piero has agreed to house, feed, and care for them. They know the way back to our property.

When the first one comes home, I'll plan to leave the next morning to see your progress and to pay you."

"I should be able to release one to you by October or mid-November."

"I'll tell my father about the progress of his investment."

"Isn't this Piero's project?"

"They're partners," she said. "My father is a merchant and banker. We limit ourselves to helping out the local poor and many of our own people. He is a great admirer of your work and a personal friend to young Piero. But that knowledge is for your ears only. It is not to be part of any discussions you might have with your former patron, Lorenzo."

"My concern is not who pays me but that the payments continue as the work continues. I have ailing parents, not to mention my other commitments. And as for sharing the details with Lorenzo, I see no need."

It was such an unlikely friendship, thought Sandro, ignorant as he was of Manfredo's rescue of Piero a few months earlier. Sandro had no idea that Piero, overheated and slimy with his own sweat as he rode in full costume on a scorching summer day, had slid off his horse on the edge of Manfredo's property. It was during that visit Piero decided to use his future inheritance as collateral to borrow money to purchase the villa away from Lorenzo.

"Though I spoke of Master Piero in jest a few short moments ago," Sandro said, "I'm most grateful for the freedom he has given me."

"Perhaps at the next scheduled payment I'll bring my father along so we can both meet your mysterious Jewess."

"That would please me greatly. And will he also need to view this work?"

"I'm afraid he'll insist, especially after I explain some of your symbolism. Artists are artists because they mask their true opinions in color, no?"

"Why do you judge me so harshly?"

"I am not judging you, Master Botticelli. If anyone is judging anyone, I'd say calling your young patron, Piero, a dog is not a sign of appreciation for the opportunity he has given you."

"You speak the truth, wise Signorina Graziella."

"Then do not bite the hands of those who feed you."

"The same words my sister spoke when she heard of my transfer here."

"You have a wise sister. I should like to meet her."

"You may meet her inside this painting. But not as the nun she is. I'll hide her religious identity too."

Who was this Graziella? A warrior of some kind. Feminine, yet not in a way he had seen before. This was not a woman to protect, for she had power on her side—more than the purse of florins neatly wrapped and boldly carried. This was not like the forcefulness of Lucrezia. Not like the gentleness of Oslavia. It was as though she needed nothing and therefore felt no need to please or flatter in the way he often found himself doing.

"Let me show you the pigeons and how to handle them," she said as they walked back toward the villa. "We want to make sure they don't all fly away when you're ready to send the first one."

"If I should have any questions, might you be available? And how might I reach you in between payments?" Sandro said.

"Piero knows how. But we prefer to keep that knowledge—forgive me—in only a few hands. Use the pigeons and I'll come to you. Although we Jews are among you, we are not of you. There are many Christians who want nothing more than to see us burn."

"My exposure to your people in the halls of the Medici Palace has been very instructive. The likes of Piccolo della Mirandola's mentor, a Jew from Prato, and several of the doctors we have, and lawyers too, have passed many days and hours there. I don't see anyone drinking blood, only stopping the flow of it out of open wounds."

"In the country, Signor Botticelli, things are otherwise. The Franciscan Bernardino is the worst offender. After he has passed through our hills, we need weeks to undo the damage wreaked by ignorant neighbors. Once you see we don't have horns, that we are just as you are—"

"Please don't compare me to ignorant country folk," Sandro said. "I think of myself as free of those prejudices."

"Don't be so arrogant. You dabble in what fascinates you, what serves you, but will you wear a yellow patch if you don't have to? I think not."

And as quickly as she stung with her words, she softened. She gave him a smile, and led him through the front door of the villa.

"Don't worry, Maestro Botticelli," she said. "You are wrinkling your face in seriousness like a monkey. Don't bother yourself about what you can't know. Use your gifts to paint what you do. You have made a wonderful beginning and I'm eager to see what you will paint next."

They climbed to the uppermost floor of the villa. At the end of a long corridor, a small door led into an unfinished section. Rough-hewn wooden rafters spanned the underside of clay roof tiles. The warbling and cooing of pigeons filled the air. A wooden ladder led to a loft a few feet from the roof. Even though the season had changed and the air outside was cooler, in this small section of the villa, the heat was intense. Graziella unlatched a small panel in the roof that opened to the sky.

"That's where you'll release them, one at a time, as your painting progresses," she said. She knelt by a large pigeon cage made of woven reeds. She opened it, quickly grasped one of the pigeons between her two hands, and brought it to Sandro's face.

Silently, she transferred the bird from her hands to his. Pressing its wings against its body, he felt its fragility, knowing he could crush it to death if he put more pressure around it. Suddenly his words to Floriana—that he had placed his own heart in the palm of her hands—came back to him. A pain pierced his chest. How easily he had given part of himself to her! Dizziness overtook him. As he handed the bird back to Graziella, he realized his sudden pain was the familiar ache of fear, made more intense by the heat and the smell of the birds.

"They are used to human touch, and they are always happy to go back to their home," she said. She placed it back into the cage, closing the tiny latch in the roof.

"I had no idea," he said.

"Most villas have these in their roofs. Piero and I decided this would be the easiest way to let me know when you're ready for each payment."

Once back in front of the villa, Graziella shook Sandro's hand as if their exchange had been without a moment's friction. For Sandro, however, a change in his mood was unmistakable. Those caged pigeons mirrored his life. A darkness descended that seemed to take the sun out of the day, the moonlight out of the night to come. His joy over Floriana had kept these darker moods at bay, but the beating of the bird's heart, and his own involuntary impulse to crush its life away, had set some deep pain in motion. He knew the pattern. This would happen whenever he encountered anyone who knew a mystery or secret he didn't. This Graziella, with her sharp tongue, had sliced into his good humor, pulling a curtain across his hopeful mood. In the past he had allowed fears and doubts to fester, interrupting his concentration, sabotaging his art. But he would fight it. After all, Floriana would be back the next day.

CHAPTER TWENTY-ONE

A Cart for Bandini

THE MORNING AFTER Floriana's return to the convent, Oslavia and Federico brought the new cart and horse to Bandini's door. Federico would cease to be the beast of burden pulling the monsignor around for his daily outing, and Floriana would have a way to go secretly back and forth to the Villa di Castello. Before they had a chance to knock, Bandini opened his door a crack, peeked out, and then shouted, "We have no funds for this!" and shut the door.

"It's a gift." Oslavia smiled as she stood outside the door. "A local nobleman had heard of your morning jaunts on the back of Federico here and he thought we might take this extra cart and old mare off his hands."

Bandini opened the door. "Who is this noble?"

"A Medici. Not Lorenzo, son of Piero the Gouty. It's his cousin Piero di Lorenzo di Piero di Cosimo di Giovanni di Bicci de' Medici, better known to all as Piero. He's a recently orphaned young Medici who has taken over Villa di Castello to offer a new home for his three younger sisters and longtime family servants. My brother Sandro resides as the court painter there, which is how Piero became aware of you."

"The orphan with such a long name thinks he can buy his way into Paradise."

"At least try the cart," Federico said, approaching the prelate. He threaded his arm through the old cleric's massive arm and gently pulled him toward the cart.

"You take your little ride with Federico and I'll send a note of thanks to Signor Piero," Oslavia said, then turned to walk away.

"No notes. A visit tomorrow is in order," Bandini said. He turned to Federico for an extra push to help him into the cart.

"He knows you're ill and expects nothing in return. Perhaps we can offer some of the woven flowers of the new novitiate. She is an accomplished weaver of religious symbols."

"Her education and conversion plans?"

"She shows great promise."

Bandini settled his corpulent body into the cart, causing the wagon and mare to lurch backward. Federico started driving slowly. Bandini waved his hands in the air as though he were controlling the beast himself, urging Federico to go faster, but no wheel would spin as fast as Oslavia's mind. *Tomorrow! That's the day Floriana is due back at the villa.*

Because of the hood of shame Floriana had worn on the grounds of the monastery, Bandini had never actually seen her face, but he had heard her name repeatedly. Scenes of an untimely meeting of Floriana and Bandini at the villa must remain just that, pictures in Oslavia's worried imagination. Oslavia inhaled deeply, and as she held her breath she sank her hand beneath the folds of her habit, her finger closing tightly around her rosary beads. With a slow exhalation she moved one bead at a time along its string in rhythm with her steps and her breathing. Soon she formed the words of a new prayer to help her through this situation: *God, I turn to thee for direction and ultimate truth. Lead me to express your love and your desire for all concerned. Thy will be done.*

As she made her way back to the convent, she passed the caretaker's cottage and decided to visit with the children, but they were nowhere to be found. Their mother, Nicola, Federico's wife, lay in bed struggling to breathe between fits of coughing. Spots of blood came up with the spittle and her skin had the yellowish hue Oslavia had seen on the faces of the dying.

CHAPTER TWENTY-TWO

Botticelli's Impatience

SANDRO WAS NOT INTERESTED in Poppi's recitation of medicinal properties for every weed and flower. His mind instead was already at his easel, where Floriana would once again be that very day. To distract him from his impatience for Floriana's arrival, Poppi had dragged Sandro uphill to a meadow behind the villa to search for carnations and the last wild flowers of the season.

"Take you, for instance," Poppi said. She had brought them to the far end of the meadow and with her back to Sandro was tying a second bright red ribbon onto one of the branches next to a granite boulder. Once the ribbon was tied, she turned to face him. "When you arrived here, full of annoyance with your young master, Piero, I had little faith you would be able to cheer yourself into work. But tea I serve you each day brewed from the stems of carnations has chased your sadness away." She stooped to gather wild oregano, shaking off any insects moving in its clouds of lavender buds. "Now I see you joyful and excited with the birth of your painting."

"It's not your tea, Poppi. It's a person who has intoxicated me. And I see no carnations here. Why the red ribbons?"

"A surprise for you when you need to get away from everyone. As good as a field of carnations, only better," Poppi said. Sandro was hardly listening.

"What is keeping Floriana?" His head was downcast as they began the descent. The villa and all approaching roads became visible, but no Floriana and no carriage.

"I'm getting a bad feeling, Poppi. Perhaps they won't make it back today. Perhaps Luigi has lost the way."

"Trust in God, Signor Sandro."

"I'll take my lunch in my room, Poppi. Don't disturb me until they arrive. If Piero asks, tell him I'm in my room working on some sketches for the painting."

"Trust, Signor Botticelli. Don't let your anxieties take over."

"That's easy for you to say, Poppi."

ONCE INSIDE HIS ROOM, Sandro paced back and forth, all the while staring out of the window and hoping to hear the dogs yelping. By two o'clock, when no sign of Floriana appeared, he defied Oslavia's ban of returning to the convent and saddled his horse.

His mind galloped faster than his horse's hooves.

First he imagined himself discovering the cart after it had toppled over a cliff: the children dead and Floriana's neck broken. Each catastrophic image drove him faster and faster along the path.

To dispel the ache of such a tragic image, he saw his long-awaited wedding day with Floriana as his bride, intelligent and full of poetry in her face and body. A Jewess would not have been a suitable mate for the princely likes of the Medici, but for an artist from the working classes, no one would care. He would wear those yellow circles on his own clothing with pride. That would shock the likes of Graziella! He imagined himself in his studio in Florence, assistants working with patrons of his choosing. Floriana would be his young, loving bride. They would ride together to scoop up her uncle and siblings in Ferrara and settle them nearby within an easy walk of his parents' house where they would live happily together and begin a family at last. These joyous thoughts brought a beaming smile to his face, and their appeal startled him. He had told his mother, only months ago, marriage would never be a part of his life. His destiny and his earthly desires lived in two separate worlds. But now they were united. He would save her, take her away with him as Fra Filippo Lippi, his teacher, had done with his wife, sweeping her away from a convent too.

As he arrived at the clearing with the monastic compound in view, Sandro laughed aloud at how his thoughts had galloped between the devastation of his worst imaginings and the ecstasy of his most idealized ones.

The cart was gone. A good sign, until he realized he should have encountered them on the path. He stopped the horse, but the animal, too, seemed to reflect his master's indecision as he swerved side to side, first facing back to the road they had traveled, and then toward the monastery.

If he sought out Oslavia directly, he would be violating her wishes. If he went to Floriana's cell, he would be violating them again. The men's compound was the answer.

He stopped first at the caretaker's cottage. The door was ajar. There was no sign of the children or their father. Instead of following his impulse to veer off to the left in the direction of the convent and Floriana's cell, he led his horse to the right to the side of the monastery. At the main entrance he dismounted and walked to an enormous wooden door. As he was about to raise the huge knocker, the door opened. Behind it was a small man who reeked of garlic. He wore cloves around his neck. At his forehead a small shiny bump the size of a cherry pushed itself out from underneath the skin—the only smooth spot on his face. His back was rounded. He looked so much like the waiter at the taverna in Piazza della Signoria that Sandro was sure the two men must be related.

"Are you brother to Faranese in Firenze?" Sandro asked.

"I am brother to my spiritual companions only, Signor . . . ?"

". . . Botticelli. I've come to make sure Father Bandini has received the cart from my master, orphan Piero de' Medici at Villa Castello. And may I speak with Father Bandini?"

"No. You may not! I'm afraid he is unavailable, Signor Botticelli. He has retired for the day."

"At five o'clock?"

"This is his custom and he takes no visitors."

"I was searching for the cart to make sure it did arrive and I did not see it, kind sir."

"It was used for a funeral."

"Someone has died?"

"Quite suddenly. One of our own."

Sandro's heart sank that it might be Floriana or Oslavia.

"My sister, Oslavia, is she . . . ?"

"She is fine. She went to officiate at the burial of the caretaker's wife, Nicola. They'll be returning soon, thanks to the generosity of your master, Piero."

"Yes, thank you. May I wait for their return by the grounds so I can get a glimpse of my beloved sister?"

"I'll tell Father Bandini of your visit. On behalf of the monsignor, I thank you," the gnarled Faranese look-alike said, and with that he closed the door on Sandro.

BEFORE SANDRO HAD A CHANCE to sneak toward Floriana's cell, he saw figures moving in the dark toward the caretaker's cottage, but no one in the shape or form of his Floriana.

Young Luigi threw himself onto Sandro, sobbing about his mother's burial.

"I told you not to come here!" Oslavia turned her back on Sandro as she whisked the children and their father into the cottage. Sandro waited at the door.

When Oslavia emerged, he spoke. "I was frantic when they didn't arrive. I thought perhaps an accident—"

"Did you talk to Bandini?"

"I tried but he was already in for the night at 5:00 p.m. I told his hunchback I had come to make sure the cart was here. He told me about the funeral. And Floriana?"

"She's waiting for you at Castello."

"Waiting for me?"

"We went there after the funeral to drop her off . . . permanently."

"Permanently? What about Bandini and the conversion?"

"Standing at the grave of the poor Nicola I decided to release Floriana to your care."

"How are you going to explain her disappearance?"

"God will show me the way. I'll do what I have to do. You go now . . . No, not yet. First, I'll take you to her cell so you can gather her personal items and give them to her when you see her."

"I'll do more than see her," Sandro said, his face in a smile. "I plan to wed her."

"Even though she's with child?"

"What! Whose?"

"The one who defiled her on her way into Tuscany. If she stays here the child will be taken from her. Trust me, I know this. I've seen more than you'll ever know. Come with me now. In darkness no one will see you."

The words "with child" erased the perfect wedding scene that had carried him to Oslavia's. As he followed his sister through the dark into the cell where he had first seen Floriana surrounded by the buds and branches as she wove the cross, it was as though his mind went numb and his heart had stopped beating.

"Are you sure she is with child?"

"The fainting, the vomiting, the slight swelling in her abdomen. Had you not noticed?"

"I saw only the perfection of her face, her expression of openness and innocence and yet the fortitude of someone who has not been told how to think or feel."

"You saw what you wanted to see. But now she is your responsibility. You must find a place to care for her at least until she's on her own, among her own. Do you even know what love is? True love of caring, not coveting?

"Did you hear me?" Oslavia asked. "Do you know what true love is?"

"I'm learning, perhaps for the first time. Pain and suffering are an unavoidable part of it. Losing and gaining at the same time."

"Make those losses and gains into teachers," Oslavia said. "It is the only salvation, Sandrolino."

Oslavia rummaged around the room with the light of a candle while Sandro stood immobilized, awash with conflicting emotions.

"Stop it!" she commanded. "You're behaving as you used to when you were a little boy and confused: you would stand as though a statue, unable to act or move. Now the most urgent thing is for you to help me search this space. Give your full attention to this, and trust God will lead you on the right path for the rest."

Oslavia handed Sandro Floriana's loosely woven shawl. It was full of brambles and thistles. He placed it under his nose to take in Floriana's scent, then gently folded it. On the floor by the straw mattress he saw a book not much larger than his own secret sketchbooks. He picked it up and saw inside it small drawings of flower shapes, insects, and some Hebrew lettering. *Such a talented hand she has! An artist for sure.* He had seen that calligraphy before in the Medici rooms. A Jewish wife would mean the children would be Jewish, and the irony that the child she carried fathered by a priest would be raised a Jew would surely be a sweet revenge for Floriana, should she desire it.

Oslavia handed Sandro a small comb. The candlelight glinted in the few golden strands of Floriana's hair.

"Do you even know, Sandro, what you were born into this world to do?"

"My destiny is to paint, but why must I do only that? Floriana has brought my destiny and my desires together at last!"

"Each of us, Sandro, is born to do something God wants of us. Our mission, dear heart, is to express that higher mission without distracting ourselves with petty desires and mean feelings."

Oslavia grabbed the small slate board and put it inside her own robes. "You are released from all vows of silence I had placed on you. But those removed, I place new ones upon you in the name of our family and decency. Do not under any conditions add to her defilement unless you plan to legitimize your love for her. Christian men in the past have been imprisoned for consorting with Jewish women."

"Years ago when adultery was the issue. Times are different now."

"Making a life with this woman, protecting her, will become a distraction from your life's purpose. Your creative fire will be consumed in your decision to wed her. Where will you live? How will you live?"

"In the way I am accustomed. The same, only finally happier and the child, our children—"

"Raised as Jews?"

"My happiness—"

"Your happiness, Sandro, is your sadness. From your gloom and darkness your genius blossoms. Your nightmares, your hovering in and out of the light, all help you to work your magic. If you were born to be a goldsmith like our brother, or a tanner like our father, you would have been married years ago. You've been singled out, lifted up to wander in the twilight between what man can be and what God can dream for him—a picture of our highest beauty, Sandro. You are dreaming for all of us."

Sandro pulled another of Floriana's hairs from her comb. "Not a hair on her head will I harm."

"Let this woman be your muse. Love her for that. Protect her with your heart, with your art. Elevate her pain in color and form, but don't make her your wife, for wife you must make her if you bed her."

"But I have the right to marry whom I please!"

"You are already married to your work, to your Florence, to your Medici. Let that be enough."

"You're saying this because you've had to renounce a family yourself. And you want me to make the same kind of sacrifice. You may be my older sister, but you've not known the longing of one body to merge with another, not out of lust, but out of something deeper, something that can't be all wrong."

Oslavia turned away from Sandro to move about Floriana's cell in a sudden burst of sweeping, dusting, and reordering the few pieces of furniture.

"How can you know what's in my heart?" he said.

She stopped her movements, then turned back to face her brother. "Think long and hard on this, Sandro. Impulse is not the way. If you're not prepared to take on all the difficulties and the public exposure you will encounter by marrying a Jewess, then you'll have to find a way to lift your love above the brutes and transform it to something higher."

After the small cell had been swept of any personal items, brother and sister made their way back toward the caretaker's cottage.

"Why do you think me a brute?" he said.

"I've heard about your raucous evenings with Lorenzo. He never hid it from the people and your name was spoken of alongside his."

"And when might you have heard this, cloistered as you were here for so long?"

"I hear the novitiates talk. I've taken trips on behalf of the church, sat in taverns, and heard coarse men drink and laugh beside me while I furiously counted my rosary beads as though in a trance of prayer. I heard every word. When I heard the name of Medici, I knew you were part of it."

"I'm a man who has given his love to art and that art to the service of others," Sandro said. "But still, I have urges and desires. Even though I've never put on the cloth, nor do I care to, a little comfort to the body with a willing, affectionate partner is not such a crime. I have hurt no one. No wife at home was I deceiving."

"My point exactly. Let that be enough. Keep your destiny and your desires separate."

"What about loneliness?"

"Both of us have lost. For me it's too late. The church has been my family," Oslavia said.

"And I have been part of another's family. But now I know I was on the outside looking in. It's only natural I yearn for my own family."

"As you should. It's not too late for you. But this girl is not for you. Finish your painting of her and see what your heart says."

Oslavia placed her arm through Sandro's arm. The talk of loneliness had dispelled any bitterness between them.

"I will not bring shame upon you, Sister."

"Nor I on you, I pray, in this most bold action I am taking on your behalf."

"Are you taking it on behalf of me or because you know it is the right thing to do?"

"I am taking it because the alternative is a sin against two lives and I have enough lives on my conscience."

Sandro stopped in the path. "What does that mean?"

"Let's say in the past I have taken my direction from my superiors and witnessed the loss of lives. Too many to count. I will not allow myself to conform this time, and with Bandini so infirm no one is watching me any longer."

"But the conversion. Now you don't even have the convert. What will you tell him?"

"I'll pray on it. I'll get the answer directly from God and not from another mortal. If I have to be excommunicated as a result, I'll throw myself on your mercy and you'll have two women to care for. In the meanwhile, be grateful Bandini has never seen Floriana, only heard her name. He insists on a visit in person. Nicola's death and our need for the new cart to take her to the burial ground prevented his visit to thank Piero himself for the cart and horse. I can put that visit off a week or two, but sooner or later, well before it turns cold, we will be making a trip to your villa and he'll surely expect me to lead the way. Luigi and the children must be told to be silent about her."

"How is the little one going to be silent? She doesn't understand deception, only affection, and she clings to Floriana, saying her name out loud over and over again whenever she sees her—as I would, too, if I had the mantle of a small child to hide my mortal desires."

"I'll take only Luigi to lead the way."

"Let me go now, dear sister. I'll pray for your safety and for the words of God to enter your mouth each time you speak about Floriana to Bandini," he said. He gently packed Floriana's personal objects into his pouch and mounted his horse.

"Godspeed," Oslavia said. "Consider wisely your words and deeds and look for spiritual light to lead you."

"You have done the right thing, dear Oslavia. You will be rewarded."

"My reward is God, my true Master, as he speaks directly to me and through me. Bernardino is a bigot against the Jews. He will be coming to claim his convert. Bandini wrote to him of Floriana days ago. I've got some time yet. You, however, have only the day, the hour, the visit of your muses, who are calling to you on this painting. God is talking to you also. You must listen to Him in your own fashion. But rein in your desires. Turn them to a higher purpose. Go do your work, my brother!"

CHAPTER TWENTY-THREE

Polishing Domestic Virtues
September 1477

"WE'RE INVISIBLE!" Piero's sister Donata whined. She punched her fists into the pasta dough Poppi had readied for the girls' domestic training. Poppi had shown them how to scoop out a crater in a mound of farina and had Renata crack several eggs into it. Poppi did the initial kneading of the ingredients, then stepped aside so each girl might take her turn to pound the mass of dough into what would become part of their dinner that night.

Poppi made no response to Donata's whine but only pushed her aside so the middle sister, Margarita, would have her turn at the soft target for the girls' rage. Margarita squeezed the dough as though she were strangling it, then said, "Now Floriana's here to stay, she's going to take all Master Botticelli's attention. He'll never see us."

Poppi's response was to hand Margarita a rolling pin and lean her body weight in toward the table, demonstrating in a rocking motion how to flatten out the dough.

"Piero has forbidden us to even ask him," Renata said. The youngest of the three girls and perhaps the wisest, she had watched her older sisters primp and preen for days, so Sandro might discover in them some glimmer of inspiration for his painting.

"Piero's such a coward!" Margarita said as she flattened the dough and held it up to the light, tearing a hole in it with her fingers.

Soon after Sandro's arrival at the villa weeks ago, the older girls had fought over perfumes and dresses, practiced smiles—each one of which was met by one of Sandro's brooding stares as though he were looking right through them. Since discovering Floriana, however, he still walked right past them, but with a smile on his face. They had become even more invisible to him. *If only he would put down his brush from the constantly blushing peasant nun and see they were the true beauties!*

"From the beginning, your brother has told Sandro he could paint whatever and whomever he wants," Poppi said. She pushed Margarita away, flattened the dough herself into a huge paper-thin circle, sprinkled it with more flour, and deftly rolled it up. She stepped aside, and handed Renata a knife.

"Straight cuts. Tiny ones," she instructed. Then, speaking to all three, she continued, "Don't underestimate your brother, young ladies! You may call him a coward, but he's clever beyond his years. Someday this painting will inspire other artists and writers for centuries to come, and if you want to be part of it you must offer yourselves as sweet helpers, especially now Filippino is back in Florence. This is your chance—if you can control your jealousies—to cultivate some patience."

"You don't know what it's like to grow up with no parents and a bunch of distant cousins who get all the glory while we are supposed to be patient," Donata said.

"You, my young ladies," Poppi said, "don't know what it's like to grow up with your hair shorn and dressed like a boy so that you can beg in the market place to support your ailing parents."

"*Che barba!* I'm so tired of hearing your story, Poppi. It's not fair!" Donata said, making the motion of her hands pulling imaginary whiskers off her chin to illustrate the expression of being so bored that she was growing a long beard.

"'Fair,' young lady, is what your skin is. If you continue with the sourness of a lemon, that is all Master Botticelli is going to see. He may even ask you to pose for him and then paint you as a lemon on the tree. He is known to do such things—a master of pranks. Be wary. Go out of your way to be sweet to Floriana, to assist with whatever she needs, and I guarantee he will notice your sweetness if you allow it to ripen."

"And how do you propose we ripen from sour to sweet if all we feel is bitterness toward her?" Margarita asked.

"And how does it happen in nature?" Poppi asked.

"It stays on the tree and takes its full time to sweeten," Renata said.

"Precisely! Attach yourselves to her. Feed off *her* sweetness, for she is a woman of sweetness. And as you do so, you'll grow sweeter still and he'll be bound to place you willingly in that painting."

"But when I see him hypnotized by her, anger strikes," Donata said.

"Your bee sting," Poppi said. "But sting yourself. Sting your thoughts, each mean and angry one into silence. Search yourself for something sweet to say or do."

"Why don't we turn her in when this Monsignor Bandini gets here?" Margarita said. "Let him take her back as a convent runaway?"

"If you do such a thing you'll lose any chance of being part of that painting. You'll enrage your brother who might decide to send you all off to separate convents for life! Your inheritance will go to building the coffers of each of your orders."

"Please don't even plant such an idea in his head!" Donata said.

"He's already thought it," Poppi said. She took the knife from Renata's hands and finished cutting the pasta noodles, then unwrapped them and laid them out on the counter to dry. "I fought for you to stay with us and not be sent off. But you must earn your keep here." She held the knife in the air and shook it as she spoke to the girls, who had gone pale. "Deceit is not an option for you if you want your freedoms."

"How dare he even consider such a thing?" Donata said.

Just then Floriana came into the room. No longer wearing her habit, she was dressed in a garment with the Medici shield across its breast.

"Good morning, ladies," she said then joined Poppi to unroll the rest of the raw pasta dough as though she had always done such a task.

"Can I tell you the joy of shedding that coarse habit! Poppi has offered to share her quarters with me and brought this dress and a scissors so I can finally cut up that heavy cloth."

"You're wearing my dress!" Donata said, as her face contorted.

"And doesn't it look so nice on Floriana?" Poppi said, glaring at Donata. "I offered it to her while you girls were at your studies yesterday. Buzz, buzz, buzz."

"She can keep it," Donata said, finally catching on. "It looks better on her anyway. Come to my closet after breakfast, Floriana, and you can pick out some more."

"There's no need," Floriana said. "This one dress will keep me just fine. My uncle taught me how to weave and sew. As soon as Poppi finds me some cloth I can sew my own dresses and dresses for you too. To be able to speak out loud is such a joy!"

Looking at Renata, Floriana said, "For you, I would weave a cloth of gold and coriander. What's your name?"

"How rude we haven't introduced ourselves to you," Donata said. "My name is Donata, which means 'to give,' so it makes sense I should give you that dress."

"It wasn't until I was in my thirties I realized my love for wearing red was connected to my name—something so obvious and yet it took someone else to tell it to me before I knew the truth, and then even more passionately I wore the color. And you, Donata, are growing into your name more than ever this morning with your generosity toward Floriana."

"And your name, how did you come to be called Floriana?" Margarita asked.

"You tell me your name first," Floriana said.

"Margarita. It means 'daisy,' and I do have yellow hair."

"You see, you didn't even have to grow into the name," Floriana said, "but the sunshine reflected in the flower must be reflected in your face too, to really grow into your name. But you've got lots of time." Margarita was confused by this. Was Floriana commenting on her pouting face, suggesting the expression was not sweet? Margarita felt a stab of annoyance even though she wore a false grin on her face as this naming game continued.

"And you?" Floriana asked, looking at the youngest, who by now had begun to blush, for all eyes were on her.

"Renata."

"Reborn," Poppi said. "We thought we had lost her when she came out of her mother's womb with the umbilical cord wrapped tightly around her neck, but she soon began to wail with full, strong lungs."

"How can I grow into that name since I was born into it?" Renata asked.

"Maybe you've got to grow into it day after day. Each day you awaken you can become a new person," Floriana said.

"How tiring!" Renata wailed.

"How thrilling!" Floriana said. "That's how I've been able to calm myself, starting my life over again each day. And now with my condition . . ." Floriana cupped her hand beneath her belly.

The girls looked to Poppi, who pantomimed the rocking of a baby in her arms.

All three girls gasped, terrified and fascinated.

"You see, girls, what could befall you too, even inside the walls of the church," Poppi said. "So you'd better do your part around here to make yourselves useful."

"The girls," Poppi said to Floriana, "have volunteered to be of total service to you while you are our guest."

At this, Floriana's eyes became teary and splotches of blush dotted her cheeks. "I only wanted a simple job weaving so I could send money back to my family in Ferrara. If I had a loom I could weave each of you treasures."

"Dry your tears, Floriana. There's an old broken-down loom in a far corner of the cantina. Perhaps we can get it working for you," Poppi said, as she handed Floriana a handkerchief.

"What are all these tears?" Sandro asked, as he stepped into the kitchen.

Poppi recounted the girls' sweetness to help Sandro and Floriana.

"The caretaker's children will not be here again to help me—unless, of course, Monsignor Bandini brings them along any day," Sandro said.

"Bandini? Any day?" Floriana said. "Who told you?"

"He insists on thanking Piero for the horse and cart we were going to use to sneak you back and forth. When you didn't come, I went looking for you at the convent. Nicola's death forced the monsignor to postpone his trip here to thank Piero for the new cart. Oslavia has told me he will be here in a week or two, and when that time comes, we must pretend you've always been here. Oslavia said we should change your name for his visit."

"We were just discussing names," Donata said.

"I shall call myself Rosanna," Floriana said after a moment. "Picking one flower instead of all, and pick the one that haunts me night and day."

"Roses haunt you night and day?" Sandro asked.

Floriana blushed. When she dropped her chin to her chest in silence it was clear she did not want to explain herself.

"Rosanna it will be," announced Sandro to end the sudden pause. Turning, he took the three sisters in for the first time with full eye contact, blinding them with the rare glow of one of his broad smiles—the kind he had shown so far only to Floriana. "And is it true you ladies, delicate and fair, truly want to assist with the painting?"

The three nodded. Renata's nod carried the most enthusiasm.

"Donata, Renata, and Margarita at your service," Poppi said as she embraced all three. "And their sweetness will so overwhelm you, Master, you may decide to include them as well. I know we do not have any right to suggest, but do consider them as available and devoted to your cause."

The three girls hugged Poppi with a ferocity she had not felt since she subdued a rattlesnake on the path. They had clung to her so tightly she could hardly move to crush the creature.

Sandro turned to Floriana to take her hand in his. "Allow me to welcome you into this family and this adventure of which you are a large player." He pulled out her comb and journal and handed them to her. "No hair on your head will be harmed here, Rosanna. I swear to you. Shall we continue today's work?"

As they turned around, Piero stood in the doorway.

"Bandini is actually coming here?" he asked.

"This is Rosanna. Bandini has never seen her, but he knows her name, so we are changing it to Rosanna until Bandini has come and gone. We shall practice with her new name from now on—for a week, or two or even a month—however long it takes him to get here, not just for today," Sandro said.

"And your work?" Piero said.

"With the help of your sweet sisters, who have volunteered to assist, it will continue splendidly."

"As long as they don't neglect their lessons," Piero said. "Master Ficino is coming here today, and they are behind in their Latin and Greek."

Out of the corner of her eye, Poppi saw the girls contort their faces into sour expressions at the mention of Ficino. She snapped her fingers, pulled her mouth into a fierce, fake smile, which made them giggle and transform their anger beneath the masks of sweetness they would try to wear, and so polishing their domestic virtues and skills, at least for that day.

CHAPTER TWENTY-FOUR

Floriana's Journal

October 1477

WHAT IS GOING TO BECOME OF ME HERE? *I've been in houses like these before, doted on the likes of these spoiled girls. How I have wanted to stick pins into them when fitting dresses for them. Dresses they have no idea are hard to sew. Bleeding fingers some cold nights. And their brother, Piero, hardly old enough to be their guardian.*

At least Poppi knows how to rein them in. I've seen those expressions of boredom and jealousy before. What am I doing here? They think a broken-down loom will appease me. My hands need to work. I need to work. Not be a thing posing for that self-important Maestro Sandro with the moony eyes. And yet when he shines them my way I forget I'm a prisoner. I've been dropped into another world to be pitied . . . and now with this baby coming I cannot run back to my uncle. I have nowhere to flee. I have no family here. This is not my family. Basta . . . Happy memories. Happy times. Looking at the habit in shreds makes me happy and yet it comes from anger. How can I be angry at Oslavia? She saved my life! She is helping. And Sandro, too, I know wants to help, and Poppi, my only true ally, knows what it's like to be a worker without a dowry. Not that I would want a dowry or to marry. And who would have me now? Soiled by a vermin. A bastard child on the way. I will get those girls to love me. Otherwise they will do everything to rid themselves of me encroaching on their lives. Roses. In the darkest days in that tower I saw roses . . . and if I want roses I must accept the thorns. Who are the thorns?

She tore out the page from her journal and ripped it into tiny pieces. Then she wrote the name *Rosanna . . . Rosanna Rosanna. My new name to help play some kind of game. At least I'm not in a tower. The tower is in me growing into what? How can it be a child of innocence born of such meanness? And yet, his hands. Sandro's hands hypnotize me. The smooth skin, confident yet gentle hands, hands that paint a better world. I see them holding me, stroking my hair, comforting me, and yet he says nothing. Does nothing. Stays distant. Only the eyes. And the hands.*

And alternating the words "Rosanna," "freedom," and "Sandro," as the outline to form a shape, she drew a hand that looked like the amulet hand with fingers pressed closely together and the thumb extended outward. The candlelight flickered while Poppi snored. A mouse scurried across the floor and burrowed into the scraps of the nun's habit. The inner darkness passed and Floriana smiled with a light of inspiration. She picked up her pen again and wrote. *Thanks to God I now know how I can turn those hateful shreds into something good.* And with that, her breath slipped into sleep.

CHAPTER TWENTY-FIVE

Poppi and Piero Prepare for Bandini's Arrival
November 7, 1477

PIERO AND POPPI worked with intense concentration and urgency at their dollmaking bench in Piero's quarters. A basket of fabric sat overturned at Poppi's feet, with scraps strewn on the floor from her rifling through to find something purple. A film of gray paste covered Piero's fingers as he molded the shape of a head intended to be a likeness of Monsignor Bandini, who was making his way to Villa di Castello a full month after he was originally expected to visit.

"His black eyes glisten like a young child's trapped inside a sea of adult flesh," Poppi said as she answered Piero's questions about the face of their imminent guest.

"So he's big? Bigger than me?" Piero asked.

"When he got into the cart, the old mare looked around to see what had lifted her front hooves off the ground."

"What else?" Piero asked. "We've only got a few minutes to finish."

"Many chins. He has at least three. And a mole right here," she said, as she touched her left eyebrow. "He also has small growths on his face like baby porcini mushrooms. If he were a tree he would be covered with fungi but he has a human face with shining eyes and a simple smile—a controlled smile to keep his teeth from showing. He's surely missing some or they might be stained from red wine."

Piero added three puffs of flesh around the doll's chin. "And his ears?"

"Covered by his hood. Everything covered except the face, large and beaming. And he has trouble breathing."

"And this Bandini hasn't discovered that Floriana's slipped out of there under his nose a full month ago! How clever of you all!"

"If we had planned it, it might never have happened so smoothly," Poppi answered. "It's far better to be in tune with nature's breezes than to try to be the wind itself."

"Imagine you! I'm the one who pays for him and her and the cart and all the other comforts he's demanding but I'm the last to see this budding masterpiece."

"One wrinkle of your brow, one twitch too strong of your head, will set the artist off in doubts. You've had the brilliance to turn him upon himself—to create something new and different that pleases his artistic nature first and foremost. You've inspired him, my clever Piero."

"It runs in the family to know how to nurture artists," Piero said, asserting his place in a long tradition.

The dogs started to yelp. "I thought he would not be here before noon," Poppi said.

Other dogs joined Piero's dogs' barking. Laughter broke from the front of the villa.

Piero and Poppi leaned out the window.

"Lorenzo and Giuliano! Here! Today! How dare they?" Piero whined.

"No warning! We have nothing special prepared for their arrival."

"Quick. Get their dolls and arrange them over there," he said.

"But your Bandini isn't finished," she said.

"No matter. We'll place him on the tray for today with the Giuliano and Lorenzo dolls. Even though Bandini's little more than a swollen apple head, I'll put him there to dry."

Poppi placed the dolls on the tray on top of a low bureau at the foot of Piero's bed. Piero kept his head out the window, taking in more and more of his uninvited guests as they soon formed a huge crowd on the grounds of the villa.

"They've brought an entire entourage! Now their dogs and our dogs are tearing up the flower beds you planted. And shipping trunks! Oh my God, they've brought their own feast with them!"

"What a blessing!" Poppi said as she joined him at the window. "And your Bandini will think this is all in his honor. What a fortuitous calamity." Poppi laughed so loudly her cackle traveled through the corridors and out the window. Lorenzo and Giuliano looked up to see Piero leaning out of the window, his head jerking a bit more dramatically with this sudden burst of excitement.

"*Scendi, Cugino!* Come! Embrace us! Welcome us on our first visit since you've moved in!" Lorenzo shouted.

Poppi flew out of the room to greet the guests. Piero took one last look at the figures she had placed on his doll tray. He rearranged them more to his liking. "Poor Bandini," he said to his work in progress. "Too bad you aren't well enough to join the fun with your whole body." He rested the half-finished lump of priest on a doll's pillow in the middle of the tray then threw a scrap of the purple cloth Poppi had rescued from the basket to cover it. Piero took a quick look at himself in the mirror, let out a long flow of gas from his colon, breathed a sigh of relief, and moved out of the room, locking the door behind him.

"Cousins!" he said out loud to himself as he raced to join them, then slowed himself down. *How dare they!* he thought. *Yet how wonderful they've brought all the food! Imagine you!*

As Piero approached his cousins, his crowd of dogs scampered over to him. Lorenzo's larger dogs jumped on him.

"Down, beasts!" Lorenzo said.

Not only did Lorenzo's dogs immediately obey but Piero's pugs did too.

"How did you do that?" Piero asked. "I've been trying to train them for years."

"Simple solution. You tie them up and starve them when they

misbehave and they get the point soon enough." Lorenzo looked at his least favorite cousin from head to toe. "Your shirt is baggy on you. The last time I saw you the buttons were bursting, and you couldn't even bend down to take off your own spurs."

Piero looked at his body in total surprise.

"Perhaps, my honored cousin, I am growing out of my baby fat without even trying. All this responsibility. I'm becoming more of a man—*padrone di casa*," Piero said, waving his hands to indicate the transformed grounds of the Villa di Castello.

"As it should be, as it should be." Lorenzo put his arm around Piero's shoulder and drew the boy toward him. Giuliano was making his way over to them, and in the moment before he was within earshot, Lorenzo whispered to Piero, "For today's party, I'd like all guests to think *I* am still the *padrone di casa*. Play along, *Cuginone*," and he released Piero with a slight push away and a glare that set the boy's head twitching and his jaw opening, but there was no time to fight back.

"It's been so many years, Piero, since I've seen you," Giuliano said. "And your sisters, how are they?"

"Becoming sweeter than you might have imagined," Piero answered even though his head was spinning inside and out. His heart pounded and all his years of jealousy and anger he had covered in politeness swirled inside him, threatening to escape in some embarrassing passage of dark internal gases. But he was able to control himself, and his lips and tongue moved as they should in polite chatter while his mind searched for a way to go along with the game.

"Take me to the studio so I might embrace my dear friend Sandro," Lorenzo said.

"I'm not allowed in there. It's part of our contract. I agreed to give him full artistic freedom. He's holding me to it."

"Show me around, then. Show me the changes you've made. God knows this place was crying out for some attention. I can see by the grounds you've already transformed our gardens."

"Poppi's area. She'll not be too thrilled with what the dogs just did."

Piero did all he could to overlook the word "our"—the same word the moneylender had used a few days earlier.

Piero watched the Medici entourage set up tables, chairs, and a regular feast, even planting decorative poles in the ground with the Medici flags and crests.

"To what do I owe this unexpected visit by my renowned cousins?" Piero asked.

"It's Plato's birthday! November seventh. And you need a housewarming. We thought, why not hold it here this year and kill two birds with one stone? And I knew that Ficino would be here to tutor your sisters. The timing was perfect."

Lorenzo turned to Giuliano. "Giuli, can you supervise this spread of food and games while Piero shows me around?"

"With pleasure, I'll set a bocce field right over there," Giuliano said.

"Imagine you! You even brought your own gravel!" Piero said.

"When we visit we want to contribute to your stores, not diminish them. I wouldn't have it any other way."

"I'm honored, Lorenzo, by the extent of your intentions. But I must say I'm not happy about your taking back ownership here, even for a day. You are only planning to stay the day, no? Are you planning to stay longer?"

"One night and then we'll head back to Florence."

"I have another guest due to arrive today. In fact, when I heard the dogs barking I thought it might have been he."

Lorenzo said nothing as though Piero had not spoken.

The two cousins entered the house and headed toward the kitchen. Poppi stirred a pot of soup she had prepared in anticipation of an ailing Bandini.

"And the Signora Poppi always in red and always creating the aromas of health," Lorenzo said.

"Actually," she said, "I do little of the cooking here. My work is mostly in the perfumery. But for Father Bandini I'm preparing a special concoction to help with his shallow breathing."

"Father Bandini?" Lorenzo said. "Is he a relation to the Bandini who came to our first Platonic Academy feast back in '68? Is he an intellectual?"

"I've not yet met him," Piero said, "but he insists on visiting us to thank us for the horse and cart we gifted his nearby monastery."

"An act of extreme generosity I would say."

"A wise political move. Since his abbess Oslavia is—"

"My sister," Sandro interrupted, stepping into the kitchen. When he saw Lorenzo, the two men embraced. "What a surprise to see you!"

"And Giuliano too!" Piero chimed in.

"We decided to give our little cousin here an official welcome to the villa before the winter sets in. This was the last possible day to come. We were making preparations for the annual Platonic feast when a brainstorm came to me. I decided late yesterday to move the preparations here instead where we could spread out across the lawn and make a party for Piero at the same time. Can I see your new painting?"

"I told you. It's off-limits," Piero said.

"To you, Piero," Sandro said. "Lorenzo may look because he has no vested interest."

When Sandro saw his young master's head twitch worsen, he put his hand on Piero's shoulder and said, "On second thought, Piero, I prefer to keep this one a surprise for all the Medicis. Only Poppi and your three sweet sisters are allowed."

"And Bandini?" Piero asked, still beaming because Sandro had chosen loyalty to him over an easy acquiescence to Lorenzo's curiosity. With Sandro as his ally, Piero could play any charade Lorenzo wanted for twenty-four hours.

"Especially not Bandini! But my sister, Oslavia, of whom you were speaking: she is allowed, for she will pose for one of the figures I have in mind."

"And which figure may I ask?" Piero said.

"You may not!" Sandro said and stuck his head into the steam of Poppi's concoction.

"Let me have some of this soup for my Floriana, please."

"And why did you not send one of the girls for it?" Poppi asked.

"Because I wanted to ask your specific advice on one of the floral details. Can you come look now?"

"Join us later, Sandro," Lorenzo said. "You will be a necessary voice in our discussions of Beauty." Turning to Piero, Lorenzo slipped his arm through Piero's and pulled him along. "Come, *Cuginone*. Let's welcome our guests."

AN HOUR AFTER the Medici brothers' arrival, Piero heard all the dogs explode into another welcoming chorus, only this time the noise came from the edge of the property at the base of the entry road. Lorenzo's clutter of tents and tables, musical instruments, animal cages, and all the fixings for the evening's celebration had made the way impassable. Breathless from his rush to quiet the dogs, Piero pushed himself past the onlookers, to see a large human body that formed a small hill on the path. Wrapped in waves of white and black cloth, Bandini tried to speak, but his tongue was useless in his mouth.

"Get Poppi!" Piero shouted, but when he looked around she was already by his side. She whispered to him that the woman on her knees tending to the huge body was Sandro's sister, Oslavia.

What Poppi had described as Bandini's laughing eyes were now filled with fear as the monsignor tried again and again to breathe and to speak.

"I should never have allowed him to make this trip," Oslavia said. After she yanked off Bandini's wraps, she tried to free his corpulent body from constricting undergarments. A stench of incense and urine rose from him. Bandini's face, a purplish red, soon turned pale. His eyes slowly lost their terror as his breathing returned to normal.

"Monsignor, can you hear me?" Oslavia asked.

He could not move his head but his right eyebrow went up and down.

"Try to speak," she said.

"Puppy," he said, spitting out words with his cheeks full and spittle slipping out of his mouth. "*Cazzo!*" he spat the obscenity for excrement with perfect clarity. His right eye showed fear as he tried to lift himself onto his elbow. He could move his right arm but his left side would not cooperate.

"He's had a shock," Poppi said. "I've seen this before. I've heard doctors call this apoplexy."

Bandini looked toward Poppi's voice in recognition of her, but he could not speak.

"Sit him up," Poppi said. "Carry him into the main room. I'll bring him some of my almond milk soup."

It took four of Lorenzo's strongest men to lift the cleric and carry him toward the villa as they weaved in and out of the party clutter.

"Who would have guessed a gift I made would cause so much pain?" Piero said to Oslavia as they followed the procession.

"When the cart couldn't make it past all this confusion, he insisted we get down and walk the rest of the way," she said.

Oslavia went on to tell Piero how happy Sandro was now that his young master had given him the freedom of his own vision. "We owe you so much."

Piero, pleased, said nothing to add to or subtract from her praise.

"Bandini is tough and pigheaded," Oslavia continued, "but I never wished him ill. This is all my fault."

"Wasn't it he who insisted on the trip?" Piero said.

"True."

"He may recover."

"He can't move his left side. His face is contorted and he can hardly speak," she said, as they made their way inside. Poppi flitted back and forth around the huge Bandini.

"Prop him up with those pillows," Poppi said once Bandini had been spread out on the floor of the main living room of the villa. "I'll add something into my almond milk soup to make him sleep for several hours. When he awakens we'll know if he can recover."

She ordered everyone out, including Oslavia. "Don't worry. He's under my control," Poppi said, but Piero and Oslavia refused to leave.

"You, sir," she said to the strongest of Lorenzo's men, "come back in fifteen minutes to help me pull him onto more cushions so he might sleep and let the soup do its magic."

Bandini grew more pallid.

"We will get you working again, Monsignor," Poppi said. She took a cloth from her pant pocket, dipped the end of it in the soup, touched Bandini's temples with it, and also dabbed the inside of his wrists.

"It heals from the outside and from the inside," she said.

With her gentle coaxing he opened the right side of his mouth to receive the spoon. The left side of his face twisted downward toward his chin, his left eyeball rolling around now, disconnected from the right one. He tried to take in the soup, but without control of his lips, most of it dribbled over his chin. A tear fell down his right cheek.

"*Poverino*," Poppi said. "Can you swallow?"

The right eyebrow rose and his lips tried to form a word, but only mumbling emerged. Then again, the word "*cazzo*" with clarity.

Poppi laughed.

"A man of the cloth with the vocabulary of a peasant today. Not to worry. You'll learn to speak again."

As soon as the first strains of music wafted in from the lawn to the villa's main room, Bandini looked less terrorized. When Lorenzo's burly assistant returned, Poppi and he, with the help of Piero, brought Bandini onto an improvised bed of pillows over which she placed a large purple blanket. Bandini let out a deep sigh as they arranged him on the floor, first lifting together one leg and then the other, one arm and then the other. Within moments, Bandini's snores set the window panes vibrating.

Piero's expression grew darker as he watched this wreck of a man on the floor half-dead and half-alive, laid out under the purple blanket exactly as Piero himself had laid out the priest's half-finished effigy that day.

"While the monsignor sleeps," Piero said to Oslavia, "why don't I show you to your brother's studio?"

Piero led Oslavia back through Lorenzo's milling entourage toward the greenhouse behind the villa and pointed her toward the large curtain that kept the work from view.

CHAPTER TWENTY-SIX

My Brother the Painter

ON TIPTOE OSLAVIA APPROACHED her brother from behind as he painted Floriana's likeness with absolute concentration. As soon as she caught Floriana's eye, she brought her finger to her lips. At a nearby table, three young girls, each with a separate bowl, ground pigments with mortars and pestles. Undistracted by the rustle of Oslavia's approaching footsteps, Sandro continued.

Oslavia pulled her rosary from her robes and counted one bead after the other. With each bead she said a silent prayer, alternating hope for Bandini's recovery with a prayer for his rapid demise and then a prayer for her brother and his genius as she witnessed it before her eyes. He was creating a being so lifelike it appeared Floriana was walking toward her from the picture.

After several moments she placed her hand on Sandro's shoulder and whispered, "God works in such mysterious ways."

Sandro did not turn his head away from his model, but answered, "God was generous, giving me Floriana, my patron, Piero, this moment, this sister, who, with boundless love, risks everything she has to help bring this painting into the world."

Oslavia released a heavy sigh.

Sandro turned his head. "What's wrong?"

"Bandini collapsed as soon as he stepped out of the cart. He's asleep inside the villa, hanging between life and death. He's lost his speech and the use of his left side and all the while Lorenzo and his men are setting up some celebration. Such commotion!"

"So you did not tell Monsignor Bandini his conversion pet had escaped a month ago and is hiding here in front of me?"

"He knows nothing. He was too sick to leave his bed for a month. This was his first day out. I should never have agreed to bring him here, but he insisted. And Luigi has sworn not to mention Floriana's name."

"Floriana has been renamed Rosanna for the day in Bandini's honor," Sandro said. Addressing Floriana, he said, "You can rest now, Rosanna, and greet my sister, Oslavia. But no hugging, please, you'll crush all the flowers!"

Floriana broke her pose and rushed toward Oslavia, grasping her rescuer's hands. Oslavia looked at Floriana's beaming face then turned toward Piero's sisters and asked, "Who are these ladies so hard at work beside you?"

"Master Sandro's helpful assistants. Piero's sisters," Floriana said.

The three girls rose, curtsied, and introduced themselves by name to Oslavia.

"Don't you want to see the games and fun out in front of your villa?" Oslavia asked.

"We would if Master Botticelli would release us," said Donata.

"Take a good hour if you like," Sandro said. "But first, bring Rosanna some water, please."

Renata did as Sandro asked while her sisters waited behind. "We can't come back, Master Botticelli," Renata said. "We have philosophy lessons with Master Ficino today."

"You with the magical name, Renata," Floriana said as she pulled a rose off her dress and handed it to the young girl. "You have the power to restore life to others. Bring this rose to Father Bandini. Place it on his chest while he is sleeping, please. If he wakes, tell him it is from Rosanna."

Renata cradled the rose in her palm, then held it at the end of its short stem to run off to join her sisters.

PIERO'S THREE SISTERS sped across the lawn away from Sandro's painting toward the commotion of Lorenzo's party. As she dangled the rose for the ailing Bandini from her fingertips, Renata whined, "Floriana's always sleeping or sitting while we grind the paints and do all the work!"

"We should tell on her," Donata said. In her bossiest voice to Renata, she said, "Go to that priest. Give him the rose. And tell him it's from his Jew-nun who was stolen right from under his nose and tell him she's here!"

"When I gave her the water, I thought I was going to choke from the smell of all those flowers," Renata said.

"You girls are stupid," Margarita told her sisters. "You heard what Poppi said. We'd be sending ourselves off to a convent. Being nice to Floriana, Rosanna, or whatever you want to call her, is the only way we're going to get into that painting. So shut up. Put the flower on his chest. Say what you're supposed to say. We've only got an hour to mingle before we'll be trapped with Ficino for his philosophy lesson."

"Margarita's right," Donata said to Renata. "We must protect 'Rosanna.' Remember, *Rosanna*."

"Shouldn't we ask Ficino what's the right moral action?" Renata said.

"Not a good idea," Margarita said. "It brings one more person into the story. And though he is a philosopher, he's still a priest."

"And her baby?" Renata said. "I want that baby! I could take care of it."

"Are you crazy?" Margarita said.

"You're crazy," Donata said to Margarita. "Pretending she's like a sister to us. That Star of David around her neck is a clear sign she can't be one of us. She should go back where she came from!"

"Are you coming inside with me?" Renata asked as they reached the villa's double doors. Rarely swayed by her sisters' opinions, in the matter of this inveigler Floriana, Renata had waffled among conflicting emotions: one day fascination, another day genuine affection for the young woman, at other moments, annoyance.

"We'll wait out here for you, but hurry," Donata said.

Renata walked inside. The sour smell of Bandini's incense and garlic-rubbed body, now sweating out Poppi's almond soup, smacked Renata in the face even before she saw his mountain of flesh draped in a purple blanket in the center of the main room. Bandini had pulled himself onto his right side, dragging the blanket with him, exposing his bare and numb left side to the world.

"NOT WISE," Oslavia told Floriana as soon as the girls had rushed off and were out of sight. "What if she says your real name instead of Rosanna and he awakens with all his faculties?"

"My father died the same way. It was a terrible thing," Floriana said. "They can hear and understand everything, but they can't speak except in nonsense words."

"I don't wish affliction on anyone, Floriana," Oslavia said, "but I have to take Bandini's new condition as a sign you and I and Sandro are doing what is for the highest good."

"That I am meant to continue with this work uninterrupted," Sandro said.

"I'm sorry to have interrupted you," Oslavia said.

"I didn't mean you. I meant the secret trips back and forth we were going to endure before you decided to risk letting her go altogether," Sandro said.

"Which brings me to another interruption for this moment," Floriana said to Oslavia. Then turning to Sandro with an expression of pleading, she said, "Can you excuse me, Sandro, for five minutes? I have something I've made for Oslavia and I must give it to her right now."

"I don't want you anywhere near Bandini, even if he's never seen you before," Oslavia said.

"Don't worry. I'm going to a tiny spot hidden away in Poppi's quarters where I have been sleeping. No one will see me and I promise, I'll be back immediately."

"Go," Sandro said. "We will wait for you." And the young girl with flowers pinned to her dress ran off in her bare feet toward the rear of the villa.

"Even at best," Oslavia said, turning back toward Sandro, "a false conversion was more than I was willing to do, once I decided to leave Floriana with you."

"Then God has simplified it for us," Sandro said.

"Unless Bandini recovers enough to realize what we've done," Oslavia said. "And enough to make an inferno for all of us."

Sandro put down his brushes, walked over to his sister, and put his arm around her, happy that he could comfort her for a change. "Don't worry," he said.

"I do worry," Oslavia said. "But when in the midst of my worrying I pray, humble as my mumblings to Him are, the fear passes. I get myself back."

Standing together they looked at the painting. "She is beautiful, Sandro."

"I'm glad you can see what I see in her," he said, then turned his head away from the painting. "Here she is!"

Breathless, Floriana carried what appeared from a distance to be a large blanket. As she drew closer, it became clearer to Oslavia it was something woven in a loose knitted pattern.

Floriana approached Oslavia and wrapped what she had been carrying around the nun's shoulders. It was a wide multicolored shawl.

"For when the winter chills come," Floriana said. "You can wrap this around you as a prayer shawl to keep you warm. I started making it soon after I arrived here for good, and finished it a few days ago."

Oslavia put the garment to her face to feel it. She pulled out her glasses to examine the fibers closely. It was not woven from yarn but from scraps of cloth. The colors ranged from deep blues to reds and yellows and against her white Dominican habit they seemed to vibrate.

"Do you like it?" Floriana asked.

"I have never seen anything like this before. What is the cloth?" Oslavia asked.

"Guess!" Floriana said, beaming at Oslavia and at Sandro.

"Poppi found the cloth for you?" Sandro said.

"No. Oslavia gave it to me," Floriana said still beaming.

"I gave you no cloth," Oslavia said.

"The habit you left me in."

"Dominican white," Oslavia said.

"I cut it into strips and soaked it in the juice of berries, and made a dye from saffron for the yellow, and Poppi helped me with some of the other tones from plants in her greenhouse. At first I cut it up out of anger. Not at you, but at the one who attacked me. But as I saw the scraps piled on the floor, the idea of making it into an object of love and not hate came to me. It became a symbol of how it had saved my life just as you told me it would. You're not angry, are you, that I cut it up?" Floriana said, a furrow of concern appearing between her eyebrows. "It was meant as a thank-you to you, Oslavia, for giving me my freedom."

"You are more than a weaver," Sandro said. "You are an artist."

"And a most daring one," Oslavia added, both shocked at the violence to the habit and yet at the same time thrilled by it.

"My hands must be busy. I make things to tell people how I'm feeling. Growing up with a deaf mother, this was the way I communicated. I wanted to change the fabric from what had been a harness to me into an instrument of comfort for you."

Oslavia closed her eyes, enjoying the feel of the shawl around her shoulders as Floriana continued to speak. "That same uncle, a traveling tailor with whom I apprenticed for three years, taught me to read and write so I could take measurements for his customers. He taught me everything I know about sewing and dying cloth and weaving. His Christian patrons gave him their old clothing, which we reworked and refashioned and gave to the poor."

"I love it, Floriana," Oslavia said. "My brother is right. You are an artist. I knew it the moment I saw you weaving those flowers in your cell. But how did you make this? It's not woven on a loom?"

"Poppi's loom was in pieces so I had to use what I could find. I tied the dyed strips of cloth together and wound the whole thing into a large ball of yarn. I used two skinny but strong branches as knitting needles. I shaved the ends to make them pointed and away I went. With each stitch, I thought of you, Oslavia, and how on that awful night you came to me in the tower cell amidst my own mud and filth. How you led me away from all of that. I thought about how, as we stood by the grave of the caretaker's wife, Nicola, you whispered in my ear you would free me that very day. And each day since I came here I've knit another row of thanks to you."

"The cloth of God is full of holes that breathe," Oslavia said. "You have opened my eyes even more to the rightness of my actions whether Bandini lives or dies."

"Amen," Sandro said.

Floriana plucked a flower from her dress, wove it into the fabric of Oslavia's new shawl, and placed a kiss on the nun's cheek.

"TILT YOUR HEAD a bit to the right and place your hand in the air as though you're blessing the universe," Sandro directed Oslavia, who had taken over as model while Floriana rested.

"Hold this part of your habit into your left hand and place your right hand about waist height," he instructed. "Don't be offended if I expose more of you than is visible today; it will be tasteful and sweet. You'll have a face of peace and serenity. Now hold still!"

"I've never held myself so still. It's an idleness I am unaccustomed to."

"Not idleness, Sister. Service. You are doing service. Now please, a little silence would be welcome."

She giggled like a young girl at her brother's reprimand, stood still, taking shallow breaths so as not to move.

"You stay," he said to Oslavia while he put down his brushes and picked up a blanket to cover Floriana, but first he removed some of the flowers on her gown and placed them back into the fountain so they might remain fresh.

"You're quite the gardener," Oslavia said once he was back at his painting.

"Silence!" he said. "It is I who can speak to you, but you must not respond. Focus on your breath. Find a point in nature and keep your head and eyes looking directly at it."

Sandro worked rapidly, placing Oslavia as the central figure on the picture plane. In broad strokes of thin iron oxide, a red watery outline, he captured the curve of her shoulders, the drape of the cloth, and the gestures of the hands and feet. For the face he merely drew in an oval indicating the placement of eyes, nose, and mouth.

"You," he said, "had the beauty and innocence rarely found in girls today, and it's a quality I wish to capture as I work on you from memory."

"Had?" she said. "What do I radiate in these later years? Surely not innocence. I have seen and lived too much." She spoke with the lips of a ventriloquist.

"You have a face of compassion, compassion that comes only from years of living. I have seen it on Lucrezia many times. She shined that light on me for years. I miss it."

Oslavia said nothing. After a few moments Sandro spoke again. "Today's question is, though, do you have compassion for the priest who holds your fate in his crippled body?"

"He does not hold my fate, Brother. God leads me and there I follow. Bandini is merely a man with limited powers as we all have limited powers."

"Stop talking. Your lips are moving too much now. Take a deep breath and breathe out through your nose so your lips don't move. Head a little more to the right."

"You asked me a question so I answered," she said, willing herself to sit still even though out of the corner of her eye she saw Luigi running toward her.

Not stopping to excuse himself for disturbing Sandro at work, Luigi rushed to Oslavia. "Monsignor Bandini is awake now and he wants you! He managed to say your name, Oslavia. And Floriana's name too."

"You mean 'Rosanna'?"

"No, 'Floriana.' He said 'Floriana'! It was mumbled but it was clearly her name."

"Take me to him now," she said, moving out of her pose. "And you, Sandro. Take Floriana somewhere, anywhere, and hide her. I don't want to know where she is if Bandini should realize what is happening." And off she went with Luigi.

CHAPTER TWENTY-SEVEN

Involuntary Speech Afflicts the Best of Us

WHEN OSLAVIA AND LUIGI reached Bandini he was reclining, propped on a huge divan surrounded by pillows. His hair had been combed, and though the left side of his face drooped in folds like a bloodhound's, the right side was alert.

"God bless that you are better, Monsignor Bandini," Oslavia said as she knelt to kiss his right hand, but he jerked it away from her.

"*Buttana!*" he spat at her.

Oslavia shrunk away from him at the garbled word for "whore." He had hissed that word—"*Puttana*"—at her years earlier when she was merely a novice about to take her vows, only to discover he had seen her that morning coming out of the forest holding the hand of a male acolyte.

She took his left hand now in both of her hands and dug her fingernails deeply into his palm.

His right eye opened wider.

"You," she said, "have no right to call me such a disgraceful word. Why do you call me this?"

He was unable to speak, so Poppi, who was taking in the whole scene, ran for a piece of slate and chalk she placed beside Bandini's good side.

With his right hand Bandini scrawled the letters of Floriana's name with a question mark. He dropped the chalk and stared at Oslavia.

"She has escaped our walls. She is gone. There will be no conversion."

I CAST YOU OUT! he wrote on the tablet. His left arm, which had been propped on a pillow, slipped and spilled the chalk and slate to the ground. He picked the left arm up as though it were a dead carcass of some small wild animal and repositioned it once again on the pillow, and again it slid off. Oslavia watched this, all sympathy drained from her.

"You're in no position to dismiss me," she said. "It is *I* who'll be in charge now of your care, so if you wish it to be proper care, you'll drop this conversion nonsense this instant." She picked up the slate and chalk and placed it on his lap.

He scrawled the name *Floriana* again with a question mark.

"I don't know where she is at this very moment," Oslavia said honestly.

Luigi, who had been watching this scene, ran out of the room.

The wilted rose lay on a table beside the divan. Once again the slate fell off his lap as he picked up the rose in his puffy palm.

"Floriana," he said, slurring the sounds, but Oslavia knew what he was trying to say.

"Rosanna," she said. "Rosanna sent you a rose when she heard you were ill. Floriana is not here. I do not know where she is at this moment. And you must not worry about it further. Drop it now, and take care of yourself."

"Home," he said. "Now!"

"You must stay the night to regain your strength. We will see how you are tomorrow."

"I have already prepared a room for him, Sister Oslavia," Poppi said. "It's behind the kitchen. I didn't think it wise to involve the stairs. And the air is getting so cold now at night, he'll be close to the fire."

"*Cazzo*," Bandini said. A tear spilled down his cheek, and Oslavia took the corner of her habit to wipe it away.

"I will pray for you that you release all worry about this conversion matter and turn all of your strength to healing," Oslavia said. "I'll bring Rosanna to meet you and you'll see for yourself she is a woman who only wishes you well."

Oslavia turned away from Bandini even though once more he had begun to scribble words on the slate. She had had enough of him and ran after Luigi.

When she caught up with Luigi at one of the food tables, she ordered him to find Renata and bring her back.

Luigi would not look at Oslavia and mumbled something about how he didn't know which of the sisters was Renata. Oslavia took him by the shoulders and turned him around to face her.

"Why are you looking at me that way?"

"Because you told a lie. I thought that you couldn't, being a woman of the cloth. Won't you go to hell?"

"There's a law, Luigi, greater than any church, greater than any man who runs the church. And that is the law of Jesus Christ, who commanded us to love one another and not to force on anyone else our thoughts or actions."

"But you told him you didn't know where Floriana was when you just saw her."

"But the truth is I do not know where she is at this moment. Do you know where your father is this very moment?"

"At home, still crying after my mother."

"Maybe he has decided to visit her grave or to take your sisters on a walk. Floriana is suffering enough without having to become a Christian because we do not understand her Jewish ways. It's not our place to force on her a life she has no preparation for or any desire to undertake."

"The way it was done to you?" he said.

"Yes, I was your age when I was sent away. Imagine if you were sent to a monastery and told you could never leave, never have a family of your own. Only God as your husband."

"It was not a sin what you did?"

"It was a sin to prevent a larger sin."

"I'm confused," Luigi said, looking up at Oslavia.

"As you should be. Go get Renata. She's the youngest of Piero's sisters and she's probably with her tutor. Tell her to go to Father Bandini immediately. Tell her he's awake now and to repeat the flower was from Rosanna. Please do this for me."

"Is he going to die?"

"We're all going to die, Luigi. Only God knows when and why. Until the last breath there is always hope."

"Well, do you hope he dies?"

"I hope he gives up his idea of conversion and lets himself regain what strength he can. Now go, please, and do not reveal what you know about Floriana, for we are performing God's work by protecting her, not man's work."

CHAPTER TWENTY-EIGHT

The Philosophy Lesson

AS LUIGI RACED to the top floor of the villa, girls' voices drew him to the end of a long corridor. With the door slightly ajar, he stood outside, listening as the sisters struggled with the pronunciation of words he'd never heard before.

"And who is out there?" a gravelly voice asked. It was a voice that sent shivers through Luigi's arms down to his fingertips.

"I've been ordered to fetch Renata. It's an emergency."

"First, come in and wait for her in here."

Luigi stepped inside a room filled with books from floor to ceiling. Charts of the heavens covered the walls. The girls sat around a table. Music still wafted through the windows. A small man, only slightly taller than Luigi himself, paced around the room as he spoke. His forehead had deep furrows in it, his eyes bulged like an old tortoise's, and he wore a red cap even though he was indoors. Straggly blonde curls spilled out from under the hat; his cheeks had deep dimples that reminded Luigi of a turtle even more. The man's lips seemed painted red and he stared at Luigi with such a smile of delight it made the boy blush.

"And you," the turtle face said, "who might you be?"

"I am Luigi, son of the caretaker at the monastery Santa Maria sopra Minerva and the convent Our Lady of the Most Holy Rosary, but my father calls it the *Chiesa dei Disgraziati*, two hours down the road. And who are you?"

"And why are they *disgraziati*? A strange name for a house of God. I have never heard of that."

"My mother died last month."

"Poor boy. Then *your* spirit is *disgraziato*. Which mine is, trying to teach these silly girls anything. I am Maestro Marsilio Ficino," the turtle man said, then reached for Luigi's hand to shake, but instead, dragged the boy to a seat at the table.

"What brings you to Maestro Marsilio Ficino's philosophy class, my handsome young Luigi?"

Luigi felt his face still prickly with heat and heard the girls squirming in their chairs. One, he could not tell which girl, clucked her tongue in disgust.

"I was guide to Monsignor Bandini, who was coming to thank Signor Piero for a cart and horse, but he fell into a shock that has frozen his left side."

"And the word for that, girls, is 'paralysis,'" Ficino said. "From what Greek root does that derive?"

The girls ignored his question. "My brother will be angry if you spend time with him without his paying for it," Donata said.

"Perhaps *I'll* pay Luigi to stay here to teach you something about the curiosity of an uncluttered mind," Ficino said. "You and your sisters will see how men think. This alone is worth quite a sum to your brother."

"Are Monsignor's clothes back on?" Renata asked Luigi and she began to cry.

"You better stop crying," Luigi said. "He wants to question you about the rose from Rosanna . . . you said Floriana."

"Her name slipped out. I immediately corrected myself," she said. Her sisters gasped and Renata cried harder.

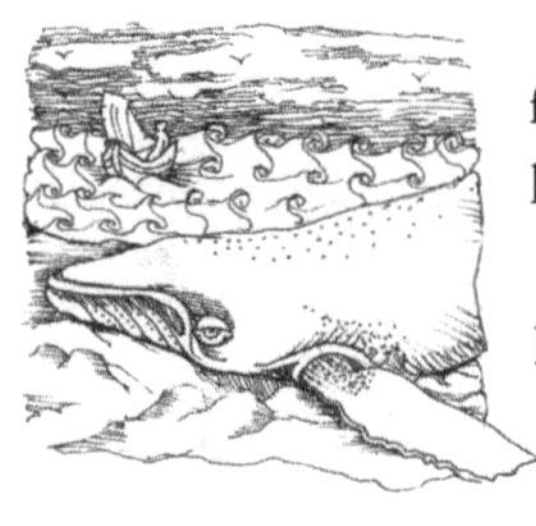

Ficino put his hands on Renata's shoulders from behind and gently prompted her to tell her story of what happened in her own words.

"I'm used to seeing large men—after all, Piero is big—but I haven't seen him naked for many years and Monsignor Bandini is double, maybe triple Piero's size. Suddenly I remembered a drawing you showed us of a huge beached whale with its small eye rolling with terror as it suffocated, stranded on dry land. I tiptoed around all sides of the huge priest and looked into his face, puffed as it was with three chins. His left eye rolled around in its socket while the right eye—wild like the eye of that whale—opened and glared at me. I stepped back, but spread my palms toward him with the rose upon them."

"'A gift to you from Floriana, I mean from Rosanna,' I said. 'From Rosanna' I said over and over again. As I heard the wrong name come out of my mouth, I felt a sharp pain run through my body from my right shoulder into my belly like a bolt of lightning crackling through me. That name, not to be spoken, had slipped out of my lips before I had a chance to say the right name. It was an accident! The pain crackling through me made me realize that over these past few weeks Floriana had won my love, a love I had just betrayed. I ran here, hoping he would die right away so no one would know what I had done."

"You go," Ficino said to Renata, "but you," he told Luigi, "must stay in her place until she returns. Now let us come back to the root of the word 'paralysis.' You do know," he said, smiling at Luigi and actually petting his hair, "who the Greeks were, don't you?"

"Were they the ones who brought the black men to Italy?"

"You see, Professor Ficino, we are slipping backwards with this simpleton," Margarita said.

"He is no simpleton, young lady. As you will learn, the simpleton is the person who claims to know all with her only experience hearsay from a professor with bubble eyes. The man of knowledge is the one who finds his way to it through action and experience."

"What do you teach them?" asked Luigi.

"I teach them how to think and reason, and we use the work of the Greek philosophers Aristotle and Plato to help figure that out."

"What is a philosopher?" Luigi asked.

"One who deliberates on good and evil. One who decides what is morally correct in particular situations."

"Then may I ask you, Maestro Ficino, a philosopher question?"

"Of course."

"Is it a sin to tell a lie even if it saves an innocent person's life?" Luigi said, happy with the way his words came out.

"Now that, my sweet Luigi, is a true philosophical question. And in the tradition of Plato we will answer it with more questions."

Ficino turned to the girls. "Do you know the difference between Plato and Aristotle?" he asked of Donata. "We went over it last week."

"Plato was Aristotle's student and Plato—"

"Whose birthday and death day is this very day, November 7," Ficino said, "which is why your cousin is bringing the festival here. But sorry for the interruption, Donata, please continue."

"So this Plato, whose birthday and death day is today, thought that in the beginning all people were half man and half woman."

"Yes," Ficino said.

Luigi watched Ficino's smile grow wider as his own eyes grew wider and his ears began to itch to catch every strange word.

"Go on," Ficino said.

"In his work, the *Symposium*, he explained why man and woman are attracted to each other. It's because the gods had punished the people and ripped them in half so the masculine part was always searching for its feminine other part."

"You didn't tell about the others?" Margarita said.

"You tell us," Ficino said without taking his eyes off Luigi.

"Well," she began, and now her cheeks turned crimson. "Well, some of the original beings were not half man and half woman. Some were two women and some were two men, so when they were torn asunder they searched for their other half among people of their own gender, which is why we have and will always have men and women of the persuasion to seek out partners of their own kind."

"So how does this answer my question about lying? I wasn't talking about lying down but telling lies," Luigi said.

"Well," said Ficino. "If the church says men should not lie with men, but one of the men is one of those originals who came from two men and not man and woman, then should that man be punished for who he is by nature?"

Luigi began, "I do not know of what you speak, Maestro Ficino. A dog cannot help being a dog and if the dog barks it is because that is what dogs do. And if the church said no dogs allowed because barking disturbs the peace but you had a dog that was going to be taken away from you, couldn't you bring that dog into the church? Would that be a sin?" Luigi asked. "If the priest asked me, 'Do you have a dog there?' and I said 'NO' and I lied, would that be a sin?"

"We are confusing the issue here," Ficino said.

"Luigi is talking, Signor Ficino, about Floriana, who is our guest," Margarita said. "She's Jewish and they allowed her to escape from the convent because they were going to force her to convert against her will. So we're all lying today, calling Floriana Rosanna so Monsignor Bandini won't take her back. Are we all sinners?"

"In this case, each of you must search inside and decide where the truth lies. If you cannot find the answer, you must pray for direct communication from God himself for the answer."

"This is exactly what the Prioress Oslavia tells us she did," Luigi said. "She says the bigger sin is to imprison an innocent against her will to satisfy a puffed-up prelate for his notches of conversions on his fat belt!"

"And who is this wise woman of the cloth?" Ficino asked.

"From our convent. The sister of Master Botticelli, who has chosen Floriana to be his model."

"I had no idea Sandro had a sister."

"She was sent away when she was our age," Margarita said.

"But now Master Botticelli is in love with Floriana and looks at no one else," Donata said. "He should be painting us too, but all we do is grind his paints and wait on Floriana hand and foot. I'm glad Renata broke the lie."

"Artists are among those closest to God, for they see beauty in everything," Ficino said. "They engage all of their senses and are thereby closest to the Divine, who knows and sees all."

"But this artist sees us not!" Donata wailed.

"I'm sure he sees you are protecting his beloved model today, and that will earn you his friendship and love over time."

"Well, that is precisely why I have offered Floriana access to all of my clothes and possessions and why the three of us have vowed to assist Master Botticelli in this great work, even if it means lying about what we really want."

"Then you are serving three masters at the same time," Ficino said approvingly. "You're serving Sandro, you're serving God by helping the artist reach closer to Him, and you're serving the attainment of your own perfection by rising above your jealousies."

"Does this mean it's all right to lie?" Luigi asked once again.

"To save an innocent life, yes. I say yes!" Ficino beamed at Luigi.

"I'm still unclear about the people who were male/male and female/female. Would they be people who live in convents? Women with women? And monasteries, men with men?" Luigi said.

"Now, my son, you are a true philosopher, and I cannot even begin to answer that one. The lesson for your mind is over for today. Let's go to the feast and have a lesson for your body with the food you will be able to sample. To dine is not merely to eat," he said, "it is to explore the fullness of harmony that comes when the body is able to harmonize from the inside out and thus the mind can remain tranquil."

CHAPTER TWENTY-NINE

The Red Ribbons

FOLLOWING OSLAVIA'S ORDER to hide Floriana away from Bandini and all the commotion on the villa grounds, Sandro approached his model with the words, "Give me your hand."

"Are you proposing?" Floriana joked. She sat on a blanket, studying the path of a tiny ladybug that explored the inside crease of her elbow.

"I'm proposing a walk—to hide you away," he said. "In case Monsignor Bandini has a miraculous recovery and insists on a search for you. If Oslavia doesn't know where we are, she won't have to lie to him."

Floriana made no move to take his hand or to rise to her feet. She had been resting while Sandro sketched Oslavia's place on the painting. When Luigi had interrupted with news of Bandini's worsening condition, Oslavia had broken her pose and rushed off toward the villa to attend to her superior.

"Oh that I might be your ladybug!" Sandro blurted out.

"I might flick you off if you bit me." She was not going to tell Sandro about her recurring daydream of his arms around her.

"Ladybugs don't bite."

"But you might, and I would have to crush you or drown you," she said, shaking the insect off as she stood.

"I'll be gentle," he said as he unpinned the flowers from her bodice and floated them in the fountain. With his muse finally all to himself for the first time, he struggled with his promise to Oslavia of chastely protecting Floriana. He had sketched her in the privacy of his room as she appeared in his mind's eye—naked. When Sandro's face and body came close to Floriana's, she seemed to shiver, then shake herself to make the shivering stop. He couldn't tell if she was nervous or fearful.

She helped Sandro tidy his brushes and cover the painting. "If I hadn't met you, this would not have been the painting it is."

"That doesn't change the fact I'm *your* prisoner," she said. As they walked toward the hills away from the villa, she felt her body being pulled toward his, and she resisted. It was as though every pulse of warmth toward him was met with a matching chill of fear instilled by the violence perpetrated against her by another.

Sandro sensed her reserve and adjusted his movements, fighting off twinges of rejection. Her fingers touched lightly where she held his arm and he allowed as much space between them as he could without breaking her fragile hold on him.

"I've missed my Sabbath and our holiest of days," she said. "I have lost a part of myself. My attacker has taken my soul away with him and I want it back."

"Do you think I'm stealing even more of your soul by painting you?"

She did not answer as they climbed the hill. Thistles stuck to her skirt and he plucked them off, throwing them into the fields. When Sandro and Floriana reached the summit, he looked down at the villa. Strains of a lute rose interspersed with marble bocce balls clacking against each other.

"These are not the sounds of a prison," he said.

"What are they doing with those balls?" she asked.

"A silly game taken very seriously by men of a certain age and income," he said.

"What is your game?"

"My game is to paint you. And yours?"

"I am the ladybug on your nose making your eyes cross," she said, then broke into a run after a rabbit that darted by.

Sandro watched her, his body and mind at war. As he was about to drown in his own internal chatter once again, the red ribbons Poppi had pointed out to him a few weeks earlier came into view and with it Poppi's words: something "beyond his imagining"—maybe some magical carnations—lay beyond it. He wished he had listened to her, drawn her out when they were there earlier, but his anxiety caused by the delay of Floriana's expected return had deafened him to Poppi's words. He had remembered only the ribbon.

When Floriana tired of chasing the rabbit, she circled back toward Sandro as he spread the branches apart. With a broad smile he said, "I have a surprise for you. It will be a surprise for both of us."

She held on to his arm willingly as he pulled her closer to what seemed to be a solid rock wall. As he groped his hands across its surface, he felt a sharp crack in the wall. They moved toward what appeared to be a narrow passageway. They slowly squeezed through it.

"Do you hear any sounds on the other side?" he asked.

"A waterfall? Where are you taking me?"

The warmth of her hand on his arm, and the closeness of their bodies as they slid through the crevice toward the sound, triggered his imagination again—their bodies side by side asleep, he with his arms wrapped around her from behind to feel the movement of the child. He brought himself back to the present as he watched Floriana's belly pressing against the side of the narrow opening.

"Can you feel the child yet?"

She looked at him with a question on her face.

"In your belly. Do you feel movement yet?"

"Not yet. Does one feel that?" she asked, then was embarrassed at the ignorance of her own question as the childhood memory of her mother's pregnancies returned.

"You'll be able to see the baby kicking and turning," Sandro said. The crevice in the stone opened into a wider passageway. She dropped her hand from his arm, stood still, and waited for him to turn back to look at her.

"And how do you know this—a man without a wife?"

"When Lorenzo's wife, Clarice, was with her first child, he had me paint a picture of her to record the large abdomen. As she posed, I watched the baby's elbow poke from inside. We laughed and she sang to the child and he settled down."

"For me this is a shame and burden I did not invite. Each day I pray to learn what good, if any, can come from it."

"Good has come to me through you and I'll protect you from harm. It's my promise to myself, my sister, to you, and to your unborn child."

She squeezed his arm to hold him back then faced him with furrowed brow. "I have never needed or wanted anyone's protection, but that was before," she whispered. She shifted her gaze to the ground. "Do you think there are any snakes in here?"

"Don't fear. Come," Sandro said before losing his balance. His right foot stepped into a deeper level on the path while his left foot hooked on tree roots at the opening. He let out a shout as his knee scraped against a cave's floor, while his ankle, caught in a tangle of roots, twisted. "What an oaf! I can't even protect myself!"

Floriana laughed as she freed his foot from the roots so he could bring himself fully into the cave. A loud roaring filled the space. Enough daylight poured from an opening in the dirt ceiling, illuminating a steaming pool, a waterfall, gnarled roots on the roof and walls of the cave, and pillars of dripping stalagmites.

"A natural spring!" Floriana said, rushing away from Sandro toward the steam, but coughing from the sulfur fumes.

"Poppi is full of surprises," Sandro said while he rubbed his ankle and watched Floriana. A rippling of mottled light from tiny openings in the cave's ceiling played across her face: *nature's brushstrokes*, Sandro thought, then looked at his blackened clothing and hands. Someone had made a fire in the spot where he sat. He laughed at himself, trying to rub the soot from his hands and clothes.

She touched him on the head lightly. "Are you all right?"

"Luckily you were there to protect *me*," he said.

Floriana sat in the ashes beside him to remove his boot. "Now we're both going to need a bath," she said as she pressed her hands with great force around his ankle, closing her eyes as she did so.

"What are you doing?" The power of her grip amazed and excited him.

"I'm sending healing to your beautiful ankle so you might not suffer. And you, Master Sandro, must think of how that ankle has supported you your whole life, how it has held you up. Send it nothing but love. Do not be angry with it or yourself for falling, but love it and it will heal faster than you can imagine."

Sandro felt a growing heat from her hands as they encircled his ankle. The warmth spread all the way up his leg toward his most personal anatomy, and so he pulled away.

"Don't move. Stay!" she said. "In your mind you must move loving thoughts to the ankle while I find something inside here to put onto your knee. It's bleeding."

He had not noticed the fabric around his right knee had frayed and a bloodstain was spreading down his shin. The sight of it brought an instant stinging sensation in his knee.

Floriana returned with roots she had torn off the lowest roof of the cave. She dipped them into the sulfur spring and dripped its healing waters onto his knee.

"I must bathe in these waters for myself and for my child," she said. "Turn around with your back to me. Promise you won't look."

"My desire to witness your beauty may not allow me to turn my head away."

"Your desire to be my friend and protector needs to be stronger. Heal yourself, while I do the same in my own way," she said.

Sandro heard her clothing, some bells, and small jewelry drop to the ground. He heard the splash of the water as she lowered herself into the bubbling hot spring. He had not intended to look upon her, but drops of moisture from the cave's roof fell on his head, and as he lifted his face to see the source, he caught her bare shoulders in his peripheral vision.

As she bobbed and floated in the steamy waters he caught the pink of her nipples, then quickly looked away.

This was the best and only *mikvah* she would find. So much to cleanse: her attraction to this non-Jewish man, her being soiled by the other one. Tears streamed down her face. She was grateful Sandro had fallen and he couldn't hold her even though she wanted him to, and that he would not turn his head. She mumbled a prayer.

"What are you saying?" he asked, still not turning around.

"Shush."

As she had instructed, he tried to concentrate his healing on himself but imagined her now in the hot spring, her hair trailing on the waters, her belly growing hard with the life inside it. They were not even touching, and yet he was able to feel a love for her and send it to her and to his ankle and to his knee all at once before his ankle throbbed so fiercely it broke his reverie. His mind raced into worry: scenes of Poppi waiting on him hand and foot, his standing at the painting with the aid of crutches. When he heard Floriana pull herself out of the pool he directed his face to the ceiling again to catch another glimpse, but then turned his head away before he saw below her waist.

"Now you," she said as she tapped him on his shoulder. Drops of the water fell off her hair onto him, each one a gift he allowed to soak through his clothing, then through his skin as he imagined it traveling into his blood stream and directly to his heart.

"I'll be your nurse." She began to remove his layers of clothing. First his belt with secret sketchbook came off and the book spilled out.

"Don't look inside," he said.

"I'll not violate you in any way. Now I am your protector, not an inquisitor." Even though his sketches of her naked body had flashed before her eyes, she pretended she hadn't seen them. She placed the small sketchbook back into its pocket in front of his eyes and laid it on the floor. Next she removed his vest, his other boot, his leggings, and all of his garments until he was naked and his maleness had grown to its full length in spite of all of his best intentions.

She looked at it and let out a sound part way between a laugh and a sigh. "How beautiful! A bird has spread its wings to become an eagle."

"He wants to fly to you!" Sandro tried to lift himself toward her but she put her hand on his shoulder to stop him.

"You can't even walk right now."

"See your power," he said, looking down.

Floriana sat beside him, curious and drawn to his nakedness. How could such a body part be so beautiful in him and yet be so ugly and loathsome when it belonged to the faceless priest who had mounted and rammed her until she bled? She reached out to touch it, petting the tip, feeling the smooth softness of the skin over such an erect branch of him. It was as though a strange and alluring creature sat between them. She tore a small square of fabric from her gauzy dress and threw it on this pulsing object that was mesmerizing both of them.

"For now we'll put this gentle cage on him and concentrate on healing your other body part," she said, smiling, and threw back her dripping hair, and helped Sandro to his feet. The flimsy cloth fell off.

"So much for caging him," he said as he limped toward the pool. "And why was I supposed to look away while you got to see and even touch all of me?"

"We are both wounded. It's not right to take advantage of anyone in a wounded state." She looked into his eyes. "I, too, have wanted you to hold me. I've dreamed it."

"Then why this game?"

"It's not a game. Unless you consider controlling desire a game."

"Oslavia says love must be greater than the desires of the body."

"Love must kill fear first. Fear in the body. Even if the body wants, fear wants more, wants confusion, wants. I don't know what it wants."

They both were quiet. He reached for her hand. She didn't pull it away but led him closer to the pool. "And I owe my freedom to your sister, freedom to leave all of you."

"I think she would be happy for us."

"She thinks you want me only as your model of the moment. And though she released me from her convent, her generosity could hardly extend to welcoming me, an impure Jew, as her sister-in-law."

"All I know is what I feel in the moment. Nothing more."

"And that is?"

"Torn between being your protector and wanting to be your lover and believing there must be some way to be both."

"Start by taking my arm in friendship, and try to lower yourself into the pool."

When Sandro placed weight onto his left foot, he noticed the throbbing had stopped. He leaned on her.

"Lower yourself slowly, Sandro, into the waters. Let your face submerge for only a moment and the rest for longer."

The sting of the hot water on his knee gave way to pleasure as his body released all tension. Pain drained out of his ankle. He closed his eyes in the penetrating steam of the bath. He would be patient with her and with himself.

Above the roar of the cave's waterfall and the bubbling of the waters, Sandro heard the sound of Floriana humming as she explored the space. Her voice became softer and softer, drifting away from him until he heard nothing. "Floriana, are you there?"

As Sandro lifted himself out of the waters to look for Floriana, she was suddenly by his side. She placed a red box, the size of a small chest, next to him. It was as wide as the span of her shoulders and about ten inches high. A tangle of frayed fabric and bones mixed together lay inside.

"A life snuffed out," she said.

"Don't touch the bones! Put it back."

"A soul unburied is a soul in continual unrest. This child deserves to be honored with a burial."

"Maybe this was a form of burial, putting him or her—"

"It was a girl."

"How do you know?"

"A small doll is with it, a few fragments of clothing, a dress has fallen away. Having the body in a place where it can be disturbed so easily means it wasn't buried properly. In my religion, the men are the ones to dig the grave but I am the only Jew here so I will do it unless—"

"I help you," he finished her sentence. "We don't have the tools. We don't know who this was."

"Shall I bury her inside or outside?" Floriana asked herself aloud, ignoring Sandro's reservations. She talked on and on about how the soul of this poor child must rest in peace, that she would wash the bones and find a place.

As he brought himself out of the waters, Sandro stepped full weight on his left ankle. No pain. He examined the knee. Although the scrape was still open and raw, there was no pain there either.

Distracted with her mission, Floriana did not even glance in Sandro's direction as he quickly dressed. He watched her tear another piece of her gown to create a shroud in which to wrap the remains after she washed them in the sulfur waters. With each ritual Floriana performed, he saw she was a person in her own right, far freer in her movements and creativity than he had ever been. The shawl she had conjured for Oslavia out of a drab religious habit, the flowers she weaved with her eyes closed—whatever she touched was instantly turned into a treasure. An alchemist she was! Turning tin into gold, weeds into wonder, and he could feel she was—without even trying to—transforming his sealed-off heart into one that beat with a desire for permanent love, the very kind of commitment he had—before knowing her—dismissed with pride.

He followed her into the far corner of the cave. Floriana pulled pebbles and rocks out of a crevice in the cave wall and ripped out a root system that had dangled from the roof of the cave and wound its way into the small opening. Sandro helped her sweep out the stones and pebbles from the clearing and together they closed in the tomb with larger stones so anyone coming upon that spot might not guess a child's corpse lay beneath the surface.

"Who was she?" Floriana asked.

"The box is typical of what gilders make when they first apprentice.

I made one like that when I was about eleven years old. It was for vestments for the priest, not for burial. I also made others the same size as dowry chests."

"Before God we are all wandering souls until we are brought to rest by those who love us," she said. "And now we need to mark the grave. Something that will not decay."

"Why don't I use my knife to draw something on one of the stones—put the words 'Rest in Peace'?"

"Add the name Empiria," she said, thinking of the infant from Oslavia's story. "It's Greek for experience."

She stepped back to allow him to take over.

"How will we explain your dress?" he asked.

"Don't talk now!" she said. "Put your spirit into the letters you write on that rock and we'll be done."

While he worked on the stone, Floriana looked toward the open spaces in the roof of the cave where bright strands of light had been coming through earlier. "It's getting dark. I'm glad we did this while we still had some daylight."

Sandro stepped back from the gravesite. "It's done."

"Do you know the twenty-third psalm?" she asked.

Together they began to recite, "The Lord is my shepherd; I shall not—"

She gasped. "The doll! I forgot to wrap the doll in it. How could I be so stupid!"

"We're losing the light."

"You take the doll," she said to him.

"I'd rather not. It belongs here.

"Which is better—to leave the body unburied but with the doll companion or to have placed the body and soul in peace?" he asked.

"What we did is better," she said, "imperfect as it was. I'll consider the doll as the soul's companion until we could put the child in her final resting place."

"I like that," he said.

"We'll leave it in the box." She ripped off another shred from her dress and, with her back to Sandro, wrapped a nearby rock as a substitute for the doll and placed it into the box and hid the actual doll in the folds of her dress. "The corpse is at peace. We'll leave the box here."

Sandro placed it under the spot of the grave and together they finished the recitation of the psalm. Floriana quickly pulled long vines and more roots from the cave, tying them with more scraps of her dress and explaining to Sandro she would use them in one of her weavings.

"You're always thinking about what you are going to create next, aren't you? I should take lessons from you."

"When you've lived so many places as I have, and hardly ever had a permanent home, you see beauty and art in every corner of nature and you burst with ways to preserve memories from special moments."

By the time they exited the cave it was dusk. Sandro took Floriana's hand, which she gave willingly as they made their way back to the villa. An energy passed through their palms—a promise that this ritual they had shared would be the first of many.

CHAPTER THIRTY

Sulfur, Sandro, and Lorenzo's Interruption

AS THEY CREPT BACK onto the villa grounds at dusk, a dark figure stepped out of the garden labyrinth to place himself before Floriana and Sandro. The shock sent Floriana rushing off toward the back of the villa. Until that moment, the couple, with their fingers entwined, had been oblivious to the cloud of sulfurous fumes that enveloped them.

"What's going on?" Lorenzo asked, looking after Floriana, who disappeared into the fading light.

"Bathing away my melancholia," Sandro answered.

"On these grounds?"

"I cannot reveal that. I'm calm and ready to take on one of your amazing feasts," Sandro said.

Lorenzo, whose sense of smell was normally weak, moved to thread his arm through Sandro's, but it was clear the sulfur smell repelled even Lorenzo, and for that Sandro was grateful.

"And the mysterious lady? Who is she?" Lorenzo asked, but Sandro said nothing.

As the two men strode toward the candlelights and torches, bright white cloths on the tables shone under the moonlight. As Sandro was about to comment on Ficino's obsession to design everything in threes, the old philosopher came toward them.

"Ah my two favorites, but what is that smell?" he said.

"Healing waters that calmed my moods," Sandro said, then changing the subject, "I can't believe the detail of your preparations, Master Ficino."

"For friendship and love, for the engagement of the senses, for healing through food, it is all in the details," Ficino said.

"As it is with me in my work," Sandro said. "Every petal of every flower must be rendered with a reverence to the unity of all."

"And it shows," Lorenzo said.

"Piero's sisters have told me how you're in love with this Floriana or Rosanna or whoever she is who is taming the other girls with her sweetness," Ficino said. "And when you're in love, you're in harmony with the universe. You've found the divine within you. Every sense, every fiber of your being, wants to merge with God through the beloved, to fuse with all the wisdom of the past and future, and you are one with it, pure light."

"Pure light! I'd say it's pure lust," Lorenzo persisted.

"Actually, it comes from an old tradition of Kabbalah. My mentor passed its wisdom to me." Ficino was eager as always to launch into one of his lectures.

"And how, Ficino, do you merge Jewish belief with your Christianity?" Sandro asked.

"And how, Master Botticelli, do *you* merge your love of this Jew with your love of paint?" Ficino answered in his Platonic style of answering a question with a question, but gave his own opinion just the same. "I'll tell you. All spiritual truths are true and have been true for centuries before the time of Christ. Before the time of language. It is how the universe operates and always has long before there were names of one religion or another."

"I must go change my clothes and shed my sulfuric cloud," Sandro said. These two men were contaminating his good mood.

"I'll walk with you, Sandro," Lorenzo pressed on as Ficino turned back toward the lights and festivities.

"I'd rather you didn't," Sandro said. His heart beat with a mix of fear and liberation.

"But we have so little time together these days," Lorenzo insisted.

"That wasn't my choice."

"I see your creative work has been twofold," Lorenzo said, mimicking Floriana's belly.

"I'm not the father."

"Who is?"

"I found her at my sister's convent."

"A Jew in a convent?"

Lorenzo's good-natured mocking had sometimes shaken Sandro from his dark mood, but tonight it blackened it. They walked in silence for a few moments until Sandro tried again to recapture his time with Floriana untarnished by Lorenzo's superficial judgments.

"Don't you agree, she's a beauty? Rare and mysterious?" he asked, still seeking approval.

"Mysterious, yes!" Lorenzo said. "A beauty, though—I could hardly see her in the darkness and she ran off like a frightened deer. Knowing you, Sandro, she will become more beautiful when you place her on your canvas."

Sandro took Lorenzo's comments as cruel and unnecessary.

"Come, Sandro. Don't be so moody. I'm joking with you. You can tell me the truth. Who is this woman?"

"An angel dropped into my life. One of the muses has taken time off from the heavens and sent herself to me in this form."

"But a Jew, Sandro."

"Your halls are full of them. Your doctors. Your lawyers. Your Piccolo della Mirandola is practically a convert to Judaism."

"This is all true, but they're not secure. And they're all men with their Jewish wives and their Jewish children. When you're done painting her, let me take her with me to Florence and bring her to my mother's house. She can stay there until the birth and then—"

"First you throw me out to the wolves and then you want to take away my first love in years!"

"I'm trying to protect you and her. And the 'wolf' I threw you to has turned out to be a lamb who baaahs to your every wish."

"I know why you're saying this. So I'll show you what I've done on the painting. You want to see it and give me your artistic advice. Well, that's not going to happen. It's no longer any of your business. The girl was taken on false pretense to begin with and violated. The only humane thing for me to do is to rescue her from proselytizing priests who still think the Jews drink blood."

"Ficino believes it helps the quality of your blood to drink others', especially the blood of young men," Lorenzo said.

"Don't joke, Lorenzo. And he recommends aging men drink milk from the breasts of wet nurses too! Are you planning to do that in your old age?"

"What happened to my fellow prankster? You've become too serious."

"This is serious."

"Then you've done a good deed by saving the girl. But don't pay for it with your life."

"How is Lucrezia?"

"She seeks counsel from soothsayers, magicians, anyone who pretends to see into the future. Ever since Milan's Galeazzo Sforza was stabbed to death by three young assassins on his way to Mass, she's convinced we're under siege, even if there's no formal army, no formal decree. We've been suffering losses inside and outside the church. As you know, that's why I agreed to sell this villa to Piero. And why I released you from my patronage. But I'll never release you from my friendship. You're as much a brother to me as Giuliano, maybe more."

"You spurned me like a chipped piece of pottery, but I'm grateful now for the way my life has changed. I owe it all to your wisdom."

"Don't call it wisdom, my friend. It was opportunity knocking for both of us. Come to our home for Christmas. You can visit your parents, and your mysterious muse can meet my Clarice and Giuliano's Claudia—"

"Claudia?"

"The masked lady. The ball. My mother's 'collapse'?"

"That was Claudia?"

"He's got her pregnant and now on our way here he got me to promise to convince our mother to let them marry. Political suicide. Claudia's a nobody."

"Like me."

"*Basta*, Sandro. You know you're like family."

"I don't know. But get on with your story. And are you going to condone this wedding?"

"Giuliano and I had a duel, an arm wrestle over it on the way here, and he won."

"You let him win. That's not like you, Lorenzo."

"It was a scorpion at Giuliano's elbow. I let him win while I sliced the insect in half. Nothing's worth the death of my brother. That's why he's so cheerful and helpful today, in case you hadn't noticed. I gave him my word."

This was too much information for Sandro to respond to. He was still stuck on Lorenzo's having labeled Claudia "a nobody." It resonated that he, too, was a nobody in Lorenzo's eyes in spite of what he was saying now. His actions weeks ago had spoken louder than his glib words today.

When Sandro remained silent, Lorenzo extended his invitation a second time. "In any case, all three ladies in waiting: Clarice, Claudia, and your lady—what's her name?"

"Floriana."

"Floriana. Yes. And your Floriana. All three ladies can discuss their pregnancies and giggle, and you and I can get a bit tipsy and sleep until noon. You have always been a buffer against my mother. Perhaps you can help Giuliano's cause and distract her with wedding banners and decorations you can offer as your gift."

"I'll do what I can," Sandro said. "I have a contract here and must finish the first third before I receive my next payment. Right now I've got to change out of these stinking clothes if you want me to join you later."

A few moments after Sandro turned away from Lorenzo to make his way into the greenhouse studio where he had extra clothes, Luigi ran to him, grabbing onto his belt. "I've been looking all over for you, Master Botticelli. Where were you?"

"Rosanna and I went for a walk to make you and my sister less than liars should anyone seek us out."

"And they did, sir. When I got myself unstuck from Master Ficino and brought Renata to see Monsignor Bandini as your sister had commanded, the monsignor wanted to know why she had used the name Floriana."

"But I thought he couldn't talk."

"He was able to draw the Star of David on his slate and add a question mark. She took the chalk and wrote the name Rosanna and he turned red all over again and went into another fit. This time his tongue got in the way and he chewed a piece of it off. There was blood everywhere. Poppi bandaged his mouth and your sister, Oslavia, tried to calm him. Poppi administered some of her flower potions and he finally went to sleep in that room off the kitchen. We tried to find you and Floriana, I mean Rosanna, but no one knew where you were so we gave up after a while. Where were you and why do you stink so of rotten eggs?"

"I was on a walk and slipped into a puddle of rotting vegetation," Sandro said. "I was going to change my clothes when you stopped me."

"A good idea," Luigi said. "I have never seen such fancy tables and food before. Maestro Ficino told me I can sit wherever I like and try anything I like. He said my complexion was perfect to try any kind of food."

"As it should be. The more time you spend among the Medicis, the more you'll see an ideal world where all are welcomed and all treated as wise men."

Before another person could stop him and comment on his stench, Sandro decided to go to the fountain in the garden among the greenhouses and take his clothes off there. He had a painting smock, sandals, and enough clothes he had kept among his supplies to make himself presentable. He found Poppi at work in her perfumery.

"How do I get rid of the stink of the sulfur spring?" he asked.

"So you found the 'carnations'? Did you bathe in them? Is Floriana now your mistress finally?" Poppi laughed.

"It's unbecoming of a woman to be so direct as you, Poppi."

"I ceased long ago to care what the men in my world think of me," she said. "I have been too busy and too far beneath any noble birth to care."

"Whose baby was that in the cave?"

"What baby?"

"We came upon a red box like the ones I made as a young boy for the priests in which they kept their vestments. Inside was a decomposing child not more than eighteen months old. A girl and a doll inside the box."

"I never saw such a thing," she said, "but I have not spent much time there. I only bathed for healing and tried to carry back some of the water from the spring, but I could not manage to lift it."

"The box was aged and the corpse mostly bones now."

"And the doll?"

"I don't remember much about that."

"What did you do?"

"Floriana insisted we bury the corpse so her soul might rest in peace. It was quite an operation but as darkness descended she realized we had left the doll outside of the burial site . . ."

"And what did you do?"

"Floriana wrapped it in scraps from her dress and left it inside the box."

"I should never have told you about that place."

"Why not?"

"Maybe it's not safe there. If I can see the doll, I will know something more, but there is no time now for those details," she said, rushing around her laboratory until she pulled out a vial of oil with herbs floating in it. "Here, place this lotion on your hands. Sprinkle this water about you and you'll obliterate the sulfur smell."

Sandro opened his hands while Poppi poured what appeared to be olive oil with rosemary and nutmeg mixed in. He rubbed it onto his hands and around his face, pulling his oiled hands through his hair as well. Then she squeezed the juice of a lemon on his head and hands. "Rub it in too, and dry your hands."

"Now this." Poppi opened a blue glass bottle and dabbed some drops around his wrists and ankles. "Black root and anise. It's been boiled down to its essence. Very masculine and perfect for a feast."

"I'm afraid Ficino and Lorenzo both guessed I had been to a hot spring, but I did not reveal its location."

"Ficino has a large mouth for such a small body," Poppi said, "but he does not use it idly and respects friends and confidences. Lorenzo is too busy to care."

"Why aren't you out among the guests?" Sandro asked. "Or with Bandini? I hear he had another fit."

"When Piero walked in on the scene and saw Bandini, he vomited some of Master Ficino's peacock tongues. After we cleaned up all the blood, Oslavia threw me out and insisted on taking over Bandini's care for the evening. And as far as tonight's festivities, I'm bored with these men of learning who think they've invented knowledge and medicine, when it is we, the women of the world, enabling them to puff and primp and take the time to read their texts. And besides, Master Piero still sees me as his nursemaid, which I have been to him for so many years. No, better I do my own calculations and salves."

"The meal will be of great interest to you, though, Poppi. Ficino prescribes special foods for special types. He says I am the melancholy type, that my brain gets dried out from too much thinking, so I need wet and warm things like eggs."

"All the medicine you need is a diet of good thoughts, like you've had lately. You have changed. You came here gloomy and rejected and now—"

"I see beauty everywhere when I—"

"Enough," Poppi stopped him in mid-sentence. "Go philosophize about Beauty with your scholars and poets and dignitaries. Don't waste your words on me."

"May I give you the kind of embrace I save for my mother only? After all, you're nurturing me as though I am one of yours." He reached out to her and she opened her arms wide, not expecting he would lift her off the ground.

"Put me down!"

"Maybe I will and maybe I won't!" He kept her feet from touching the floor. "Do not ask about my relations with Floriana. I have pledged her protection above all else, and you must be my ally on this. Do you understand?" He squeezed her a bit tighter.

"Release me now!" she said. "I promise to speak no more of what goes on between you two and vow to be your ally and your friend."

He held on a moment more. "And the cave?" he asked.

"I'll tell you if and when I go there. Now put me down!"

"And Bandini?" He held her still in the air.

"What about him, the poor piglet, he is useless to this world."

"That you not reveal—"

"It is I who have tamed the three she-beasts to work for you and lie for you. How dare you even think I would betray you?"

He placed her back on the ground. She shook herself like a bird shaking out its feathers.

"You are right," he said. "Still, we must be careful, even if Bandini is silenced."

"Trust me," she said. "Now go before I spray you with the nectar of a skunk!"

CHAPTER THIRTY-ONE

Oslavia Confronts Bandini

AS THE STRAINS OF FICINO'S LYRE filled the late evening air and the dogs yelped and barked along with the music, Oslavia sat beside the great mass of Bandini as he slept. Her hands held rosary beads. She counted each bead over and over again, pleading with God to lead her to the next step. Surely Bandini's speech would never be the same. His days of morning outings, with or without the cart, had come to an end.

Just as a child weeps for an aging abusive parent who now suffers in his last hours—so, too, she wept. Her tears were not only for him but also for her years of confinement under his rule. Still, loving scenes returned to her: he had comforted her with a huge hug as she slobbered on his shoulder and he whispered into her ear that God had given her strength and power to lead the others, to teach the others, that she was his jewel among the stones. She had witnessed acts of compassion he had performed in spite of his controlling and avaricious tendencies. It was as always a case of degree. We all had that mix of light and darkness in us. He, too, had his moments in the sun, and for those she wept.

"I forgive you," she said to him, thinking he could not hear her. "I forgive your cruelty, your punishments, the time you confined me to a cell for three months to test my character. 'To build it,' you said. I forgive the letters from my home you burned so I would think my family had abandoned me, so I would make of you and our houses of worship my only family."

"Stop!" he said, only it sounded like "Pop!"

His right eye opened. It had a pleading look. His good arm reached toward her rosary and his head twitched slightly.

She knew he wanted her to perform the last rites. She placed his hands together on his chest. He breathed in shallow breaths. A rumbling sound came from deep within him.

She had no oil with her but made the motions of anointing him. He closed his eyes as she performed the rite. When she was done, he took one last inhalation and released his last breath. Both eyes opened wide at that final moment as though a shock of lightning had passed through him, restoring sense to every cell, and he died with his eyes fixed on her.

She closed the door and settled back into the seat beside him, gathering herself into a prayer of release for his soul and a prayer of thanksgiving he had left the world so efficiently.

From her place beside the corpse she heard the music stop and several rousing cheers. This was to be the philosophical part of the evening when the big questions about the meaning of love and life would be discussed, and she knew the news of Bandini's demise would be announced soon enough. She would not interrupt the festivities. It could wait until the morning.

After about an hour she closed Bandini's eyes and knelt beside him to pray for direction. The longer she put off reporting his death, the longer it would take to set the wheels in motion for his replacement. She would have to send a message to the pope or at the very least to a nearby monastery. The closest of the same order was the one in Bologna. But at this moment she allowed herself permission to stop time and to taste a delicious freedom from action. Prayer was that refuge—a pause from the world, and a way to quiet the urgency of anything. With rosary in hand, she prayed by the dead Bandini, losing her sense of time until dawn. She lifted herself off her knees, opened the door a crack to bring in fresh air, and laid herself on the floor beside the bedding and fell asleep.

CHAPTER THIRTY-TWO

Savonarola Wanders

WITH SMILING HEARTS and saddlebags full of bread and wine from the Bologna monastery's storehouse, Savonarola and his two brothers in faith rode off slowly into the chilly afternoon. The first stop on their wandering mission was to be Imola by nightfall, in time to find merchants and traders finishing their day and heading for home.

"But first," Savonarola said, "we must give you new names, for your new life. Especially since neither of you has taken his vows. You can choose your own name or I can choose it for you. What is your wish?"

The two young men exchanged glances, then said in unison, "You, Brother Gerome." One added, "You have brought us out of the darkness—" The other one finished his sentence with, "And it is only right you name us also."

"Tell me your worst weakness, and I will make a name that turns your weakness into your greatest strength," Gerome said.

The one who had first wept pitifully at his confession with Gerome said, "I have a fixation for women's breasts. When I used to see them or a hint of them, I became so aroused I was not able to control myself."

"*Il Petto*—the name for such a thing. All right. Instead of your given name of Silvestro, I will call you Brother *Pettipiatto*—breasts as flat as a plate."

"It is such a long name. Why not something shorter? *Piattino*? Little plate, and only we three will know the roundness of the plate suggests the fullness of the breast which I will have left behind me," Silvestro said.

"I like that," Gerome said, "and the flatness of the plate suggests it is empty waiting for you to receive spiritual food in exchange for sensual pleasure. But let's make it plural, two plates. Piattini it is." Facing the other acolyte, he said, "And you, Domenico?"

"My crime has been to steal, to hoard, to covet things of beauty, especially objects that belong to rich people. Now I know we cannot steal forgiveness or purity. It must come from God by putting Him first above any and all possessions."

"I don't want to give you the name Brother *Ladro*—the brother who thieves—for that would frighten our followers."

"Why not use its opposite?" Piattini said. "*Donare*—to give gifts."

"You will be Brother Dono," Gerome said.

"It's so simple, but I like it," Domenico said. "Dono," he repeated. "Every time someone addresses me as Dono it will remind me to give something instead of to take something. And you, Gerome. What shall we call you?"

"My family name of Savonarola is always appropriate, but some have known me already as Brother Gerome and I have taken my vows with that name and shall keep it."

"And your sins?" both men asked of their teacher.

"I have my dark spots in the past, but they have brought me to the passion I now feel. My biggest weakness was to hide inside the books, inside the walls, and inside my own mind, avoiding contact with others, but God has now chosen me and thrust me out among the living with Brothers Piattini and Dono. We'll bring our stories of transformation to all, and in the process, lead them back to the kingdom of heaven."

As they continued on their journey, the taking of new names was followed by songs learned behind church walls, but when they were through with those, they tried to create a new song that would spread their word and leave a haunting refrain behind them so all who heard it might recall the pious trio. It would take more time and experience together before such lyrics might take form.

By three o'clock they came to a house along the road. Their plan was always to bring gifts rather than to expect to receive them, though they did hope the gifts they gave might be exchanged for gifts from their host, and then those gifts might be offered to the next generous host and so on and so on.

Gerome and Piattini remained on their donkeys while Dono, fully ready to reenact with every human contact the significance of his new name, strode forth to the modest cottage. He knocked at the door but no one came. As a young boy he would have taken such silence as an opportunity to steal something, assuming an elderly infirm person might be behind the door. This time, he left one of the fresh breads from the monastery on the porch with its note attached. "May the bread of our Lord feed you forever, Brothers of Salvation."

Dono felt a surge of joy as he left this gift without any fanfare or excitement. As he turned back toward his traveling companions, he did not hear the door open nor see a small hand reach out to snatch the bread. His companions had watched the whole thing and were laughing at Dono's elevated chest as he walked back toward them.

"What?" he demanded as he heard them laughing.

"You missed the receiver's joy," Piattini said.

As the three watched the house, the door opened again and three young children stepped onto the porch to watch the men in clerical robes who sat on their donkeys and stared back at them.

"Aren't we done here?" Piattini asked.

"These children hold the future," Gerome answered, "we must practice first on them."

"But what do they know of sin at such an early age?" Dono said.

"They know right from wrong, for God places that knowledge deep into our hearts even though the world covers it over. And we must do the right thing."

Gerome got down from his donkey. The children ran inside and slammed the door. The note still lay on the porch floor of the cottage. *Surely they cannot even read!*

He unbuckled the saddlebag to take out a sweet. From the corner of his eye he watched the door open a tiny bit as the children's eyes riveted on him.

Dono and Piattini watched their master approach the door.

Gerome placed three sweets in his palms and showed them to the door as though it had eyes. It opened a small crack. Gerome saw flies swarming around the children even though the season was a cold one. He took a step toward the house, and the door slammed shut again. He took three large steps closer now and stood motionless in the spot, waiting for the door to open once again. He stretched out his hands again, showing his offerings.

The door opened a crack. One by one each child ventured forward, took a sweet from his hand, and then retreated.

Each child gave off a sour stench of urine. Gerome smiled at them, silently praying for the wisdom to help them and not frighten them.

They were between the ages of four and six. He did not speak, but stood still, watching them eat the sweets and bread.

"Where is your mother?"

"Inside," they said, and opened the door wider. Gerome walked into the home. The body of the mother, partially decomposed, lay on the floor.

Gerome quickly knelt beside her and prayed. The children clung to his robes. All three cried, their wails growing louder and louder. The sound traveled to Dono and Piattini, who got off their donkeys and made their way into the house. When they entered, the little ones stopped crying and huddled against Gerome.

"Dono and Piattini," he ordered, "come and remove the children. Pick them up so I can wrap and clean the body."

Unprepared for the filth and lice they were about to take on, the young acolytes did not move. Gerome brought himself back to his feet while the children clung to him.

"Sit!" he shouted to the children, who started wailing again.

"Now listen!" he continued, but with a softer tone, which quieted them. "This is Brother Dono and this is Brother Piattini and I am Brother Gerome. We are here to help you, but you must allow us to." When the children's chests stopped heaving, Gerome continued.

"Your mother must rest in the ground. We will dig a hole and bury her here on your land, and we will take you on a trip with us. Where is your father?"

"We have no father, only mother," the eldest said. The three clung to each other as they sat obediently in front of Gerome.

"Dono, take the little one in your arms, please," Gerome said.

"But, Brother Gerome, she is crawling with lice."

"As you will be in a few moments. Do it!" he commanded. "How can you save souls if you are afraid to touch the bodies that house them?"

Tentatively Dono approached the little child, who could not be more than four. He crouched down so his eyes and hers were at the same level and said, "*Vieni*. Come to me." He forced a smile and she hugged his chest.

As he held her he could see the lice in her hair. The smell of her body made him gag but he willed himself not to retch.

"Gentleness," instructed Gerome. "Rise above your senses. Send God's love to her."

Dono heaved a deep sigh, closed his eyes, and held the young body close.

"Now you, Piattini, take the other two into your bosom also while I wash and prepare the body. We must find some water here."

"We have a well," said the eldest, a boy of not more than six years.

"Show me," Gerome opened his arms so the boy might leave Piattini's hug and come to him.

The young boy took Gerome's hand and led him outside of the house to a small water hole that had grown over with the rot of decaying leaves. "More water?" he asked and the boy led him to a shallow ledge below which a stream of fresh water flowed. Savonarola jumped down the ledge and waded into the stream.

"Go tell the others to come here, and tell them to bring a basin, please," Gerome said. The little boy turned back from the rocky ledge and ran off toward the house while Gerome removed his robes and soaked them in the stream. He hung his wet robes on some nearby branches. When the others came he instructed them to disrobe the children as well and all waded into the cold stream, shivering.

"Keep moving and you will not go numb in the feet," Gerome said. "The cold water will kill the bugs but not the body. Wash their heads and bodies."

When the bathing was through, Gerome led the group to the saddlebags of his donkey and had each person, including the acolytes, rub red wine into their heads. The children laughed at this. He rubbed a lotion of olive oil and rosemary and mint on himself and the children. The movements were brisk and the children laughed as though they were being tickled. Dono and Piattini joined in.

"Now for clothes," Gerome said. "You, Dono and Piattini, put on fresh and clean robes and use our sacrament cloths to fashion something for the children."

"We need them to hold Mass," Dono said.

"These children need them more," Gerome answered. "I'll carry the body to the stream, and bathe it and wrap it in my robes, and we three shall dig a grave and bury her. Cover the children in the extra blankets, then come and assist me."

And so the trio of friars in their zeal to perform acts of salvation completed their first ones in ways they had never imagined.

"We must be ready to respond where we are called. God will protect us and lift us above the filth on earth to return lost souls to Him," Gerome said.

"But, Father Gerome, how are we to move on to Imola with these children? Are we to leave them alone again?"

"We'll take them with us. They will be gifts of the spirit we will offer to our hosts in Imola. Surely some childless family will take them in."

"I think," Piattini said, "we should take them back to Bologna and start over again."

"I thought of this myself," Gerome said, "but we must move forward toward the unknown and mold ourselves to what we find, and trust along the way we will be renewed sufficiently to be able to do our calling."

"I was hoping at least when we got to Imola we might set ourselves up in a proper manner," Piattini said. "To look worthy of respect. Now we'll appear to be beggars."

"But remember," said Dono, "we are not going to beg. We're going to give and give and give."

"And when there is nothing left to give," said Gerome, "our God will fill us with more love so we can give that. Just as those lice were infesting the bodies of these children, so, too, the craving and lewdness of a life misspent infests the spirit, and our mission is to wash away infestation even though the waters may be icy cold."

IMOLA WAS A SMALL TOWN with two churches in the center. One had been built centuries earlier, and its façade had never received the striated marble top layer the one facing it got generations later.

Gerome led his team to the church without the marble, the humbler of the two.

Because of the late hour, he did not want to sound the bell. Since the door was ajar, he made his way with a sleeping child in his arms into an inner courtyard. From a nearby room, he could hear the low murmuring of several men's voices. He waited outside, silently hoping they might take a break from the liturgy or whatever it was they were doing. Soon, however, the child in Gerome's arms awoke and let out a whine. The voices stopped and someone stepped into the courtyard.

"Who goes there?" a voice came from the dark.

"Three men of God in search of a place to lay our heads and a spot on the floor for three orphan children."

"We meet again," the monk said. "You're the one who's going to put God in power. Have you come to join us after all?"

"Ah, Stefano da Bagnone. My bruised groin remembers you."

"And you, too good for us, if I remember correctly. And now you are playing baby-sitter."

"We took them with us after setting the soul of the mother to rest. Can you give us a floor to sleep upon?"

"Where are the others?"

"In the street," Gerome said.

Stefano stepped outside to look, then came back and quickly disappeared. Gerome could hear men quarreling. Scenes of the campfire, the blood dripping from the fox and the kicks and blows Gerome had suffered at the hands of Stefano's companions brought back a wave of intense fear. But he was determined that, standing in a house of God, these men of the cloth would not touch him in violence.

A large young man in robes and jewelry appeared. The candlelight exaggerated his features, making his eyes appear to be deep black holes, his chins full and stacked like carved melon, fleshy and moist. He announced himself as Girolamo Riario, prelate of the town.

"My sincere young man," he said. "Come with me."

Riario led the way out the front door, gathering the rest of Gerome's companions, and showed them to his chambers in a house behind the marble-faced church. By now all the children were awake and whining.

"You are literally saving souls one at a time," Riario said.

"We could not leave them on their own. Perhaps you have an orphanage in town or some ideas for a home, some childless couple who might want to take them on."

"We will discuss this in the morning. Lay yourselves in front of the hearth and sleep. I must return to an important meeting. We'll talk in the morning."

"May God be with you," Gerome said with a bow. Riario bowed in return.

In front of the hearth, the trio found pillows and blankets and set themselves and the children upon them. Within a few moments all had fallen fast asleep, while a few paces away the plot to overthrow the Medici grew.

CHAPTER THIRTY-THREE

Daylight Shows True Colors

DAWN'S LIGHT ENTERED Monsignor Riario's house, revealing a place of opulence. Large, hand-woven rugs covered marble floors inlaid with gold bands between the slabs of stone. The orphans awakened, but when the eldest boy tried to stand, the loosened sacrament cloths fell around his ankles and tripped him. The youngest had soiled hers during the night.

"Nursemaids, are we?" Dono said to no one in particular. It was more an exclamation than a question.

"If you want to call yourself that," Gerome said. "Name yourself carefully, for what you call yourself is what you become."

"Protectors," Piattini said. His attention left the children as he rose and fondled the candlesticks, the curtains. "I feel as though I am at the Vatican."

"Riario is the pope's nephew," Gerome said.

"And how do you know this?" Dono asked.

"In my travels I have heard and seen much. The pope, as much as any simple man, wants to take care of his own. This is sacred ground according to Rome."

"And according to you, Brother Savonarola? Would you call it sacred?"

"I prefer not to tell you what I call it. I prefer to suspend judgment until we see Riario in the light of day among his own."

"They judged us to be nursemaids."

"Man likes to name and blame rather than look in the mirror and take account—"

"Yes, you don't have to say it again. I remember what you tell us constantly," Dono said. "To spread light in the world you must be a candle or a mirror, and which you are you cannot change. It is the Almighty who chooses the time and place you are the flame, the time and place you are the mirror. The rest is about keeping busy in between those opportunities."

"Keeping busy? Is that what this is all about?" Piattini said. "I kept busy rolling in bosoms. A nice busy."

"But where did it take you?" Gerome asked.

"To you. And I still don't know exactly how," Piattini said, "but I believe my joy is greater with you. I have a future."

"When you are a sinner you only have the past," said Gerome. "When you are on the path of God you have a future."

"I like that," Dono said. "Shall we use that phrase?"

"If and when it serves you, use it, but do not make a mockery of it by using it without thought," Gerome said. "Then you are a talking bird, a parrot who watches the world but never leaves his perch because his wings are clipped. We, my dear brothers, are to soar like falcons higher and higher toward the Almighty, carrying in our talons the souls of the drowning above the floods."

"I see no floods," Riario said as he entered the room in the midst of Gerome's poetics. "The only flood is one I smell on the sacrament cloths you've wrapped around those children."

"We used what we had, Your Holiness," Gerome said.

"Do not address me so, please. Call me Father Riario, but do not give me rank over you. I am, as you are, finding my way to God."

"And so many paths there are," Piattini said.

"And so few who follow any one," Riario answered.

"But isn't that the problem, Father Riario, so many follow the few?" Gerome asked.

"I was referring to so few people following one path. They are led down the path of the past with the classics and words of heretics and nonbelievers who prefer the world of ideas over the word of God. Christ has said 'Follow me!' and do not stray into the forests of your own doubts," Riario said.

"I agree precisely," Gerome said.

"If we place Rome as our guide, we will not falter, and we will lose no one," Riario said.

"I fear Rome and the church—or shall I say Christ—are not always one and the same," Gerome said, too late remembering the warning of his mentor in Bologna when the two had discussed the hypocrisies in Rome. He couldn't take those words back now that he was in the home of a miniature Rome. "But that is our task—to prove they are the same, I suppose—to keep the message clear."

"What message might that be, Brother Gerome?"

"That Christ is the Leader, our Prince, our King, our Ultimate Ruler."

"We try to spread that message so we can unify our countries and bring harmony," Riario said, "but there are those among us who disagree and think they have the power to appoint without the faith. To them it is mere politics and position."

"I try to keep my own geography pure," Gerome said.

"What do you mean?"

"To confine myself to the world I can see and feel within the town I am traveling, the house I am visiting, the people before me. You, for example."

"Me?"

"Yes, you are before me and we are at this moment brothers in a cause for faith and salvation. How we approach it is very different."

When the orphans' whining grew louder, a small child dressed in a heavy brocaded smock ran into the room.

"Father," he said, addressing Riario. "Can I play with them?"

"After they get some clothes on," Riario answered, then turned back to his guests. "Enough politics and priests," he said. "Let's find clothes for these children."

"And a home for them, please. Do you have any ideas?" Gerome asked.

A woman ran into the room. She was clearly in charge of the child and scooped him into her arms. He struggled to pull himself free. She looked at the other children then at Riario questioningly. She was young, under twenty, and wore the simple dress of a servant.

"Take them all if you can," Riario said. "Find some clothes for them and we must find them a home. Their mother has died."

"Poor babies," she said, "come and follow me. I will give you some porridge and some new clothes."

"You are most generous to open your home to us, to feed and clothe the children," Gerome said.

"When you are the heart of the town," he said, "you must not be hard-hearted to those who pass through. You are *passing through*?"

"Yes, if we can release the children to safety we will take up our itinerary of soul-catching."

"And once you catch them, what do you do with them?"

"Why, they are free to be reborn and return to their Maker—"

"*Basta!* Enough!" Riario said in a sudden change of voice. "All this is giving me a headache too early in the morning. Come and share some food with us, and you can be on your way. We will find a home for the children. Do not worry."

Though his words were cordial and sweet in meaning, his presence seemed dark.

Savonarola had been a reader of souls for a long time now. It was part of his handicap that he could feel the pain of those he wanted to save. And this was not the time or place to unleash his passions and his visions. Already Riario had overheard a tiny piece of it when entering the room. This was a time for diplomacy among the clerics. Respecting the boundaries. For surely this was Riario's pasture and these Imolians were his flock.

"Your generosity, Father Riario, will smooth our path," Gerome said. "Please allow me to give you some wine from our humble monastery of Bologna." He snapped his fingers at Dono, who, after a moment of confusion, shot out of the room to retrieve some stores from his donkey's saddlebags.

"And I, Brother Gerome, will give you sacrament cloths directly from Rome to replace the ones soiled by the children."

"I cannot accept those, Father Riario. Your generosity has already exceeded what we might have hoped for."

"I insist. If you are spreading the word, you represent us large and small. From the village priest to the pope, we are all connected to the primary source, our Savior. The rituals we have forged over the centuries must continue, so I command you to take our sacrament cloths and to keep them holy. Come, Brother Gerome, I will personally bring you to them and let you choose the three you like most, one for each of you."

Riario led Gerome into the dark, cold chapel. More gold and opulence filled this church than he had ever seen short of Rome itself. Riario led Gerome through a small door behind the altar. He pulled a long chain of keys from his waist and unlocked the door. The two men stepped through into a small closet. Riario carried a candle. Gold threads shimmered in its light.

"I prefer the most humble," Gerome said. "Plain, white, without adornment."

"That will be hard to find in here. We have my uncle's insignia on all. Why do you object to giving the best to God?"

Closed in this tiny room, Gerome felt the weight of Riario's personality on him. The glitter of the gold sickened him. He wanted to say how displaying so much opulence encouraged greed in the simple-minded and would surely lead them away from the spirit. Instead, he tried to speak a nicety about the supply he was about to receive, but his stutter returned. His jaw opened and closed as he tried to get the word "Father" out. "Fa-Fa-Fa-," he said, then took a deep breath and tried again.

Riario waited, then slammed his hand on Gerome's back. "Spit it out, boy."

"Father Riario," he got out, then continued to falter. God had stopped him from falsifying his true feelings in conventional politeness.

"I prefer the simplest, whitest ones, please," Gerome said as he regained enough composure to speak his own truth.

"Simple it will be," Riario said as he slammed the cabinet door shut and quickly stepped out of the small room, waiting for Gerome to exit.

As Gerome silently followed his host, he felt the chill of Riario's anger. Even though decorum dictated he ask forgiveness in case he had offended, he knew to attempt to speak insincere words would only lead to more stuttering, and so he kept quiet.

Riario's rage filled every part of the church. It was as though he alone consumed the air, leaving none for anyone else. He waved Gerome on to follow him. Neither man was about to make light conversation. Gerome followed him through the center of the chapel and down a back stairway into a dusty cellar. Beams of morning light filtered in through tiny windows close to the top of the room where the street outside met the roof level of the small storage area. Rough wooden shelves lined one wall against the stone foundation.

"There," Riario said, pointing to dust-covered mounds of cloth. "Just as we found them when we came into the city. Threadbare, yellowed with time, and carrying the musty smell of this cantina. Take as many as you like."

"I'm sorry to see I have offended you, Father, but I—"

"No explanations necessary, Brother Savonarola. Each spirit seeks his own level, and surely yours has its purpose in the world."

As he spoke, he lifted one sacrament cloth after another, piling them onto Gerome's outstretched arms.

"Please," Gerome said. "This is far more than we will need."

"You are helping me to get rid of them," Riario said. "I had been meaning to throw them out and now you have helped me do it!"

"Very well. I thank you. The people in the towns I will visit thank you. You have increased my supply so abundantly."

"I have increased your supply so abundantly? Let me make something abundantly clear, Savonarola. I want you to take these and get out. Take these moth-eaten rags with your outmoded hysterics and don't let me hear of you blaspheming my uncle—the pope—and his opulence directly or indirectly again. Remember, I have the power to excommunicate you at will."

"I only meant—"

"I don't care what you meant. I care whether you support us or are against us. And, dear fellow gentleman of the cloth, I care not to discuss it today. Pack up and be on your way. I will find a loving mother for the little ones."

Gerome's cheeks filled with blood and he knew the high color in them would shout his rage and embarrassment, his passionate revulsion for Riario's definition of what it meant to be a priest, a saver of souls. To Riario, saving souls meant to be a shepherd penning them in; to Savonarola it was to be a rescuer releasing them from the confines of the worldly and leading them into the spiritual realm. Fearing any further expression of disobedience would reflect unkindly on his mentor in Bologna and thereby impede his mission, Gerome prayed for the blood to recede from his cheeks, and for the patience to remain silent, so that he might escape the wrath of this generous yet intimidating host.

When they exited the church, Riario said to Gerome, "Go to your donkeys, and I will send out the other two-legged asses to join the four-legged ones. Do not set foot inside again, please . . . and may God protect us all."

As Riario slipped inside his house, Gerome made his way to the three donkeys and stuffed the musty sacrament cloths into the side bags.

Moments later, Dono and Piattini, half-dressed, spilled out onto the street.

"What did you say to him that made him turn from sweet to sour?" asked Piattini.

"I refused his riches for rags, and he was offended. Did you at least say goodbye to the children?"

"They were gone, off with the nanny or whoever the young girl was."

"I suspect she was his woman, or perhaps one of several," Gerome said. He had let slide from his tongue a tiny piece of his rage. "Excuse such cruel words. The man has taken the children and given us gifts of a night's lodging, sacrament cloths to replace our own, and above all, the gift of experience to see what we are up against when we are up against Rome."

"He looked as though he wanted to kill us all," Piattini said.

"We are an annoyance, we are not his target. His target is much larger; his prize much bigger. We were like the lice on the heads of the children—repulsive, annoying, and easily flushed out. He is after larger game and we, my brothers, are fighting for the unseen to be felt, the inaudible to be heard in the hearts of the weak and humble as well as in the hearts of the strong."

"What if we encounter this kind of rage everywhere we go?" Dono asked.

"We are not in the business of converting those already converted to prayer, as he is. We seek the common man and woman, the innocent children. I only pray in spite of his hoarding and posturing, those children will find a good home."

"Whatever home they find will be better than the one they left," Dono said.

"Let us pray for their souls that you speak the truth," Gerome said. "Are you still with me, Brothers?"

"I liked the comfort of that room. The fires burning to warm us, the sweet-fruits, and snacks they offered us," Dono said.

"I liked the look of that young nanny, also, and the innocence of the young boy weighed down in brocades. But all of that washed away when I saw the rage in the face of one who offered us a gift and then so cruelly ripped it from us," Piattini said.

"He did not rip it from us," Gerome said. "Truth came into the scene. The invisible presence of pure Truth angers those whose motives are suspect. But enough! Let it slide off us like water from the duck's back. The oil of our mission, the truth of our Director, the Almighty, will protect us again and again. Take this experience as a warning, for what we say and believe is against the priests in high places. We will keep our movements out of their view to build an army of the pious."

Overloaded with the threadbare sacrament cloths, the trio went off, deeper into the hills toward Tuscany and the unsuspecting, simple people on whose souls they would prey, while the army of Riario's faction—bearers of the pope's holy insignia and support—gained momentum.

Winter

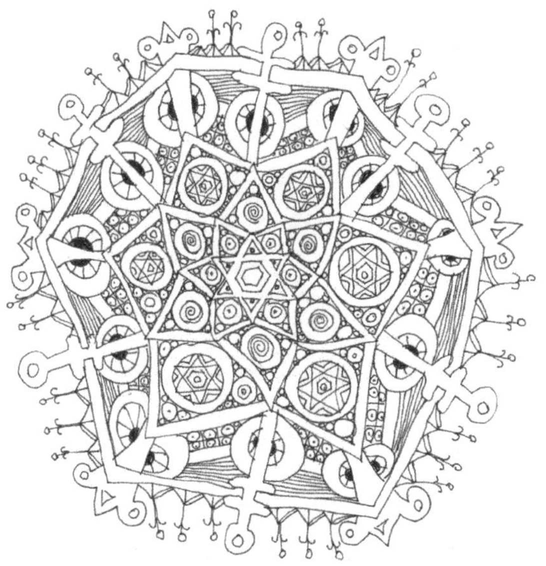

CHAPTER THIRTY-FOUR

Floriana's Dread

CHILLING DAYS FORCED SANDRO to move his work inside the villa. He commandeered the largest room, the very same one where the dying Bandini had been laid out like Piero's unfinished effigy doll, draped in purple. Poppi helped Sandro hang heavy fabrics over the doorways to keep the heat from the hearth fires in and intruders out.

Piero cooperated fully with Sandro's restrictions. Not seeing the progress of the work brought him relief. As the painting's expectant father, he was unable to know the sex or temperament of his offspring until the actual birth. He did know that his three younger sisters—always spoiled, complaining, and uncooperative—had become, under the influence of this artistic event, sweeter, less self-centered, and more attentive to their studies. Piero almost dreaded the completion of the painting. All would change again; the equilibrium of his household would be lost.

Sandro had given himself until Christmas to complete the first third of the painting and was pleased with his progress. All conversations about Floriana's condition were suspended as everyone focused instead on the longer gestation of the art.

Poppi had become a confidante to the expectant mother. As the winter cold deepened, more people shared large beds for common warmth. Poppi and Floriana lay side by side most nights. Often, before dawn, while still dreaming, Floriana would thrash in the bed, waking Poppi. Always it was her faceless attacker who had returned, threatening to kill her or the child within her, or to imprison her again. Poppi would promise to hide her and the child, to do whatever was in her power to warn her in advance, should she hear of any such person making his way toward them.

During the daily sittings, Floriana had seemed content, disconnected from the terror of her dreams, and even happy. When, in late November, Sandro began the section of the picture where she was posing as Chloris, the one who is impregnated by the fierce and dark forces of the Wind, Floriana's mood changed. Even though the theme of the scene was a positive one—the cold blast of winter wind turning the victimized Chloris into the resplendent Flora, goddess of spring—Floriana suffered.

OBLIVIOUS TO HER INNER TURMOIL, Sandro painted on, going deeper into his imaginary world. He painted the wings of the wind creature in dark green tones, blending and blurring him into the forest in which Sandro imagined the scene. Soon after arriving at the villa, Sandro had lost his way among the thick branches and low vegetation, the undeveloped part of the property Lorenzo had neglected due to waning finances. Sandro had felt even then that this jungle of green would somehow be part of his next work. Now, the wind figure emerged from the forest half human, half demon or divine. Sometimes he even used two brushes, one in each hand, as he painted deeper and deeper into the story. Then one late afternoon, as daylight waned, Floriana broke his concentration when she shouted, "*Basta!* Enough!"

Sandro dropped his brushes and rushed to her side.

"He's coming back," Floriana whispered into Sandro's ear. "That evil force is entering me again and again. Today it was like a kick to my belly from the inside."

"Because I am about to finish a turbulent scene," Sandro said, and he tried to explain the symbolism, but Floriana would not listen.

"He's coming back for me" is all Floriana could say. She couldn't explain the scream she had released underwater after the rape. She had been left alone to dress herself and instead had stepped back into the waters to wash off the dirt and blood. She had sunk below the surface to release her rage and felt it reverberating like ripples, not only in the small lake, but deep into the earth, sending its vibrations to some unknown place of release. Each day while Sandro painted the Wind, that smothered cry echoed inside her. An uncontrollable need to release that scream once again had been building inside her.

"You don't even know who he is," Sandro said. "We're here to shelter and protect you."

"You can't protect me from forces you can't see and touch. Forces I can feel. Every hair on my body, every part of me, knows the truth. Trust me, Sandro. I must leave this place."

Sandro stayed silent, unable to translate into words or actions the swirl of emotions passing through him.

Floriana plucked the flowers from her dress and combed her fingers through her hair to remove the leaves. "Do you need your muse so much you don't care if I'm snatched away from you?" she asked. "Can't you finish my part of the work from memory? Please, I beg you on the life of this unborn innocent, on the life of your ailing parents, on the life of your own talent, help me leave here or I'll do it on my own."

"We're going to Lorenzo's for Christmas. Five days from now. He has already extended an invitation to you to stay there until the birth if you want."

"I need to leave now, not in five days. Besides, I don't know anyone there. I don't think *I*, or shall I say *we*—my unborn child and I—can bear the gloom that has suddenly descended. Today's the worst. Too many days are passing since Father Bandini's death. A darkness is moving closer."

Before Sandro could say a word, she ran out of the room.

SANDRO'S JOY IN HIS WORK and his satisfaction with the painting vanished. Even though his first impulse was to run after her, he determined he would rise above the bruising her words had inflicted upon him. Painting was the way he made order out of chaos, especially the chaos inside him. What was in front of him became his single point of focus, allowing other concerns to fade. And so he kept painting. He was not going to run after her. Maybe she would calm down, but in the meantime, with only a bit of natural light left on this short winter day, he decided to carry on.

He rescued Donata from the paint-grinding bench, placing her in the spot where Floriana had stood. He tried to reignite the concentration he had lost. "A thousand voices," he told himself, "demand everything of me, all at the same time. I must quiet them, otherwise they will rule me. That's why I paint. To shut the voices down." He tried to resume, following his inner words of reason, but it was impossible.

"I'm done for today," he told Donata, as he put his brushes down, grateful she took her disappointment quietly. Donata assisted him as he covered the painting. "Tonight I'll paint by candlelight to finish some of the darker areas I can do without any models."

As palpable as the Wind he had painted, a black mood descended, a brewing storm choking off the sun. The thought of separation from Floriana pained him. She had spoken one truth. He *could* finish without her, but she had taken up residence in the deepest chamber of his heart— a pose, a posture, a tenant he hoped he might never evict.

Dark and morose, he walked through the villa, passing those he might have saluted with joy that very morning. In the kitchen, he found Poppi braiding Renata's hair.

"Oh that I had the soul of Renata!" he said. "To begin again with sunshine each new moment of the day!"

The young girl smiled at him, then cried, "Ouch!" as Poppi yanked her head back by pulling the braids.

"What's come over you, Master Botticelli?" Poppi asked.

"Floriana's part of the painting is almost done." While Renata's head was turned away from him, he motioned to Poppi to send the child out of the room so he could talk to her alone.

"That's it for you, my sweet," Poppi told Renata. "Go do your lessons. Tomorrow Master Botticelli will want your help with the painting."

"But if he's done with Floriana," Renata said, "does that mean we don't have to be nice to her anymore?"

"Your sweetness was a duty?" Sandro asked.

"It was that or be sent off to the nunnery," Renata said.

"You've said enough. Go!" Poppi tried to push Renata out of the room but the girl babbled a breathless stream of apologies. "But I do like her. In fact, I have grown to love her at least as much as a half sister. I can tease her and fight with her to prove it. She made this dress for me and we sewed on each of the beads by hand," she said, trying to take back the ugliness she had let slip out like the disturbing shadow of a mouse that darts across a room.

"I'll need your help tomorrow. And your sisters as well. Be at the painting room after breakfast, please. And bring your finest gauzes if you have any," Sandro said.

With a gasp of elation, Renata ran off to find her two sisters.

"News they've been wanting for weeks and months now," Poppi said, "but you, Master Botticelli, look as though your best friend—"

"Floriana's leaving."

"And where is she going?"

"I offered to send her to Lorenzo's house to help Giuliano's Claudia, who also expects a child around the same time. Together they could have readied themselves. She'd be safe, away from the man she fears."

"Ah, the faceless priest with the long and probing member."

"She fears his return and senses he's coming here."

Poppi stirred a pot of broth.

"Graziella and her father!" Sandro said. "They could take her for a while. She'd be with her own kind and I'd have news of her. How am I going to go on with this work?"

"Master Piero has mortgaged his life to Graziella and her father—this whole villa, his inheritance—on the strength of the art you are going to embellish it with, so you must complete it."

"I thought they were 'partners,' not moneylenders."

"And if you want *them* to care for your dear Floriana, you must find a way to carry on with your life here and the life of your painting. Let Floriana's presence in the work be your muse to finish the rest."

"You're so wise, Poppi. I'll finish the first third, get my money, and send Floriana off with them. If she'll agree, if she'll wait until then."

"I'll tell her the plan tonight as we wrap each other in blankets to keep off winter's chill," Poppi said.

"I'm jealous of your blanket."

"Do you want to be her lover or protector?"

"Both. Both is surely possible. But, would she have me?"

"Go to her and talk with her."

"But I did try to talk with her. She's determined to leave. She ran away from me!"

"That's what she said, but not what she wants. You men are so dense. Never believe a woman's words."

"No wonder I never married."

"You're already married to your art, to your city, to your life with the Medici. And she knows that, too."

"I'll go to her. Plead my case."

"But how will you take away the fear?"

"Hers or mine?"

"Both. Fear blinds and obscures as love clouds and colors the truth."

"Enough. Where is she?"

"Try the sewing room, the flower room. If she's not there, try the cantina. I've found her down there some mornings praying to her Hebrew God, rocking her head. She could be anywhere."

Sandro wrapped a woolen cloak around his shoulders as he went off to find Floriana. In the flower room he found stems strewn on the floor. The sewing room also showed some recent activity, the threads still crumpled in piles on the cold tile floor like crushed beetles. His skills around Floriana had been hardly better than those insects. One of nature's creatures destined to die if it were rolled on its back, unable to lift its own top-heavy armor. *I should have run after her instead of continuing with the painting!*

Poppi's words, how women do not say what they mean, echoed through his head. He saw himself as an overturned turtle, already slow, but now, stopped dead by his stupidity. His heart beat with fear of finding Floriana and fear of not finding her. Finding her, he would blurt out what he wanted. But what did he want? Surely without a doubt to protect, but to marry? Yes, if it would help. What was this—a negotiation, a business deal? Hardly. And yet, his need for her equaled his need for a muse to help him finish his work, which would help him get paid, so yes, it was a kind of business deal. He had motives other than her protection. The rapid movement up and down the villa stairs had added to the beating of his heart.

He exited the back door of the villa and walked toward the greenhouses, then turned around abruptly. She would never be there in this extreme cold. He turned around again, heading toward the cave, but stopped himself, then turned back toward the villa.

Off to the right, about thirty feet from the villa's rear wall, he noticed a large door that appeared to be hinged to the earth. He had surely walked past that spot hundreds of times with the door closed. He had never seen it opened before.

The cantina! As he approached it, he stood at the mouth of the doorway looking down a dark stone staircase. A grinding sound suggested wine-making, but it was far too late in the day for that. As he descended into the black corridor he felt as though he were lowering himself into a well of emotions so strong and deep he held his breath in order not to drown.

He entered a labyrinth of corridors with walls of rough-hewn stones. The last bits of late afternoon light slivered through the ground level entrance, illuminating the mouth of the tunnels clearly, but then it seemed total blackness awaited him until he saw a tiny flame. It was a wick floating on a small vessel of oil that hung from an iron hook hammered into the space between two of the foundation stones. Next to this faint flame a torch stick sat in a metal holder. He lit the torch, stood still, closed his eyes, and waited for some bodily sensation to lead him on, or some sound to offer a clue.

He heard again the far-off scraping from the left corridor, so he moved along it slowly, both shoulders touching the walls. The torch crackled and spit. The cold walls seeped drops of moisture onto the dirt floor that smelled of damp earth. The scraping sound grew louder.

At the end of the corridor he saw a flickering light coming from an opening. He peered through the opening to see Floriana intently weaving on a large loom that filled most of the space. The shuttle of the loom had been causing the sound, and her control of it with her foot added another clacking sound. The whole mechanism sat on a wood slatted floor that elevated her above the damp earth.

Small candles sat on a stone shelf around the circumference of the chamber. Stacks of multicolored wools along with dried vines and roots lay on a table beside her.

She was humming a barely audible tune. A pang of pure joy pulsated from Sandro's heart to the tip of his tongue, coming out in the words, "Marry me!"

She jumped with fear at the sound of his voice, wrapped her shawls around her shoulders, and then smiled at him.

"No one will harm you if you're my wife."

"Is that why you want to marry me?" she said. Her hands in gloves with cut off fingers went still in her lap.

"Your leaving is nonsense."

"To protect myself and my child is not nonsense." Her heartbeat shook her chest. Heat filled her cheeks. His closeness left her open to him in a way she had always tried to prevent. She felt herself being pulled toward him.

"Marry me and let me do the protecting," he insisted.

"I will and I won't," she said, toying with him as she regained her composure and leaned toward her loom, picking up the shuttle and reaching toward the spot of entry for it.

"What does that mean?"

"I will it. My heart has seen us married already in my imagination. A momentary spark of fantasy when I sat in front of you while you painted me and watched every move of an eyelash, every rise and fall of my breath." She did not look at him, only at the loom. She reached toward the floor to lift a new color yarn and turned her head to face him. "I'm not of your world."

"What is my world but you?" A glow emanated from her, and he saw the colors of the wool, her hair, her clothes, in a blur of hazy longing. He drank her in and with that inhalation lost his words. Her confession of having thought of him as husband shocked, delighted, and terrified him all at once.

"How can I marry someone already married? You have made a life of this art and it's your spouse." She grabbed a dried root, turned back to the loom, and wove it through the loom's warp.

He wanted to say how he was tired of yet another person telling him he was married to his art. Instead, he took strands of her hair into his hands. "You weave gold."

She shook her head to free her hair from his fingers. "Hardly. This is weaving to move my hands, steady my heart, to calm me. I grab anything I can find. See these vines I have woven in too? Those came from that cave, remember?" She ran her fingers over her work, avoiding his eyes.

"You went back there?"

"I remembered the way. I thought about hiding there. It would be too cold. Without you there I would be a trapped animal in hiding."

"You're not listening to me. There's no need to hide. You must stay with me."

"But you have not said why you want me. Is it for protection? Pity? Guilt? Or because I'm your pretty model of the moment?"

"Oslavia put those words into your head, didn't she?"

"But it's true, isn't it?"

"How do you know it's true if *I* don't know it is true? It could be true. But I don't want it to be all there is." He hated himself for the hesitation in his words. "At this moment I feel a love for you so deep I'll do whatever you want."

"Take me away from here. Leave your painting unfinished and take me to a safe place."

"I can't leave it undone. That's how I make my living. That's how I can provide for you. If you love me, you wouldn't force me to make such a choice."

"Exactly. And that's why I said I will and I won't marry you. I want to, but I won't because I love you."

"Now I'm confused by your words. Go with Graziella the Jew and her father, Manfredo."

"So there, you don't really want to marry me!" She suddenly laughed like a child. "Pluck the daisy. He loves me. He loves me not. He loves me. He loves me not!"

"Your laughter is tying my heart into a knot!"

"You want me to stop laughing?"

"Don't stop laughing because you are so delicious when you do, but listen to me. I'm trying to finish the third of the painting that will enable me to have my next installment. You'll be safe with them. I'll know where you are and be able to have word of you and the child. We don't need to marry—"

"There he goes again! He loves me, he loves me not."

"We must be together in spirit, at least."

"And is this just a spirit that sits inside my womb? An imaginary painting about to come forth like one of your Botticelli cherubs?" She was angry and smiling and fluttering all at the same time, teasing and trying to play, but still her eyes watered. He caught the first tear with his finger and tasted its salty flavor. She turned away from him, facing her weaving. He grabbed her by the shoulders from behind but she continued to weave.

He knelt on the wooden floor to kiss her hair and her neck. She turned her head toward his and their lips met. He moved his arm from behind, grazing her breast, then rested his hand on her hard belly.

They stayed like this in silence, their breaths in complete rhythm and harmony until the candles started to sputter.

AS THE LAST CANDLE'S LIGHT GREW DIMMER, Floriana felt a chill seep through the foundation walls like a blot of crystallizing ink bleeding across the floor and into the hem of her gown. In the comfort of Sandro's embrace—a comfort to which she released herself fully for the first time—she had fallen into the hazy cavern between sleep and wakefulness. Even though the chill passed over her as the light dimmed more and more, the weight and heat of his hand on her shoulder stopped her from shivering. She imagined his powerful hand—tendrils of heat, light, and blood flowing with hers, now together, inside and out. His warm hand was permanently attached to her now. They were one body. Both hearts beating in twin rhythms. Warm enough to melt the imaginary crystals of fear, to banish the cold. When he lifted his hand to pull her closer, the spark fired, the fusion broken.

She turned her head to look in his eyes, but he would not release her. The tendrils gone, she pushed herself free of him at last.

"Don't leave," he said.

"I'm just getting up to light one more candle," she said as she pulled her shawl tighter around her shoulders. "With this last candle we must bring our embrace to an end, at least in the physical realm."

Without speech, without discussion, without promises to one another, the silence had cemented between them a ferocious attachment interrupted only by the movements of the child within Floriana's belly.

Standing now, he wrapped his arms around her again, but she could not get warm. The cold brought back her fears and with them an urgency to leave. A tear fell from her face onto Sandro's hand.

"Happiness tears," she said. "That you are wrapped here around me with such affection and without direction. That you have ceased to instruct me, that you hold me and hold me and hold me."

"And that you hold me and hold me and hold me," he said. "If I knew the man who ravaged you I would kill him, but thank him first for making more of you."

"What do you mean more of me?"

"Making you bursting with a new life. But also if you hadn't been saved and cared for by Oslavia, I would not have met you."

"I can't believe the soul growing within me is evil. It enlivens me. I dared not say it to anyone lest they think I had invited that animal to—"

"We have treasures thrust upon us so often in the guise of affliction, while the gifts for which we have hungered and prayed, and finally received, so often, are curses. Curses born from misplaced desires," he said.

"Am I not good for you?" she asked.

"You make me ill with desire and yet rob me of any way to satisfy it in the ways I have known before. And still, can you feel my desire for you pressing hard against your body?"

"Yes, I feel him too. Your bird creature wanting to burst forth from his cage," she said, and held Sandro even tighter.

"My caged bird is ready to take flight to you whenever you release him—"

"Tonight, here, is not the place. But press him closer and hold me tight."

"I'll keep hold of you like this in my heart." He fumbled in his belt where he kept his tiny sketchbook. He pulled out a small golden band that might have come from the finger of a child.

"It was Oslavia's when she went off to the convent. She gave it to me to hold her close. Please take it now."

"It just fits here," she said, placing it on her tiniest finger, then kissed the ring. "Dear Oslavia. She has saved my life and risked her own to do it."

"The kind of saint who talks to God. She carries that power beyond any church walls."

"Church walls," Floriana repeated, remembering Oslavia's story of one young girl's sacrifice to the church walls, and how she had sworn to Oslavia not to speak of this to anyone.

"What about church walls?"

"If they could speak, we would know so many more truths than what the people say, those people of the cloth."

"And in your faith, is it the same?" he asked.

"I have little knowledge of my faith. Mostly the men dominate it. There were secret meetings my father attended, but he never discussed them. We were always hiding away in one way or another. Let's not speak.

Speech takes us into the future and the past. What we have, holding each other, is the beauty of the moment."

Sandro tightened his arms around Floriana. He opened his mouth to speak, but she placed her finger on his lips. "No more words! I must decide what I must decide and you must believe me and let me go in love."

Sandro tried to speak again, but she placed her hand over his mouth and wrapped the corner of her shawl over his head.

"You'll be my blindfolded prisoner," she said, "and I'll take you with me." She tickled him until he laughed.

"Your laughter cheers me. I want to see in my mind's eye only your smile and hear in my ear only your laughter."

Again Sandro tried to speak but she stopped him. "You cannot! It's my turn now to tell you what you must do. So be still."

She unwrapped her shawl from his head and held his face in her hands. "Keep this moment of our togetherness inside you no matter what comes next." She unhooked the chain around her neck and slid the tiny star from it into his palm, closing his fingers around it.

"It's all I can give you to remember me by. Keep it until we meet again," she said, as she returned the tiny chain to her neck. "Take no action. You have done enough. Go out the way you came in. I'll head back the way I came here. The less you know about where I am, the more protected you'll be."

As the last candle flared, she grabbed it to ignite his torch before lighting her own. Sandro watched her turn away from the weaving and all the yarns as her image faded into another long, dark tunnel.

"My sweet," he said. His words echoed down the corridor.

She did not answer.

CHAPTER THIRTY-FIVE

Savonarola on the Prowl

WRAPPED IN SEVERAL LAYERS of woolen robes, Gerome knocked at the huge door of the late Bandini's parsonage. Piattini and Dono shivered a few yards behind him in the cold. The door opened a crack.

"Monsignor Bandini, please," Gerome said. He saw no one, only smelled the stench of garlic.

"Bandini passed on in November. Sorry." It was the voice of an old man, who coughed and shut the door.

Gerome rang the bell. The door opened again, a bit more than before. "And the young woman convert, the Jew. Is she still in the tower?"

A face appeared about the height of a child's. "No one here like that. Ask of Sister Oslavia over there in the convent." A scrawny hand with long fingernails emerged, pointing across the rose nettles toward the convent side of the compound. All the roses had faded, the leaves were gone, and the mass of bushes appeared to Gerome impossible to cross. The door slammed shut.

He knocked again but the door stayed closed. "A passageway connecting to the convent?" Savonarola asked.

"Not for you!" the voice said. The door opened wide enough for Gerome to see the hump of the old man's back.

"Go away please. I can't host any traveling priests. We're not set up for it. Sleep on the caretaker's floor. That's the best we can do."

"We have not asked to be hosted. Perhaps we assumed there would be no need to ask—all of us being Dominican. And I've been here before." Gerome placed his foot across the threshold then noticed a cart with no horse stood outside the monastery. "May we buy that cart from you? We can pay in supplies."

"We're waiting for Monsignor Bandini's replacement from Bologna." The elderly man would not move the door an inch to allow Gerome to pass into the hall, nor would he respond to the offer to buy the cart.

"We are from Bologna," Gerome said.

"With orders from Rome?"

"Aren't all orders in church matters from Rome? We've been traveling for weeks, awakening and saving souls along the way. We're heading toward Florence."

The man stepped aside to allow Gerome to stand in the hallway.

"I beg you," Gerome continued. "Allow us to stay the night. Perhaps we can help you prepare for the Bolognese. His name?"

"I was told from Bologna it would be by Christmas, but maybe not until the spring." The old man peeked around Gerome's body. "And those. Who are they?"

"Spiritual soldiers, building a tide of reverence to the Almighty. When we enter Florence we'll have God's energy with us through all those we have touched and converted."

"But they're already Catholic . . . all of them."

"And they have lived as heathen!" Gerome said as he stood in the cold, dark entryway of the large stone priory so different from Riario's home, which had been dripping with gold, silver, and purple. This simple place, aside from the hovering clouds of garlic, was unadorned.

"We can rest right here if you might allow it, sir." Gerome pointed to the hearth with a few sparks smoldering in its pit. "No need to prepare anything for us. It is we who want to cook for you tonight and offer some gifts from our travels."

"No trinkets, please," the old man said, opening the door and waving in Gerome's companions. "I'll get some covers and pillows, but you can't enter the chapel if you don't mind. First, what is your name?"

"Gerome Savonarola, from Ferrara. Originally, son of Savonarola, doctor of Ferrara. I even have some salves to make a nice hot plaster for your back."

"One night only, Brother Gerome. I've seen you before from a distance. This summer, no? You brought the hooded whore to the tower, no?"

"That's the woman I seek."

"Long gone. Long gone. And the others. What are their names?"

"Brother Dono, and Brother Piattini."

"Strange names."

"They chose their names for their ministries."

"And yours, Savonarola? What does that mean?"

"You could say it means to save on and on and on."

The old man made a sound part guffaw, part pained exclamation.

"And you, my kind host, what's your name?"

"Petrarchio." He lifted his head as high as he could above the hump in his back to see how Gerome's face might change. "Bandini gave me the name in memory of Petrarch because I liked to collect books even though I cannot read. I found volumes hidden here and Monsignor Bandini called me that ever since."

"And are you also a poet?"

"Not exactly," Petrarchio said.

"We will reward you for your efforts, Petrarchio," Gerome said as he watched his companions move toward the sputtering hearth.

"This is Petrarchio," Gerome said to his men, whose nostrils dilated visibly from the garlic cloud that filled the room and reeked off the thick stone walls.

"Piattini," said the first, and approached Petrarchio with a humble bow, then returned to the hearth.

"May I?" Piattini asked when he saw a log beside the hearth.

"Our last dry wood," Petrarchio said, "but go ahead. It should take you through the night."

"We will cut you some fresh wood if you might provide me with an ax."

"Now? In the dark?"

"Yes. This very hour, since the sun is about to set I could go into the forest and chop down a small tree, gather some kindling. Before we go tomorrow, we'll fill your wagon with wood if you let us," Dono said.

"No kindling left," Petrarchio said.

"We're here to give, not to receive," Gerome said.

Piattini placed the large log on the cinders. It burst into flame. Insects and sap ran out of the log, which crackled and hissed.

"Lend me a cauldron. I'll put some special powders in it and make a paste for your back if you wish," Gerome said.

"Not so fast," Petrarchio said. "One thing at a time. Let me get you some soup." He turned to disappear behind a heavy black velvet curtain.

A cat with a mouse in its jaws sat beside the flaming hearth. It dropped its prize at Piattini's feet.

"Our first gift." Piattini smiled, then sat in front of the hearth to warm himself while Dono waited with his scarf and gloves still on, ready to fulfill his offer to gather more wood.

Gerome spoke, barely above a whisper. "Although we have asked for one night's lodging, I predict we'll stay a week or even a month. Perhaps we can endear ourselves to Petrarchio enough to stay until Bandini's replacement arrives from Bologna."

"Might we become the permanent head?" Piattini asked.

"Hardly," Gerome said. "Our mission is to take over Florence."

"But this is closer and it is a place needing a leader," Dono said.

"I wouldn't mind staying here for a while," Piattini said, "sleeping in a normal bed and—"

He stopped when Petrarchio walked into the room with three bowls. "Black bean soup. Hearty and good for frostbite."

"Thanks to you, we're not worrying about frostbite tonight," Gerome said as he looked into his bowl of soup—a reddish-black paste with small lumps in it.

"My ears are as sharp as they were when I was twelve years old," Petrarchio said. "I've promised one night. Now eat."

"And the ax?" Dono asked. "The firewood?"

"Yes, the ax. Come with me." Petrarchio held the curtain aside for Dono to follow.

They walked through a narrow corridor filled with braided garlic, which hung on metal spikes driven into the stone walls.

"To ward off illness, death, and bad odors," Petrarchio said as he and Dono entered the parish kitchen where another hearth roared. A pile of wood, freshly cut, stood beside it.

"You've got plenty of wood," Dono said.

"For this hearth only. The caretaker's son, Luigi, is strong and he cut this today. That's how I know there's no kindling left."

Petrarchio motioned toward the ax that stood against the woodpile. "If you want your own, go get it. A wheelbarrow is outside the back door."

As Dono moved toward the ax, Petrarchio continued, "Your boss, this Savonarola. Is he a pious man?"

"Of course, why do you ask?"

"I've seen these traveling priests who go about the countryside converting peasant girls to their beds, and robbing homes of their treasures in the name of the Lord. The cloak of the church blinds people to the fact these are men, corrupt as the others, only pretending to be protectors of children and virgins."

"Brother Gerome is on a mission to save souls, not to wreck them. He's saved mine and Piattini's. We were not much more than two constant erections hiding under brown frocks until he saved each of us. Our message of repentance comes from righting our own transgressions."

"You, too, have been what I fear—"

"A saint is a sinner who keeps on trying to stop," Dono said before Petrarchio finished his sentence.

"And you have stopped?"

"Since our time with Gerome we have only saved souls. From town to town. Though we have been tempted, our brotherhood is stronger than any pull of the devil."

"And what about Gerome? Has he sinned?"

"He says he's tempted daily as we all are in the course of living, but we can choose to side with God or hide from God."

"Don't be blind to your leader's imperfections," Petrarchio said. "Ask him where he was five months ago. I have seen him before on these grounds delivering a hooded woman we fed for a month before she went off to the convent. He did not speak, nor look one in the eye as he does today. Bandini was the one who spoke with him but I saw him from a distance. Ask him about that. How else do you think he found us?"

"Brother Gerome is beyond suspicion. He was sent home to Ferrara to die but God wanted him to lead us and healed him, healed his mind and his stutter, and now he's a lightning rod of God's truth."

"Ask him about his other rod."

"Ask him yourself," Dono said.

"He asked about her and I told him there was no one here like that."

"So where'd she go?"

"Transferred into the convent with strict orders for conversion, but Bandini died and I don't know any more about it," Petrarchio said.

"What you say is all idle conjecture."

"Take it for what it's worth, Brother Dono, and keep your distance from him long enough to take a look at him with your eyes open."

THE NEXT MORNING the kitchen hearth was well fed and spat sparks onto the tile floor. Drool slipped out of the side of Petrarchio's mouth as he allowed himself to be touched and worked upon for the first time in his adult life. Gerome had prepared the plaster the night before and explained to Petrarchio the need for it to set in the pot outside in the cold air before they applied it at dawn.

"Please don't press too hard on me," he said. "I'm so brittle, I'll crack into pieces."

"No speaking, please, Petrarchio. You must try to relax your muscles and bones and take in the healing of this compress."

Gerome worked with a light touch and spread the chilled paste over Petrarchio's back. The addition of the garlic had been Petrarchio's suggestion and Gerome adopted it readily, knowing from his father that if the patient has faith in the medicine, it will work better.

"Try not to shiver from the cold," Gerome said. "In a few minutes a powerful heat bubbling in the plaster will travel into your bones. You must lie still for a full hour to let it work. And you must not speak or move once I cover the plaster with blankets."

"The place is like a tomb at this hour; it should be all right. Are you going to leave me alone?"

"You are never alone, my dear Petrarchio. God is always with you. I must do my prayers and meditations and meet with my brothers to plan our next destination. So stay still now," he said, finally placing the last of three blankets on top of the plaster.

"The aroma of eucalyptus leaves I've left steaming in a pot for you will clear your sinuses also. Now rest." Petrarchio's eyes began to close. He ran his tongue over his lips to catch dripping saliva. His breathing soon deepened into a snore. Gerome tiptoed out of the room, gave instructions to Piattini on how to remove the plaster if he did not return in an hour to do it himself. He was soon out the front door, into the cold, misty dawn as he made his way across the field to the caretaker's cottage and to the road leading to the convent.

Vines, still green even in the winter months, climbed the thick walls of the main building. This complex was spread out in small bungalows and buildings. Once workers' cottages, they had been strung together over the years. Unlike the monasteries in the major cities, the acolyte cells were individual houses, each isolated from the rest. Only the main building had two stories and a small bell tower to one side. In between the two centers of spiritual retreat spread the spiked rose bushes, most at this time of year barren of leaves, though some buds here and there had remained frozen onto their branches.

Not knowing what he was about to say or do, the young Friar Gerome knocked on the door of the main house.

With her prayers for the morning already completed, Oslavia opened the door with a calm and open spirit. The unfamiliar face that greeted her changed her mood instantly.

"Brother Savonarola," he said as he bowed slightly in front of her after crossing himself.

"Abbess Oslavia at your service," she said. "How can I help you?"

"We are guests at the monastery and I came to inquire of the health of one of my fellow citizens of Ferrara brought here over the summer with a group of brothers of which I was one. Her father has been asking for her, and I wanted to bring back news of the sweet young woman."

Oslavia stood still, staring at this small man of the cloth. She peered deeply into Gerome's dark eyes, seeing an intensity and fire that sent a sharp ache to her heart.

"Do come in," she said, stepping back. "And sit down, please." She looked him over. His eyes swept every inch of her sacred, private space as though he were measuring it.

"So you are from Ferrara," she said. This could be the perpetrator, this could be a friend, and yet hadn't Floriana's parents died? That was why the young girl had been brought so far from her home to weave.

"The girl, do you know of her? Where is she? Is she converted yet?"

"I know of no one here from Ferrara. Perhaps you are mistaken," Oslavia said. "Are you sure this is the right convent? We have no one like that. What does she look like?"

"Reddish cheeks, long hair, and she wore a Star of David, though we tried to remove it from her when she came here."

"There is no one here matching your description. And Monsignor Bandini has passed away. If anyone knew of it, it would have been he."

Gerome's face was turning white. "What shall I tell her family? That she is missing, that she is dead?"

"I'm afraid you must continue your search elsewhere. Our newest novitiate came eighteen months ago. Can I get you some tea or morning cakes?"

"N . . . no," he said. "Perhaps she escaped."

"What was her name? And why would your group have left such a woman with a Star of David here among the priests and nuns?"

"For her own improvement, of course. To encourage her conversion."

"To what? Pray tell me, to what?" Oslavia said. She did not like this man pressing her with questions. His intentions were becoming clearer to her. "Would you like to meet our other novitiates?"

"Why would I do that? I'm simply hoping to send word to her family and now I cannot do this."

"Better no word than a false word, don't you think, Brother . . . what did you say your name was?"

"Sav . . . va . . . va . . . vona . . . rola," he said with difficulty.

"Are you traveling alone?"

"I have other brothers with me from Bologna."

"Are you the replacements for Father Bandini?"

"I would like to be, but our mission is to go from village to village to save souls from the destruction and debauchery of Florence, where we plan to settle."

"And these two companions, were they with you when you brought this—you did not say her name. What was her name? Were the others with you then?"

"They were still in Bologna where I returned after accompanying the other women to their destinations."

"So who determined to bring this girl here?" she asked, not wanting to dwell on the topic too long and yet she couldn't help herself for she wanted to hear it in his own voice.

"It was I," he said. "Considering her poor background and the unlikely prospect of marriage, I brought her here out of compassion."

"Well, I'm sorry that this woman whose name you have not surrendered is not among my fold. I have much to do today, so please excuse me," she said, standing close to him, hoping he might rise and depart. "It is wise to be leaving early in the morning so you can make Florence in time for Christmas."

"I'm actually hoping we might fill in here until the Bolognese replacement arrives."

"We have few provisions and we wouldn't want to interrupt your traveling mission."

"I think you're hiding something from me," Gerome said.

"I think you're overstaying your welcome," Oslavia said. "Please go now before I ask the groundskeeper to escort you away."

Savonarola did not leave his chair.

Oslavia waited beside it, not taking her eyes off him. It was surely he, the perpetrator, the cause of so much havoc and pain, the very man claiming to save souls. Her body quivered with rage as she tried to contain it with some kind of silent prayer of acceptance.

As she gazed at him, his eyes were closed and moist with tears. His starched and stiff demeanor melted as he began to weep.

"I'm such a failure," he said.

"You have simply come to find someone who is no longer here," she said, taken off guard.

"You admit she was here!"

"You told me you left her here. I assume she was under the care of Bandini and no longer is. Now please," she said, touching his elbow slightly. "Pray for direction, my young man, and you'll find her if you will. I cannot help you except to urge you to return to your mission."

Gerome straightened himself in the chair. "I'm quite able to lift myself out of this chair. A sadness and regret overwhelmed me for I had so hoped the young woman might be saved, and now for sure she is among the lost."

"Perhaps you'll come upon her yourself in your wanderings and get news of her firsthand."

Still, Gerome did not stand.

"And how is Petrarchio as a host to you?" she asked, changing the subject.

Savonarola did not answer but dried his eyes and adjusted his robes, then looked at Oslavia. "He's under a soothing plaster for his back. I must return there and remove it now."

"And you're a doctor as well as a priest, are you? Physician of body as well as spirit?"

"I do what I'm called to do, Sister Oslavia."

Gerome had lost his fire. His dark eyes stared out into space.

"Shall we pray together for those whose lives we touch?" Oslavia said.

"I always pray for all the children of God, and I will pray for you, Sister Oslavia, that the truth you speak will bring me further on my search to the truth I know."

With that, he stood at last. He smoothed his robe, and withdrew one of the sacrament cloths Riario had given him. "A gift for you. This comes from a humble church in Imola, from Father Riario, nephew of the pope. May you use it as you pray today."

Oslavia took the battered and threadbare cloth into her hands and trembled. The mention of the pope and any connection of influence usually sent a tremor of fear into her, but this trembling was not fear, it was not honor; it was more a sense that he had removed the cloth from a sacred tomb where it should have remained.

"I will care for this and keep it apart and safe from contamination," she said. She walked over to the door and opened it, waiting for the young man to leave. Scenes of her own violation by a priest all those years ago welled inside her and she wanted to injure this evil young man, to poke him, to hurl him, to kick him out of her sacred space; to wrap the foul cloth around his face, to cover those beady eyes, to smother him and choke him with his own words and spittle, to mummify him as other flesh and blood had been mummified in the walls of the very building in which she was standing.

"Go now! Please," she said. "And I pray God will be with you."

Once he was finally outside and she could close the door, she slipped into the chair and allowed herself to muffle a scream into the cloth. She pulled at the loose threads of the sacrament cloth until she found its weakest place. Then, with her teeth, she made the first rip. With her hands still shaking, she tore his gift to shreds. Emotions crashed inside her: fear of the power of this young man who had caught her in a lie, fear that her cooperation to free Floriana would be discovered and punished, and with those emotions mixed a deep wailing from the core of her belly. She muffled her sobs into the scraps of cloth as she tore them.

Once she regained her composure, her only impulse was to warn Floriana, to warn her brother, but she was a prisoner as long as the three visitors stayed on the grounds. She would have to wait, or go to Luigi and send him to Castello with a note. But to commit to writing anything with this nosy young insect around would be too great a risk.

There was no time for her Peredexion tree. She must calm herself without it. But first, she must find Luigi and his father to make certain they would not reveal anything of Floriana's whereabouts to this too-curious visitor who had openly revealed his deviousness. Leaving Petrarchio alone on the slab, not standing beside his "patient," told her volumes of how this young priest could mold circumstances to fit his plans. She was prisoner in the chair, in the habit she wore, and she prayed for a sign to guide her to her next action.

CHAPTER THIRTY-SIX

Piero and Sandro Exchange Needs

PIERO COULD TELL by the fierceness of the knock on his door it was Sandro. With doll parts drying on his workbench and his hands covered in paper paste, Piero's first impulse was to rush around hiding all traces of his eccentricity, but something close to confidence welled within him and kept him in his chair. He wiped his hands, stood, and not even taking a second for his habitual glance in the mirror to check himself, walked to the door and opened it wide.

"Promise what you see here remains here in this room," Piero said.

"Have you lovers?"

"Many. But none of them breathes."

Sandro peered into the room.

"What brings you here at this hour?"

"A personal favor, my Dream Patron," Sandro said. "For if I have not said so plainly I'll say it now. You've given me the freedom to create—without your influence and direction, yet fueled by your infinite trust in me—perhaps my greatest work."

Piero's head twitched under the glow of such a heavy compliment. "You honor me."

Sandro walked around the room. He sunk his hand into a bowl of wet paper pulp, then sniffed his fingers.

"Even though you keep your work secret from me, I don't want to keep my work secret from you any longer," Piero said, then led Sandro through the closet door into the chamber that stored the collection of dolls he and Poppi had created. It was a menagerie of two-legged and four-legged creatures, some primitive while others had the intricate decoration and detail of fine jewelry.

"Where am I?" Sandro asked. "Show me to myself."

"You're on the 'active' tray—the people here and now in my life. These others are people long gone or those I speak with or see from time to time." Piero closed the closet door and moved toward a tall privacy screen in his main bedroom. He folded back one of the tapestry panels and there on a huge silver tray sat the miniature members of the household. Sandro's effigy was dressed in deerskin clothes like the ones he wore on his arrival. Floriana posed in front of him, her belly round, and her hair flowing in yellow silk and tiny flowers strewn over her from head to foot.

"May I?" Sandro took Floriana's tiny double in his hands. "Show me now, the moneylender, and Graziella, his daughter."

Piero's head twitched. "They are business partners. Secret ones. Friends, not usurers," he said.

"I don't care who pays me as long as I get paid. Where you get the money is your business. But now show me the moneylender, I mean your friend who happens to be a moneylender, please."

"Manfredo," Piero said as he walked back inside the closet to retrieve the doll.

"And bring the daughter too."

When Piero brought the dolls out, Sandro said, "Now another tray, please. A small one."

Piero pulled out a small silver tray with a sweet upon it from underneath his bed. He popped the pastry in his mouth, then spilled the crumbs into a nearby plant and handed the tray to Sandro.

Sandro placed the three dolls, Manfredo, Graziella, and Floriana, together on the small silver tray.

"This transfer," he told Piero, "must happen within the next twenty-four hours. And *you* must do it. Only *you* know the way and only you can offer the protection."

"Why the sudden casting out of the one who so inspires you?"

"To keep the inspiration alive and well, we must remove her to safety among her own people."

"I'm scheduled for a hunt tomorrow!"

"Cancel it! This is a matter of life and death."

Piero flinched under the force of Sandro's voice.

"I can't cancel. Unless of course it rains or snows."

"If the sun shines, I'll hunt in your place," Sandro said. "Tell Poppi of this tonight and tell her to prepare Floriana for the trip. You must leave at dawn."

"And if I don't cooperate?"

"I won't cooperate. You can't afford that, can you?"

Piero's head twitch worsened. "You have taken me by surprise. Who is the master here?"

"We are both servants of a higher good, to save a life, possibly two or more."

"Why all of a sudden? Isn't she safe here now that Bandini died so conveniently?"

"That's the problem. His replacement is due, but more pressing than that, Floriana senses the return of her cleric rapist. If he finds out she's pregnant, even more disaster could befall her."

"Why don't you just marry her, Master Botticelli? You are obviously in love with her."

"All she can think about is to leave here. We must assist her. It's precisely because I'm so committed to you and my work here that I'm not going to take her myself. I must stay and finish in time for my Christmas visit to Florence. Lorenzo has insisted I come. I considered taking Floriana and leaving her there, but I don't trust him any longer."

"Your precious Lorenzo, not trustworthy? That's the first time I've heard you say anything bad about him! And don't you need Floriana for the painting?"

"I've completed enough to finish the rest from memory."

Sandro got on his knees for the second time that day. "I beg you."

"Get up. Get up! But you must swear on your parents' lives you'll never tell Lorenzo about my relationship with Manfredo. It's none of his business!"

"On my parents' lives, not a word about your business dealings."

"Never, ever, ever."

"Never, ever."

"One more question," Piero said.

"Anything you ask."

"What do you think of my dolls, my artwork here?"

"It's magical. I can't believe you have created all these beings on your own."

"I haven't done it alone. I do the faces and hands, and Poppi sews the clothing. We've been doing it since I was five, but my parents expected me to outgrow the passion. Instead it has become more intense, especially since their death, but I've kept it a secret even from my sisters. In an effort to be manly and to take on manly pursuits, I've kept this part of me locked away."

"Taking up manly pursuits for which you have no interest or talent is hardly a manly action," Sandro said. "Making a proper show of these dolls, making them public, would be most manly of you."

"Imagine you! That manly I am not yet. But thank you for your confidence. Still, I implore you, not a word of this to anyone. Floriana knows too. Poppi knew she would welcome the chance to add her talented hands to the task. Always humming while she works. I will miss her. She hasn't told you?"

"Not a word. You do me my personal favor tomorrow, summoning all your manly protection, sacrificing your newest collaborator, Floriana, and delivering her into Manfredo's care, and I'll help you in any way I can. Not only the painting, but whatever else I can do for you. And as for Lorenzo, I'm happy to keep your private business deals from him. He thinks he knows everyone's deepest, darkest secrets, and can make any one of us do whatever he wants. Trust me, Piero, I'm more your ally than his."

"I'll do it. But what if Floriana refuses to go with me?"

"I doubt that will be the case," Sandro said, "unless she's already gone."

CHAPTER THIRTY-SEVEN

The Too-Quick Savonarola

NCE SAVONAROLA WAS OUT of her space, Oslavia decided she would go to Villa di Castello herself. She opened the door, half expecting young Savonarola to be crouching there, listening. He was gone. The winter air chilled her, the wind howling, the sun hidden behind clouds. She placed the heavy shawl Floriana had made for her about her shoulders and hurried to Federico's hut. As she approached, she saw Savonarola leaving it.

Face and eyes red from crying, Federico crossed himself. Savonarola held the hands of the two little girls. Oslavia watched the prelate head back toward the monastery with one small child on either side of him. He was so involved with the girls, he did not see Oslavia approaching.

She greeted Federico, offering her handkerchief to wipe his tears.

"Such a pious young man," he said. "He has given me new hope. I haven't felt this clean since Nicola and I were married."

Luigi stood by his father's side, trying to comfort him, not comprehending these were tears of joy.

"God bless," Oslavia said. "What did he say to you?"

"He asked about my sins of longing and lust. I have begun to have them now that Nicola's no longer with me. I found myself confessing thoughts I hadn't even remembered having. He pulled them out of me like a rotten tooth from my gums. And I wept. He held me. He took my mourning of Nicola into his body and carried it away. He told me God will provide for me and the children."

"Did he ask you questions about Floriana?"

"None. Only about me and about how Bandini died. I told him he had gone to your brother's to thank them for the cart and had come back in the cart as a corpse. I was guilty I hadn't gone with him but Father Savonarola absolved me totally. He wiped away my sin. I have a new beginning. I asked him if he was to be the new monsignor. He said no, that he had received a message from God to abide in Florence to save the people, the children, the buildings, lest sin become incarnate and devour all in a ghastly fire."

"I don't trust him, Federico. Perhaps for you today he was God's messenger, but I don't believe he always was. He's hunting for Floriana. Luigi and the girls must not say anything."

"I fear, Sister Oslavia, it's too late. As you can see the little girls are right at this moment his guests. He promised them sweets. He left this sacrament cloth. He said it was his last—a gift from Rome, he said."

"I must see my brother today, Federico. I must take Luigi with me to the Medici Villa di Castello."

"But I'm already taking Brother Savonarola there," Federico said. "He insisted. He wanted to find out the details of Bandini's last moments. Luigi told him he knew the way there and we would take him."

Oslavia glared at Luigi. "Did you mention Floriana?"

"No. I only talked about the artist and how I had assisted him."

"Did he ask about a Jewish lady?" she pressed, but Luigi looked away.

"You must stall him," Oslavia told Federico. "You cannot take him. You must take me. I command you. Tell him you forgot I had an important visit I must make and it will not be possible to carry us both."

"How can I deny one who has saved my life?"

"Because another life, maybe two, are at stake here, and because you must. Trust me. In memory of your departed Nicola, I beg you to do this."

"No one is going anywhere," Federico said, "until all the wood is removed from the cart and the horse is harnessed to it again. I'll go and tell them. And see what I can do."

Federico went off to the monastery. As soon as he was out of sight, Oslavia took Luigi by the shoulders and shook him. "Tell me you said nothing."

"I said only—" He started to cry. "I can't remember what I said. I said there was a party. I said I tasted foods I had never seen before. I said I helped the sisters assist Master Botticelli with the flowers of his model. I did not mention her name. Why are you hurting me?"

Oslavia released her grasp then pulled Luigi to her bosom and almost suffocated him with her embrace.

"Sweet Luigi. You don't understand that all who seem of God are not always of God. Though they wear the robes of God and know all the prayers, sometimes inside their hearts lives an evil as great as any other mortal's. That evil can jump out and take over the body and the soul even without the person wanting it to."

Luigi pulled himself out of her grasp to face her.

"Dear Mother Oslavia. Do not cry. I'll go with you today. I'll help you."

"You must take the horse *now* while they are unloading the cart. Take the horse and ride as fast as you can to Sandro and tell him the priest is coming for Floriana. Tell him to hide her."

"But, Mother Oslavia. I don't know how to ride a horse. We have no saddle. I can whip him from the cart fast. But if I try to ride him bareback I'll fall to the ground and no one will reach Master Sandro's."

"Let them follow us on their donkeys and we'll lead in the cart. As soon as we get to the property you must bolt ahead like lightning and warn Sandro to hide Floriana. Do you understand?"

"I'm fast. And Master Botticelli and I have a secret code, a special whistle I can make so he'll know we're there. You know I'm fast on my feet."

"Now it's winter, they won't be set up outside as before. You'll have to search the villa quickly and let them know. You must find Poppi first."

"I can do that," he said.

Oslavia had released her hold on Luigi's shoulders but now held both his hands as they spoke.

"And if anyone asks for the name of the model, you must call her Rosanna as we did that night when Monsignor Bandini died. Do you remember?"

"I remember. I won't disappoint you. I'll go now and suggest they follow us."

"Don't do that. Perhaps your father will have success in convincing them to stay here, but I doubt it."

Oslavia and Luigi walked from the cottage toward the cart.

"I'll place myself inside the cart the moment the wood has been unloaded. You grab the horse and bring him to the cart. Tell your father of the plan, but do not, I tell you, do not discuss it within earshot of that friar."

Oslavia whispered to herself over and over again: *Save me, Father, for I have sinned. Truth will set me free. Save me, Father, for I have sinned. Truth will set me free.* She spoke in rhythm with her pulse as it throbbed in her neck and her heart. There was no time for Peredexion trees. She would announce her intention to pose for her brother's painting. *No not the painting! Surely they would want to see it and once that happens all will be lost.*

Oslavia stopped herself outside of her house. *If I trust in God, I should allow Him to work His ways, for now I'm surely attempting to be God, orchestrating all of this.*

The thought of staying at home to pray crossed her mind. The thought of the hours of travel under the gaze of the young friar with the piercing eyes terrified her. He would know she had lied to him. She entered her home and walked to the main altar of the convent. This was her castle. She was the abbess, after all of these years, and yet she had no power, no control.

She wrapped the woolen shawl around herself more tightly and decided to act with respect even though she had no trust for this Savonarola. Perhaps on some level she was mistaken, perhaps even if he was the perpetrator, the father of Floriana's baby, perhaps he might be sincere and remorseful at the same time. All these thoughts flushed through her at once as she walked toward the monastery. There was no need to use the lower passageway, and there was no need, with someone as sneaky as he on the grounds, to call attention to it. Yes, he did look like a rodent. With those beady eyes and long nose.

As she strode up to the cart, she saw the other friars, Piattini and Dono, unloading branches cut from what she recognized to be her Peredexion tree.

"Did you cut down the entire tree?" she asked.

"No," Piattini said, "only the lowest branches. Why?"

"It is a sacred tree, don't you know? The Peredexion under whose shadow evil dragons die."

"I haven't seen any dragons around here," Piattini said. He laughed, throwing more cuttings onto the ground.

Your master is one, she thought.

"We're going to see Floriana!" Luigi's little sisters squealed as they ran to her. "Father Gerome is taking us with Daddy!"

Oslavia scooped both girls into her arms and as they nestled into her bosom she saw the piercing gaze of Savonarola.

"Out of the mouths of babes comes the truth," he said.

"I am taking you myself," Oslavia said. "I need to see my brother, and Federico has too much to do. Luigi and I will be in the cart and you and your companions can follow on your donkeys, please. I'm due to be painted by my brother, so this way we will kill two birds with one stone."

"We want to go!" the girls screamed.

"Take the girls back to the cottage, Federico. Luigi knows the way and these gentlemen of God will follow us."

The small girls didn't budge. Instead they clung to Oslavia's robes. Any attempt to wrench them away by their father created screams and tears.

"They haven't been on a trip since the cemetery," Federico said.

"Very well, then," Oslavia said. "But only if we play a game. We'll all stay silent the whole way there. Not a word until we see the little dogs." The two girls barked and growled like Piero's pug dogs and laughed. They were so happy to be on the cart and eating the sweet candies Savonarola had given to them—a tiny cost for the information he gained.

"I hope you'll not be disappointed when you see the person you seek is not the person you'll find," Oslavia said to Gerome.

"I am not going to seek anyone. I am going on a mission of God's work to spread forgiveness and allow people to confess to me and my brothers that which most troubles their hearts. We bring gifts wherever we go."

"Shall we begin then?" he asked Oslavia with a smile and voice free of any sarcasm or anger toward her obvious lie. His deep, dark eyes seemed to be telling her, *I have understood your need to protect and lie, and I forgive you.*

"All we have," he said, "is the human heart reaching for God. I can see in your face, Sister Oslavia, you are one who shares this belief. So do not worry. I am after the same thing you are. Salvation and peace. God's love above man's love."

As the cart slowly made its way to the Villa di Castello, and she smelled the fresh sap from the Peredexion tree on the wagon, tears of confusion streamed down Oslavia's face. The turmoil inside her settled into a quiet hope that all would resolve itself in God's plan. The little girls kissed her cheeks, giggling, as they pretended to be cats lapping up her tears. Oslavia placed her finger on her lips to plead with them to be still and quiet. When the girls snuggled and relaxed against her, her body melted into the soft cushions Luigi had placed into the cart for her. Following behind, the friars from Bologna sang a slow and long Latin chant, one she hadn't heard in years.

In her state between wakefulness and sleep, a recurrent, haunting image returned: she is still young, and Empiria is freshly buried inside the wall of the convent, but in the dream she, Oslavia, is growing older and the baby is growing older and older, pushing away the blocks the way a stubborn root breaks through the stone of a foundation wall. First a baby's hand punches through the stone. The hand grows, matures—nails wrapping around the fingertips. Time passes in this dream so fast.

A foot breaks through, a whole section of wall comes down, the stones tumbling onto Oslavia, who is now too old to move. The child, turned monster, rises up. Lacerations in her flesh from scraping through the stone add to the horror of the image as she opens her enormous maw of a mouth from which she releases an inhuman shriek like the sound of a thousand crows, shattering the convent walls in a wail that reaches to the ends of the world.

CHAPTER THIRTY-EIGHT

Claudia and Giuliano at Medici Palace

CLAUDIA AND GIULIANO lay in bed as the morning light burned around the edges of shuttered windows. A smoky scent came from the glowing hearth, sending wispy threads of black charcoal into the room. Giuliano wrapped his arms around Claudia's belly and waited for the baby's movement.

"There," he said. "I felt it. Sssh! Don't say a word!"

"Don't shush me!" Claudia said as she took his hands off her.

"Let's not fight," he said. "The baby can hear us and that's not good for him."

"And how do you know it's going to be a boy? Because you want one?"

"I know. I feel it's going to be a Giulio."

"If anyone feels anything it is I, who am carrying Giulio or Giulietta, and you don't seem to care what I feel."

"I've told you over and over again. We must wait until after the baby's birth for the wedding. My mother will not have it any other way."

"Your mother. Your mother!"

"Don't speak ill of her. We've won. Lorenzo's convinced her to give up on the arranged marriage for me. All we're talking about is a mild concession to the calendar."

"I'll be weak for a while after the birth. How can I be a bride then?"

"You'll be a spring flower in the full bloom of motherhood." He walked his fingers slowly again around her belly, then whispered in her ear, "We're already married in our hearts. You are here. We are together."

"But I can't go out. I'm a prisoner."

"For your protection, my sweet."

"Don't *my sweet* me!" Claudia threw the covers off the bed and stood, but Giuliano pulled on her sleeping gown and she fell back laughing. The second he let go, she jumped up to face him. "You promised at the very least to register our engagement. When are you going to do that?"

"When I'm sure no one knows what I'm doing. It will be our secret. You know it's supposed to be part of the ritual to do it in front of a crowd with bells ringing and everything."

"Just do it. And I'll be happy. No one needs to know about it." She sat back onto the bed and curled herself around Giuliano's back. "You will do it, won't you, my muffin, my *pasticciotto*!" she said, nibbling his ear.

"That's the sweet girl I'm going to marry. Come, come, let us pleasure ourselves before the sun is full, before I must pretend to care about helping Lorenzo run this family business."

"Pleasure you, you mean. I'm afraid of hurting Giulio."

"Let me hold you both," he said. "Forget about the pleasure. Forget about the wedding, the engagement papers, and lie still. I want to feel him again." Giuliano tried to turn himself around to face Claudia, but she fought him.

"What do you mean forget about the wedding! Now is it off altogether?"

"No. I mean forget about discussing it this moment, this day. Trust all will unfold as it should. I want to say good morning to my son."

"Or daughter."

As he wrapped his arms more around her, she drew her arms about his head and pulled his face to hers and licked his nose.

"Stop!" he said. "Let me concentrate."

"I concentrate on him or her all day and night. Now I want to concentrate on your nose, your lips."

Giuliano became hard against her side.

"So much for simple hugging," she said. "I'm getting up now."

"And abandoning us both," he said, looking down at the bulge under his nightshirt.

"Tell that one to put his clothes on. And as for you, you can hold me all night long tonight. You'll feel him kicking me as I try to sleep. You can stay awake with us both."

"But I won't be here tonight," he said, and they started in on an argument about how he was still spending so much time in diplomacy with his brother, Lorenzo, how Claudia feared it would get even worse rather than better after the baby was born. "I'll be a stranger in a stranger's house," she said, her refrain every time Giuliano refused to give her a date when they might move out to a villa of their own.

When their words solved nothing, they let their touch create whatever limited form of lovemaking they could manage.

Moments later, the couple lay in silence, as the light of day, now brighter, sliced its way past the closed wooden shutters, sending shards of sun onto the floor and walls. Giuliano reached under the bed to pull out a small scroll tied with a blue silk ribbon and an official seal dangling from the knot.

"I told you I'd pleasure you after," Giuliano said then handed the scroll to Claudia. "Open it!"

While Claudia slowly and carefully untied the ribbon, Giuliano continued, "You have no idea how I wish we had a normal life. I've never wanted this pomp and the adoration of the crowds. I play the part. But inside I count the minutes until I can be back in my private quarters stripping off the crest and the shield and the helmet."

Claudia put the parchment to her breast. "It's official? When did you do this?"

"I snuck out yesterday. I got the clerk to file it without anyone's noticing and to swear he would say nothing to anyone."

Claudia held the engagement certificate to her chest, smiling at Giuliano with a river of love flowing from her eyes.

"I've seen so much faithlessness," he said. "I've watched my own brother go out whoring when he was younger, even while Clarice was pregnant. I want no part of that life."

Still Claudia said nothing, only shone her smile on Giuliano.

"Do you trust me now?" he said while he wrapped his arms once again around her from behind. He did not see the worried expression on her face or hear the nagging thoughts that troubled her.

CHAPTER THIRTY-NINE

Gerome and Oslavia Reach the Villa di Castello

ULLED BY THE FRIARS' CHANTING close behind them, Oslavia and the young girls slept the rest of the way to Villa di Castello until Piero's dogs awakened them. Before Gerome could catch up to the cart, Luigi stopped the horse and jumped onto the ground, while Oslavia lifted herself into the driver's seat to take the reins.

Luigi ran to Poppi, who appeared at the door, then continued past her until he disappeared into the house with his little sisters and the dogs running after him. Soon his whistle—the signal to Sandro—filled the air, but there was no sign of the artist.

Piero's younger sisters watched from the doorway. When they saw the three monks they turned and ran into the house, yelling, "Piero, where are you?"

Poppi walked to the cart to greet Oslavia. "Your brother isn't here today, nor is Master Piero. No one but me and the girls and the other servants."

"We have come to see the Jewess," Gerome said, as he pushed his way forward, a stern expression on his face.

Poppi and Oslavia looked at each other but said nothing.

"I think he's referring to Rosanna," Oslavia said, using Floriana's alias.

"No one here by that name," Poppi said. "Too bad you came on a day Master Piero is out on a diplomatic trip and your brother Sandro is filling in for him at the hunt."

"Hunting! I never knew he liked it," Oslavia said.

"It was a favor he offered to young Master Piero," Poppi said.

"The girl. Where is she?" repeated Gerome. "I know Bandini was in charge of her, and she's disappeared from the monastery. This was the last place Bandini was alive, so there must be a connection."

"And if there was," Oslavia said, glaring at him now, "why is it so important for you to find her?"

"It's a mission from God that I see her and make sure she's alive and well."

"She is," Poppi said, "and not anywhere to be found here. I fear you'll have to take my word for it, sir, or should I call you Father? Though you are young enough to be my grandson."

"I must find her."

"You'll not find her here," Poppi said. "You can search high and low and you will not find her."

"Why don't you listen to what this wise woman has to say?" Oslavia told Gerome. "We each must live with our disappointments. You, to find your imaginary lady, and I, to lose the opportunity to visit my brother the artist."

"In Florence—a few short months ago, in the staggering heat, Master Botticelli begged me to share a meal with him and instead I starved myself and slept on rocks until I almost died," Savonarola said.

"And why did you deny yourself so much?" Poppi asked.

"I thought abstinence from any sense of pleasure would cure me, but it almost killed me. Now I focus on helping others rather than on my own past. That is why I am seeking the young woman. The little children told me she was here. May I search this house for traces of her?"

"I doubt my master would be pleased if I gave free rein to a stranger to search through our villa."

"I must find her."

"And I'm sure you will if you're so determined," Poppi said, "but not here. Come inside. Rest. I'll prepare some food and you can tell the master's young sisters you are not here to take them away to a convent."

Gerome relented, and the group made its way inside.

"Trusting God to reveal what we need is part of accepting His will for us," Oslavia said. "Perhaps you're not meant to see her again."

"What are you suggesting, Sister Oslavia? I did nothing to her but bring her to a place of refuge."

"Enough about the past," Poppi said. "Come and sit in the parlor and warm your feet against the hearth before you head back."

"I'll wait for the master's arrival if I might," he said as he settled into a chair.

"I'd rather you didn't," Poppi said. "I'm happy to serve you and your companions a bit of food and drink, but I cannot offer hospitality in a home that is not mine."

Grateful for Poppi's sense of control, Oslavia went off with her into the large kitchen.

"He could be the one who violated our Floriana," Oslavia said, "and yet I cannot tell if he is lying, if he's remorseful, if he wants to see her to apologize, or to take her away."

"What's a traveling priest going to do with a pregnant Jewess?" Poppi asked. Just then, the two women looked at each other in panic. They both rushed into the parlor where Savonarola stood with the corner of the cloth meant to cover Sandro's painting in one hand in the air.

"I wouldn't do that," Poppi said. "Master Botticelli would be most incensed. It's not his style to let a stranger view his work in progress."

"I've seen all I need to see," Gerome Savonarola said. Piattini and Dono stood beside him. "He has painted her in the style of a woman in waiting."

"It is the style of artists to render young women so," Poppi said. "Don't think she's truly in that condition."

"But she is, thanks to one of your kind," Oslavia said, glaring at him.

"You accuse me falsely," Gerome said.

"I did not accuse you," Oslavia said. "I merely said 'one of your kind.'"

INSIDE GEROME'S HEAD a terrible pulsing began as the sounds of voices outside of him grew muffled. It seemed blood might spill out of his ears at any moment from the ache behind his eyes. When he opened his mouth to speak, nothing came out, his eyes rolled in their sockets, and he dropped to the floor.

Dono and Piattini fell to their knees and tried to rouse him.

"You have blasphemed such a holy man," Piattini said, looking at Oslavia.

"I did not accuse him directly. Perhaps his 'holiness' is not without a past of sin," she answered.

"As is true of any saint. One who reforms and places his indiscretions behind him and is a shining beacon to others to do the same," Dono said.

"And you believe this about him?" Oslavia said.

"We know this about him. He has told us as much," Piattini said.

"This is why we are bound to him till death, for he has awakened us from our own folly," Dono added.

"The folly, however—his or yours or whoever it was in clerical robes who took her—has planted a seed."

"I'm sure he knew nothing of this," Dono said.

"How could he have?" Oslavia said. "Whoever it was did his dirty work, then abandoned her in a prison and went on his way to redemption while she was left carrying his evil."

Dono and Piattini lifted the small, limp body of their spiritual guide to a couch, the very same one where Bandini had all but expired.

Poppi ran off to the kitchen and came back carrying an herb. As soon as she placed it under Gerome's nose, he awoke.

"Please ask the others to leave," Gerome said to Oslavia. "I'll tell you my side of this if you'll listen—but only you." He glared at everyone else. Poppi led Dono, Piattini, and now Luigi and his little sisters out of the parlor and into the kitchen area.

Head in his hands, Gerome looked at the floor, his body slumped into a chair. "What have I done?"

"You have planted the fruits of your wicked impulses and she carries it into the real world for the rest of her life," Oslavia said.

"I must see her."

"Never! She does not know it's you. She did not see your face. If you go away and leave us and her in peace you'll be left alone."

"Except for the conscience of God, which torments me for my moment of temptation."

"And what about the moments after that—the moments of rational thought that caused you to take a life and confine it against its will to a future you thought was best, a future of silence and isolation?"

All blood seemed to have drained from Gerome's face. His chest rose and fell as he struggled to regain his composure.

"Sin is an ink blot that seeps into the future, staining your life in every direction," Oslavia said. "Now do you understand why I defied Bandini and allowed Floriana her freedom? He claimed her like chattel to display as his convert. Heaven knows what they would have done to the child."

Savonarola wept openly. "I was an animal. I couldn't let anyone find out about this. It kept haunting me. Instead of feeling satisfied and finished with it, my lust became worse, and with each episode of desire I punished myself more until I had sores on my body, no food in my belly, and I was taken back to my home in Ferrara to die."

"At least you had a conscience. Did you pray for forgiveness?"

"I prayed for death. To be released from my sins of desire and my acts of carnality."

"And never did you ask for forgiveness for how you had destroyed another's life?"

"I honestly thought bringing her to the monastery, converting her, would make her see her nakedness had also been a sin."

"Her nakedness was not meant to be an act of seduction, but one of cleansing."

"I know. I know. Still, I must see her."

"That's the last thing you should do. What you have seen in this painting is more than you deserve, if you're truly remorseful. Have you confessed this?"

"I have been absolved by others, but I have not been able to absolve myself. As my family nursed me back to health I received a direct vision from God of how I, as sinner reformed, could rouse others to choose a purer way."

"Do your penance with renunciation, then," Oslavia said. "You must release her to freedom, limited though it will surely be, now with child and no husband and on the run out of fear of your return."

"One act of impulse—succumbing to temptation in one moment—can change the world forever."

"And violence in thought ranks close behind."

"You must forgive me, Sister Oslavia."

"Why is my forgiveness of any weight to you?"

"Because others have heard a story, where you have seen the consequences."

"It is not my place to forgive you," she said. "It's my job to speak the truth. To forgive you would be to forgive others before you who have so abused their trust as servants of God. You are not the first I have encountered, and I fear you will not be the last. You must relinquish any connection to her and the child. God assisted you by because she never saw your face and so you must release her and yourself, and you must rededicate yourself to preventing others of your kind from similar actions. If you could but put the fear into them, or better yet, the faith into them to ride out those moments of temptation, perhaps they can teach others by example. Otherwise you are teaching sin and the joy of absolution from it without concern for those you have victimized."

"Yet you lied to me just this morning."

"Because I sensed you were devious."

"How so?"

"You wanted news to take to her father. Her father has long been dead."

"So you set yourself up as God, deciding when and where to follow His bidding."

"You're mistaken, my young and naive Friar Savonarola, for it is He who shows me the folly of man, especially men in robes. The truth is not an opinion."

"Confess to me a sin of your own. Make us equal," Gerome said.

"For years I harbored a desire to leave the convent."

"And what else? That is not in any way equal to what I have done. I want to know your deepest and darkest blot."

"And why should I share such a thing with you?"

"To make us equal!"

"We will never be."

"I know you are hiding something. Something big."

"On the day Bandini fell, there was a voice inside me wishing for his death."

"What else?"

"Is this a contest of evil? Isn't that enough?"

"I have admitted to you this sin that could destroy my whole life. You must share something not even your brother knows."

"My brother was never a part of my life in the convent. I would not share with him even half of what I've done or learned there."

"I'm waiting, Sister Oslavia," Gerome said. "And I am very patient."

"I'm taking the opportunity to right a wrong. A wrong I was too young and too stupid to handle when it was done to me."

Oslavia turned away from Gerome as her shoulders rose and fell as the suppressed sobs from her past surfaced. Still with her back to him, she began, "My sin was silence. My sin was submission to someone much like you."

"A priest?"

"An acolyte who lured me to his cell for contemplation, only to take me against my will."

"But, Sister Oslavia, was it completely against your will? Was it fully without your complicity? Turn to me. I will not judge you."

Oslavia shuddered to speak what she had kept in a haze of memory. The sweat, the smell of the semen spilled on her fourteen-year-old body, and she had, in spite of the violation, in spite of her knowledge this was a sin, she had taken a moment of pleasure from it.

"Why the tears?"

"For my ignorance. My willingness to allow the syrup of youth to enter me. I knew to be alone with him was in itself cause for remorse, and yet I did it."

"And what came of this union?" Gerome pressed her.

"A child."

"From one time?"

"It does happen like that," she said. "You're not the only one."

"The child?"

"Ripped from my breast, and placed inside the walls for eternity."

"Buried inside the convent walls?"

"Exactly."

"Alive?"

"Her cries contained by bricks I fear. I only know the resting place for her body, but not for my soul. Time had healed me by covering it over until I saw Floriana's pain." Resuscitated with the knowledge of Oslavia's secret, Gerome pressed her again. "And so you took it upon yourself to reverse the will of your superior."

Silence fell between the two—she recovering her composure and he calmer now.

"And now?" he asked of her.

"Just as I was forced to release my own flesh and blood, you, too, must do the same."

"I cannot."

"And what would you do? Are you to wed her? Bring a child along with you? Kidnap the child? Kill the child? I pray, young friar, fuel your rapture with release!"

"I'll only agree to this if you agree not to identify me to anyone as the father. Not to your brother, his master, and especially not to Floriana herself."

"As for my brother, he knows nothing of my past shame, and I prefer it that way. You, too, must swear a silence about what I have confessed to you."

"I do not like this pact," Gerome said. "I must think about this."

"That is precisely what you must *not* do. You must move ahead as I have done. Your secret will die with me and mine with you."

"Does this make us allies?" he said.

"It makes us equal under God's grace. Erase all memory of this conversation except in the depths of your soul."

"But I recount my story of sin and portray my absolution as part of how I entice others toward our Savior. I keep the victim of my story faceless and nameless."

"As you should. You must tell your cohorts they, too, must die with the secret inside them, for they surely suspected the truth by your reaction to the painting."

"I will deny it. They will believe whatever I tell them," Gerome said. "And what about the housekeeper, Poppi?"

"Her heart is a vault," Oslavia said.

"You must be sure. If I renounce all claim to your Floriana and the child here and now."

"We must live in the present and move forward from this as I am prepared to do."

"And I, I am prepared for nothing except to dedicate my life to saving others from becoming wasted souls. I want to save Florentines from themselves. I want to make a world where God is King and all others his subjects."

"You aim high, my young Dominican, for such a fallen angel."

"I am a chosen one."

"Chosen to rape an innocent girl?" she said.

"Chosen to learn and to teach others to save themselves."

The dogs yelped, and Sandro's voice boomed at them from outside. "Holding down the fort are you, puppies?" His tone was bright and cheerful.

"My brother. And you must agree to what we said this moment or I will tell him what you've done. Who you really are. What's your choice?" Oslavia said.

"Silence. I'll take myself from here with sealed lips about your secret, and trust you'll keep mine."

"Now swear!" she said, "with the sign of the cross. A vow once taken not to be broken."

As the two mendicants faced each other, they made the silent sign of the cross upon themselves. Their solemn faces wore no cover of propriety or attitude, stripped as each was in front of the other and each holding the fate of the other in silence.

AS SOON AS SANDRO WALKED INTO THE ROOM where his sister and Savonarola stood, he smiled with a greeting. "What brings the starving brother from Ferrara here? No rags? No sores. No longer a mere skeleton. What changed you?"

While Sandro hugged Oslavia, he kept his eyes on Gerome.

"I'm here to meet the Master Piero who was so generous to Bandini."

"Bandini? The poor fellow choked on his own vomit," Sandro said.

Oslavia glared at her brother. "Please don't joke about the departed." She turned to Gerome. "My brother often makes light of the most serious matters."

Turning back to Sandro, she continued, "This young priest and his two acolytes are making their way through Tuscany, saving lost souls with prayer. As for me, I was coming to surprise you with a visit, but you were gone."

"I've suffered separation pangs from my mistress," Sandro said. "My painting, of course, which is my mistress hoping to be my masterpiece."

"And the subject matter?" asked Gerome.

"Not of your liking I'm sure," Sandro said. "Wasn't it you who accused artists of painting Madonnas as whores? Though, this, too, will have its Virgin Mary disguised as Venus among the cast of characters. Would you like to see it?"

"No. I might urge you to change it. I might want to save the souls of those you paint."

"I'll take your decision then," Sandro said, "as a compliment of faith since I seek divine guidance during every brushstroke."

"The girls, your master's young sisters, are afraid this Father Savonarola has come to take them away to a convent," Poppi said as she entered the room.

"Bring them in right away," Sandro said, always ripe for a prank.

Poppi left the room to fetch the girls. Luigi followed her close behind.

Sandro looked into the young friar's eyes. "You seem disturbed. Are you?"

"Do I?" Gerome said. "I'm disturbed I have missed Master Piero today. I promised Bandini's houseboy—not a boy—but an old man who wears garlic about him. Have you met him?"

"Petrarchio?"

"Yes, Petrarchio. I promised Petrarchio I would bring back news of the young woman who had been brought here from the convent."

"Who was asking?" Sandro said.

"The one who cared for Bandini says there was a young convert who escaped here, and Monsignor Bernardino is coming one of these days to witness and record her conversion, but she is no longer here."

"Well then, Bernardino will be minus a convert," Sandro said. "She's long gone from here, I know not where."

"Perhaps you could take one of the master's young sisters back in her place," Sandro said, raising his voice, as he heard the girls coming into the room.

He reached out his hand and grabbed the wrist of the eldest, Donata. She let out a scream and then a giggle. Dono and Piattini entered the room followed by Poppi, who brought in Sandro's catch for the day—some birds on a string.

"The game you found on your hunt?" Poppi asked Sandro.

"I'll not hunt for anything larger than my fist," he said. "But these men of the cloth are hunting for a young woman escaped from the convent, and I offered up the three girls." Sandro turned to Poppi with a wink.

"And with their older brother gone for the day. What do you say?" he said to Gerome, inviting him to play along.

Gerome walked up to the three girls, turning his most piercing gaze on them at close range.

"I can see by the look in their eyes their prayers are recited from memory without any heart in them. They worry more about their gowns and makeup than their place in heaven with the Almighty."

The two youngest girls burst into tears, but the eldest, Donata, said, looking directly at Sandro, "Don't even think we would go for one moment without the consent of our brother. He has promised us he would never send us away."

"But if—" Sandro said, "if he found something about your lives, some deceit or scheming, especially against him or against his pocketbook, I'm sure he would send you away."

"That's enough!" Oslavia said. "They're joking with you, girls. Don't worry. Master Botticelli did this even in his youth to me. I've had my share of frogs and mice placed between my bed sheets." Turning to her baby brother, she said, "I haven't seen that side of you in years. You must be pleased about something."

"I am," he said. "The first third of my painting—the one this gentleman of the cloth has no interest in viewing—is nearing its completion and Christmas is in three days. As a present to all I'm leaving you to yourselves while I take off for Florence."

"Shall we travel together?" Gerome said.

"I think not," Oslavia said. "For you, my dear Brother Gerome, are leaving today, remember, while I plan to rest the night and my brother will be painting me. He has cast me as his Mary in disguise as Venus."

"And a good subject you'll be," Gerome said. "You have a heart free of malice with gentleness to all you meet."

"And I can see in you, dear Brother Savonarola, a man clearly on a mission for God, sweeping cobwebs out of any unbelieving mind you meet," Oslavia answered.

"Precisely. Which is why I should take confession from the three sisters before I leave," Gerome said.

"That's not necessary," Oslavia said.

"Don't you trust me?" Gerome asked.

"I trust you are a man united with your nature, and if that unity is fully with God, then I trust you."

"I do not wish it," Donata said.

"Nor I," Margarita added.

"I want to give a confession," Renata said, and walked over to take Gerome's hand.

"I can't refuse any soul who seeks me out," Gerome said.

"She's a child!" Oslavia said.

"We're all children of God," he said. Looking at Poppi, "Is there some quiet spot where we might go to talk. Some place private?"

Poppi led the way as Gerome took the young girl off with him.

Oslavia would pump Renata later to make sure the rodent priest had not used his clerical privilege for interrogation.

"Now, the rest of you, sit down," Poppi said, "while I make a quick snack of these poor winged creatures caught by the master painter."

THE MOMENT SAVONAROLA left the room with Renata, Piattini told Sandro, "Your painting is very beautiful!"

"You have *seen* it?" Sandro said. "Why didn't he say so?"

"When Poppi and your sister were out of the room we took a quick look," Piattini said. "He condones painting of religious subjects only. He says artists are speaking for those who cannot read and therefore they should use their talents only to praise the Lord. The painting disturbed him."

"Your priest is blind to beauty!" Donata said. "Master Botticelli sees beauty everywhere, not just in the church!"

"Brother Gerome is not blind," Dono said. "He sees the blindness of others and helps them to shine a light into their darkness."

Margarita and Donata twittered, shining adoring smiles at Master Botticelli, posing as though they were showing off their own earthly beauty to emphasize Donata's words.

Old desires stirred in Piattini as Donata walked closer to him. The eyes of the fresh-faced mendicant could not move away from the blossoming bosom that crept out of the top of her dress.

"Brother Dono," Piattini said, "shall we take a little walk around the grounds until Father Gerome is ready to depart?"

Donata grabbed Margarita's hand. "Better that we play hostesses while our brother is away. He would be annoyed if we didn't fulfill our role in his absence."

Donata glared at Margarita, who refused to move.

"Actually," Dono said, "Brother Piattini was suggesting the walk so we might not invade your home any further."

"Nonsense! My name is Donata so it is only correct that I accompany Brother Dono and Brother Piattini. Are those your real names?"

"Our chosen names. Brother Gerome gave them to us when we decided to travel together through the countryside," Piattini explained, as the four young people walked out of the villa toward the winding garden paths behind it.

Piattini's plea had been to walk away from the sexual pull of these young women, but now they were alone with them. To fight his urges, he sang a psalm and was relieved when Dono joined in with the words, "*Oh God, lead me not into temptation. Lead me not, lead me not.*"

The girls, walking ahead arm in arm, laughed while the two men slipped into a rhythmic step side by side. The girls' perfume pulled the young men by their noses and sent jolts to their private parts.

Dono held Piattini back. "What do you think we're doing?"

"We're being sociable. Polite. That's all."

"And what polite thoughts are running through your head?"

"The same as yours," Piattini said. "The sin of thoughts is not the sin of action."

"But only a human hair's breadth divides them. A hair easily made invisible in the presence of these temptresses," Dono said.

Donata and Margarita had stopped to wait for the men to catch up. One could always be oneself around these young men of the cloth because one expected them to be pure of heart and motive, protectors of their virginity—or so they assumed.

The men stood still, watching the girls.

"You know they want this attention from us," Piattini said. "Don't you hear the giggling?"

"Giggling is not the same as spreading their legs to us. We have sworn off this."

"But even the master has succumbed. You saw that painting," Piattini said.

"He never admitted anything. We don't know if it was he, or that she is really—"

"Enough! That was the past. This is now. We have sworn to celibacy as a power of example." Dono held on to Piattini's robes to keep him back.

"We haven't officially taken our vows yet anyway," Piattini said. "Is touching a young woman's flesh violating that vow if no seed is spilled, but merely a 'fatherly' embrace now and then?"

"Yes, if what you say is not what you carry in your crotch. Better to forgo this titillation. The more you give in to it, the longer it will take you to recover."

The girls were suddenly beside them.

"What's the matter? Are you ill? What do you need to recover from?" Margarita said.

"You girls are too beautiful for us to be alone with you," Dono said. "We're only human, after all, and the thoughts you evoke are beyond—"

"So we must take our walk alone without the joy of your companionship," Piattini said.

"How stupid!" Margarita said.

"That's rude," Donata added.

"You have it all wrong, my sweet innocents," Dono said. "We're protecting you from our lustful eyes by looking away. So be grateful we do so."

"We're so bored here!" Margarita said. "We're trapped with our studies and our paint grinding while you get to travel about. Tell us a story about what you have seen."

"People estranged from their God and slipping into slimy pits of sin and avarice. We want to pull them out, clean them off, and send them to the Almighty, pure and cleansed." Dono welcomed the chance to hide his own impulses with a sermon.

"Well then, clean us!" Donata shouted. "But we're already too clean. It's dull as paint drying!"

"Clean us some more," Margarita said, "and at least that might put us into some kind of rapture. I've heard it's possible to experience passion through the church."

The girls exchanged a quick moment of double daring and jumped into the icy waters of the round fountain. The wet clothing clung to their young bodies. They splashed at each other and posed, sticking their bosoms out at the young priests, who took in every curve and hardened nipple, before the girls ran into the house screaming, "We're cleansed, we are cleansed!" Piero's noisy pugs followed them in a cacophony of doggy yelps through the villa doorway.

"On fire," Piattini said, as he held his crotch.

"As is mine," Dono added.

"Shall we go into the bushes and relieve ourselves?" Piattini said. "It would help me to calm down."

"It would help you to take your lust to a lower level," Dono said. "Our challenge is to raise our spiritual condition toward the heavens in the presence of such temptation. Each time we do so we'll be stronger and more spiritually fit and more convincing in our presentation to the peasants and all we meet."

"But we haven't succumbed in weeks, months now."

"And are you worse off for it?"

"I'm feeling worse off for it this minute."

"And if Brother Gerome were standing here," Dono said, "what would he say?"

"To answer your question—" Gerome said as his two companions jumped at the unexpected sound of his voice. "Young Renata's confession was a short one. And to answer your question, Dono, I would say temptation is not a curse. God repeatedly visits us with temptations so we can choose again and again, not the direction our anatomical compass has chosen."

Piattini and Dono stayed silent. Gerome continued, "What if one of these young things were to become with child from your probing? Are you going to drop out of your God-given work to make a family—to narrow your life to one humble existence? Overcoming temptations builds spiritual progress. Succumbing to temptation in the real world will distance you from the very souls we are trying to reach."

"And what of self-satisfying in such a circumstance as this one when the devil has turned our members into signposts of lust?" Piattini asked, still holding his crotch.

"There are ways to quiet the beast."

"And they are?" Dono asked.

"Food is a good one," Savonarola said. "I learned this at death's door. Until then, my repentance, remorse, guilt for my actions, brought no relief from nightly rampages of my fleshy member. The more I starved myself, the harder the floor on which I slept, the more open sores I collected, the more I fell prey to dark angels of desire."

"You mean that when we took you to your home in Ferrara and you were at death's door, even in your weak state, you were more lustful than we as we flirted with your sisters?" Dono said.

"The stronger the guilt, the stronger the bulge. It was my father who told me if I looked more like the dead than the living, no one would listen to me, so I began to build myself up. With food."

"So we're supposed to eat to be relieved instead of spilling our seed in the forest?" Piattini asked.

"You make it seem so simple, Brother Gerome," Dono said.

"It is simple, but it's not easy. The devil aligns with all our darker forces. Moving to God is so much harder than slipping into the slime of human gluttony."

"But isn't eating for pleasure gluttony?"

"Not if you pray first. If you ask that the food fill you physically and spiritually you will not eat for the taste but as a sacrament."

"And you, Brother Gerome. Are you tempted?"

"Not at the moment, but my thoughts can arouse me and pull me away from my mission. I pray to be redirected to take those thoughts merely as God's testing so I can move toward God's pleasing. Let's get out of here!"

"But we just got here," Piattini said. "The old lady Poppi is preparing food for us. You just said we should eat rather than cheat."

"And haven't you eaten enough with your eyes? We've all learned enough today to know it's best to keep moving," Gerome said.

As he led his followers back to their donkeys and provisions, the indelible image of Floriana in Sandro's painting intensified his sense of revulsion and shame and yet aroused him. Prayer and performance had been for naught when that ugliest of all heads decided to rise with a will of its own. If he could hack it off his body, he would.

He wrapped his cape more fully around himself to cover his own unruly body part. Over the months since his fall into sin, especially between waking and sleep, he had been visited by images of her. Sometimes she had transmogrified into the mother church herself and he was penetrating the Vatican as though it were some whore begging him to do so. Awakening from those dreams, he found only long periods of prayer and silence could restore his composure.

He often lagged behind Dono and Piattini as he contemplated the mystery of these recurring images. How in one moment he had turned from sincere acolyte to rapist still tormented him. To offset the unruliness of his body, he often sat by candlelight to write his instructions and philosophy. During those times, Dono and Piattini left him to his own solitude. By the power of his example, they studied the Bible and rehearsed the scenes they were to reenact in front of peasants who listened and watched intently. Until this visit to Villa di Castello, in all their travels, there had never been a night the trio was not invited to sleep at the hearth, to share a meal, or to help nurse some ailing family member back to health.

This visit to Villa di Castello had brought him reeling back to the agony of his own lapse of the flesh. With it came a shudder of desire to see Floriana again. This sin, now blacker than he had ever imagined—a child from his own seed, growing in the belly of a Jew—could not be erased by prayer or confession.

Not only had his companions lost their way, but he himself had seen proof of the evil fruit of his actions, the public knowledge of which could destroy his sacred mission.

CHAPTER FORTY

Oslavia Keeps Her Word

SANDRO UNCOVERED THE PAINTING while Oslavia prepared herself to be his model. No shadow of guilt hovered above her as she stripped off her religious habit from her head, replacing it with a gold-toned headscarf.

"I've decided to place a cupid child above you," Sandro said. Oslavia's belly lurched. It was as though he knew about the topic of her confession to Gerome, and yet he could never have heard it. She calmed herself by keeping her back to her brother as she wrapped her shoulders with a rose-colored velvet blanket fringed with small bells around the edges.

"Strange one, that Savonarola," Sandro said. "He could hardly have been Floriana's perpetrator, don't you agree?"

Still with her back to her brother, pretending to adjust her costume, she said, "All priests who seek converts of those they know not are perpetrators more or less."

"He's not your usual young friar," Sandro said, then went on to share his memory of the young prelate he had encountered the night before he left Florence: emaciated, delirious, and in rags. Sandro stopped to show her his sketch of him with the nose of a penis. She looked away, busying herself more with her preparations.

As much as she wanted to applaud Sandro's psychic ability, she had promised to keep her lips sealed.

"I suspect," Oslavia said, still with her back to her brother, "all those he touches and speaks to melt into tears of repentance and remorse, confessing the deepest and darkest of their pasts to him without any power to stop their tongues."

"Then he is truly gifted," Sandro said. "I should seek him out."

"I caution you, sweet Brother. You commune already with the Almighty through your art. Don't surrender it to the edict of someone who could sweep you away from yourself."

"But a deeper connection to God can only add more to the art."

"It has to be *your* connection," she said, now turning to face her brother, "not a connection that uses your gifts for someone else's ends."

"Sadly what I've done most of my life."

"Exactly," she agreed. "But you're not doing it now. On this work you call your first masterpiece, the images have come from your heart."

"And God has been my partner, and continues to be."

"Yes, yes," she said. "Come here, my sweet brother, and give your sister, who is weary and weak from all of this talk, an embrace. Let's forget the priest from Ferrara and all his fiery words."

Oslavia held on to her brother. To confess to him now what really went on between her and Gerome would open up too much pain again. She had given her word.

"Why the tears?"

"When you weren't here I was worried and I had come to warn Floriana about this meddling beady-eyed priest, but God had already protected her once again by sending her to another place. Why is life so complicated?"

"You should know, Sister. You who have been talking to God for so many years." Sandro took his sister by her shoulders. "Come, I want to paint you."

"But it's not part of the third you're trying to finish," she said.

"I'm ahead of schedule, and now I'm moving to your part, so I want to at least place you there, get your lines. You're the central figure, inspiring love all around. And what better symbol than to have a child of love hovering above you? Perfect timing that you arrived today!"

He came over to adjust the folds on her shawl. Once he began to paint he said, "I wish we had some musicians to accompany us today to raise your spirits and calm mine."

"And why do your spirits need calming?" Oslavia asked.

"Because every time things are going along well, I fear some calamity is making its way toward me. It always does. Even though today I am relieved Floriana is with those who will care for her for now. Even though I am joyful you are here before me as my Venus—"

"Madonna, you mean," she corrected.

"Venus. Madonna. They're the same to me today. Even though I am happy my youthful, twitching patron is a greater man than he realizes—I dread the darkness that inevitably follows these rare occasions of happiness. Music helps me to stop these forebodings."

"Even with your forebodings, Sandro, I've not seen you this content and still so far from the one you care for most."

"And who is that?" he joked with her.

"The one who has so captured you. Are you through with her now?"

"Stand still and close your mouth. It's precisely because of her and my love for her I'm so full of happiness. For the moment."

"Even though she's not here? How so?"

"Because she dwells here." Sandro placed his hand over his heart.

"And she for you?"

"She says she does love me but she says she can never be my wife."

"Because . . . ?"

"Because she sees me as already married to my work, and she does not wish to compete with my art."

"Mature beyond her years."

"She is." He put his brushes down, went to Oslavia to rearrange her costume, and whispered, "I am full and content."

"For now."

"No wonder I have my forebodings! I've learned that kind of thinking from you. Maybe it's in our family blood. What else is there but one moment, one now, following the other?"

"Happy is he who blinks sideways at the clouds, for there he sees the rainbow," Oslavia said, with her eyes closed.

"Who said that?" Sandro asked, as he slipped deeper into his work. "And what does it mean?"

"One day when I was weeping over something, I cannot even remember what the cause was," she said, opening her eyes again and trying to stay as still as she could for her brother. "But through the glistening of my tears, I looked at the clouds. The sun was breaking through, and there inside my tiny tear I saw a full rainbow form in the light. It was not in the sky but in my eye, my tear. That's when I learned about patience."

"Floriana is teaching me patience."

"A virtue in short supply," Oslavia said. "And one I surely need this afternoon so I can pose for you for hours."

Toward the end of the day's light, Piero's three sisters tiptoed into the room, placing themselves behind the master to look at his work. "And you lovelies," he said. "Did you win over those handsome priests?"

"Yes," Donata said, "we made them uncomfortable enough so they had to walk by themselves, and when they left, they would not gaze into our eyes."

"I liked the confession I got," Renata said.

"And why is that?" Oslavia asked, looking straight ahead as the pose required and not at Renata.

"Because Father Savonarola said how the children must teach the adults about purity and truth."

"And did he make you cry?" Oslavia asked.

"How did you know?" Renata said.

"That's his specialty. His talent."

"You mean like Master Botticelli's talent is to paint and Master Ficino's talent is to teach Greek, Father Savonarola's talent is to make you cry?" Renata asked.

"He makes you speak of what you didn't even know you wanted to say and then all of a sudden you're crying and then he forgives you and then you feel better."

"That's it exactly!" said Renata. "I want to see him again."

"Enough to live in a convent?" Donata asked.

"I don't want to be locked up," Renata said.

"Imagine being locked up with handsome men around who can never touch you," Margarita said to Renata. "Ever! And you cannot touch them."

"That would be hell on earth, not a doorway to heaven," Donata said.

"There are those of the cloth who don't behave so well," Oslavia said.

"Like the one who soiled Floriana," Renata said.

"How do you know about that?" Sandro asked.

"We all know about it. Floriana told us herself. She said he was like an animal, ugly and hairy, but she did not see his face."

"Father Savonarola could never do that," Renata said.

"That kind of impulse can jump into anyone's body," Oslavia said. "That's why they call it the devil."

CHAPTER FORTY-ONE

Christmas Preparations at the Medici Palace

CLAUDIA FOLLOWED LUCREZIA up and down the palace stairs as the two women wrapped the marble banister with Christmas greens of rosemary and laurel. Lucrezia issued precise, curt directions. Claudia accidentally dropped the greens and ribbons repeatedly. At one point, three of the ropes of greens Claudia had tied onto the banister came loose and drooped. Lucrezia had launched into a lecture of how important patience was to the process of doing things right and that Claudia needed to cultivate it.

"Patience is not one of my talents," Claudia said.

"I promise you. One cannot have children without developing patience. You are never free to think and feel alone in your own heart without concern for them. Even with all the help of nannies and wet nurses, yours is still the milk that spills out at your baby's cry."

"I'm tired all the time now," Claudia said. "My food never seems to digest itself after I eat. There's a constant burning in my chest."

"Keep in your mind's eye the beautiful and healthy baby you're about to see."

"Four long months away."

Claudia sat on the stairs, placing the box that carried the greens at her feet. "You have no patience for me, Lucrezia!"

"I'm trying to train you, girl! I've learned through experience when to shut up, when to sit down, when to make a fuss, and when to rest. I've learned that no one listens to a woman after a certain point, no matter what she knows."

"Who isn't listening?"

Lucrezia stopped her work and sat next to Claudia. "Your Sweet Giuliano doesn't listen. He walks about the city as though he owns it, as though no one's jealous of him. There are those who want the Medicis sent into exile or worse."

"Everyone seems at peace who visits here."

"There's so much below the surface, my naive Claudia, bubbling in a cauldron of greed and envy."

"Lorenzo has won many hearts with his magnetic personality and his lack of snobbery."

"There are those who hate him for that. We are no monarchs, no queens and kings with absolute rule. We are merchants and bankers who did well. Others wait to see what we do. We have power, but it's not official."

"You have banks all over the world. Isn't it true France is in your debt?"

"One of our biggest defaulters! I don't venture into that arena. My job is to maintain our image to the outside, our behavior in front of the public under control and in good taste, so as to keep a sociable peace. To maintain the proper decorum."

"I ruined your 'decorum' plans with my child," Claudia said as she lifted herself up and continued to wrap the banister.

"Better that Giuliano be with you, my sweet, simple Claudia, than be carousing like his older brother in brothels, and rolling about in the countryside with milk maidens."

"How does Clarice stand it? Especially in her current condition?"

"Being married to an oversexed man can have its benefits once you adjust to it, as long as your needs and the needs of your children are met."

"I would die if Giuliano hopped in and out of beds."

"He's tied to you. Count yourself lucky, simple Claudia."

"Why do you keep calling me 'simple'? I do have the ability to form a thought."

"I meant it affectionately."

"It makes me feel as though you view me as the carrier of your grandchild and not a person."

"Maybe that's how you see yourself," Lucrezia said as she got up to assist Claudia's wrapping. "What else do you wish me to see?"

"I'd like you to see what Giuliano loves in me."

"I see your sweetness and simplicity, not in nature, but in life plans and hopes that Giuliano has wanted from the first time my Piero took him to court and the toddler hid under his father's cape. You're his way to escape all of this," she said, motioning to the stairs and into the courtyard. "You keep his life simple and for this he loves you."

"Am I just an object or an animal like a horse on which he can escape?" Claudia asked, stopping her work.

"Sweet Claudia, I'm speaking with spelt mush in my mouth to your ears! I'm praising you for making my son happy and you're taking offense."

"And you, future mother-in-law, how do *you* see me?" Claudia threw her hair off her shoulders, refusing to follow Lucrezia up any more stairs. The greens fell out of her box, trailing onto the steps as the distance between the two women widened and Lucrezia continued to wrap. A wave of exhaustion passed through Claudia's body. She sat on the stairs. The engagement certificate safely hidden under her bed had given Claudia more confidence than usual to speak her mind. "I'm no good with my hands today."

Once again Lucrezia sat beside Claudia. "I see you as a gift to us all because of the happiness you bring to Giuliano and thereby to each of us and in the good mother I know you'll be."

"But what about me myself? Do you like me or hate me?"

"I like your directness, your devotion, but I hate your family background," Lucrezia said.

Claudia's face contorted to keep her tears from dripping onto her cheeks.

"Your ignorance of this life is not your fault. Not a moral issue. Not stupidity. A matter of experience. Dry your eyes and send your love and goodness to your unborn baby and to your heart's desire, *my baby*, Giuliano. I'm here to protect and love you just as you are, and to nurture you into this world. For, dear Claudia, you'll be ushered into it, like it or not."

Lucrezia stood back from Claudia so she could look into her eyes. "Stop those tears, and help me dress this place for our company. Without Sandro here to do the decorations on the banisters and hallways, I can hardly keep my head up with pride. We're going to introduce you formally to our visitors tonight. No masks. And when I say the time is right, your public engagement will follow. We don't want you to be a weepy, swollen wench, now do we?"

Claudia shook her head and wiped her eyes. "I think it's going to be a boy," she said with a proud smile. "In fact, I know it is going to be a boy!"

"How wonderful," Lucrezia said, "and we'll call him—"

"Giulio," both women said at the same time. Even though the two sparring women had spoken in agreement, Lucrezia's naming of the child made Claudia feel as though a hand had reached inside her womb to take control.

CHAPTER FORTY-TWO

The Medici Christmas

RESSED IN HIS FINEST boots and tunic, Sandro glided down the streets of Florence on his way to the Medici Palace. Winter winds swirled about him carrying sand and dirt up to his face. The cold air had frozen and dulled the usual putrid smell of rotting debris that covered the streets of the city; a dusting of snow masked imperfections lying beneath it. To Sandro's eyes, the world sparkled. And with his painting progressing well, his declarations of love toward Floriana spoken and received, and her safely sheltered from harm at Graziella's, Sandro's life sparkled too.

His fingertips felt for Floriana's tiny Star of David, which he now wore around his neck. As he held on to its sharp points, he remembered his last visit to the palace and the creative turmoil he had suffered then. *Now I'm at a pinnacle doing my best work,* he thought. In love—even though it be a love ill-defined, it was a love, for sure.

The closer he came to the entrance on Via Cavour, the more the memory of Lorenzo's sarcastic jest about Floriana's belly returned. *How dare he!* And after he and Floriana had had their first time alone at the cave. He decided at that moment he would not allow any bullying words to touch him or to ruin his good mood.

As he passed in front of San Marco's Church, he crossed himself and prayed for balance. *Please, God, fill me with love and appreciation and take away my fears.* When he turned the next corner, he saw a band of soldiers surrounding the walls of the palace. Not only at the entrance, but apparently winding its way, rope-like, around all four sides of the building. These guards were not the same he had encountered in the fall. This group was much greater in number, clearly mercenaries; he could tell by their uniforms and threatening voices spoken in a foreign language. Strains of music came out of the windows, trumpets blared in short spurts, so it was clear no emergency was in progress.

As he approached the door he saw the guards were laughing and carousing. After all, it was Christmas Eve. His sparkling mood and confidence in the face of Lorenzo's unpredictability—plummeted when a guard put his hand in front of Sandro's face and shouted, "Wait!"

After sending his name up through another guard, Sandro adjusted his cape, his hat, then pulled the star again from inside his shirt and held on to it while he stood shivering for five minutes until Lucrezia herself pulled him inside. She hugged him, then stepped back to look him over from head to toe. "What took you so long?"

"Your guards are ferocious. I almost gave up and turned around! There are three times the number you had watching the palace the last time I was here!"

"Dangerous times," Lucrezia said.

"Let's hope your enemy is not one of your own, this very moment guarding your palace."

"Don't say that, Sandro. We're prey to the envy of the lowest of the low and the highest of the high."

"Why don't you move the children to one of the villas on the outskirts of the city? Piero has more rooms than he knows what to do with and the cousins could get to know each other out there."

"That's like inviting the enemy in the front door and giving them the key to everything we own here in Florence, Sandro. No, we watch and wait and we are careful," Lucrezia said, pulling him up the stairs toward Lorenzo's Salon of the Intellectuals.

"Even my father has heard something at the tannery not meant for his ears," Sandro said.

"Tell Lorenzo," Lucrezia said. "He thinks everything I say is a product of my imagination and fear. He loves you and respects you. And he misses you. He'll listen to you."

"And I miss him too, though the work is going well. You'd be proud."

Lucrezia led Sandro into the room of Neo Platonists, where Lorenzo, his hand on a cane, brooded in the back of the room while Ficino, engaged with a Kabbalist of the moment, Rebbe Abramo, stood at the front.

"A Jew on Christmas Eve?" Sandro whispered to Lorenzo, who pulled him close but shushed him at the same time.

"He's about to tell one of his stories," Lorenzo said.

The old rebbe stood in front of the crowd of men.

"Thank you, Prince Lorenzo, for inviting me here to shed some light on the evening," the old man said.

"I'm no prince. I'm your student, so do teach me and the rest of us," Lorenzo answered, waving his arm about the room in an all-inclusive gesture.

"First, before I tell the story," Rebbe Abramo said, "I must explain why a Jew is honored to be here on the eve of your Savior's birth. In Kabbalah we do not exclude anyone for his beliefs. Instead, we encourage all to move toward the light of the Creator. We all have such a light dwelling within, and because we meet tonight as equals moving toward the light, we are all one."

"Even the enemies?" Lorenzo asked.

"They are moving toward the light, but must remove the darkness first. But that's another discussion."

"Do begin," Lorenzo said, "I consider your stories gifts to us for the whole coming year."

"Once, there was a very busy man who suffered from gout in his feet," the seer began.

"Sounds like me," interjected Lorenzo.

"Many suffer and few are cured," said the wise man. "But now, if I may continue . . ." and he waited until the voices and movements in the room settled into silence.

"There was this merchant with painful gout in his feet. Walking had become more and more difficult. But he had heard of a wise man many miles from his home who was supposed to be able to heal anyone of anything merely by his touch. So the man limped his way to the wise man's house. When he arrived, the wise man's wife ushered him into the front sitting room where there were beautiful soft chairs and pillows. The merchant was told to make himself comfortable, the wise man was still busy, but would be there eventually.

"The merchant soon fell into a deep sleep and began to dream. He saw in his dream a large clearing in the middle of a town he did not recognize. Dark horses drew dark wooden carts into the space and each cart had a sign on it. One said, 'adultery with the wet nurse.' Another said, 'unfair interest rates on loans.' Another, 'hoarding money away from the family and wife.' As the merchant looked deeper into his dream, he realized that these were sins he had committed in his life. Out of each dark cart stepped a dark angel. The parade of dark angels now climbed onto a platform in the center of the square and stepped onto one side of a huge scale.

"Next, white carts came with signs on them also. 'Contributions to the poor,' 'caring for old Auntie,' 'feeding the workers on their holidays.' And there were all the wonderful things the merchant had done in his life listed on the sides of those carts, and out of those carts stepped the white angels and they climbed the stairs and placed themselves onto the other side of the balance. But, alas, there just were not enough light angels to equal the weight of the dark angels. The merchant in his dream could see that his sins had far outweighed his good works and he could see he was headed for hellfire in his afterlife. This was, he realized, his day of judgment.

"Then, unexpectedly, gray carts came into the space. Each cart had a sign on it of all the suffering the merchant had endured. 'The loss of his first born to the Plague.' His wife's sterility after that; his father's early death, and so on. Each of the merchant's sufferings was represented by the gray angels who approached the scale. Each gray angel walked up to the dark angel's side of the scale and removed one of the dark angels and took it away. Soon the scales began to change. The merchant in the dream understood that each of his sufferings had the power to reduce his sins. The dream ended as the wise man tapped the sleeping merchant on the shoulder.

"'And how can I help you?' the wise man asked.

"'Just show me the door,' the merchant answered as he walked away, suddenly grateful for the gout, which by way of the dream's wisdom, was helping him get closer to heaven."

Raucous applause followed. When it died down, Lorenzo shook his cane above his head so all could see and told the group, "Alas, I should be grateful for the gout that's got me limping tonight. Now I know the light of forgiveness will shine ever bright!"

Everyone cheered Lorenzo's interpretation of the rabbi's story.

As the crowd moved upstairs toward the music and dancing, and Lorenzo and Sandro were the only two left in the room, Lorenzo turned to his friend. "Enough stories. We're in danger. And when they strike I would like to have you by my side."

"It's you who sent me away. Now you want me back for what? Distraction? Protection? I'm no soldier, Lorenzo."

"I miss our times together," Lorenzo said. "My destiny is to be a target. A target of envy as well as love."

"The love the people of Florence have for you and Giuliano and your whole family is a protection stronger than any mercenary at your door."

"Come," said Lorenzo. "I'm in no dancing mood. I need to walk and talk without anyone listening. Wait for me by the balcony."

Sandro watched Lorenzo hobble up the stairs while he waited below by the railing that overlooked the central courtyard. More than five hundred candles illuminated small patches of green from the gardens.

The water fountain in the center still bubbled. On it floated wreaths of myrrh. Aromas of all the past Christmases caressed Sandro's senses with their perfume.

Although he was relieved by Lorenzo's welcome, Sandro was not at ease. As he stared into the courtyard, the burning candles reminded him of the candles he and Floriana had watched together. Lost in the memories of that night, he was startled when a priest in Dominican robes approached him.

"God bless," the priest said, then made the sign of the cross on his heart. "Are you ready?"

"Things really are dangerous!" Sandro said when he realized the cleric standing before him was Lorenzo in disguise.

WITH THE PACE OF TWO OLD MEN, Lorenzo and Sandro moved arm in arm along the Arno toward Forte Belvedere. A sharp wind cut through the layers of their wraps. When they reached the top, Lorenzo looked down at the city. The full moon illuminated the Duomo's cupola.

"Do you believe the fable the rebbe told?" Lorenzo asked.

"I believe good things happen to bad people and bad things happen to good people and then they are cursed by them for the rest of their lives."

"Who are you talking about?"

"I'm talking about Floriana. You saw her for a moment at Castello. An innocent girl. Through no fault of her own, raped and left for conversion at my sister's convent. Now with child, she's cowering from the constant fear the priest who spilled his seed in her is going to come back to harm her again."

"And who's this wolf in Christ's clothing?"

"She didn't see his face. I've put the story into my painting."

"You've painted a rape?"

"No. I've taken the act and turned the villain into a creature who impregnates all the earth with seed so we can have spring over and over again. Just as she is doing with her adversity, turning it into a mission to mother the child she carries. Out of darkness is coming the light of spring."

"You're such a romantic, Sandro. To turn a rape into a celebration of spring!"

"Why not turn our adversities into something beautiful rather than be silenced by them?"

"So you believe that if you illustrate this cruel act as the wrath of Nature in your painting you will have taken the poison out of the actual rape?"

"Not exactly. By confining the act within the height and width of a painting, I change its name and nature."

"And what is the name of the painting?"

"I have not named it. I've painted one third of it, and I'm not sure what other stories I will add to this one."

"At your whim, then?" Lorenzo asked.

"No. The whim of the One who fills my brushes with ideas that I paint through a fog. I am not ever sure what subject I'll entertain in it next. No patron dictates, and no models are waiting in the wings—though, don't mention this to Piero, but I do believe I'm going to incorporate his three sisters into it as well."

"Those spoiled, scrawny chicks?"

"They're blossoming, at least Donata and Margarita."

There was a rustling in some nearby bushes. Still quick on his feet if fear summoned, Lorenzo leapt toward the sound and opened the bushes with his knife raised for protection.

A fat raccoon scrambled away. "I'm looking behind every tree, expecting someone to strike me down at any moment. No pope with his illegitimate pen of bastards is going to defeat us! He gives his nephews cities and states as though they were peaches and apples or toys. Who is he to say I can't appoint a prelate in my own territory?"

"That's the spirit. That's the Lorenzo I know," Sandro said.

"I'm going to see the pope myself and work this out with him face to face, tell him to call off his henchmen."

"And when do you propose this?"

"Soon. Once this gout attack settles down. My father and his father before him have both been pious men. We've supported the churches in Florence. We've sent gifts to Rome. I just couldn't allow that greedy pope to buy the town of Imola."

"But he did anyway."

"I'll offer him an opportunity he won't reject."

"What opportunity?"

"A celebration, perhaps for the whole city, and with Sixtus IV as honored guest. Let him christen the new child that Claudia is carrying. Let him perform the wedding."

"And you think he'll come and do this?"

"If Giuliano had married a Pazzi, we would be assured of our place for a couple more generations, but the good will we bought with my marriage to Clarice has worn thin. Her Orsini blood is no longer in favor with the pope."

"Let's enjoy this winter night and pray that the Savior's birth we celebrate tomorrow will illuminate your way," Sandro offered, but Lorenzo ignored the sentiment.

While they walked back toward the palace, Sandro weighed whether or not to tell Lorenzo what news he intended to bring from his father, Mariano. To stay silent would be a betrayal, and so he began, "My father has heard things in the tannery. Mercenaries. Chatting, talking, and laughing. Montesecco is here, Lorenzo. My father says he's a professional assassin. And there's more: the pope turned his back to some soldiers in his presence who were speaking of acts of violence. Instead of forbidding it, he said 'do what you must.' Shall I go on?"

"Not now, Sandro. You were right. You're not a soldier. I must get back to the palace to introduce Claudia officially to our guests. I'll announce, too, my plan to have the pope officiate as our special guest. And I'll hand deliver the invitation to him myself as soon as I'm able. I'll want you to accompany me there, Sandro."

"I'm no soldier, and I'm also no diplomat. The painting must proceed," Sandro said. "There's a momentum I can't lose. When you released me to Piero, I felt like a pawn, a piece of property, but I rose above that and am in debt to you for having done it. Now the fruits are ripening. I'm creating a legacy for all of us. Don't ask me to interrupt it."

"A trip to Rome with me now could benefit you, Sandro. It could lead to some commissions in the future." Lorenzo stood still and turned to face Sandro. "When I call you, if I do call you, you'll know it is an emergency and you must come to me. You owe me that much!"

CHAPTER FORTY-THREE

Graziella's Attachment to Floriana Changes

RAZIELLA HESITATED behind the thick carpet wall that separated Floriana's sleeping area from her own. She could hear her father, Manfredo, reciting his morning prayers in a distant part of the house. A faint aroma of the sweet apricot jam she had left by Floriana's bed still hung in the air. That morning Graziella had awakened startled, finding her hand rubbing her woman's place and herself breathless and overwhelmed with images of Floriana. The familiarity of sisters that they had developed over the first short weeks since their meeting would no longer be so easy.

Hiding behind the carpet wall, Graziella searched her heart to find her way between desire and affection. *Pure unselfish love draws to itself its own; it does not seek or demand,* she told herself. If she did not speak it, it would not be real. She heard Floriana stirring behind the curtain.

Unaware of Graziella's nearness, Floriana spoke to her unborn. "Good morning, Sister. I'll call you Sister, for you will surely be a girl and we'll soon be running and playing together." She hummed to the baby inside her as she moved around the room tidying her covers and arranging pillows on her bed. As she stood sideways looking in a mirror at the profile of her body, she said to herself, "How can I have them both at the same time? Full of life and yet my heart is a desert without Sandro!"

Graziella cleared her throat to signal her presence, then moved the carpet wall aside to enter.

"Now she's safe at last," Floriana said, looking at her belly, and then into the face of Graziella, who averted her gaze, "and yet an emptiness remains."

Floriana motioned for Graziella to come sit on the end of the bed.

"Shall we ask her if she wants to bathe?" Graziella said.

"You're encouraging the child to control me, Graziella, when it should be I who set the rules!" Floriana said.

"Who will answer my question?"

"Come closer. Put your ear to my belly and ask her if she wants to bathe. If she moves, that means yes. If she sleeps still, that means no."

Graziella laid her head on Floriana's belly.

"Lower." Floriana lifted all her bed clothing out of the way. "Now ask the question."

"Little princess of gold, shall we wash your mother or not?" Graziella asked.

Floriana's belly changed shape as a little knee or elbow made its way around her womb. "You see," Floriana said, "she hears everything and already has opinions."

"So bath it is!" Graziella held her hand out to help Floriana off the bed.

"You can sponge me down. I'm too exhausted for a full bath."

"Baby Princess wills a true bath," Graziella said with her new resolve to distance her longing. "You must wrap yourselves and walk outside to our bathhouse. The small fire inside it has been heating the water for you all morning."

Floriana did not move.

"Are those tears on your pillow, sweet Floriana? Aren't you happy to be safe with us, your own people?"

"Truly I am, but I miss Sandro. Without his help I might have been an unwilling convert sealed up forever in that convent."

"And instead, you're the inspiration for a Botticelli painting, and we are honored to have you!"

Floriana made no move toward Graziella.

"He's forgotten me. I know it," Floriana said.

"It was you who decided to leave him."

"And it was the right thing to do. You told me so yourself. Haven't you ever loved someone you couldn't have?"

"I did not live the life of a typical woman groomed for marriage. With no son, no brother, my father made me his heir, deciding long ago I would inherit all he could teach me, not only about business, but also about the mysteries in life."

"Is that why you have never loved another, Graziella? Out of loyalty to him?"

"I did not say I've never loved another. I don't want to talk about it at this moment. I have not yearned to care for a man. Especially after all the mysteries I've learned, it would be hard to be subservient—to watch the prayer, instead of perform it myself." *And besides, my sweet and silky maiden*, she wanted to say, *I'd sooner sleep beside you than any hairy man!*

"Maybe someday you will tell me who it was," Floriana said, raising herself to her feet and throwing off her nightshirt. She stood naked, waiting for Graziella to prepare her for the bath.

Graziella averted her eyes from the redness of Floriana's swollen nipples and the pale velvet of the young woman's flesh. "Wrap yourself in these blankets because the bath is outside and you'll need protection from the cold."

"What about you? Won't you be cold?" Floriana said as she covered herself.

"Only for a moment. You'll be sitting long in the tub and then must cover yourself when you come out."

As the two women made their way through a rocky yard, then up a slight hill to a hut with a red tile roof, Graziella said, "Perhaps in the convent you forgot your Jewish roots enough to want someone outside our faith."

Floriana answered, "Oslavia rescued me when I was delirious from starvation and brought me back to myself. Whatever charity she possesses is fine for me. I don't care whether it is Christian or Jewish or heathen. It's the same with Sandro's concern for me."

Graziella continued to lead Floriana forward along the path. Steam rose from a hole in the roof's center. Graziella opened a small door, and led Floriana up several stairs attached to the inside of the shed's walls. These stairs circled around a huge cauldron on loose stone slabs spanning across a pit filled with logs that were now glowing embers. At the top of the stairs was a wooden platform level with the top of the cauldron. Steam exited through a large window and an even larger opening in the hut's roof into the cold winter air.

"You're sure you're not a witch about to cook me alive?" Floriana asked. "I had nightmares of such things when I was a small child."

Graziella, not her usual playful self that morning, did not respond to Floriana's teasing and instead flashed on the scenes from her erotic dream. She led Floriana to the platform and helped her remove the blankets. "You tip yourself over the side, head first," Graziella said. "It's easy."

"Easy for you," Floriana said as she watched Graziella sprinkle rose petals and lilac oil into the bathwater.

"Once you enter, the extra water spills over the top and puts out the logs so you won't burn your feet. For the first few moments, keep your feet off the bottom and hold the sides. When you're ready to come out, ring this bell and I'll come back to help you."

Enticed by the sweet-smelling water, Floriana sat on the edge of the warm clay cauldron and let herself slide into it. She surfaced immediately with her hair dripping as she held on to the sides.

The coals sizzled and steamed and Graziella said, "Excellent. The fire is out. Let yourself sink to the bottom slowly and rest and relax. All is fine now."

WHEN FLORIANA HEARD the small door shut, leaving her alone inside the bath, she closed her eyes as her hips sank to the bottom of the clay cauldron. Gradually she released her arms from the side to float in the water.

Never in her life had she been inside a bath like this one. The rose petal perfume added to her rapture until she drifted off into a sleepy haze. Half-conscious, she felt a thrusting inside her body. As the sensation of the attack by the young monk revisited her, she jerked awake, spilling more of the hot water over the edges, causing more of the wood underneath to sizzle and pop. She looked up. Small snowflakes fell through the air and dropped onto her face and around the bath. She held the sides of her belly and felt a wave of tears overtake her. She was tired of allowing anyone to see her cry and had determined she would control herself, but inside the bath she let herself go. She felt torn into so many pieces: eagerness for the baby growing inside her. Longing for Sandro. The loss of her father. Anger and rage at the faceless monk. A yearning, too, for Oslavia, whose compassion had given her a chance for freedom.

Alone in the cauldron of heat, she wished for a transformation to bring the disparate parts of her into harmony.

She closed her eyes, determined to allow sensations or scenes from her attack to pass through her rather than to turn away from them. She was cooking all the parts of herself: bitter and sweet, salty and sour, with enough of each to balance. Just as these jewel-like snowflakes could rest on her warmed flesh, so, too, could she house in her body and mind opposites in nature. Balance, order, calm. The tops of her hands had snowflakes dropping on them. To warm them she plunged them into her soup, which quickly lost its heat. Not sure how to pull herself out, she rang the bell. Soon the warm blankets Graziella had kept near the coals and wood fuel were wrapped around her.

Graziella led her into her own chambers, dried her hair, and then dressed her in a heavily beaded gown. The beads formed geometric patterns in gold and deep reds. Graziella placed a matching tiara on Floriana's head. From the middle, a Star of David hung onto her forehead. "It was my mother's. We've kept it in the family for special occasions like this."

"This is a special occasion? The New Year?" Floriana asked, still carrying the warmth and calm from the bath and her thoughts of balance within her.

"We are going to offer Hebrew names for your baby today and to bless her or him for protection during these last three months."

"I've already named her," Floriana said.

"But you must have a Hebrew name ready for a boy and girl since we don't know which it will be."

"Doesn't naming happen after the baby is born?"

"It does, but given these circumstances, my father said that preparing the names now is better protection so when the child is born he'll—"

"She! I know it's going to be a girl!"

"Well, this way, she'll have a name and a welcoming family awaiting her."

Dressed in beads and silks, Floriana made her way into Manfredo's chambers. The same question that had challenged her in the bath returned, so she asked the old man how to rise above the fear and hate that had so often descended upon her at the thought of the child who grew and moved inside her, a child conceived out of violence.

"We must dance with what comes to us," Manfredo instructed her. "We must move into it with illumination. Without regret or remorse, resentment or anger, for those emotions bind us to the past." Each moment, he told her, she had the choice of which to follow—the darkness or the light. If she was to love this child she must love the other soul that created it. She must move to the light freed of all hatred and fear and only cultivate the best in herself and her child.

"We shall name him Uriel if he is a boy because that means light," Manfredo said. "Devorah of the Palms if she is a girl. In our Zohar, Devorah was the one who was able to shine her light on all without judgment. Through your child, your love will bring you the light and clarity you'll need to illuminate your way."

"Devorah of the Palms," Floriana whispered to herself and to the baby as she walked out of Manfredo's section of the house. "Devorah of the Palms," she repeated to her unborn. "May you teach me how to walk toward the light and free me from any rush to judgment."

CHAPTER FORTY-FOUR

A New Doll and a Miracle for the New Year

ONE BY ONE, Piero handed Poppi each doll to dust its parts, and then she handed each back to him to place on one of the many shelves of his secret doll closet at Villa di Castello.

"We haven't made any new ones in so long. Perhaps we should do some infants to replicate the two babies we're expecting," Piero said.

"Two? There are three if you count Lorenzo's newest arrival, Contessina. Better to wait and know they have survived the birth, that mother and child and father are all fine," Poppi said.

"We don't know the father of Floriana's."

"I don't have a clue," she said, "unless it could be that beady-eyed priest who visited the day you took her to Manfredo's. He has an odd personality—intense. He brought poor Renata to tears, but she loved it!"

"Imagine you! Let's do him! I'll do his face. You can sew the robe. What was his name?"

"Savonarola. His two handsome companions melted in the presence of your beautiful sisters, who teased them mercilessly."

"Tell me about his face. What distinguishing characteristic does he have along with the eyes?"

"His nose. His nose is like a large hook."

"A hook? If I make it too large out of this simple clay it could break off. Let me think how I can make it stronger."

"His nose looks almost like a beak," she said, "and with those beady eyes he could be a rodent or a bird."

"Rodent is too lowly. But a bird does have lofty possibilities. And I like the idea of how the bird eats with the beak. Tiny little pieces of its food. What kind of bird would he be, Poppi?"

"An eagle? A crow? No, a falcon! He would be a falcon because, though his nose is strong and sharp, he carries himself with a straight spine, head high as he looks around, taking in every detail, and then goes in for the kill—with that beak."

"Bring me the ailing falcon that was wounded on the hunt," Piero said. "Is he still living?"

Poppi sped down the steps to retrieve the bird. A few moments later, she returned with a red cloth wrapped about something. "He was already beginning to decompose, and the others in the cage had picked his eyes out," she said, putting the bundle on the table.

"Dare I look? Put him over there, by the window, please."

Poppi moved it from the table to the windowsill, where she unwrapped the creature with most of its feathers disheveled. When he gazed upon the bird, Piero's head twitched more, as it did in any stressful moment.

"It's dead, Piero. Nothing to fear."

"Does it resemble this Savonarola enough? Is the beak the right one?"

"It's not only the right one," Poppi said, "it's the only one we have on hand unless you want to slaughter something healthy. And look, his mates have done most of the work for you. His head hangs by a thread. You'll have to replace the eyes."

Piero pulled a glove over his hand, then touched what was left of the bird's head.

"I'll hold the body," Poppi said. "You hold the head."

All the while, Piero's head twitched and his breathing was shallow as he sucked air through his teeth.

The bird's head separated from the body easily. Poppi placed it onto her master's gloved palm.

"It resembles him too well," she said. "It's as though he were here among us at this very moment."

Just then the dogs released their high-pitched yelps. Poppi looked out the window. "Speak of the devil, that fiery Dominican has returned once again!"

"I tell you, Poppi, we are making magic here. Whenever we make a new doll, the human model appears. How strange was that unfinished Bandini?"

"I'll not forget. Now you can view today's subject firsthand and this will make the face even more authentic."

"You go downstairs," Piero said. "I'll watch him from the window to see if he holds himself with a straight spine, head high as he looks around, taking in every detail. Then he goes for the kill with that beak! He's quite thin and small, isn't he?" Piero spoke to the air, because Poppi had already left to run down the hall, down the steps, and through the inner courtyard, to meet the priest with the beady eyes at the great door.

As Piero watched from the window, he noticed that the priest made no attempt to befriend the yelping dogs. They soon gave up and ran away from him back toward some winter crows that fed on the lawn.

"Perfect timing," Piero said. With Floriana gone, and Sandro still not back from Florence, and the usual routines suspended by the celebratory days of the new year, Piero would have hours to work on his hobby without interruption. Sandro had inspired him to consider displaying his handiwork in a great cabinet someday instead of hiding it from view as he had done for too many years.

A bird's beak for a nose excited him. He had never seen such a thing. The fact the idea came directly from his own imagination caused Piero to puff with pride. He pulled the glove off his hand, covered the bird's carcass with the red cloth, and turned to examine himself in the mirror.

"Stop it! Stop the shaking. I demand it!" Piero told his reflection. He placed his hands over his ears to hold his head still. He took a deep breath and exhaled slowly so the twitching diminished. He sprayed some perfume under his armpits and onto his crotch. Even though it was a winter day, Piero often perspired, and a sour sweetness emanated from him. He pulled the curtains to hide the doll collection, then waited a moment to release a long burst of flatulence before heading to meet the inspiration for his bird-beak doll.

ALTHOUGH POPPI HAD INVITED GEROME to sit in the parlor, he paced around the room. He stopped in front of the painting as though he were about to lift the cloth, but did not.

When Piero walked in, Savonarola turned to him and gave him one of his most piercing stares.

Piero's twitch worsened. He hit himself on the side of the head as though it were a tiny child or pet he was disciplining.

"And why do you slap yourself, Master Piero?" Gerome asked. He had turned away from the painting to focus on Piero.

Piero's head kept moving. When he opened his mouth to speak, all the years of pretending no one cared about his tic melted away and he felt as though this priest with a nose, yes, a beak of a nose, was seeing his twitching head in a way no one had ever seen it before—without any revulsion, without the need to look away, or to pretend it wasn't happening.

"Come here," Savonarola said. "Come and sit and I will pray for your nervous head. Together we can bring Jesus Christ into this room and heal you."

"Imagine you!" Piero said. "I've had this affliction since I was a young child. All the doctors have given up on me. Since my brain is working fine and I have speech and all my other faculties, people have accepted me this way."

"And no one has ever teased you?"

Piero's eyes filled with tears and his head twitched more than he had ever remembered.

"Come and sit," insisted Savonarola. "If God has taken away my stuttering, he can take away your shaking."

"You stuttered?"

"Since childhood. And it grew worse as I got older and worse still in the monastery. But I was healed and it only comes back in rare moments."

Savonarola approached Piero, who had resisted the invitation to sit in his own chair. The young priest placed his hands on the sides of Piero's head and slowly pressed them against the temples. He led Piero to the chair, never once removing his hands and never once taking his eyes off the face of the young man as he guided him into the chair.

"Now we both must close our eyes and pray," Savonarola said.

Piero felt warmth coming from the palms of Gerome's hands. The heat penetrated through his temples, circling his eyes, filling the cavities in his head with a burning sensation.

"Drop your jaw and open your mouth. Relax your tongue," Gerome ordered. "Let it hang out of your mouth."

"Father Gerome, sit, sit," Poppi said as she watched all of this, then pulled a small chair behind Savonarola so his eyes might be level with Piero's. He sat without removing his hands from Piero's head.

"I'm going to pray now. It's going to be a prayer you have never before heard, but you must open your mind and your heart to it," Gerome said, "and you must pray with me. Are you ready?"

Piero nodded, but Savonarola jerked his head still. "I'm sending Jesus Christ our Lord directly through my hands into your head this moment. I call on you Almighty of the mighty. Shepherd. Lead this soul to salvation. Carpenter. Build his character to reflect your divine nature. Servant of the poor and weak that You are, come now my liege, allow Your heavenly light to descend and fill all of his graces in the light of transfusion and transfiguration. Stop his shaking NOW! I implore You so he too can be your soldier." As Piero's head drooped, Gerome loosened his grip. Piero's breathing slowed, and as he slept, his head made one last twitch and then fell lower onto his chest.

"Sleep, my kind and good young master. May the light of the Father, the Son, and the Holy Spirit light your way through darkness and may the force of the Lord keep your head lifted high and strong with no tremor from His force either from the top of your head to the bottoms of your feet. I say it is done!"

Gerome sat facing the sleeping Piero for several minutes, then said, "Dream yourself tall and strong with no shaking or infirmity. Only with the willingness and passion to join the army of Christ."

While Piero snored, a slight bubble of flatulence released itself.

"You'll never rouse him," Poppi said. "Once he sleeps he is deep into his dream life and cannot be roused except by all his dogs barking at him at once."

"Scoop up one of his canine companions and bring it to me," Savonarola ordered.

Outside, Poppi grabbed the first beast that made his way into her arms. She was back before the smell of Piero's latest emanation had dispersed.

"Eeyuuwee," Poppi said as she entered the room.

"This smell is a good sign," Savonarola said. "He's expelling his fears and his mistaken thinking. Bring me the pup."

As soon as the dog lay in Savonarola's arms it became docile. "Go to your master and lick his face and eyelids to awaken him slowly, please," he told the dog as though it were a small intelligent child. He placed it on Piero's ample belly. The dog made muted whimpering sounds and licked Piero's nose, then his cheeks. Piero snored. His head lay undisturbed on his chest, but soon the left eye opened. He embraced his small dog as the other eye opened and a smile broke across his face.

"I am so calm and at peace," he said. "And my head is still. Totally still. What did you do?"

"I did only what can be done with one who is willing to be healed," Savonarola said. "I called on the physician of your soul, Jesus Christ, and implored him to heal you. Did you not hear me?"

"Only a tremendous heat from your hands went into my head. Then I fell asleep," Piero said. He turned to Poppi. "He's healed me!"

"No. You have heard and felt the power of the Lord and allowed your natural state to be restored. You were willing, and so it worked," Savonarola said.

"You've cured me!" shouted Piero. "You've cured me!"

"I've quieted your mind to allow God to work through you in His perfection. Know that the shaking is caused by doubts—the work of the devil—that cause you to hesitate between what you are called by God to do and what you think your rich world wants you to do. Stop when the shaking starts and always go with God's voice within you."

"But what if I don't hear God's voice?"

"Stop what you are doing. Drop to your knees and pray wherever you find yourself, and the trembling, which is a trembling between right and wrong, will go away. It is God's way of getting your attention."

The dogs outside yelped and the little one on Piero's lap jumped off and scratched at the front door until Poppi opened it.

"You've been missed," she said when she saw Sandro and his assistant, Filippino, about to enter as the little dog scampered outside. "The place is crowding up once again."

"Who else is here?" Sandro asked.

"The fiery priest from Ferrara, Savonarola, is back."

"Asking more questions?"

"He's just performed a healing on your master."

"And that being?"

"His twitching head. Stilled and calm for the first time since he was a young child."

"That qualifies as a miracle, wouldn't you say?" Sandro asked, walking into the room as Savonarola stood up.

"I see our Ferrarian is back," Sandro said, offering a slight bow to him.

"My twitching head, Sandro! Stilled and calm for the first time since I was a boy," Piero said. He stood and walked around the room with an easy posture, head held high and steady.

Piero sat again with hands resting on his legs and a sweet smile on his face. He turned his head tentatively as though the twitching might return if he moved too fast. "Can you believe it?" he said to Sandro.

"We asked and we received," Gerome said in a modest tone, then looking at Piero, "We did it together."

"I've asked so many times, but never have I received like this," Piero said, "so it must be your magic."

"Please don't use that word! Magic defies belief in the ordinary. What we did here is very ordinary. We restored Piero to his ordinary self and scraped the scab of longing off his soul."

Gerome placed his arm around the seated Piero. "You're quite young, so there was only a thin layer of the scum."

"Whatever you want to call it," Piero said, "I'm indebted to you. You're always welcome here."

"The last time I was here I didn't feel so welcome," Gerome said.

"That's because you were probing into personal matters," Sandro said, "about those whose whereabouts we wish to protect."

"And who was that?" Piero said, still in a daze of calm.

"Think hard, my dear patron!" Sandro was not going to volunteer a name.

"Oh, yes. But this man of such strong faith could only help her," Piero said.

"It's a matter of honor, not of faith. And I'm happy for you in your newfound calm," Sandro said, glaring at Piero so that he might not say another word about Floriana. "Perhaps this powerful healer knows how to heal the Medici household from its fears. There's a definite rumble in the air of an imminent attack on the family."

"Are you sure?" Piero asked.

Sandro retold the news from his father, the sense of fear in the palace. "There was talk of the pope being behind the plot."

"And his army of clerics too," added Gerome.

"I hadn't heard about that part," Sandro said, directing his attention to Gerome.

"After almost dying, when the healing of my stutter was given to me, I happened to meet along the road to Bologna a small group of clerics camping out in the field with some unlikely partners. They tried to enlist me to join them to bring down the Medicis. When I refused they attacked me."

"Their names!" Sandro said. "You must remember!"

"I was getting my strength back. I don't remember their names but I would recognize their faces. The younger one had a hand like a claw. But I can tell you, from my own travels since, that the one who rules the little town of Imola is involved."

"The pope's nephew Riario!" Sandro said.

"I was warned by him never to show my face in Imola when I refused his sacrament cloths with the pope's insignia all over them. Instead he gave me all the threadbare ones which had been washed and scrubbed by the knuckles of the humble. I chose those over the pope's issue, and he took it as an affront."

"You must warn Lorenzo. Tell him what you've seen and heard," Sandro said.

"If he'll see me."

"I'll write a note for you. Give it to the guard at the door. They have soldiers surrounding the palace night and day. I'll explain you have an important message for him and his mother, Lucrezia. She should be present. Actually, on second thought, don't include her. Just go see Lorenzo and tell him you are from God directly and you have bypassed the pope. I'll write to him of how you have cured Piero. Maybe you can heal his feet—swollen and crippled from gout."

"I'll leave immediately, collect my two companions to assist me."

"We still do not know what inspired your visit today?" Poppi said.

"What I had thought was bringing me here is no longer relevant."

"A curiosity about the well-being of the young Jewish woman?" Poppi asked.

"We have not seen her for weeks," Piero said, adding, "Perhaps she's reunited with her mother in Ferrara."

Sandro was surprised by this cooperation though distressed by its inaccuracies since all knew Floriana was, like Piero himself, an orphan. Yet, Sandro noted with amazement, Piero's words were spoken without the slightest shake or twitch of the head.

"Shall we share a meal together before you leave?" Piero asked.

"I know now why I have been led here today," Gerome said as he placed his arm around Piero while turning his falcon gaze onto Sandro. "No time for food, only time enough to wait for you, Master Botticelli, to write that letter."

CHAPTER FORTY-FIVE

Savonarola Meets Lorenzo

AS HE MOUNTED the interior staircase of the Medici Palace, the chill on Gerome Savonarola's feet lessened. A strong voice with high, raspy tones beckoned him into the room from which he had heard the sounds of a lyre. He removed the hood from his cape, gathering up his robe to enter.

Once inside Lorenzo's chambers, Gerome saw fire blazing in the primary hearth and felt a blanket of warmth enfold him. At least twenty boxes of glowing coals surrounded the perimeter of the room, each one giving off its own spurt of heat. Gerome had heard the voice but still could not see Lorenzo anywhere.

"Over here," the voice said. "On my bed. Pull aside the curtain. Bring over a stool so I can see this famous healer of my twitching baby cousin."

"He healed himself," Savonarola said as he opened the curtains on one side and gazed at Lorenzo, then continued, "for he had the faith he could be healed."

Gerome had never seen a face as out of the ordinary as Lorenzo's. His nose was as long as Gerome's nose was hooked, but Lorenzo's had the opposite nature in that it was flattened and close to his face, as though the bridge of it had been crushed and all the fullness exploded at the tip like the opening spread of a trumpet flower. Below the nose, however, Gerome was surprised by Lorenzo's jutting chin and broad, welcoming smile—an expression he had not anticipated from someone who was supposed to be suffering so much pain. Gazing at Lorenzo, Gerome felt himself delighted as though he were a child again stumbling upon an unexpected playmate. Sharing the same birth year could hardly be enough to explain the instant attraction the two men seemed to share.

"I'm afraid my gout, which my father had, and his father before him, is going to age me before my time," Lorenzo said.

"It's a simple thing to correct," Gerome said. "I've watched my physician father offer relief to many with the same affliction."

"Relief and not cure?"

"Relief creates the opportunity for the body to heal itself. Only God can cure, and that is a test of faith."

"I've had the best doctors in all of Europe treat me. Still, these joints swell and cripple me. It's only going to get worse. I need to leave for Rome for a meeting with Pope Sixtus, but I can't even stand."

"Gout is a disease of excess, your most honored potentate of this city. Forgive my directness, but surgery with words is the scalpel I prefer over steel."

"Excess! Ridiculous!"

"Look around this palace. Excess. Do you need twenty coal tubs to warm you?"

"Sandro wrote you have important news for me as well as healing hands."

"I do not have healing hands, but I do have healing words for those who are capable of listening. But about the news: it's about a plot brewing with Pope Sixtus behind it."

"What could you possibly have heard that my informants haven't yet discovered?"

"In addition to Vatican soldiers on his team connected to the family

Pazzi, there are members of the clergy who form part of it. I met two of them. Franciscans in the forest several months ago. They tried to recruit me, but I declined, suffering blows to my body."

"I appreciate the support."

"It wasn't in support of you that I declined. I declined because I believe—in fact, I have an overwhelming premonition—that if this entire city does not rid itself of its excesses of pride and vanity and, and, and, I could go on—"

"Please do," Lorenzo said with his eyes reddening from pain or lost sleep.

"I see things you don't want to hear, Master Lorenzo."

"And what have you seen?"

"I've seen blood, like a river flowing through the streets of this city. I've seen the death of this city, the drowning of the city in the vomit of its own excesses. And you, dear Signor Lorenzo, who are loved by the masses, have a unique opportunity to stop the blood by divesting yourself of your own excesses. And you can start with your own body."

Lorenzo's eyes opened wide, and he lifted himself on his elbows.

"Stop eating meat and fowl!" Gerome commanded. "Extra meat and fowl cause so much stress on the body, and those with gout cannot digest it. You don't have enough urine to wash that out of your system, so it goes to the joints. The more you drink and eat, the more the joints swell."

"That is too simple an explanation," Lorenzo said. "Marsilio Ficino has written extensively, advising me to eat more pork!"

"Has it helped you?"

Lorenzo changed the subject. "And what did you hear out in that forest? What are the names of these two clerics?"

"I can't remember their names, but I would remember their faces in an instant as they would remember mine. The younger one had a malformed hand with the fingers fused together. It looked like a claw."

"You'll excuse me, Brother, or should I call you Father Savonarola, you do have a face and eyes one cannot forget."

"That's because God is speaking through me. Believe me."

"And the pope?" Lorenzo asked. "What's your stand on the pope?"

"The pope's excesses," he said, magnetizing Lorenzo's eyes with the power of his own, "make yours seem petty by comparison."

"And yours, Father Gerome? What of your excesses?"

"I have had them. I have sinned with my body, but I am stronger for rising above it. I have learned that excess—even excess prayer—weakens the spirit."

"What an odd thing for a cleric to say!"

"Prayer without action is a meaningless whimper."

"I like your spirit," Lorenzo said.

"I like your power and charisma, Master Lorenzo. And I would like to enroll you in God's army to rid the city of its poison."

"Can you start with my feet? Can you help me to rid myself of the excess in my ankles and toes?"

"Are you willing to give me and my two assistants four days alone with you to do the work?"

"Tell me more."

"I'll not criticize the theories of others about medical matters, I'll merely suggest what to do. But if you take away the excesses of the body and not of the spirit, not of the mind, then the healing of the body will be pointless."

Lorenzo placed his stringed instrument on the floor beside the bed and turned to Gerome. "What else will you need?"

"I have some personal favor in mind, but I will refrain from asking it until you are satisfied with our treatments. First, I must ask you a question."

"Ask away," Lorenzo said.

"Why would you be going to visit a pope who has contracted soldiers to remove you from Florence?"

"I want peace, not war."

"But is it true you have appointed your own bishops without the pope's consent?"

"I have."

"And is it true you denied his nephew Riario, whom I have had the direct misfortune to encounter in Imola, a post in Pisa?"

"I did."

"And is it true your brother's Claudia is with child and that the wedding is scheduled to take place after the birth of what, according to the church, would be a bastard?"

"This is true."

"And what are you going to offer this pope to prove you are contrite?"

"Nothing."

"Why would you go there?"

"If it's public knowledge that I am seeking him out to make peace and for him to perform Giuliano's marriage, he would not dare to snuff me out. The city would be enraged. If I'm on the side of reaching out, all favor will be with me. And most importantly, I'll buy my mother's tranquility. She's convinced we're sitting targets."

"Before you go anywhere, Master Lorenzo, you must be able to walk and, if need be, to run for your life. Let's get started. Tell your guards to bring in my companions. Your protection out there is fierce. It took me a full hour—even with Signor Botticelli's letter—to be admitted. Next, you must tell your people we'll be working on you intensely for four days and you should not be disturbed."

"I'm in your hands," Lorenzo said, then rang the bell beside his bed.

HAVING RAISED HIMSELF into a seated position on his bed, Lorenzo de' Medici turned so his legs dangled from the side. Gerome Savonarola carefully unwrapped the rags and bunting from Lorenzo's feet. The joints were red, the toes enlarged.

"You see this is no imaginary affliction," Lorenzo said.

"I see an opportunity for healing." Gerome held Lorenzo's feet in his two hands, closed his eyes, and did not move. After a moment he uttered, "God, put the words into my mouth that will heal this man and restore his power so that out of gratitude for Your intervention he will help us do Your work."

Gerome took a deep breath, then let it out very slowly as he released Lorenzo's crippled feet and stood. He grabbed several pillows off the bed to make a path of them to the nearest chair. "Step, if you can, on each of the cushions and we'll sit you over there," he said.

Lorenzo groaned. "Those ten feet might as well be ten leagues."

"We'll do it together," Gerome said, then placed his arm beneath Lorenzo's shoulder to lift his patient to his feet. The joy Gerome was feeling lifted both men up so that Lorenzo was able to walk quickly to the chair.

"Those were the easiest steps I've taken all week," Lorenzo said.

"Because you were walking with our Lord. He was carrying you through me."

"I don't care how you did it, but do whatever you can to heal me—I mean, to allow God to heal me through you."

"I need my men to help us."

"Ring the bell yourself one more time. One of the soldiers will come and I'll tell him to bring in your companions."

"And don't forget the hot water. We need a large tub and some pork fat to rub into those joints."

"I thought I was to stay away from pork."

"On the inside. How we use it on the outside is another matter."

"Having my feet down like this makes them throb worse than ever," Lorenzo said.

"That will change soon enough."

When the soldier arrived, Lorenzo told him to summon Gerome's companions, but before he left, Savonarola stopped the guard and gave him the plate of breakfast meats that had been beside the bed.

"What are you doing? That was my meal!" Lorenzo said.

"The last thing you need."

"Bring him instead water with pomegranate juice in it."

"I do not do these tasks," the soldier said. "I will send one of the servants."

"You must do it," Lorenzo said. "And don't speak to anyone of what you see in here."

"I know, sir. To all who ask, you are at the bank."

"Exactly," Lorenzo said.

Turning to Gerome, Lorenzo continued, "No one must know I'm so incapacitated, or they'll lock me in the palace and throw away the key while they take over the city."

"You'll be back to yourself in four days, I'm certain," Gerome said.

Within moments, Piattini and Dono arrived. Upon seeing the famous Lorenzo, they appeared overcome, as though seeing the pope himself.

"Our mission," Gerome said, "is to heal Master Lorenzo's gout. We have four days to do it, and with God's help working through our hands and hearts and our commitment it will be done."

"Piattini. You're in charge of the right foot. And, Dono, you're going to be in charge of the left foot."

"And you?" Lorenzo asked.

"I," Gerome said, "I am in charge of your heart, your soul, your passion. You must talk about all your excesses the whole time we are working on you. Everything you tell us will be held in confidence."

"It will take me four days to recite it all—to dredge it from memory," Lorenzo said.

"Exactly. This is a confession that will go on for days as we rid your body of poisons. You'll speak them out of your mouth. Each day we'll ask God and His only son, Jesus Christ, to fill you with courage and the gift of truth and we'll be witnesses for you."

"Are you going to write down what I say?"

"I thought of that," Gerome said, "and then commit it to flame, but instead I decided our hands must be on you full time so the wails your body will release will travel to their rightful place in the heavens, and you will be liberated."

"It sounds excruciating."

"Or you might view it as an ecstasy of release and cleansing. But you must keep your body and soul pure after this and engage only in restraint from sex and food and drink," Gerome said.

"But I need all those as part of how I move in the world!"

"And how are you moving now?" Gerome asked.

"You've won your case," Lorenzo said.

At that moment, three servants entered the room. Two carried a tub of steaming water and one carried three pomegranates. All looked to Gerome for direction.

"Place the tub at the master's feet and give me the pomegranates and a knife. Tell the master's wife and mother we are deep in prayer and not to disturb us for four days. Be sure to leave more pomegranates and water at the door and bring a tub of hot water once every three hours." Gerome, the meek stutterer, was surely someone of the past. The servants responded at once, crossing themselves each time they neared either of the three holy men.

"You must keep this session to yourselves and not gossip about it to your fellow servants or your families," added Savonarola, as they were about to leave. "Our Lord looks angrily at those who carry tales, and we are doing the Lord's work here, so do not betray or belittle it with idle chatter."

One of the servants suddenly hiccupped and her face turned red. "Ah, so gossiping is one of your weaknesses?" Gerome asked, and the woman burst into tears.

"How long have you been working for me?" Lorenzo asked her.

"Fifteen years. For your father first and his father also and now for you. I wouldn't betray your trust. I would rather die first," she said, wringing her hands on her clothes.

"Idle chatter swells and distorts the truth, and then it flows into the wrong ears and, before you know, people believe things that never happened," Gerome said. "Let what you see here remain here. Do you understand?"

All the servants bowed, crossed themselves, and said, "We do, Monsignor."

"I'm not a monsignor, and I'm not a doctor, but I am a doctor of souls and I can see ailing souls inside seemingly healthy bodies, so be careful!"

The servants exited silently, closing the door with great care.

Turning to his companions and to Lorenzo, Gerome said, "Are you ready?"

"My feet are already so hot I fear placing them in more hot water will make me pass out."

"Heat to neutralize the heat," Gerome said. He stationed each of his helpers by his assigned foot.

"When I wave my hand," he told Piattini and Dono, "lift his foot gently and place it in the water. I'll squeeze the pomegranate juice and seeds into it as well."

Lorenzo closed his eyes in anticipation of great pain, and the ritual began.

"Oh Heavenly Father, pour down on all of us the power and the wisdom to remove from the beautiful Lorenzo, one of your most perfect creatures, all of the vices and flaws that are keeping Your joy from speaking through his body. He is offering his soul to you now, supplicant and servant to you, our Almighty Leader."

Piattini and Dono recited "amen" and plunged the feet into the hot bath.

"Do not bite your lip," Gerome said, "but scream out in pain if that is what you feel. This is about releasing all the parts God wishes to wash away now."

Lorenzo let out a deep wail as the pain of the hot water intensified the pain in his swollen feet.

"Now let yourself weep, not only for your own pain, but for all those who suffered before you, and all the unborn of your family who might carry this burden of excess. Weep now!"

Lorenzo's nose dripped, and his eyes burned as the tears streamed down his face.

"I am sorry for all the excesses of my life, but most about my infidelities to my faithful Clarice," Lorenzo confessed.

"Now describe each and every one of your sins in detail," commanded Savonarola, "and pull up the ones furthest from your memory, even as a child. The farther back you go, the more will surface and this will start the healing process."

Lorenzo confessed his infidelity to Clarice on the morning of their wedding day and then delved deeper into his past, confessing to locking his baby brother, Giuliano, in a closet, and even dangling him with bedclothes out of a window. As he focused on these memories and gave voice to them, the pain of his feet in the water began to subside.

After about fifteen minutes of this, Gerome instructed Piattini and Dono to lift up each foot and to massage each part of it, each toe and each bone. As they did so, shooting pains passed through Lorenzo's legs, and he kicked back against the pain, twice knocking over his helpers.

"Keep going!" Gerome said. "Start softly with your massaging, and then press harder and harder, moving all the swelling and congestion back from the ends of his toes toward his heart to cleanse the toxins and remove them through his bowels and urine. Now drink water between your confessions," he continued, as he handed Lorenzo the first of many cups of water, saying, "Drink until your bladder is about to burst, and then drink past that point." Gerome squeezed some of the pomegranate juice into the drinking water as well.

As soon as Lorenzo gulped the water, he was overcome by a huge wave of nausea, which leapt out of his body as vomit, spilling over him and hitting Piattini and Dono and the floor.

"Excellent," Savonarola said. "The Father is pleased for He is working quickly, faster than I would have thought."

"I'm so sorry," Lorenzo said to the two priests.

"They have known far worse," Gerome said. "They've seen half-rotted corpses covered with flies, and beside them crying children who were starving, surrounded by their own feces. This is nothing. Continue. All the emanations of the body are part of God's design, so none is to be hated."

"Then why do you scorn adultery and lewdness?" Lorenzo asked, still coughing up more of his vomit.

"Don't question me at this moment, Lorenzo. Now is your time to cough up your own history, to release the poison of your own life. Continue!"

Lorenzo's chest heaved a deep sigh as he took in a large breath and wiped away some of the vomit.

"Can't you clean me up?" he said. "The smell of this is making me sicker."

"You must not forget this smell, for it is the outward manifestation of your wrongdoing. Now, when you even think of working against your spirit's journey toward your true master, Jesus Christ, you will smell in the nostrils of your imagination this putrid smell and you'll choose instead the sweetness of prayer and submission."

Even though Gerome saw in Lorenzo's face an expression of incredulousness at having surrendered himself to the care of a madman, he knew Lorenzo would continue, doubts and all, as long as he harbored even the slightest faith in Gerome's ability to heal him of his Medici family curse.

"Your city has been filled with followers of yours, crazy for you and Giuliano, laughing at your pranks and prancing, never blaming you for anything. And now with the stench of your own vomit dousing you to the bone, you will know some measure of regret and remorse. Let's continue with the confessional, or the healing will not take," Gerome said.

Lorenzo recounted how one night when his second child was with fever, he had left Clarice and gone off with some of his men friends and bedded a peasant woman, and when he had returned the baby was dead.

"I killed one of my own children," he said, then collapsed in tears, recounting in detail what he had done and how only now, under these circumstances, was he able to say those words and feel the guilt.

"Guilt," Gerome said, "is useless before God. Action is the only redemption. The act of reform in your life, the amends you make from this day forward. You are forgiven. You are cleansed."

Savonarola wiped off Lorenzo's bedclothes as well as the pieces of clothing on Dono and Piattini where Lorenzo's purged matter had landed.

"You are serving all of us with the foulness of your vomit too," Gerome said, "for we smell in it the foulness of our own thoughts, our own transgressions, our own sins, and are reminded we must keep that poison out of us. So though we may flinch as it hurtles toward us, we are grateful your cleansing cleans us as well."

"May I please lie down or change my clothes?" Lorenzo asked.

"The point is not to relieve the discomfort, but to use it to dig deeper and deeper into your soul. Let us continue." And so continue it did, with all four men sleeping in the midst of Lorenzo's waste.

ON THE MORNING OF THE FOURTH DAY, Lorenzo was able to grab his foot and bring it close to his face. All the swelling was gone and the toes moved freely with no pain. He examined the other foot as well. It had become restored save for the smallest, stubborn toe, which still had some redness and a slight puffiness. The other toes moved painlessly.

He released his foot from his grasp and lay back under the covers. Tears of gratitude trickled down the sides of his face as he lay in silence, eyes open, looking at the painted ceiling, the cherubs, the violent thrashing of bodies he had been seeing for years. Suddenly they looked ugly to him and he resolved to have Sandro repaint it as the huge expanse and stillness of the heavens with stars and no people.

"Master Lorenzo is awake and well?" Gerome whispered.

"I've had a revelation, Brother Gerome."

"And your feet?"

"They are healed except for one toe that still swells. How long will it take to heal?"

"The rest of your life," Gerome said. "It's the poison waiting in reserve. Waiting to come out of its retreat and fill you again, quicker and more crippling than before."

"Then I am not healed."

"You are relieved of the poisons, but the tendency is in your nature and only God can change your nature."

"But didn't God give me my nature?"

"True. He gave you a mirror to choose. We must always choose."

"I choose to simplify. To stay close to my family, to rely less on my smiles and personality and more on my actions, and I'm determined to set a good example."

"And Rome? Will you be leaving tomorrow?"

"No. Rome is not necessary. I'll not play that game and kiss the feet of one I despise or one who despises me."

"How are you going to protect yourself?"

"With prayer, moderation, perfect attention. You have given me not only new feet but new eyes." Lorenzo raised himself onto his feet painlessly. He took steps carefully. "The one toe aches, but I can ignore it."

"Do not ignore it. Tend to it."

"But a tiny spot of suffering to remind me is better than removing all of it so I will not forget."

"As you wish," Gerome said. "To clean that last stronghold will take a month of spiritual retreat for you and it will change your life to put all of your politics on hold and become a servant of the Master."

"I think not, my dear Brother Savonarola. For you have given me exactly what I needed. Now I'll go with you and your colleagues to the church of San Marco and assign you permanent cells in which you can stay whenever you like. You will always be welcomed in this city. And instead of the pope, I choose you to marry my brother and Claudia in June."

"Let's see how you are in a month or two. It will be spring, and the temptations of that blossoming time will test you. Besides, my followers and I are meant to travel about the whole of Tuscany for a while longer. One day, however, we'll want to return permanently, but this is not the time or season. Your offer shows me you have intuited the very request I was about to make if you are happy with our services for you. And your offer tells me you are. Have your local priest perform the wedding and we will come to give our blessings. We do not want to usurp the place of those who came before us."

"We shall see," Lorenzo said. "And now let us all go to the baths and shed the stench of our work together."

CHAPTER FORTY-SIX

Gerome Leaves Florence and His Acolytes

BATHED, FED, AND RENEWED, the three clerics trekked into the hills of Fiesole whipped by chilly February winds.

As he stopped to watch a scattering of snowflakes flutter in the air, Dono spoke. "Was it worth all that vomit? All that scalding pomegranate juice! I'm exhausted!"

"You are missing our victory, Dono!" Savonarola said, so elated from his success with Lorenzo de' Medici's cure, he appeared to feel no cold or fatigue. "We've earned a permanent home in Florence, and you're complaining!"

"After all that discomfort, you could move us into our promised cells in San Marco," Piattini said. Prolonged immersion in the hot waters used to heal Lorenzo had dried out his hands, which were now chapped and cracking as he tried to warm them.

"Not before you two have been ordained! When we return to Florence to live, it will be with the respect, the power, and the following we crave to do our work."

"Isn't craving a bad thing, Brother Savonarola?" Piattini said.

"When the craving is for God's work, there is no bad," Gerome said.

At the end of the climb to Fiesole, the trio arrived at the ruins of a small Roman amphitheater. Rays of winter sun broke through the clouds. Gerome and his companions laid themselves on the cold stone benches to soak in the sun's warmth.

"Where next?" Dono said. He removed his shoes and wrapped his feet with a scarf he had pulled from his neck. He drew a silver candlestick from his robes and began to polish it with the edge of his cape.

"What is that?" Gerome asked.

"A trinket. I did not steal it. One of the maids saw me eyeing it and she put it into my hands. This will hardly send me to hell. Isn't it better to help myself to something like this than to some young maiden's undergarments?" Dono looked to Piattini for agreement.

"So she stole it *for* you!" Gerome said just as a dozen feral cats ran onto the theater's proscenium. With matted fur and open wounds, they fought and clawed at each other.

"I've been waiting for a sign to teach you one more lesson," Gerome said, "and now it has arrived. What do these cats who feed on each other remind you of?"

Dono and Piattini said nothing.

"These feral cats' true nature is to be one of God's creatures first. Their culture is to be wild and that is why they are so good at it. But soon they'll die, each feeding on the other for entertainment as well as survival."

"Where are you going with this?" Piattini said. "You are always going somewhere with your words."

"You tell me," Gerome said.

"Maybe my nature is to be a thief after all," Dono said.

"And mine is to dream of breasts," Piattini said. "Swimming in them. Being pummeled by them. Licking them and sucking them."

"What's got into you men?" Gerome asked. "Have you forgotten all the work we've done to turn our nature to God?" He could see their exhaustion, but they had been exhausted before. This time, however, both of his followers averted their eyes, ignored the cats, and turned away from their leader as they curled into fetal positions against the cold.

Gerome returned to his saddlebags and pulled something from his pack while his two young followers tried to snooze.

With a quick flick of his wrist, Gerome snapped the edge of a whip first at the bottom of Dono's feet and then instantly at Piattini's shoulder. Both prelates sat at attention.

Gerome threw the whip down, then jumped into the center of the theater toward the cats. "Watch," he said, then took off his outer robes and got on his hands and knees to crawl toward the cats. He lay next to them. They stopped and jumped back as he neared them. Out of his belt, he let roll a small piece of cheese. He sat up to watch. One cat approached and hit the small piece of cheese with its paw. The others jumped him and the cheese shot into the air. Two of the cats jumped to catch it and collided in flight. Gerome made a mewing sound. He took another piece of cheese out of his belt and placed it in his mouth. The cats ignored him. He stood and put on his robes.

"If these cats were mice," he said, "then we would have tamed them with the cheese, but they are cats and must be fed some raw meat or a bird or some milk, but we have none of those things so we cannot entice and if we imitate their antics we gain nothing. We must find what it is they lack and bring it to them to get their attention."

Dono stopped rubbing his feet, threw his hands up as if to say, *I have no idea what lesson you're going to give us with this story!*

Gerome closed his eyes, as he often did when he was about to enter his most inspired oratory. Until this day his men would have been mesmerized. Today, however, he sensed his words were about to fall on deaf ears, and yet he continued, "All things on high pull us toward them, pull us and pull us until the weight we use to keep ourselves within the devil's reach gives out and we are swept into the glory to another force, larger and bigger than what those cats are doing. God pulls us up from the mud and sets us upon our paths to tame the other animals . . . the human animals."

He stopped to take a deep breath, opened his eyes, and saw Piattini and Dono had returned to their sleeping postures with their backs to him. Gerome snapped the whip in the air to get their attention. "God has given us the ability to love Him and to love the idea of Him," Gerome said. "In doing so we raise ourselves above these cats. And we can raise ourselves above the devil—"

"Why didn't you raise yourself above the devil? That was your handiwork in that painting, wasn't it?" Dono asked as he stuck his belly out and rolled his eyes, smirking at his fellow sidekick, Piattini. "Even old Petrarchio said you weren't so holy."

"So, if these cats were people, then how could we attract them?" asked Piattini.

"We've been discussing this forever, but you tell me, Piattini, from what you've seen in our humble travels, when have we succeeded and when have we failed?"

Dono stepped forward. "Even if it appeared we failed, we let people know we were concerned for their spiritual survival. They will not forget this."

"But when did we succeed?"

"When we helped the children and buried their mother and found them a home," Dono said.

"But what of that home? Who knows what influences may form them under the pope's Riario?" Gerome said.

"We are a mirror?" Dono asked.

"Are we a mirror then?" Piattini ventured.

"We hold the mirror," Gerome said. "Confession is a way to hold the mirror, but—"

"I'm so bored hearing this!" Dono said. "We say these things, but look at us, three scruffy priests ourselves without even milk to tempt your feral cats. I could sell this candlestick to feed us for a week. Is that a sin? Is that stealing?"

"We have no place to stay but these hard seats tonight. We could be covered in snow by the morning," Piattini said. "Dono has a point. We should sell the candlestick, not give it back. We should consider it a gift like all the others."

"As winter closes, the blossoms will open on the trees. Let the blossoms open inside your hearts. If you wish to leave you can. You have not sworn your life to me in chains."

"The chains are chains we've chosen," Dono said. "But the only thing I'm feeling now is exhaustion. The only thing that gives me any comfort at this moment is to polish this trophy rescued from all that vomit."

"Let's pray in silence, please," Gerome said, "here and now, and ask for more direction."

"I'd like to take a direction toward those young girls again at the Villa di Castello and offer ourselves to them as tutors, not as starving cats. I want to practice overcoming temptation on them," Piattini said. "And since you cured the master's twitching, perhaps we might enjoy a few days of comfort there before we move on."

"A few days of comfort. A soft bed in a Piazza San Marco cell—if that's all you boys want, then I want no part of you. I break your chains to me here and now. This very moment," Gerome said. He rolled up his whip and walked back toward the donkeys, leaving his charges alone.

They followed him, but he would no longer look into their faces.

"Go back to Bologna and return your robes or take your vows," Gerome said. "Six months are up. It's time you decided. I have no more patience for aspiring priests. I need full soldiers in my army. Consider long and hard about what you want. If you come back to me, come back ordained!"

Piattini and Dono looked at each other. "We will need your blessing for our ordination," Piattini said.

"Look at the two of you! You act as one man, not two individuals. You are like these cats, part of a litter, tumbling and wrestling with souls, your own and others'. For you, it's just a game."

"We're just tired!" Dono said.

Without responding, Gerome mounted his donkey while Dono and Piattini watched him in disbelief. When they tried to speak, Gerome put his hand up.

"Silence! Tell the monsignor I've sent you back for your ordination if you choose it. That will be my recommendation. And if you choose otherwise, I bless you and will pray for you. For now, we are through. I'm in need of men, not boys who whimper in the back of the choir."

CHAPTER FORTY-SEVEN

The Sisters Scheme to Reconnect with Floriana

WITH FLORIANA GONE and Sandro working again with Filippino instead of them, Piero's sisters, Donata, Margarita, and Renata, had too much time on their hands. Like the feral cats that entertained Gerome and his cohorts in the Roman theater in Fiesole, Piero's younger sisters attacked each other and sparred incessantly in front of the kitchen hearth where they hovered, waiting for the warmth of spring to arrive.

One day when Poppi tried to give them tasks to distract them, Donata announced to Poppi, "We need to visit our friend Floriana!"

"Your friend!" Poppi said as she dusted the charcoal that had settled around the floor. "We had to force you to be sweet to her!"

"But we grew to love her," Renata said.

"Friends do not betray each other," Poppi said, glaring at Renata.

"I didn't say anything bad."

"You let it slip with Bandini when we were supposed to refer to Floriana as Rosanna, and then you cried about it."

"But he died anyway," Renata said.

"Luckily," Donata added.

"What do you mean *luckily*? It was a great weight on all of us to deal with him," Poppi said.

"A great weight, indeed," Margarita said, puffing out her cheeks and doing a waddling fall to the ground. All four women laughed.

"That's the first time we've laughed in weeks," Donata said. "And the last time was with Floriana. Master Botticelli stays days locked in that room. He's refused our help."

"Because he's got his assistant, Filippino, here again."

"The one we doctored after he scraped his knee?" Renata said. "I've never even seen him all these weeks!"

"That dreamy boy with the curly hair and kissable lips? How could we not know he's been here? We've become the walking dead!" Margarita said.

"Together they're painting flowers along the bottom of the picture and all the rest is still only sketched in," Poppi said.

"We grew to love her, and now this place is so boring, and Master Botticelli, who was all smiles to us and nice to us and let us help him when she was here, now avoids us. He walks around glum and sad," Donata said.

"Because he needs to see her as much as we do," Renata added.

"Let me dream on it," Poppi said. "Tomorrow I'll have a plan. In the meantime, prepare a loving note and some gifts for Floriana we can give to Graziella for her, in case she knows where Floriana is."

Renata, Margarita, and Donata, busy with their studies, primping, and sparring with each other, had not paid much attention to Graziella's coming and going. With no knowledge of the homing pigeons tucked under the roof of the villa, they had no way of tracking Graziella's appearance. With Sandro and Filippino hidden away from them, they had lost track of the painting's progress. Now that they had a purpose, they argued amongst themselves about the timing of Graziella's visits. Each had remembered a different time. One recalled the morning, the other the middle of the day, and Poppi, who had been busy at her perfumery, had not seen Graziella at all after the first couple of times. Only Sandro controlled the schedule as he released the homing pigeons. By the end of winter, he had released only two of the six birds.

The girls created a package of trinkets and books for Floriana. Renata donated one of her dolls, and Margarita a tiara. Donata created a card with flowers pressed into it and delicately attached with some rabbit's skin glue she had "borrowed" from Sandro's studio.

Piero, free of his twitching, enjoyed life in a cloud of rapture. Now he dared to see himself as attractive and to consider marriage as a possible plan to speed up his inheritance or, better yet, to increase his own wealth by obtaining a substantial dowry. Knowing the painting was progressing, that his artist was honoring the contract, his concern for the work was satisfied. He became more absorbed in Poppi's perfumery and less involved in the drama of Sandro's life, which, much to Piero's liking, had returned to a more normal and predictable pattern.

As for his sisters, he had delegated their care and grooming to Poppi. What he did not see, he did not wish to know. The flurry in the house as they prepared for Graziella's next arrival never caught his attention. They had convinced themselves she would be there on the first of March. Piero went off falconing that day with neighbors. His sisters and Poppi were content with the perfection of their plans, especially with Piero away from home.

By four o'clock, Graziella had not yet arrived. Frustrated, they fought with each other, screaming and pulling hair and even tearing their clothes. The noise was so disturbing that Sandro sent Filippino out to see what was going on.

The girls did not hear his approach. Margarita had yanked off Donata's hair ribbon. Renata turned to see Filippino watching them. She did not speak or move—her sudden quiet stance signaled the others to be silent.

Barely in his twenties and not being a priest, Filippino was openly affected by the girls' high emotional pitch. Watching in fascination he stood still until the three grew silent. "Your screaming interrupted us," he said.

"We're so sorry," Margarita said. The sight of Filippino, even covered in paint and dressed in rags, silenced the girls, who looked at him with longing.

"I'm Filippino. You three nursed me back to health several months ago. Have you forgotten me entirely?"

"Never!" Renata said.

"Why haven't you come to see us, say hello to us? Show us your knee all healed?" Donata asked.

"Master Sandro and I have been working night and day to finish more of the painting, while it seems all you've been doing is fighting," Filippino said. "What's the matter?"

"We want very much to see Signorina Graziella today when she comes to see Master Botticelli," Margarita said, "but she has not arrived, so we're growing impatient."

"She has come and gone," Filippino said. "She was here at dawn. You were probably sleeping. Master Sandro sent for her yesterday."

"Sent for her?" Renata said. "How's that possible? We have no runners or messengers here."

"With the pigeons. He releases one when he's finished with a section."

"What pigeons?" Donata asked. "We have no pigeons here!"

Renata dropped to the ground, lowered her head to her knees, and whimpered.

"How could we have missed her? We have messages for her to take to Floriana," Margarita said.

"And what makes you think Graziella knows where Floriana is?" Sandro asked, as he stepped into the circle of commotion. He had given up waiting for Filippino and had come out to see for himself what was going on.

The girls said nothing, only wore expressions of shock on their faces. Sandro realized his unkempt, wild-eyed appearance must have horrified them. "You all look lovely," he said, noticing them for the first time in weeks since Floriana's departure.

"We miss Floriana and wanted to send her a message and some gifts," Renata said.

"We figured Graziella, being a Jew and all that," Donata said, "would know her whereabouts. She must be lonely."

"We don't know her whereabouts," Sandro said. Turning to Filippino, he waved him back toward the studio. When Filippino was out of sight, Sandro turned to the girls and in a soft voice, barely above a whisper, said, "Graziella won't be here until the first week of spring and not before I finish the entire foreground." He looked at the girls. "I'll ask Graziella myself if she knows anything about Floriana."

Donata stepped forward. "That is generous of you, but we have some feminine issues we wish to discuss with Graziella anyway and would like to talk with her ourselves if you wouldn't mind. May we send off one of those pigeons?"

"Never! And who told you about the pigeons?" Sandro asked. "I don't like your meddling in my business relationship with Graziella. Be here in two weeks at noon. She should be back then. I'm sure she'll be kind enough to speak with you. Now quiet down and let me get some work done."

As soon as Sandro was out of earshot, Donata said, "He's going to let us speak to Graziella! We just have to hold on."

"Isn't there anything we could be doing now to find her?" asked Margarita. "We could let one of those pigeons go by mistake, of course! And she'd be here the next day!"

"Sandro himself might want to send a message to her," Renata said.

"He'll never do that," Donata said.

"Never say never," Poppi said. "You've planted a seed in his heart. If he knows your gifts are going to her, he'll be sure to make one of his own."

"I say we find the pigeons," Donata said, "and let one go today so she'll come tomorrow!"

"I say wait until he's ready," Margarita said. "You do that kind of sneaky thing, and you'll ruin it for all of us. We'll never find our way into his painting!"

"Where are those birds anyway?" Renata said. "I want to at least see them."

"No you don't. Not now you don't," Poppi said. "Patience, more presents, that's all you want to concentrate on, not meddling with Master Sandro's artistic life."

"He needs help with his love life," Renata said.

"Settle down," Poppi said.

"But before that, he needs a bath!" Margarita said.

"Amen!" all four women said in unison, then the three sisters laughed, breaking into a spontaneous dance, hand in hand, circling Poppi.

CHAPTER FORTY-EIGHT

Lorenzo's First Journal Entry

March 1, 1478

"WHAT DO YOU MEAN *you're not going to Rome?" Clarice asked me—her newly attentive husband. I tried to explain to her I'm a different man now. Though I can walk and even run, I choose to stay close to home, to enjoy her and the children and the arrival of our next child. To finally be there for her instead of riding all over the countryside.*

I told her how I've changed my mind about going to Rome, which I had been so certain was the only way to resolve current hostilities, or at least to quiet them. It's time to honor the church in this city. To keep it in our Florentine family. I don't wish to kiss the hand of my enemy and have decided not to visit the pope to beg for anything.

I told her how the pope has been jealous of our family for decades. He covets our libraries, our devoted admirers. He's toothless and fat and balding and aging and all he cares about is total obedience to his every whim while he showers money and land on his assorted nephews. I won't betray myself any longer by pandering for support from one who has no regard for the soul of the common man and no love for our family.

"That priest from Ferrara has turned you upside down. I hardly recognize

my husband," Clarice said and I agreed he has done so in a good way—how he turned me against the poison in my own life and gave me a path to avoid it by turning inward and monitoring my own values and my own life. He has put me on a path of self-reflection, which is why I am writing in a journal rather than searching for rhymes for my superficial songs that I have pursued without any real passion. No longer will I write poetry to romantic love. I will record each lapse in my thinking, so that in writing them down, I will not have to act on it.

March 14, 1478

When I hold our new infant daughter, Contessina, in my arms and look at her with attention and fascination, it is as though I've never before seen such a child.

I need to balance my outer life with the inner life of my family and stay close to home. Clarice confessed she has been praying for these changes in attitude for years.

All those around me have begun to think I have finally listened to each of them, when in reality I have begun to listen to some inner voice in myself. The word that voice keeps repeating over and over again is—Simplify.

Not having even met him, Clarice said she liked "this priest from Ferrara," as she identifies him, and in response, I assured her we will surely see more of him.

CHAPTER FORTY-NINE

Graziella and Floriana Talk

EVEN THOUGH EARLY MARCH had brought them some hints of the spring weather to come, Graziella and Floriana were wrapped in woolen blankets as they walked arm in arm through the open fields around Manfredo's house.

"You've been such a comfort to me, Graziella," Floriana said. "Yet every few weeks you see Master Sandro and you give me no news."

"You told me you refused his marriage proposal, so I purposely say nothing about him to you."

"Tell me what he's doing. Any detail!"

"I see him lost in the flowers of the painting, doing one more blade of grass or leaf on a tree. Anything but the people in the picture. He's losing himself in the sea of details and he has his assistant, Filippino, there with him. The two are like recluses, with their beards full-grown now, and you'll excuse my saying this, but they have forgotten about bathing or even washing, and the smell is not a pleasant one."

Floriana laughed.

"And what's so funny?"

"They're painting flowers, and they stink like beasts."

"And with a perfumery right on the grounds."

"You must bring him something from me. He doesn't have to know I prepared it, but let's dry some flowers and make a mixture of something, sew it into a little pouch, and he can drop it into the water and the scent will fill the house."

"Don't you care about his not being a Jew?"

"I should care, but that's the last of my worries. I think of him."

"At least as an older brother or a father, he loves you and wants to protect you. That alone might be a reason to resume contact."

"I hope he feels more than that. I feel more than that toward him. My dreams bring him to me over and over again. I am torn between reconnecting and closing him off."

"What happens in the dreams?" Graziella asked.

"We're together, admiring the child. We're happy and yet there's a dark cloud hovering in those dreams. I awaken relieved I'm safe here with you. And yet it does pain me to be cut away from him and from my sisters and brothers in Ferrara."

"Once the baby comes and you have your strength back we can get you back to Ferrara."

"Never! All my misfortune came from there. It's not safe to even think about such a reunion. And I would be ashamed of what's happened to me. I don't want anyone there to know, especially my uncle."

"What's safe for you now?"

"To make a tiny pillow of scents for you to bring to Sandro on your next visit. And I want you to bring one to each of the girls, too, who in the end were like loving sisters to me."

Once back in her room, Floriana sat on the floor on pillows of silk and searched through her basket of dresses. She pulled out one Margarita had given her. With it on her lap, she delicately tore away threads to create small squares of fabric she would use to make the sachet bags. She would send a sachet to each of the girls and one to Poppi and one to Sandro. Inside the sachet she would fold a message into tiny squares and place it in with the herbs and dried flowers. If they never saw the note, that would be fine, but if they looked they would find it too.

As Floriana's fingers worked on the fabric, her mind raced forward to the words she would write. A sadness came over her as she remembered she hadn't said goodbye to the girls, to Poppi, or even to Sandro. And of course, how could she forget Piero! He had valiantly carried her here in the middle of the night. She could sense he was relieved to have her and all her complications away from the villa. He had been cordial but distant when they worked together on his doll collection. When she wept off and on during the journey, he had ignored her tears and repeated his silly, strange expression, "Imagine you! We're almost there."

She was sure her pregnancy, her Jewishness, her neediness, had put him into an uncomfortable state. Already in debt to Manfredo, Piero perhaps did not want to ask another favor. He had dropped her on the edge of the property and had not accompanied her into the homestead. She had suddenly appeared with her few possessions.

But Manfredo, and especially Graziella, had taken her in without hesitation.

CHAPTER FIFTY

Sandro and Poppi

POPPI EMPTIED AN APRON full of cuttings from her plants onto Sandro's studio worktable and spread them out across the table's surface. Still camped out in the main room in these last days of winter, Filippino sat in a corner grinding pigments to blend the greens they were going to use for that day. Poppi transferred some of the less hardy flowers into a large metal bowl of water to keep them fresh. Sandro sat alone by the window, apart from his work. He made no attempt to acknowledge Poppi until she said, "Why so glum this morning, Master Botticelli?" at which point he jumped and grabbed her by the arm, saying, "Take me to your greenhouse. Perhaps I will find something I want to paint today."

Sandro yanked her so hard some of the flowers fell onto the ground. She tried to pick them up, but Sandro said, "Never mind. Filippino will get them." He snapped his fingers, and pointed to the spilled flowers. "Keep grinding and pick these up. I'll be back in a few minutes, and we will paint."

As Poppi and Sandro walked toward the greenhouse, Sandro said, "Please don't ever discuss my emotions in front of Filippino."

"You fool yourself," Poppi said. "Anyone working around you can see you're miserable."

"As far as Filippino knows, she was a sweet model who came and went. He doesn't know what's happened here, and he does not know the condition of my heart."

"He's not stupid, Sandro. He probably knows something's wrong."

"He's seen me ecstatic and seen me this way before, enough times not to question it. But I can tell you, Poppi, I'm suffering. I was supposed to say nothing and do nothing. To honor and protect her, but instead I feel as though I have abandoned her. I must see her or talk with her or send her some note, some gift, some word from me to her."

"And she's so close to her time now," Poppi said.

"Don't make me feel worse!"

"I'm glad you're hurting."

"How could I not be?"

"Master Piero feels nothing but relief at her absence."

"Master Piero is not in love with her. Master Piero is more in love with himself, especially now without the twitching—"

"Master Piero is looking for a wife!" Poppi said.

"Good luck to him and the woman he marries."

"To him you're a symbol of his success. As long as you are here and producing, he'll be content. But let's get back to you and Floriana. You aren't the only one who misses her."

"I know, the girls miss her too," Sandro said.

"They plan to visit her."

"Impossible. I gave my word that no one would follow her, not even me!"

"And only Piero knows her whereabouts," Poppi said.

"Piero and Graziella," Sandro said.

"What if—?"

"I've sworn to be a protector. The less I know the safer she'll be."

"Do you believe that?"

"Not anymore. A note. Something. Some contact."

"And Graziella? Has she brought you news of Floriana?"

"Not a word. We keep the conversation exclusively on the business at hand, and my next installment is due when most of the foreground is finished."

By then they were inside the greenhouse. They walked among the rows of seedlings and flowers. The stench of Sandro's unwashed body mixed with his paints and binding oils made her cough. She shoved a vial of purple water at him, coughing again. "Why have you not shaved or bathed? It's most difficult to stand beside you or your assistant, Filippino. Out of respect to the others who share the house, if you're not going to bathe, at least use some of my perfume."

"I've been working night and day to finish the next installment. I've not wanted to think of anything else."

"So you've chosen to avoid remembering Floriana?"

"I've substituted work to take away the pain of her absence."

"Show me the work," Poppi said. "I might have a suggestion."

"But you've seen it every day."

"I have seen what you and Filippino are doing: painting the grass one blade at a time. Are you waiting for an inspiration for the next figure?"

"Are you referring to the one I'm painting of Oslavia, as Mary/Venus?"

"Is that who you're painting? But there's no face yet."

"Because I want to depict Oslavia as she was before she left our home. I'm trying to remember her as a girl, but it does not come back to me. I have the figure, the flowing garments, but no face. I can't bring anyone to mind for it."

"Use the young Renata. She's full of innocence."

"Renata! Of course," he said. "Is there anything you don't know, my wise crone Poppi?"

"Many things. Some are a mystery. Others, clear as spring water to me, while still others are mud. You, for example—"

"What about me?"

"You're a man of two worlds."

"Only two? I fancy myself as a member of at least four."

"Four?"

"Tell me what you see first," he said, "and then I'll tell you what I am."

"I see the man, the son of the tanner, the simple worker who must have his work to fill his days. He must produce or he has nothing."

"And the other?"

"The other is the sea sponge who takes in all he sees, every petal on this flower, every sigh of the woman you most admire, every twitch and fart of your master. Busy, busy, busy—you're soaking up, listening and watching, and then you go to your work and regurgitate it onto the canvas, into your tiny sketchbooks, even in the arrangement of the food on your plate. The maker and the one who takes in what God has made."

"You flatter me. And are these two selves at war?"

"Only under certain conditions," Poppi said.

"And what are those conditions?"

"You tell me," she said.

"Sometimes I want to be that sponge to join with the ocean of life and soak up more and more of the experience and flow with it as others do. Not to have to stop to translate it into the art, the making, the doing. I want to be in that flow of life."

"But?"

"Well, sometimes the doing of the art feels like all of life itself. It's the only place I want to be. As a sponge, I soak up from one sense to the next, from one breast to the next, until after a while all are the same and my memory fogs over and the senses collide." All the time Sandro spoke he pinched off dead blossoms from one of Poppi's nearby flowering plants. She stood next to him doing the same.

"When I make the art," Sandro continued, looking at the dead blossom heads in his palm, "I slow it down and savor and record what I see and feel and understand, but the effort takes me away from more of the ocean."

"And what about Floriana? Are you at peace or war concerning her?" Poppi asked.

"At first when she left I was relieved she would be safe, that I had held myself back and chosen protection instead of seduction. Not that she would have been one to seduce, given her condition and misfortunes. But as each day passed, the satisfaction of my right action paled as my heart suffered from her absence. Then the art was not coming from the same place and the war seemed waged and twisted."

"You sound confused."

"Some contact with her would be enough to lift me from painting the earth of flowers and petals and give me the courage to face the people I must paint. A word from her or even to her might set the balance straight for me."

"Contact her through Graziella. We both know she knows the whereabouts of Floriana, even if you pretend otherwise."

"I don't technically know the whereabouts of Graziella's home."

"Which you could easily obtain from Piero."

"Or from Graziella herself. Just to consider it, my mood is lifting—light comes back into me. I'm tired of being the worm crawling through the earth of this painting. Let me finally get off my knees and stand tall once again. Enough war!"

"Enough war," Poppi repeated.

"Enough war," Sandro said. As though waking from a dream, he asked Poppi, "Where are we?"

"Here in the glass gardens. We came to speak away from Filippino, but also to gather flowers for more of your painting."

"Even if I'm not to see her immediately, I want to make myself ready and presentable. I'll take a bath! Forgive the neglect and odor of neglect I have inflicted on you."

"Go tell your Filippino to ready himself for a bath also. Then, come to the kitchen for a decent meal. I'll tell Renata you'll start painting her tomorrow."

As Sandro's face brightened, he tried to hug Poppi. "After your bath," she said, shrinking away from him. "When Graziella comes the first day of spring, we'll shower her with gifts for Floriana—both from you and the girls, who miss her terribly. Go now and let me prepare a nice mix of bath scents for you and Filippino."

"I can see now why Piero has wisdom beyond his years. It's because of you, Poppi."

"You flatter me. I water flowers and watch them grow. Now go and water your own flower before all the petals fall off!"

Spring

CHAPTER FIFTY-ONE

Spring at Villa di Castello Begins with an Unexpected Guest

ON THE FIRST DAY OF SPRING at the Villa di Castello, Piero and Poppi sat at their workbench in Piero's chambers. In order to fashion a more human head for the priest who had healed him of his nervous tic, Piero had removed the bird beak head from Savonarola's effigy when the dogs barked and a clock chimed twelve.

"Could that be Father Gerome himself attracted by our magic?" Piero asked.

"No. It's Graziella," Poppi said with certainty. Graziella's arrival had been anticipated for days. The girls had forced Poppi to look at every thread of every gift they had prepared for Floriana. She got up from the workbench, leaned out the window, and saw Piero's three sisters running toward the pugs. They stopped short, changed direction, and ran back inside the villa, wailing Poppi's name.

"And Father Gerome Savonarola it is, but without his helpers!" Poppi said. "You greet him while I round up the girls."

"Yes, round them up," Piero repeated. Before he ran downstairs to meet his unexpected guest, Piero positioned Gerome's unattached new head with its unfinished nose on the tray which had so many times before acted as a miniature stage for the day's activities.

"AND HOW IS YOUNG MASTER PIERO THIS MORNING?" Gerome asked as soon as Piero collided with him at the entrance.

"There's less of me. And no more shakes!" Piero paraded in front of his hero. "Imagine you! I'm a new man."

"He no longer eats all day long. Now he takes meals at regular times like the rest of us," Poppi said as she settled in beside Piero.

"Your more balanced nature has emerged," Gerome said.

"With God's help," Piero added.

"With God's help."

Piero scooped up one of his favorite pugs and held it as it squirmed and whimpered in his arms. "*Silenzio!*" he ordered. The dog obeyed. With a smile of pride Piero said, "I am indebted to you. And to what do I owe your visit?"

"You owe me nothing," Gerome said. "But if it is your wish, I am asking of you today a large favor."

"Anything!"

"Now that my helpers have gone to become officially ordained, I'm taking a small rest from my travels and had hoped you might host me for a few days."

"We'd be honored to do so," Piero said. "Poppi will prepare a suite of rooms for you."

"A few pillows and enough floor space to spread myself out is all I need."

"Nothing but the best for you," Piero said, turning to Poppi, who glared at him and said, "Impossible!"

Piero's jaw fell open as Poppi spun a tale.

"The girls are preparing for their recital, and many of their friends are scheduled to arrive any minute and stay. They have been planning this for months."

"And why have I heard nothing of this?" Piero said. "What friends?"

"I'll explain it all to you," she said, still smiling at the fiery priest.

"Even a shed on the grounds would be more than enough," Gerome said. "The climate is almost mild."

"Will you excuse us for a moment, Father Gerome?" Poppi said. "Stay for lunch. You can rest yourself in the greenhouse for now. We'll catch up with you there." She pointed the way around the side of the villa. "The master and I will join you very soon."

"I'm grateful for whatever you can offer—a day, or a week," Gerome said as he headed toward the greenhouse.

Once Gerome was out of earshot, Piero said, "What are you doing, Poppi, defying me like that?" His head did not twitch.

Poppi hooked her arm through Piero's, then pulled him forward into a brisk walk toward the greenhouse. "Calm yourself!" She yanked his arm each time he looked forward at Savonarola. "Today's the day Graziella arrives!"

"What's the problem?"

"Your sisters and Master Botticelli have planned to offer gifts and greetings to Floriana in the main house through Graziella, and now with your priest of the bird face, all plans are interrupted."

"And why is that?"

"Because he's always on the lookout for Floriana. We have sworn to protect her, and now he's here. If they don't get their gifts to Graziella this time, it will be another month, and by then Floriana's baby will have already been born."

"He's the most devout Christian I have met."

"He's a saint who wants us all to forget he was a sinner."

"You have no proof of that."

"If it isn't he, then it's one of his group. He comes from Ferrara. She came from Ferrara. He came looking for her the first time he was here and he saw her in the painting and knows we know where she is. Maybe he wants to murder the baby!"

"He's a healer. Beyond reproach!" Piero said.

"Are you willing to jeopardize the flow of money from Manfredo? If this priest, no matter how devout and gifted he is, finds her and, God forbid, harms her, you'll lose the support of Manfredo and Graziella, not to mention the cooperation of your resident artist, Sandro. And furthermore, you'll incur the rage of your sisters, who have lately set Floriana as some kind of goddess of purity."

"Hardly."

"Send him away! Tell him he can return in three days' time and stay as long as he likes."

The dogs started barking again. "Graziella!" Poppi said. "Go to the greenhouse and detain your healer monk there for at least two hours. I'll keep the girls and Graziella distracted in the house. Don't let him move from that spot. I'll bring food there. After two hours, you can let him stay in the house. Do you understand?"

"I don't like when you order me."

"When it's necessary, I do it. When it's for your own good and the good of your family, I do it. Trust me. Lock him in if you must!"

"I'll ask him to give me his views on marriage since I'm considering it."

"Now you're using your brain. Tell him we've decided to postpone the girls' party until after he leaves and his quarters will be ready by dusk, that he needs to rest there until then."

"You're such a schemer, Poppi. I'm glad you are on my side."

"I am. Believe me, I am. Now go before he starts wandering around the gardens."

Piero rushed off in the direction of the greenhouse while Poppi hurried back toward the main villa and the barking dogs. Visions of Graziella being attacked with gifts for Floriana by three screeching girls under the sly eye of Savonarola made her break into a run. There Sandro would be, too, with his gift. Floriana's secret hiding place would be compromised. Only she, Poppi, had the power to keep them all apart, to orchestrate the next few hours without any problems. Distracted by all her chattering thoughts, Poppi slipped on a patch of muddy earth, landing her in one of the new holes the gardeners had dug that morning.

She pulled herself into a seated position, rolled up her red leggings, and removed a shoe. She hobbled toward the front door and into the main room. Empty. She limped to the kitchen, where she kept her healing salves and balms. Her ankle and knee throbbed. The dogs were not out front, nor in the house. Through the silence, she called out, "Renata,

Margarita, Donata? Where are you? Sandro? Filippino? Where are you?" She slathered some mutton fat mixed with lilac powders onto her leg, then ran upstairs, searching through every room, even heading toward Sandro's room. Not a sound of anyone stirring. She flew into Piero's room, looked out the back window of the doll closet, and saw Sandro, Graziella, and the three girls walking toward the greenhouse. She leaned out the window, and shouted, but it was too late.

SANDRO HAD WORKED ALL NIGHT in a frenzy preparing his gift for Floriana. He'd torn apart the shirt he had worn their last time together and used a scrap of the cloth to wrap the gift, then further wrapped it with his neck scarf, and finally sewed that shut with silk threads.

In the light of day, hazy from so little sleep, he watched Renata pull Graziella through the new garden paths toward the greenhouse. He left his gift behind. He'd assign it to Graziella's care outside of the chatter of the girls. Let them have their twittering and comparing of gifts to themselves without his being part of it. Still, he wanted to witness their excitement, so he ran to join them. With each long stride to catch up, he questioned his middle-of-the-night inspiration. It was intimate and personal, and he feared it might have been in bad taste. But it was too late to make something else. *Basta! Stai calmo!* he ordered himself. He shifted his thoughts to more purposeful subjects: moving the painting back to the greenhouse studio later that week, the hope of a positive reaction by Graziella to his progress on the painting, the money he would send to his parents through Ficino.

The jumble of inside and outside chatter went silent, however, as he reached the greenhouse door only to see Piero rush out, blocking the entrance with his body. "You can't come in!"

"Graziella's going to bring our presents to Floriana, and they're inside," Renata said, pushing past her brother.

Gerome stepped out from behind the door, shoving Piero aside. "So you've found the young Jewish woman?" he said to Renata as the rest of the group stopped short in front of him. Graziella stepped forward.

"Who is inquiring?" Graziella asked.

"And who might you be?" Savonarola said.

"One who has her best interests in mind," Graziella answered.

Piero's head twitched. His sisters ran inside, trying to pull Graziella with them, but she wouldn't budge. She glared at Gerome, then stepped aside to allow Sandro to come forward. He placed himself in front of Savonarola.

"It is I who have Floriana's well-being most in mind, but I have not seen her for weeks, nor have any of the others. Forget her. Let me show you my recently completed Madonna."

"I prefer to learn more about this Floriana."

"And why is that?" Sandro asked.

"She's from my hometown and her mother yearns for news of her."

"Her mother's dead," Sandro said, suddenly attaching Savonarola's face onto Floriana's attacker. It was he, Gerome Savonarola, the one who had pressed her head into the sand, the faceless clergy who had mounted her from behind against her will. The image nauseated Sandro, but he would not turn away.

"And how was your visit with my cousin Lorenzo, Father Gerome?" Piero said to break the tension.

Without taking his eyes off Sandro, Gerome answered, "Master Botticelli's letter brought me right into Lorenzo's chambers where I was able to assist in the healing of—" but Sandro clamped his large hands around Gerome's bony throat.

"You're the one who left her to die!" Sandro said. "And I, the blind one, sending your evil into the house of my best friend, Lorenzo!"

Gerome's face did not change expression. His eyes, the eyes of a rat, moved from side to side, avoiding the gaze that wanted to make him bleed, to crack his liquid speech back into stuttering stones.

Squeezing his words out in a raspy whisper through the vice of Sandro's hands he said, "You accuse me falsely. I want her to know I have forgiven her for tempting my brothers to sin."

Sandro watched Gerome's eyes stop their movement and try to burn through Sandro's rage. "She's bursting with the fruits of *your* temptation."

"I thought you painted her that way—"

"You've seen it, after all. Liar!" Sandro said. "Another proof you're a criminal. You stole her innocence! And now you probably want to kill the child!"

With one hand, Sandro pressed Gerome's bony shoulder, holding him still, and with his other in a fist, he struck the priest in the face, downing him in one blow.

"She never saw your face. Never," Sandro said, standing over his victim. When Gerome turned away Sandro dropped to his knees and turned the priest's face toward his own and said, "And she never will! I'll kill you if you set foot near her."

When Sandro got to his feet, Gerome said, "I want only to ask her forgiveness," then wiped the blood from his face.

Sandro could see he had broken Gerome's nose. He felt a rattling in his own body as the images of this snake of a cleric slithering on Floriana's naked body played in his mind's eye. "How could you leave her in that filthy tower to die?"

"I left her to be cleansed and saved. Not one day has passed without my praying for her."

Sandro knelt again, but the priest cowered and Sandro stood up.

"Have you never given in to the flesh?" Savonarola raised himself into a seated position.

"I don't call myself a saver of souls and then rape a woman who tempts me."

"I'll pray for—"

"You should pray for yourself. I can't even look at your face without wanting to hit you again and again."

"I've been forgiven. I walk with that forgiveness. Guilt will not heal any soul."

"And who has forgiven you?"

"Your sister."

"She knows?"

"She suspected, and she took my confession, and I took hers."

"And she, what did she have to confess?"

"That's for me to know," Gerome said. He winced when Sandro fell back to his knees, raising his fist in the air to deliver yet another blow.

"I promised her I would not seek out Floriana or the child."

"And yet here you are doing just that! Your lies mangle my mind, Brother Gerome."

"Have you forgiven *yourself* for your lapses into the flesh?"

"I have through my actions toward Floriana. I have a new life since knowing her."

"And I have done the same," Gerome said.

Torn between his two heroes, Piero knelt to lift Savonarola. "How dare you strike him," he said, glaring at Sandro.

"He's the vermin who raped Floriana."

"And if he hadn't done it, you would not have met her! Your sister would not have found her," Piero said.

"Am I supposed to thank him for ruining her life and shaming the cloth he wears? No wonder he calls my Madonnas whores. His own eyes see lust everywhere!"

Looking at Gerome's bloodied face, Sandro felt his hands tremble as though the rage itself were becoming another being separate from him, with its own will to do more violence, but he resisted its pull.

"You disgust me," Sandro said, getting to his feet. He stomped off toward the house, blind to Poppi, who was limping toward her master. As Sandro disappeared into the house, he shook his hands to shed the trembling, willing the rage to leave through his fingertips.

Moments later, he stood in front of the painting, focusing on Floriana's face. *If he hadn't raped her, you wouldn't have painted it this way*, he heard himself saying. Still, his breathing was rapid. He knelt beside Filippino, grabbed a brush, and tried to paint the foreground, but his hands still trembled.

"That's enough for today. I need to be alone," he told Filippino, who knew his master's moods well enough to leave quickly.

Just as water reaches a rolling boil and then turns to steam, anger had risen in Sandro and he had struck without forethought. The shaking spread to his entire body as he saw Gerome's blood on his hands.

He ran to his room to scrape himself clean, to calm himself. Floriana's gift lay on his bed. It now assumed an even greater importance. He went to the balcony to breathe more deeply, but his eyes took in the greenhouse, and he watched as Piero, with his head astir, came running after Savonarola as the priest neared his donkey. Sandro felt a tiny twinge at having broken the spell of his young master's cure. Savonarola placed his hands on either side of Piero's head. Both men stood still. When Savonarola removed his hands, Piero's twitching stopped. The young man knelt to kiss the priest's robes, but Savonarola lifted Piero up by the elbow. The two embraced, and Piero headed back toward the greenhouse and his sisters as Savonarola disappeared.

Still trembling with anger, Sandro tried to calm himself. Piero's allegiance to both him and Savonarola nagged at him and yet he knew the boy could hardly choose between them. Feelings of satisfaction for having struck Savonarola swam through him along with a sense of shame at having lost control. Yet another part wished he had attacked more ferociously the vermin who had soiled Floriana. He was glad he had hurt him. Sandro watched Graziella, her arms full of the girls' presents, walk toward the house. He took Floriana's gift from his bed and carried it downstairs to meet her in his studio.

When Graziella entered the main room of the villa where Sandro worked, she heard Sandro mumbling as his head almost touched the picture, "Sister, oh sister, what could you have confessed to that chameleon priest, that defiler and healer all mixed in together?"

"Master Botticelli?" Graziella stood beside him with her gaze on the central figure.

"My sister, Oslavia."

"Floriana has told me how Oslavia saved her life and released her at risk of her own station."

"I've tried to recapture her courage using Renata's face. The spirit here is Oslavia's as much as I can remember her when she was sent to convent."

"And the arching tree trunks?"

"Anyone who stands in the shade of the Peredexion can speak only the truth. Oslavia relies heavily on its powers."

"Now we know the truth of Floriana's attacker—"

"You must swear you'll not tell Floriana what took place today. We've not seen the last of this priest. His words of confession and apology may be real, but she needn't hear them. What would your father say about this?"

"He might ask you why it's so important she not know."

"It can't change anything. She's suffered enough."

"She does not seem to be frightened any longer, only sad and lonely for this place. For you."

"As you can see today from the girls' gifts, we all miss her."

"She gave presents to everyone through me, but you ran off before I could give you this." Graziella placed a small silk bag into his palm.

"For me?"

"From Floriana."

"I'm still shaking with rage. I could have killed him."

"Murder rarely solves anything."

"He deserved at least my anger."

"But did it change anything?"

"He left."

"Physical assaults never erase thoughts," she said.

"What do *you* think about him?"

"I think he'll come back. I think he'll continue to search for her and the child."

"Are you saying I should have killed him?"

"I never said that. I said he's not through with her."

"Nor am I. Now you're here with gifts from the woman I love and admire."

"And what kind of love is it, Master Botticelli?"

"The most chaste of which I'm capable. Our separation keeps it so. If she were with me, I would still urge her to be my wife."

Graziella said nothing.

"You know her. Do you think she'd have me?"

"I think she's lonely. I think she doesn't know what is best for her."

"Your words pain me. I love her in more ways than I've ever loved anyone. Even in her absence I feel—" Sandro stopped himself and instead said, "Tell me what you think of this face, this Madonna."

Graziella turned her attention to the painting. She did not want to hear about Sandro's love for Floriana. She did not want to consider the words from one of the holy texts that had spoken to the root of her longing: "Pure, unselfish love draws to itself its own; it does not seek or demand." Still, she did not care to be "unselfish." She did not need to help another's love blossom. She did not need to be Sandro's ally. The less said the better. The more doubt she could create in Floriana about Sandro's intentions, the more she could press her own affections onto Floriana, and keep her close.

"This is a sad Madonna," she said. "She's right in the middle, but all alone in her shrine of trees."

"As Oslavia has been."

Sandro reached into his shirt and pulled out the small silk-wrapped item. "I have sewn it shut. It's meant for her eyes only."

Graziella removed Sandro's payment from her satchel before she put his gift for Floriana inside. "She'll be buoyed by your thoughtfulness."

Tears filled Sandro's eyes, and he turned away to keep from showing any more of his emotion.

CHAPTER FIFTY-TWO

Puzzles of the Heart

MOMENTS AFTER Graziella's departure, Sandro heard Piero's three sisters chattering and laughing their way toward him. He darted out of the salon, taking two steps at a time up the staircase to his private quarters.

Once inside his room, he closed the door, and placed a chair in front of it. He took Floriana's gift into the bed with him and threw the covers over his head. He brought the small silk bundle to his nose to breathe in the perfume.

He sat up and took out his tiny sketchbook, drawing a picture of her with the bag pressed to her belly. A tear down her left cheek. He pulled the leaf of paper from the sketchbook and placed it inside his shirt. Holding her gift in his hands, he savored the moment of imminent surprise, which was interrupted by the low whistle of a dove outside his door. *Luigi!*

Sandro leapt from the bed to pull the chair out of the way and open the door. "Let me see you!"

"Petrarchio told us Bernardino is on his way. He's coming to witness Floriana's conversion. Oslavia's praying night and day."

"Doesn't she always pray night and day?"

"She usually prays with her hands busy on her embroideries or studying the books, but now I see her go off to her forest sanctuary night and day, day and night. And old garlic man Petrarchio is missing, so she asked me to beg you to help her any way you can."

"You must go find Brother Savonarola. He was just here. Beg *him* to return with you to Oslavia's. Tell him she needs his help with Bernardino. Tell Oslavia I'll come to her tomorrow."

Sandro brought Luigi to the window to point out the direction the priest had taken as he left the estate. "He's traveling alone. You've got the cart and horse. You'll overtake him easily. But before you leave, Luigi, let me take a look at you." A few facial hairs had sprouted on the young boy's chin, and he had grown taller. "In another year you'll be ready for a decent apprenticeship."

"An apprenticeship for what?" Luigi asked.

"An art studio, perhaps. You'd be most sought after in Florence." The scene of his last visit to the artists' guild, the Company of Saint Luke, flashed through his memory, complete with pretty boys half as beautiful as Luigi, fawning over their masters—kisses and hugs and pats on the asses in easy supply in that all-male institution.

"The only apprenticeship I want, Master Botticelli, is with Master Ficino. I love his ideas about how to run the world. I'd love to be his student. Sister Oslavia says I'm meant for better things than groundskeeper. I even use a fork with my meals. I keep it here in my pocket and take it with me everywhere."

"I'll introduce you to others when the time is right," Sandro said. "Hurry to catch up with Brother Gerome. He'll be happy and grateful to follow you."

"Grateful?"

Sandro was not going to recount the nose-crushing scene. "Priests are always happy to make themselves useful where needed," he said, making a gesture with his hand to brush Luigi out of the room. *"Sbrigati!"* Sandro said while thinking: *let this devoted and deluded priest make himself useful once and for all!*

Once he closed the door, Sandro rescued Floriana's gift from under the covers. He sat at his little desk by the window. She too had sewn her gift shut. He brought the fabric to his teeth and bit the silk thread to break the seal. It appeared nothing was inside but scraps of torn paper, cypress nuts, and a small pearl. In addition, some dried rose petals had been thrown in.

He took the scraps of paper and began to arrange them. "Such a puzzle and a puzzler she is!" he said as he pieced the papers together. A gust of wind blew through the window, scattering the scraps. He dropped to his hands and knees to collect them. He sensed someone outside his door. "Who's there?" he demanded, annoyed for this second interruption.

"Renata. Can you open the door and talk to me?"

He gathered the scraps and placed them into the gift cloth with the cypress nuts.

A red-eyed Renata stood with tracks of her tears spread across her face.

"The girls have been teasing me about your 'Virgin.' They say because you painted me as one, I'll never marry. I'll be sent to a convent, as Oslavia was."

"Renata. You're beautiful in your own right before man and before God. Every woman, virgin or not, is a blessing from our Lord. Only He can determine your fate. It is your duty to cooperate with His voice within you."

"Which voice? They've told me I'm going to be a nun."

"There are worse things you could be," he said. "But a nun is not something you will be forced to become. If Piero has not sent your older sisters off, he won't send you."

"I posed as the Virgin!"

"I painted you more as the goddess of love, Venus. Soon I'll place the baby Cupid over your head."

"But how can Mary the Virgin also be Venus?"

"Because pure love and pure beauty are all one and the same. You, my sweet Renata, possess beauty and the capacity for much love. I've seen you and Floriana together."

"But what about what *I* want?"

"What do you want?"

"I want a husband and some power. Children too."

"So be it, if that is God's plan."

"And how do I know God's plan?" she asked.

"Come sit with me on the floor." He cleared a space for her amid his clutter of papers and bedsheets strewn about the room. "What did Floriana send you for a gift?"

"It was a bit strange. She sent me cypress pine nuts and a small doll she made out of them. One pine nut for a head, two pine nuts for the breasts. She had painted all of them. Attached to the leg she had sewn a miniature book with one embroidered letter on each page."

"And what did the letters spell?" he asked.

"Well they didn't spell anything."

"What were the letters?"

"e, m, o, r, a. Emora . . . what does that mean? Oh, I know," she said. "It's AMORE, love."

"Exactly! And you had to move things around to figure it out. It didn't come the way you expected."

"That's true," she said.

"And it's the same for what you love and what you want to do. The pieces come to us slowly, one at a time. If you decide to become a nun, then that is going to come from inside you and not from someone making you do it. Floriana said it. Love. You are love. She sends you love. All is love."

"My sisters have been jealous you have not yet painted them. They're getting back at me."

"You tell them that if they behave and are sweet and gracious with you and each other and everyone here, especially Filippino, that they just may find their way into my painting."

"Really?"

"Only if you all return to the sweetness and cooperation you had when you were helping me with Floriana."

"What did she give you? A romantic letter, I bet."

"No. I got a puzzle too. I was trying to figure it out when you knocked."

"Can I help?"

"You can help by leaving right now and telling your sisters what I told you. I'll work on the secret code of what she's sent me and if I need some help I'll come to no one but you."

"I love you, Master Botticelli," Renata said, and threw her arms about him.

"See?" he said. "Love, love, love is everywhere."

As she turned to run out of his room, he grabbed the glue to work on Floriana's gift.

Piecing the scraps together, he realized why she had gone to such lengths. To have sent a plain letter that could have been used to trace her whereabouts or embarrass him would have been too risky. With his heart beating somewhere between fear and anticipation of what she was going to say—if in fact he would be able to decipher it—he tried to stay calm, shifting his focus between the puzzle and his sense of urgency to help his sister as soon as possible. He must protect her from Bernardino's wrath. And if Luigi hadn't found Savonarola, then Sandro himself would have to seek out the victim of his rage, apologize, and ask a favor at the same time. All these thoughts scrambled through his head as he continued piecing the scraps together until the last piece was attached. Sandro sat back to squint, blurring away the torn edges and concentrating on the words that emerged:

Dearest Sandro,

If you have taken the time to piece this together you will know the content of my heart. Just as the words have been torn into so many pieces, so too is my heart torn with thoughts to bolster me and make me brave, but when I put the pieces together I don't feel strong, but weak, for I cannot make myself whole. When I was with you I felt whole. Even though I say you are married to your work, I know and I feel that your spirit and mine are married in some larger place with God. I am frightened for the baby who is almost here. I wish you could hold me again and reassure me and nurture me the way you have, petting my head and weaving flowers into my hair, and I wish I could calm you and nurture you, too, in your work. I curse him who brought me to this place of motherhood uninvited, and yet I bless him for having done so, for if he hadn't, I would not have known you or loved you. Graziella has told me God punishes with one hand, with the other he embraces. So there, if you read this, please come to me at the month's end to be with me when the baby is due, if you can. In any way you can, Floriana

"Silly beauty!" he said as though she were right there with him. "No need to be so doubting to test my love with your puzzle, but so . . ." He kissed the scarred letter and held it to his forehead and then to his heart. "So . . . loveable! So adorable you are, my sweet puzzler Floriana!"

What a day of emotion he was having! Almost killing a man with his anger one moment and now weak in his limbs, overcome with instant happiness the next. "*Your spirit and mine are married in some larger place with God*," she had written, and his fear about the intimacy of his gift to her melted away.

CHAPTER FIFTY-THREE

Savonarola on the Road Again

EXHAUSTED AND SHAKEN from Sandro's blows to his face, Savonarola stopped at the first clearing beside a stream. While the donkey drank, Gerome gathered a few soft branches to lay on the ground under blankets. The pain in his cheeks and nose and behind his eyes raged with such a force he could feel its ripples in his tongue and teeth. He let out a gasp as he stretched out on his makeshift bed. The memories of all his earlier self-inflicted austerities returned and he smiled with nostalgia. This was another tip of the whip, only this time it had come through Sandro.

As he dozed, the fantasy of Sandro heaving his lewd paintings into a bonfire calmed Savonarola. A parade of other artists, known and unknown, followed Sandro's lead. As Gerome drifted into unconsciousness, he felt the heat of flames on his fingertips and listened to the sound of water boiling over a pot, sizzling with embers beneath it. The hissing sound became the sound of twigs and branches cracking under someone's foot. Gerome opened his eyes to see Luigi wearing an expression of horror as he looked at the battered priest.

"Don't be frightened. It probably looks worse than it is," Gerome told the boy. "I fell on some rocks."

"Do you remember Bandini's helper, Petrarchio, whose back you worked on?"

"How is the garlic man?"

"Missing! And Sister Oslavia needs your help to find him. Master Botticelli sent me to you so you could help her. Bernardino is finally coming for the Jew girl, Floriana, and she's no longer there, as you know, and Bandini died, and Bernardino is going to hold Oslavia responsible and you must come to protect her. Sandro said you would do it. That you owe him one."

"One what?"

"One act of kindness and forgiveness. That you'd be the best one to turn Bernardino away. Please come."

"I was awaiting my next assignment, and you've brought it. Tell Sister Oslavia I'll be there by nightfall. I'll stay as long as needed."

"Are you sure you know the way?" Luigi asked.

"How can I be lost when God himself is calling me through you and another of his special children, Sister Oslavia?"

"What about Petrarchio?" Luigi asked.

"I'll keep my eyes open for him. You go on ahead now and put Sister Oslavia's heart at ease. Tell her I'll protect her from the raging Bernardino."

WHEN GEROME REACHED the fork in the road at the crest of the hill about a mile from the entrance to the monastery, he saw Piattini and Dono approaching him from the Bologna road. The three priests merged their paths and continued on in silence toward the compound.

Gerome knew his pummeled face and broken nose would be a topic of alarm for his companions, who now wore the robes of ordained priests. Gerome put his finger to his lips to insist on no speaking.

After a few moments, he simply said, "Sandro Botticelli. It will bring us closer."

"Bring you closer?" Piattini and Dono asked in unison.

"God has more in mind for him and me. The violence that spewed forth from him was a good sign."

"How?" Dono asked.

"He and I have the same impulses. He knows how I live my life now that I have succeeded in squelching carnality for the higher plane. He'll come to follow."

Before they were able to say any more, the three of them saw what appeared to be a huge sack on the side of the road.

"Supplies might have slipped off someone's cart," Dono said. "We won't arrive empty-handed."

"Unchanged you are," Gerome said. "You're suggesting we steal another's supply and claim it as our own?"

Before any of them could say another word, the sack moved.

"An animal trapped inside," Piattini said. "Let's set it free." The three moved closer, then jerked backwards when a feeble, gnarled human hand shot out of the open sack.

"Petrarchio?" Gerome asked. He kicked the side of his donkey to get closer but the beast wanted none of it.

"Petrarchio, is that you?" shouted Gerome once again.

The hand raised into the air followed by a faint groan.

The familiar stench hit them—garlic, only now it was mixed with the smell of urine and feces. Flies buzzed around the sack. Gerome pulled down a side of the cloth, which turned out to be no sack at all, but a coarse blanket in which Petrarchio had become entangled, tripping himself. He must have been lying on the ground for hours. Gerome pulled off enough of the blanket to expose the old man's face, which was covered in scratches. Blotches of blood dotted his robes.

"What have you done? What are you doing?" Gerome asked the old man. To Dono he said, "Bring water and a blanket."

"Don't touch him!" Dono said as he drew away in revulsion from the sight.

"Did your ordination mean nothing to you? He's one of God's creatures, and one of the more faithful. Water!"

Dono extended the water cup.

"We have one blanket left," Piattini said. "None for ourselves."

"God will provide," Gerome said, then turned back to Petrarchio.

"I was coming to get Bandini," the old man said.

The three prelates looked at each other. Petrarchio had lost his hold on the real world.

"And what were you wanting to tell him?" Gerome asked as he brought the water to Petrarchio's mouth, then peeled off the old clothing, exposing a body covered with scars and sores, some oozing. Gerome fought off the flies. "The vultures almost had you for breakfast!" Gerome undressed him and wrapped him in the blanket.

"You're the vultures," Petrarchio said. "Pick at me and let me go to heaven. I want to go to heaven, but first I have to find Bandini and tell him Bernardino is coming."

"Where do you think Bandini is?" Gerome asked. Piattini knelt to peel off Petrarchio's mud-encrusted sandals, then washed his feet.

"Not the garlic!" Petrarchio said as Gerome removed the braided garlic bulbs, covered with blood and spittle, from around the old man's neck.

"We need to clean you off. We'll get fresh cloves once we get back to the convent."

"Bandini. I must tell him."

"We'll tell him." Gerome hoisted Petrarchio onto his donkey and walked beside it. He sent Piattini and Dono ahead to give news of Petrarchio with orders that Luigi should return with the cart to help. As pain in Gerome's face and temples returned, reminding him how he'd forgotten it when attending to someone else in far greater pain, he recited to himself a silent blessing and thanks to God that, unlike Petrarchio's condition, his pain was only temporary.

CHAPTER FIFTY-FOUR

Graziella Brings Floriana Her Gifts

NABLE TO CALM HER FEARS of Sandro's indifference to her note, or worse, that it had come into the wrong hands, Floriana paced until she saw Graziella's form take shape through the dusk.

"What news have you for me?" she asked as she ran to Graziella's side.

Graziella led Floriana by the hand to a clearing in the yard and sat her at the foot of a tree. "Close your eyes, and I'll be right back. Don't open them, please."

Floriana leaned her head against the trunk of the tree. *I'll pretend this is the Peredexion tree and I can only speak the truth underneath it,* she thought, and a flash of longing for Oslavia, whom she had not seen for months, overcame her. *Tears again! Why am I always crying! I'm happy and cry, or frightened and cry, or I think of someone and cry.*

She decided her tears must be part of being with child, so she wouldn't stop them. This thought alone dried her eyes and made her laugh until she heard Graziella approaching.

"Don't open your eyes," Graziella ordered.

Floriana sat with open palms on her lap. "I'm ready," she said.

"Imagine the energy of the being inside that tree."

"Must you make everything into a ritual?" Floriana laughed, but she had grown impatient with Graziella's games.

"It heightens the senses and helps you remember every second of every day. And besides," Graziella added, "it will make your inner powers stronger if and when you're alone defending yourself and your child."

"You're frightening me!"

"I mean only to educate you in the secrets my father has shown to me. Imagine God's presence moving from the leaves through the branches into the trunk and into the depths of the roots. Can you feel it?"

Floriana took a deep breath and feigned concentration. "I can feel it."

"Imagine that energy coming from deep in the earth, passing through the roots up the trunk and out through the tips of the branches and leaves."

Floriana was silent for a while. "I feel it," Floriana said, knowing she would say whatever it took to move this game along.

"Now draw from the heavens once again the power through the branches and have the force go through your back and spine as it travels below the earth."

"And now?"

"Now we're almost there," Graziella said. "Now imagine the darkest night of evil seeping into the roots from the bowels of the earth and passing into the trunk and into your spine as well, and as it passes through you and the tree it releases the darkness into the heavens, and the light of day."

"It's already night," Floriana said.

"We're releasing your fears and the fears and darkness of the deepest places, and sending it out to the moon, to the sun, to the last light of this day and once it is all released I want you to breathe in and pull in all the beauty of this night and this season of spring into the tips of those leaves, into the top of your head, and now you're one with the tree. You are the tree. You are filled with the peace and patience and power of this tree constantly fed by the air, the sun, and the rain. Feel it with your whole self."

"I am the tree. I am strong and powerful and I need say nothing. My roots are deep," she said, tears in her eyes again! She held her hands out. Graziella placed something on her outstretched arms. With her eyes closed, Floriana said, "From Renata? It's small and sweet just as she is."

"Open it with your eyes closed," Graziella said.

"It is from Renata, isn't it?"

"Yes. Open your eyes."

Inside the cloth envelope, wrapped with a narrow pink ribbon, Floriana found dried rose petals and a tiny gold ring.

"Hers since birth," Graziella said. "She had worn it around her neck but it should fit you."

"How can I take this?"

"She wanted you to give it to the baby. She said the ring will fit your tiniest finger." Floriana placed it on her hand, next to the ring Sandro had given her.

"She hoped you might return it to her when she has her first child."

Floriana said nothing. How could she know where she would be, or if she would be near enough to satisfy that request?

"Close your eyes!" Graziella said, and Floriana returned to their game with her empty hands outstretched to receive the next gift, a round bumpy object.

She brought it to her nose to breathe in the scent of oranges and cloves.

"They thought the sweetness might help you. Hang it over the crib and the baby will digest his food correctly, for the clove and the orange combine to give off the fruit of sweet gold."

"I don't know if I'll place it above *her* head. What if it were to drop onto Devorah's head? From Donata and Margarita?"

"Yes, and this third one is from Master Piero. He was stung by the beauty of the bee you made him whereupon he strode instantly to his chambers and sent this to you from himself and Poppi."

It was a miniature replica of one of Piero's pug dogs. "Now close your eyes again and I'll bring Master Botticelli's gift."

"Oh, what joy!"

Graziella placed onto Floriana's palms the silk packet Sandro had sewn lovingly out of the scarf he always wore tied to his neck.

"This package alone is enough!" she said, then brought the silk cloth to her nose. "The scent of him is so strong! I can smell his world, the pigments of the colors, the perspiration as he worked."

"I'll leave you alone with it, but it's so dark now you won't be able to see it. He also gave me the gift of a hug to give to you if I may."

Floriana opened her arms wide, holding on to Graziella, imagining the sensation of Sandro's strong body against hers, remembering their last night together and how hard it had been to let go of him. Graziella held on a bit longer than Floriana wanted her to, so she pulled away. "I can smell him on you, on this gift. I'll take it with me to my bed and by candlelight I'll open it if you don't mind," Floriana said, looking at it even more closely. "You opened his gift! How could you?"

"I didn't!"

"I can see these golden threads are broken. How could you?"

"It fell from my purse while I was galloping. It was the last to go in, so it fell out. I brushed off the earth and the thread broke."

"You opened my gift!"

"The thread was coming loose when I picked it up off the ground. I tried to pull it tighter but it came loose."

"You opened his gift! Did you open the one I sent with you for him?"

"No. I gave it to him. He was happy that you were thinking of him."

"Swear you did not open it!"

"I swear. It was sealed with your threads. I opened none of the gifts. I would never."

"But this one. Why this one?"

"Trust me, Floriana. It fell. I didn't look inside."

"Not even a glimpse?"

"I wanted to but I held myself back."

"Thank you," Floriana said.

GRAZIELLA SAW even in the dark of night that Floriana's face had turned red again the way it did whenever she became agitated or upset. She had opened a crack of doubt in Floriana. One crack narrower than Sandro's golden thread, but wide enough to carve a river of regret between her and her beloved Floriana.

"I must re-shoe the horse before he throws me the next time," she said, but Floriana was no longer listening. She had put Sandro's gift up to her nose to take in any hint of Sandro's skin, any scent of his paints, his touch. Floriana was lost to her for sure.

An ache encircled Graziella's heart, pinching it tighter, piercing the center so she was forced to hold her breath. Any attempt to inhale or exhale pushed the pain deeper.

Graziella could see a curtain of doubt cloud Floriana's eyes as she sat as still as a stone, waiting patiently for Graziella to leave her alone.

Instead of their usual sisterly embrace at bedtime, Graziella turned away, covering the stain of her discolored cheek with her hand. She had carried the flaw all her life as a mark of pride, but now it became its own vast lake of shame and ugliness in which she might drown.

FLORIANA SAT BY CANDLELIGHT, summoning the courage to open Sandro's present. Even though the threads of the gift's packaging had been broken, she decided to pretend her trust in Graziella had not been bruised.

Sandro's gift could not have been an answer to her gift. Surely he hadn't had the time to piece her love letter together. And if he had, and his gift was fatherly instead of romantic, she would feel shame for what she had written.

If, instead, his letter or gift was openly loving in a romantic way, and he had risked telling her of his true heart, then she would feel shame at having been so careful to have protected herself by tearing up her own love letter.

She paced. *Better to not open it.* She soon abandoned that idea.

If he no longer loves me, or if he loves me only as a father and protector, I have not lost, I have gained. And if he loves me as a lover, and longs for me as much as I for him, then what are we to do? As she vacillated with a shawl about her shoulders, the child in her belly moved as if it had an opinion. *And what do you wish, my unborn jewel?* she asked. *Shall I open it? If you move that means yes. If you are still that means no.*

The child moved and turned once more in her womb. She took a deep breath and delicately brought the scarf-wrapped object to her face.

She pulled at the broken gold thread that formed the outer wrapping, then pulled out another small object wrapped many times over. Inside she found a small folio of sketches and the same golden threads that had sewn the booklet together. She tore open the tops of the folios so she could see on the inside of the pages. *At least if Graziella looked inside the gift, she didn't look all the way in.* The inside leaf had the words, *To my beloved Floriana, my muse and savior.*

She tore the top fold open and saw lilac pressed between the pages. He had secured it to the page with rabbit's skin glue. She turned the next page. On one side was a profile of Sandro blowing a kiss with wings on it across the page to the opposite side where a sketch of her with outstretched palms was catching it.

"*For you to feel the warmth of my breath on your lips,*" he had written.

The next page held the image of a penis with wings and it was blurred. "*He yearns for you so much that tears have smeared this drawing,*" he wrote.

On the next page, he wrote, "*But my organ of delight is hardly worth satisfying without your willing love and devotion to set him free if you long for me in that way. Let me come to you in whatever way you choose.*" More petals, fallen petals of flowers drawn and tears smearing that as well.

In the last page, he had drawn the picture of a dove carrying the Star of David, and written the words, "*To my sweet Jewess, I await your command.*"

If he had read her letter, he would surely come to her. She regretted tearing it up. If he loved her half as much as she loved him, he would have realized it was a puzzle for him to solve and he would have read her words.

One last object was in the package, so small she almost missed it. A seed. A tiny mustard seed glued onto the back of the folio. "*Do not underestimate the power of the mustard seed,*" he wrote. "*Plant it inside your heart for me and let it grow. I will water it if you but allow me to.*"

She pulled the seed off the card to put it inside her mouth, but then ran out into the night with a drinking cup and filled it with the soft spring earth. She returned to her room and planted the seed deep into the cup and placed it by a wall under the light of the moon. "Grow!" she whispered to it. "Grow and fill us both with a way to bring us together if it is our Almighty's wish."

She tied the silk scarf around her neck to have Sandro's scent on her and she crawled under the covers, bringing the candle beside her, and opened the page to the picture of the blurry penis with wings. Her muffled sighs alternated with laughter. The baby turned and kicked as Floriana slipped into a dream. A soft wind blew out the candlelight.

CHAPTER FIFTY-FIVE

Oslavia Encounters Gerome

STILL IGNORANT OF SANDRO'S ATTACK on her fellow cleric, Oslavia hurried through the secret tunnel from the convent into the monastery cellar. She was grateful Gerome had brought Petrarchio back alive and that he was back to help her face the proselytizing and bigoted Bernardino.

Once above ground she encountered Piattini and Dono.

"And bless this day," she said.

"And bless this day," they answered.

"Is Father Savonarola up and about?" she asked.

"Since dawn, Sister, he's been ministering to Petrarchio's sores and raving tongue. He fears the old man will let slip some words about the young Jewess and Bernardino will interrogate us all to find what actually happened to her."

"Tell Bernardino to come to me with his questions," Oslavia said. "I'm the only one who knows what was going on here. Bandini was a recluse most of the time. Floriana arrived wearing the hood of shame, so neither Bandini nor Petrarchio ever set eyes on her. No one can be certain who the young woman actually is."

"And lying doesn't bother you, Sister Oslavia?" Dono asked.

"No God would judge her a harlot. She is what she is, and we're called on to conceal her whereabouts."

"And where might that whereabouts be?" Piattini asked.

"Not even I know."

"What will you tell Bernardino?"

"Never mind," Oslavia said. "Just direct all inquiries to me and say nothing. The truth is, you've never set eyes on this person."

"We've seen Master Botticelli's painting of her."

"My brother also painted me in that painting as a fourteen-year-old virgin."

"You're still a virgin," Dono said.

"After a life of suffering, one piece of skin does not a virgin make."

Piattini shushed her. "We're in a house of God."

"This house," she answered, "has been my home since the age of twelve. I can raise my voice as I please for God's sake."

"We've been told that in the house of God we don't invoke the devil."

"Talking about a flap of skin is not devilish. The sin resides in your own imagination, Brother Piattini."

He bowed to her, exchanging glances with Dono as the two newly ordained priests began to walk away.

"One minute," she said as she grabbed the edge of Piattini's robe and pulled him closer to her. "What are you devout men about to do?"

"Heading for more prayer out on the grounds."

"Since you're here to help out, I would like to ask you for something more than your prayers, if you don't mind," she said.

"And how can we serve you, Abbess Oslavia?"

"Don't call me abbess!" she said with a wave of the hand. "I have heard you three go about presenting plays of conversions and redemption, or moments of salvation."

"We do."

"I want you to prepare a performance for Bernardino. It might distract him from his mission here."

"What kind of performance?" Dono asked.

"Something unexpected, of course. Something entertaining. You can work on it today, and when Bernardino arrives, you'll be ready."

"And if he arrives this today?" Piattini asked.

"You'll improvise. Do something you've already done but you must add in a conversion of a Jew to a Christian. One of you will have to play the young girl. A pity about those beards. Recruit a young man with peach fuzz."

"We could enlist one of your novitiates to play the part," Dono said.

"Absolutely not!" Oslavia said. "And get to it. *Subito!* Make it brilliant so Bernardino will be mesmerized."

Oslavia walked with a force inside her body that made her feel taller. She breathed deeply and held her head high. Talking openly to Dono and Piattini peeled away yet another layer of scar tissue that had grown over her heart muscle from years of repression and resignation. With Bandini gone, and with the freeing of Floriana, and with the emergence of her own independence beyond the men of the cloth who had weighed her down, Oslavia felt herself defying gravity, her body at the point of levitation. She had confessed her youthful blot to Savonarola, and he had confessed his to her. At the very least, they were comrades against the edicts of the pope. In spite of her earlier loathing of him, her mistrust of his lies and manipulations, he *had* returned to help her.

As she walked toward Gerome's chamber, she allowed her heart to open to him and his work, to forgive him and to join with him as his equal. All this she constructed in her imagination, and with communion in their common love for God, she was fused to him, supported by him.

She had intended to pass the monastic cells on her way to find him as he was ministering to Petrarchio but sensed someone's presence inside one of the rooms. Even though the door was open, she hesitated. It was Brother Gerome; she could tell even though his back was to her. He was sitting on a cot. He swayed from left to right and then circled. *Was he in prayer?*

She had never seen that type of prayer movement and so she waited, holding back the excitement she had wanted to share. A heavy cloth, one of his habits, hung over the window and he had candles burning even though it was morning.

He turned his body toward her so she could see his profile. With his eyes closed, he let a hissing sound out slowly from his mouth. With one quick jerk of his hand he threw his robe off and stiffened his naked back, lifting his legs in the air stiffly. He held his pulsing member, pulling it and taming it like a small beast, a viper, a dragon, and she saw it in a last spasm. A convulsion. His toes curling, his hissing louder, and now his entire robe lay on the bed. The candlelight caught a small path of scarred flesh on his back as he slapped himself hard on his thigh, his chest, until the creamy white fluid spilled in clumps out of the mouth of the viper.

Oslavia dared not move. No saliva in her mouth. The sound of metal hitting the floor. It was a crucifix he had slapped against his thigh. Gerome had become the viper, its head now drooping, his breath soft and a faint sigh of pleasure—eerie and evil on his lips—between Latin syllables.

Oslavia's hair, her scalp under the habit, itched as she prayed for herself to vanish, to return to their upcoming theatrical conversion skit for Bernardino, but she dared not move or make a sound.

"You!" he said, looking around and throwing his robes on. "Can you not announce yourself!"

All that sea of religious ecstasy that had carried her through the tunnel emptied from her mind and she stood there unable to speak, gazing into Gerome's bruised and distorted face.

"I'm still a man," he said. "And what I do in private I must do sometimes to hold off a bigger flood of recklessness. Better that I release myself from time to time than to bottle it up and lose myself—"

"Onto some innocent woman's back," she said, finishing his sentence. "You are a hypocrite like all the others," she said, and turned to leave.

"Stop! I command it!" he said, but she ran away into the dark tunnel.

NOW HER HEART, which had soared moments earlier, beat loudly in her chest, in her ears, in her wrists. A wave of fear and nausea overcame her. *But this is the best we have*, she told herself. Then, everything turned yet again in her favor as her mind shifted. She had seen him at his weakest moment. This became one more act to bind them. She knew more of his secrets, and this knowledge she could use to her advantage. She laughed out loud, picturing him, for he had looked silly and hairy and his toes had spread apart in his onanistic reverie. After another deep breath, calm returned as she whispered "amen" to herself, then, "Thank you. Thank you. Thank you," to God on high and the newer, more intimate God in her heart.

This concept of switching from one way of thinking to its opposite was not a new concept for Oslavia. She had been switching year after year from her own young girl thoughts into the mental garment of the church. She was well practiced in sublimation, redirection, shifting from self to God. But this was a new side of the talent and once again the power returned as she claimed her confidence, hard won after all these years, to follow her truth.

Oslavia made her way through the tunnel into the convent side of the complex, then above ground into the abbey, then outside to breathe the warm spring air. As she exited the door, Sandro's loving face beamed at her.

He had galloped from the Villa di Castello toward his sister's convent on the wings of romantic bliss. His love, Floriana, loved him. There was no doubt. It was all that mattered. But moments after Oslavia set eyes on him, his mood shifted as she trembled in his arms.

"Your heart's jumping out of your chest," he said. "Is this about Bernardino?"

She pulled away. "I'm happy you're here. I'm happy Brother Gerome brought Petrarchio back alive. But to put my fate in that priest's hands—I don't trust him."

"You don't have to keep his secret. When I realized it was he who attacked Floriana, I broke his nose—"

"No wonder his face is such a bruised mess!" she said, then laughed out loud with pleasure from learning the cause of Gerome's smashed face.

"Had I not torn myself away from him, I might have done worse. When Luigi asked me to help you, I sent him after the beast even though I had just wanted to kill him."

"I've drafted his new 'priests' to stage a mock conversion for Bernardino."

"First tell me the secret he pulled out of you."

Before he could say another word, Oslavia grabbed Sandro's hand and pulled him toward the forest.

"We must go to the Peredexion," she said. "There's only a stump! Damn that Gerome! With one hand he punishes and the other he heals. His men cut it down for firewood this winter."

Once inside the forest, seated at the spot of the former Peredexion tree, brother and sister formed a circle with their hands around what was left of its trunk. Small shoots and new leaves grew toward the light.

"Pretend the tree's inside your heart," Sandro said. "I've painted you underneath one. All the philosophers concur: love and friendship are what carry human beings above—"

"You're not the only one who has left a loved one."

"You had a lover?" Sandro asked.

"I had a child. A daughter. She did not survive. I called her Empiria."

"You told Floriana about this but not me? When? How did this happen?" Sandro said, breaking the chain of their hands. "I carved that name on a grave Floriana and I made together."

"I told Floriana of a child born on the convent grounds. I told her someone else was the mother. I wanted her to understand why I agreed to help her. Where was this grave?"

"It was inside a cave on Piero's land. The remains we found were of a child no more than two years old. And with a doll. Both interred in a sacrament box."

"They bound my breasts to stop my milk. They buried her in these walls. When a vow of chastity is the order of the convent, the secret stays inside."

"The pope and others have their secret babies and their mistresses. Why were you not able to keep her?"

"I was fourteen years old! I had no say. They decided for me, while a piece of my soul was torn from me. Now you know why I let Floriana go. It was the first act of freedom I had taken—an act of saving another baby when I could not save my own."

"And the father?"

"One who wore the cloak of clergy but had no spirit for it. He soon left the church never knowing he had impregnated me."

"Who knows of this?"

"Only you and now that silver-tongued priest half saint, half satyr."

"How did you survive?"

"Prayer, prayer, and more prayer."

"I don't want to lay eyes on Savonarola if I don't have to. It would make me want to kill him for the wrongs one of his kind has done to you."

"There's no need for you to see him. What about Floriana?"

"I'm going to her when the baby's due," Sandro said.

"What would you like me to say?"

"I remember only the kindness you have offered to her, the freedom she owes to you."

"And to you, Sandro, for letting her go."

"I did let her go. But she's asked me in a letter to come to her in whatever way I choose—protector, lover. But to go to her when the baby is due, which is soon."

"I can't advise you, Sandro. I've been in a closed world too long to know what to tell you."

The words "whatever way I choose" set off a sudden wave of anxiety about the gift he had prepared for Floriana, especially the drawing of the winged penis. A pain pierced his chest and with it a wave of doubts. In spite of that brief moment in their embrace in the cantina of Villa di Castello when she referred to his male member pressing against her as a caged bird, had he been too insensitive to have held on to her words and then to have illustrated such an intimate part of himself? Might she have been so revolted by its impropriety, especially given the trauma of her rape, that her affections would sour?

He noticed rosary beads tied around Oslavia's robes, and for instant relief, he imagined himself counting one bead at a time to the rhythm of Floriana's tease: "He loves me. He loves me not," only substituting the words: "She loves the drawing. She hates the drawing."

"I can see you've gone off into one of your dream worlds. Where are you?" Oslavia said.

"Who am I? There are so many warring parts of me. It's hard to know the true voice to listen to."

Oslavia made no attempt to lead him through his confusion. Instead she listened to the morning birds. "Hear those birds who sing without ceasing?" Oslavia said. "We're meant to do that, yet we stop ourselves. I never found my true voice until I let Floriana go."

"And I, too, felt that. As much as I wanted to possess her and save her, and to make her be a part of my life, loving her and releasing her seemed purer. But things can change."

"They always do," she said with a voice of surrender.

As they exited the forest and walked toward a courtyard, bells were ringing.

"Whoever thought Petrarchio would be able to climb that bell tower again? Gerome—a physician of the soul, he also knows how to heal the body," Oslavia said.

"You were just saying before the bells started that letting Floriana go helped you to find your own true voice."

"I've only begun to hear it. The challenge is to use it."

"Leaving the convent?"

"What I know is I'll not be subjected to anyone's definition of God when He lives inside my heart the way He does since I freed Floriana. There's no turning back for me. What about you?"

"What about me?"

"Trust yourself and move from your heart, as you do with your work. For a life is surely a continuous work of art."

"But we can only stand back and study it when we're almost dead," he said. "If we want guarantees—"

"Yes? Go on?"

"If we want guarantees, we'll never move ahead."

"Yes, and when you came to your young patron, weren't you sad and bemoaning your fate? Now you're not only in love, but you're creating a work that is truly your own."

"We must always leave the future open. No certainty of the outcome of our choices." Sandro stood still, contemplating the weight of his own words—words, at least for the moment, gave him confidence. He would trust Floriana. She understood him and his intentions. She would see that mustard seed.

CHAPTER FIFTY-SIX

The Conversion

A FEW DAYS BEFORE EASTER—Petrarchio rang the bells with enormous force, signaling the feared Franciscan Bernardino's arrival.

Oslavia walked toward the caretaker's cottage just as Bernardino's cart arrived. A primitive cage woven from twigs and thorny rose stalks, it sat on top of two large wooden wheels, and it lurched backward when Bernardino's men unhitched it from the donkeys. A tall Bernardino walked toward her, leaving his entourage behind. As they neared each other, Oslavia could see that, although his mouth formed a smile, his eyes, a cerulean blue, were more like ice than sky. His ruddy cheeks brought back the memory of Bandini's apoplexy. At that moment she hoped for a repeat performance of Bandini's demise by this new Franciscan rather than the performance of the mock conversion she and Brother Gerome's men had concocted. Although neither she nor Brother Gerome, nor any of the residents of their religious compound, had witnessed Bernardino in action, Bandini had praised Bernardino's violence and the results it produced. The memory of those stories caused her chest to quiver and her jaw to clench.

"*Salve,*" Oslavia said and bowed, "Abbess Oslavia Filipepi at your service."

In spite of the warm spring day, the Bishop Bernardino threw a red bishop's cloak over his shoulders and said, "Show me the way to the Jew! What did you say your name was, Sister?"

"Oslavia."

"Is your name not German?" Bernardino said.

"My parents are simple Florentines and have never revealed the source of my name, so it has always seemed normal to me."

"It is unusual," he said.

"I was happy that I might keep it as it is."

"I say we add Maria in front of it. I name you Maria Oslavia and you will be more pleasing to the Lord for this."

Imaginary straps of confinement wrapped around Oslavia's wrists and shoulders. In that moment, she knew Bernardino would take great offense at what had seemed to her earlier as God's sense of humor working through her. But it was too late.

"Maria Oslavia it is, Monsignor Bernardino," she said even though she had no intention to obey his absurd suggestion.

"Let the conversion begin," she said. "I'll lead you to our Jew! We have been preparing for your visit for months, Monsignor Bernardino. At last we hope to entertain you with our presentation."

When they reached the clearing designated as the stage—the one patch of meadow below the dense and thorny rose bushes that separated the monastery from the convent—Gerome stepped onto the stage area and spoke. "Greetings, Monsignor Bernardino."

Bernardino came forward to embrace Gerome, but the younger held his palm toward the large cleric to keep him from coming any closer.

"Stop in the name of conversions!" Gerome said, almost hissing the words. "We are so honored by your arrival that we have prepared our own proper greeting to one who has done so much to increase the reach of the church."

Gerome raised and lowered his head, then pointed to the bell tower where Petrarchio's wobbly head peered out the small window in anticipation of the agreed upon signal. The bells rang in a smooth, even-paced rhythm: three bells, then five bells, then three.

The men and women from both orders paraded in silence onto the lawn. A large carpet hung from a rope tied between two trees, separating the seating of men and women. Oslavia motioned for Bernardino to sit in a throne-like chair that had been placed at the head of the separating panel. The right side of Bernardino's back was visible to the men and the left to the women.

Luigi-as-Floriana stepped into the circle of the stage. He wore a wig made of blonde horsehair cut from the old mare's tail and a long dress Oslavia had found among the leftover garments that had belonged to Luigi's mother, Nicola. Dono had painted the boy's lips red with the juice of a berry plant. Strands of Luigi's dark curls protruded under the yellow mass. He walked about the stage dragging a huge wooden Star of David half his height, then sat in front of the star, bowed his head, and placed his hands together in prayer.

Dono appeared dressed as the devil in red leggings. A large twig-stuffed pointed tail wagged behind him. The devil's vest, covered with the blood of a goose they'd sacrificed for Bernardino's dinner, added a touch of gore. Oslavia had tied short twigs into Dono's hair.

Sitting just behind and to the left of Bernardino, Oslavia heard her novitiates stirring.

"How dare you think of converting!" the devil said. "You must keep your faith in Israel."

"But," Luigi answered in as high a voice as he could. It cracked from high to low and back to high again. "I know nothing of Judaism. They're going to kill me if I don't do it."

Piattini as an angel fluttered on stage. He wore shimmering robes and the wings strapped to his back had been fashioned from young tree branches tied into hoops with green leaves to form the wings' centers. Onto this they had glued white feathers from the unfortunate goose.

One of the male novitiates coughed and sneezed. A number of the men fought back laughter.

The women kept their silence. Oslavia turned and nodded her approval.

Petrarchio, who had not been cast for the performance, shuffled across the stage unannounced with three rows of garlic around his neck. He presented a wide grin full of rotted teeth, while making a continuous popping sound with his lips as he smiled at Bernardino. The devil shooed him away. He turned and ran back toward the bell tower.

Bernardino cleared his throat, then lifted himself out of the chair, but sat back when Oslavia placed her hand on his shoulder and whispered, "Give them a chance, Monsignor. They're a little nervous."

Savonarola stepped forward. He had placed a large pillow under his belt to simulate the girth of the deceased Bandini. "My wicked woman of sin," he said to the wilting convert. "Arise and choose! One way is to salvation and the other damnation to be chained to your religion, which has long ago died and lost its meaning."

"I am following the instructions of my family, who have loved me and cared for me," Luigi said as Floriana.

The false Bandini said, "See how little that protection has brought you. Join the church, and you will find at last your true home."

Savonarola as the Converter stepped forward, and with his gaze glued on the cerulean magnets inside Bernardino's face, he launched a fiery and convincing oratory about the sins of the world and the secret sins we all carry moment by moment inside our hearts.

In the end, instead of laughter, Oslavia heard sighs and whimpering, noses sniffling, and communal muffled wailing sounds from the audience.

Oslavia herself, in spite of her misgivings toward her religious partner, had come under his spell. The Luigi/Floriana character broke the chain with her bare hands and ran to kiss the feet of the passionate priest, Bandini. The devil, too, ripped off his tail, his mask, his clothes and fell to the feet of the Almighty Converter.

After a short delay, Bernardino, too, applauded. A roar of appreciation filled the audience as the novitiates and monks rose to their feet. Oslavia experienced it as a wave of unity so strong, so high, she was confident they had won over Bernardino, and with that victory, her own release from his power over her.

Bernardino rose from his chair to walk to the middle of the makeshift stage. Arms thrust in the air, he motioned for all to sit. He turned behind him to wave the actors to sit at his feet, then waited for all to settle onto the ground.

"That, my brothers and sisters, was a performance that taught me I am never too far above you to learn. But as you can expect, most conversions hardly happen so easily. It is a deep, dark conviction the Jews possess. A belief they are a people chosen by God, that the Christ our Savior is not the messiah, so how can they be deluded so easily? We must enter into their dreams and pull out of them their mistaken memories. This takes time and when they come to the church they must be convinced."

"But, Monsignor, what if they are not open to it?" Luigi asked.

"We make an example of them to the others. The fear we place in them prepares them for conversion." Turning to Gerome, he said, "Bring me your true subject, Floriana, about whom our dearly departed Bandini had written to me, and I'll show you what I mean."

"You have seen her," Gerome said as he pointed to Luigi. "We have no converts here, only willing participants among our cloisters."

"The Jewess Bandini promised. Where is she?"

Oslavia stepped forward. "I let her go, Monsignor, for she was clearly not a willing convert."

"You what? Maria Oslavia!"

"I released her after the death of Bandini."

A silence fell into the space.

"Send your followers back to their cells. Then we'll talk about your impudence," Bernardino said.

Oslavia saw this as the last act of civility before Bernardino would declare himself a tyrant. She set her feet apart, sending her determination deep into the earth, for she felt with every part of her the rightness of what she had done. She would not cower under the gaze or edicts of such a one as this tall and bearded priest who stood before her as her authority. She, who had grown up in this place and whose presence in it had nurtured so many novitiates inside these walls, was not going to allow this imposing Bernardino to press her into the earth.

"My novitiates can hear what you have to say," she said.

Gerome stepped forward to face Bernardino, but at the last moment turned toward Oslavia, piercing her conviction with the full focus of his eyes.

"Release them as I will release mine," he said. "We should talk in private with Monsignor Bernardino."

Oslavia absorbed Gerome's stare. Without a sense of diminishing her resolve, but more as one seeing a clearer logic, she turned to wave her charges back into the convent. As they rose to their feet, Gerome did the same for his side.

The actors remained. Gerome turned to them, and with his eyes and a loving smile he sent them on their way.

"Being three devout followers of Christ," Oslavia said, "we should be able to find a place of agreement."

"You both are young," Bernardino said. "I have seen more of the world. We cannot be freeing those who oppose the foundations on which our religion is built."

"I'm sure you and I are closer in age than you think," Oslavia said. "Christ himself did all his work and died in his thirty-third year, so age is not the arbiter of wisdom."

"Are you challenging me?" Bernardino said.

"I'm challenging your arrogance!" she said.

A thin layer of perspiration covered Bernardino's brow, and the line between his eyebrows furrowed deeply as a flush of blood reddened his face. "Did you hear the impertinence of this woman, Brother Gerome?"

"I heard her words only," Gerome said.

"You two Dominicans are a disgrace to our pope. What kind of order do you follow?"

"After thirty-five years of worship, if I cannot hear the Lord from within, then where will I hear Him?" Oslavia said.

"From without!" Bernardino glared. "From those who have gone before you who are your superiors. In order for the church to remain strong we must keep the orders strong, and that means you stay in your place."

"My only place is with the Almighty, and my only discourse is a direct one with Him."

"And you?" Bernardino said, turning to Savonarola.

"Let me place the question back to you," Gerome said. "Whom do you listen to?"

"I build my knowledge on studies and the wisdom that has come to me through my years of watching the lost souls around me," Bernardino said. "The Jews are the worst of the lost souls. Being separate, they give others too many ideas. I have known since I was a young priest that it is my mission to bring them into the church and in so doing bring the others of our own who might be lapsing into the worship of money and material objects back to their spiritual home."

"You and I are not so different," Gerome said. "I do not focus on those separate from us, I focus on those among us who think that because they say their prayers they are pure, while in their hearts they are asleep. I try to awaken them."

"And I want you both to wake up! The greatest threat, I tell you, is not the ones among us who sleep. The greatest threat is those apart from us who awaken in others the belief that there is no hell."

Bernardino's angry tone carried Oslavia back in time to the days she first joined the convent. Someone had told her about hell in graphic detail. For many years she'd felt its heat burning through the soles of her feet. She often wanted to escape or cry out to go home.

Other girls had done and said those things and they suffered consequences. One had escaped, but when found was placed in a room and the wall sealed, leaving only a small place for food to pass. After a while a foul odor came from the opening. The wall came down and her remains were buried as though she were a martyr, along the row where previous abbesses had gone. This show of respect in death had offered little consolation to the young Oslavia. Hell, she concluded, was on this earth if one cared to look around. The evil in others wreaked hell upon the innocent. Then there was the hell inside one's own heart—an internal bleeding when what you know to be true is repudiated by some higher authority.

Bernardino's reprimand became a waterfall of words, Oslavia the rock over which his condemnations spilled without effect.

"You're not listening!" he said.

"I *am* listening, Monsignor, but I am not hearing. You preach fear and I preach love. How can we ever meet?"

"We'll meet in the chambers of the pope, for I'll report you to him. Both of you."

Savonarola moved closer to Bernardino, glaring. "Until that day, until that edict," he said, "we'll continue to do God's work as we see it. And since we have no converts here, perhaps we can accompany you to your next destination."

"What about dinner?" Oslavia asked Bernardino. "We've prepared a special meal in your honor."

Bernardino sat himself back into his chair. "You both will be eliminated. It's just a matter of time."

"Perhaps, Monsignor, we can help you to make it sooner rather than later," Oslavia said. "Would you like an entourage to bring you straightway to Rome?"

"I'll have dinner as planned and stay the night," Bernardino said.

"We have prepared Bandini's room for you," Oslavia said.

"I prefer not to rest in the bed of one so recently deceased."

"You can stay on our side," Oslavia said. "In the cell where our Jewess slept." She wished she had not uttered those last words.

"What Sister Oslavia is implying," Gerome quickly added, "is, if you care to, we can offer you the simplest of accommodations." He turned to glare at Oslavia. Now, surely, their fates were joined together in the eyes of Bernardino.

So practiced in the art of submission, Oslavia decided in that moment to put on a second performance off stage with a sudden drop to her knees. She kissed the hem of Monsignor Bernardino's cape. "Forgive us, Monsignor, for disappointing you. Please understand that after the untimely death of Bandini we were without direction except for the promptings of our own hearts. We waited for Father Bandini's replacement. It is only from the generosity of his soul that Father Savonarola has left his wandering ministry to help us. When we heard of your imminent arrival we tried as best we could to honor you."

Before Bernardino had a chance to respond, bells started to ring in no set rhythm.

"Petrarchio!" Gerome said, looking at Oslavia. There had been no signal for the bells to be sounded, and they were being rung with no pattern or precision, which meant Petrarchio had either lost his senses again or he was trying to send some kind of message to them or to Bernardino, which might confuse the delicate situation further. With a quick bow to Bernardino, Oslavia and Gerome ran off toward the bells.

As soon as Oslavia entered the bell tower she saw Petrarchio's dangling feet. He had tied himself to one rope at the neck, with one of his arms tangled in the rope of the opposite bell. His body had been swinging between the two. As she reached the top she saw Petrarchio's eyes bulging inside a red, swollen face. His eyes darted from Oslavia to Gerome.

If she released his hand from one rope, the full weight of his body on the other rope would strangle him. From Gerome's vantage point, if he were to grab Petrarchio's feet, he would pull the old man's arm out of its socket.

The clanging bells had summoned Monsignor Bernardino and several of the novitiates, and Gerome's helpers, Piattini and Dono. Gerome ordered them to hold out their arms to make a safety net to catch Petrarchio.

"The curtain!" Dono said.

"Yes," Gerome shouted down the bell tower, "but be quick about it!"

While Oslavia and Gerome hovered close to Petrarchio, the others ran toward the performance space and quickly dismantled the carpet between the men and women's sides of the audience. Moments later, they held it like a safety net at the bottom of the bell tower stairwell.

Gerome set a knife against the neck cord, and Oslavia readied hers against the wrist cord. Bernardino counted: one, two, and on the count of three, both ropes were cut, and Petrarchio fell into the carpet.

As Bernardino approached him, waving away the stench of the garlic, he loosened the rope around Petrarchio's neck. The old man's tongue had swollen so large he couldn't speak. The blood drained from his cheeks, and with it, his last breath of life.

Luigi, still wearing the horsehair wig and costume, whimpered.

"*Zitto!*" Monsignor Bernardino said. "Let me give the last rites to this poor unfortunate."

Luigi ripped off his wig and stood at attention like a soldier beside the huge prelate. Gerome and Oslavia stood by while Bernardino's Latin phrases put closure on a life. All present gave a faint "amen," while Piattini and Dono stood ready to carry off the body.

"You seem to have your share of death here," Bernardino said.

"Brother Gerome has saved him from it twice before," Oslavia said.

"It was his time," Gerome said.

"As it was Bandini's time when he perished," Oslavia said.

"How did it happen?" the monsignor asked, the earlier rage gone from his voice.

"Because of the generosity of a nearby nobleman, we had come into the possession of a horse and cart. Rather than take a simple drive around the grounds as was his daily habit, he insisted on a trip to the noble's villa to thank him in person. It was on the grounds of that villa Father Bandini expired.

"His weight had become a terrible burden," she added.

"The weight of your souls pressed heavily on Bandini," Bernardino said.

"I hardly knew the man," Gerome said.

"I had been under his charge for many years," Oslavia said. "He had little grief from my life here. It was he who promoted me to abbess."

"He gave you permission to release the Jew?" Bernardino glared at her.

"God gave me permission, and I am prepared to stand in front of any tribunal to prove it."

"You may have to," Bernardino said.

"Can't we honor the soul of this dear departed servant, Petrarchio, with some silent contemplation and clear the animosity from the air?" Gerome asked.

"Yes, Brother Gerome Savonarola," Bernardino said. "You can silence this inquiry now, but I promise you both, it will return to haunt you. No one interferes with my conversion quotas."

With that, Bernardino grabbed the robes trailing behind him and made his way to his entourage. "Our work is finished here," Bernardino said. "Let us continue on."

"But the convert?" asked one of them who was in charge of the small cage on wheels. The door had been propped open in anticipation of their catch.

"Escaped," Bernardino said. "We'll find another soon enough."

CHAPTER FIFTY-SEVEN

Renata Sells Herself and Her Sisters to Sandro

ONCE FILIPPINO RETURNED TO FLORENCE, Renata forced herself on Sandro as an assistant. As he moved the great painting from the villa back to the privacy of the greenhouse studio, he allowed her to carry small items, like rags and brushes, vials of pigment, wire baskets of eggs. She asked him why he seemed so gloomy. He pretended not to hear her.

Standing in front of the painting, staring at Floriana's likeness, Renata said, "Didn't it help to get Floriana's present?"

"It made me happy. Then it made me sad. But I'm going to her in a few days for the birth."

"Why don't you go now?"

"I wanted to set this up before I left. I have no idea how long I'll be away."

"This is not up to you, Master Sandro. You're under contract with my brother, are you not?"

"And I'm ahead of schedule."

"Why so gloomy?"

"I've lost my ability to focus on one subject and obliterate all others.

You females do this all the time, balancing chores, and politics, and children, and food. All going round in your head and still you accomplish everything with ease and grace."

"We're taught from an early age, and you are taught to do one manly thing at a time. One stab to the heart, one thrust of the hips into one woman at a time."

"Aren't you too young to be talking like that?"

"I may lack experience, but I know what men and women do together."

"This painting pulls me forward and the duty to my chosen muse—" he mumbled.

"You need other muses to amuse you! Why not consider me and my sisters? A little chatter and laughing and grace combined to lift the rhythm of a serious work. And the mood of a melancholy artist!"

"Since when are you an authority not only on artistic composition, but artistic temperament?"

"I know what pleases me," Renata said. "Oslavia's stillness as Venus requires some lively movement to help her balance all the magic of the Flora figure."

"What do you suggest?"

"If you can't focus on one thing at a time, focus on three! Me and my sisters: your resident Graces. You can sketch us in with your iron oxide color, go off to be with Floriana, and when you return, you can do each of us one by one. I may only be nine years old, but I know what I like. If you don't want my advice, use your own."

"I choose your advice. Bring on the dancing nymphs large and small. With a stroke of paint, we'll make each one a breath of joy grown tall."

Renata let out a squeal of laughter at Sandro's rhyme. "The three Graces dancing in your painting!"

"You've read my mind," Sandro said with a smile.

"Why didn't you tell us before we were going to be in the painting? How mean!"

"I wasn't sure until now." Sandro stirred the iron oxide wash Renata had prepared for him the day before. Satisfied with her ability to lighten his spirits, Renata ran off to tell her sisters the news.

MOMENTS LATER, as soon as the three girls returned hand in hand to his studio, Donata said, "I want to be Euphrosyne, the Grace of Beauty that arouses desire."

"And I want to be Love, Thalia," Margarita said.

"*I* want to be Love! I refuse to be Chastity, Alglaia, I can't even say her name!" Renata said as Margarita pulled her to the ground. From chirping hand in hand they had turned against each other in a knot of wrestling and hair pulling.

"I'll decide who is who!" Sandro shouted and put down his brushes in order to untangle the three girls. "You're acting more like the three Fates. First you'll help me mix some of these pigments."

"Didn't you want to paint us?" Margarita whined, shaking the dirt from her dress. "Let Renata mix your paint!" She twirled on her toes with her arms flung out, imagining how Love would look.

"I'd give anything to be your full-time assistant, Master Botticelli," Renata said, "but you told me you're going to paint us. Helping with the pigments is something I already know how to do, but posing for the next arrangement, that's new; even if I have to be Chastity I'll do whatever you want."

Sandro handed Renata a mixing knife. "Concentrate on mixing this vermilion with the oil and egg yolk until every particle of powder has blended with it. See that bubble of vermilion dust? Burst it gently so all particles are combined."

"It stinks," Donata said.

"It's the resin and varnish we mix in to help the colors dry and never change tone," Renata said.

Margarita and Donata watched, pointing to different bumps in the mixture, directing their younger sister in doing something about which they knew nothing.

"Leave that for now," Sandro said. "This next subject I'm about to paint is going to pull the whole painting together, and you will have to work very hard. Though the painting will capture a moment, you'll have to practice the moment over and over again."

"We know enough about standing still," Donata said.

"Exactly the opposite," Sandro said. "You must be music in motion. I can't paint sound, so I must feel it as I watch you dance and dance. Throw your heads back, laugh in your hearts. Serve Venus as a sacred mission. Each of you will be a special muse, but at the same time you must move as one body with three parts—like the three stages of love: beholding the beauty, arousing desire in the eyes of the beholder, and then leading to fulfillment—all separate and yet parts of the whole of the magic of love. I will decide which one you will be after I see you dance and laugh. This is going to be a lot of work."

"Don't you believe we're up to the task?" Donata asked.

"Don't question him," Margarita said. "We've been waiting for this."

"But we're such different heights," Renata said.

"Don't worry. Stand on your toes, and I'll paint in the rest. In my hands you'll each be full-grown, from the world of mystery, and very beautiful. What I need from you, however, my Graces, is to put on your sheerest gowns and come back here ready to dance and sing."

Renata broke from the group to throw her arms around Sandro. "You see, I *can* make you laugh. Gloom be gone!" she said, waving a twig like a magic wand. "And when you finish sketching us, I give you permission to go see Floriana!"

"Thank you, thank you, thank you, my princess of pity and paint. I will wait for you three to return to dance and sing and twist until you faint!" Sandro said, almost singing as he recited another spontaneous rhyme—finally in a lighter mood. At last he had found a moment of balance between his passion for his work and his passion for the woman who had inspired it.

CHAPTER FIFTY-EIGHT

Graziella Helps Floriana Ready for the Birth

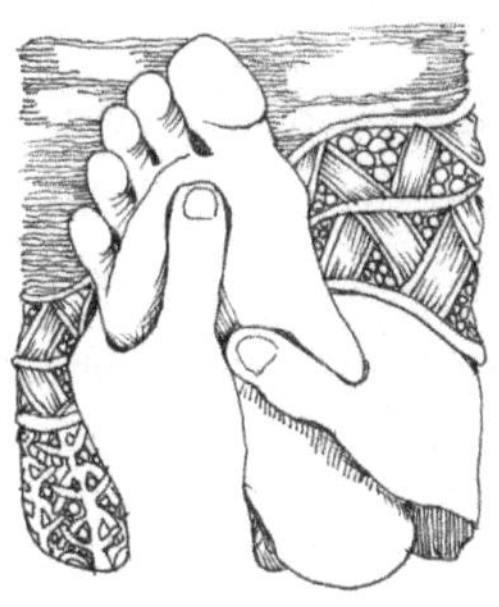

IN DREAMS, Graziella felt skin on skin as she and Floriana held each other. By day she nurtured and comforted Floriana as a sister. Memories of the night images traveled into her fingertips, her mouth, and the deepest recesses of her sex. Alone in her room upon awakening, words came to her, none of which made sense, but when she wrote them down they reined in her desire while capturing it:

Waters rise with the whistling lap of your tongue.
Splash me into your pale-toothed grin. Fence my
body inside your grasp. Contain me soft as baby's breath.
Incestuous shame spills from eyes enticed by you.
Whistling mouths bite through my flesh. You
wash me blind. Fear dissolves the waters of your
wingspan. River, ocean merge under the hood of
my loins. Kisses. Your hands ride my valleys, landscape
of us. Together . . .

Floriana's growing reluctance to be touched relieved Graziella's night images by day. Still, her offers of massage and baths increased.

"Not now!" Floriana whined to Graziella, who knew on this day Floriana's need for comfort outweighed her recent tendency to withdraw.

"We must calm you and the baby for the work ahead. In the Jewish faith, we anoint the body that is about to receive one of God's major blessings, carrying on the seed."

"But the father is not one of us."

"The baby takes the faith of the mother. She'll be one of us," Graziella said as she sprinkled drops of gardenia oil onto Floriana's ankles. Floriana did not pull away.

"Why, when I know so little about my own faith, would I still not take on another?"

"You know the answer," Graziella said, moving her hands up Floriana's leg and gently removing the fabric from her hips and thighs.

Floriana rolled onto her back. All tension released from her body as she gave in to Graziella's stroking.

"It's something about telling a lie. About saying I had no parents, or that I had no God. God has been with me forever, but not the one I recognized in the convent. I don't know enough to argue. I knew I had already lost something of my private self when that Dominican rammed me with his seed. How could I ever take on the faith of someone so faithless?"

"We all have our battles." Graziella moved in closer and removed some of her own more confining clothes.

"You talk as if you know him."

"And if I did, would that matter? Would that change anything for you?"

"Change anything? I might want to kill him! Why would you hide that from me?"

"I am just saying *if. If* I knew him, not that I know him, but *if* I knew him, what difference would that make to you this day, this hour? The child is coming. The child is yours. This is what is real, here and now. As real as my hands on you, calming you."

"I am calmer now, except for that moment when you spoke of him as though you knew him and were hiding it from me."

"I hide nothing except what is hidden to me as well."

Graziella gently placed the fabric back onto one leg and started on the other, enjoying for the first time in days Floriana's lack of resistance. "If he's a man of the cloth, the time for remorse and redemption has surely come to him."

"Are you saying he regrets?" Floriana asked.

"Enough talk about some faceless person. Let's think the best of even him. Take off your gown and let me prepare you. Sunday is the Passover, so we want you to be done with your journey through the Red Sea. We want you to be on the other shore by then." Graziella straddled Floriana's legs so she could work with both her hands for a while, stroking Floriana's shoulders, moving her own hands along Floriana's arms right to her fingertips. Her own belly pressed against Floriana's. A stirring in her empty womb sent an ache of guilt, the very words she had written that morning, *incestuous shame*, coming back to her. She lifted herself away from Floriana.

"Roll onto your side," Graziella said. "Place your hand under your head, close your eyes. Let me give you all the blessings I can transfer with my touch."

"My mother used to do this to me when I was young and could not sleep," Floriana said. "She would hum to me also, and I would be contained as though I had reentered her womb, calm and still, floating on water."

"Think of me as your mother. Let yourself go back to a time of safety and calm. Keep your breath soft and easy."

Graziella interlaced her fingers with Floriana's right hand, working her touch through the fingers and wrist.

"I smell roses again," Floriana said.

"Rose oil in with the rosemary salts and gardenia oil to calm and refresh your skin. Don't speak. Let yourself be anointed, be fed and prepared, for the moment is at hand."

Graziella continued her massage in silence for a while and then said, "I can hear your words spinning, as though you were speaking aloud."

"What are they saying?"

"I see your eyes darting around in their sockets even though they are closed. Move inward and to the center of your deepest shadow of fear and release it, let it go to the joy of a new life."

"What do you see darting around in my eyes?"

"I see questions about Sandro. About the unknown father."

Graziella stood with her hands slightly above Floriana's forearms. She closed her eyes, opened her palms to the heavens to draw inspiration from above. After a few moments of this supplication, Graziella turned her palms back toward Floriana's arm. As though performing a sacred rite, she placed her hands above Floriana's wrist. With each of Graziella's strokes, Floriana breathed deeper, then exhaled with a soft humming sound.

Graziella moved to Floriana's upper arm and shoulder, with each stroke coming closer to the breast. She, too, hummed along with Floriana, the two voices blending into a hymn of the body.

"Now imagine yourself in hot springs, in a safe and private place where no one is watching you. Go back to that pond where you first sought relief from the heat that July day. Banish any fear of the place."

"I was in an actual hot spring one day in a secret place Sandro took me soon after I came to the villa."

"Go on," Graziella said. "Can you smell the place?"

"The sulfur, like spoiled eggs. It filled my chest, in good ways. Sandro protected my modesty by looking away from me. I was safe with him there in the dark cave with the moisture dripping from the earthen roof. We had left the villa to be out of harm's way on the day of a big banquet. It was a place filled with darkness and light together and it was the first time since being attacked I did not fear, even with the presence of death around us."

"You just said it was safe."

"It was dark and light at the same time."

"Describe it more." Graziella had worked her hands along Floriana's back where she had complained of aches from the baby's weight. "Relax more," she said, "as you tell me. Go into the space and tell me how your body felt in the hot spring."

"As though my flesh were melting and floating at the same time. I had broken the bounds of my body. Even though we weren't touching, with just a few shards of daylight coming from above, our union seemed complete. At that moment I wished the child I was carrying might be his."

"Did you tell him?"

"It was too perfect for that."

"And the darkness?"

"As we explored we found the body of a young child, a girl, and her doll. Some of the clothing was remaining though the flesh had decomposed."

"And what did you do?" Graziella sat back to listen to this story.

"I insisted we bury the child properly, and when I explained this part of our faith, Sandro assisted me. We forgot to bury the doll. We said someday we would go back there and get the doll, but I had laid the child to rest and didn't want to disturb her any further. So I took the doll at the last minute. He didn't see me gather it up in my skirts."

"And were you sad?" Now Graziella was lovingly caressing Floriana's right foot again, working the oils around each toe, the instep, and the ankle. Once she pressed lightly on the side of the ankle, Floriana opened her eyes.

"What did you just do?" she asked. "A wave of sadness and fear passed through me when you touched my ankle."

"The feet are the home of so many of our deepest fears and emotions, perhaps I opened something there."

"Do you think that dead child was a sign from God my child will be born dead?"

"A dead child was there to show you that even a child from wealth and favor still faces death like the rest. Even though your child has been conceived in violence she can be delivered in peace and love. Stay with the feeling of safety you had in that hot pool. When the child's time has come, let her float in that liquid, filled with healing and magic. We are blessing this child before she takes her first breath of life."

"May she know only beauty and light and love but also may she have wisdom to spare. Wisdom from within, wisdom from without, and above all," Floriana said, "let her have patience, what I lack the most."

"Yes, patience." Graziella said as she took her hands off Floriana's skin, pulling the garments back over the nakedness into which she so yearned to escape.

CHAPTER FIFTY-NINE

Lorenzo's Journal

March 28, 1478

NOT SINCE MY FIFTEENTH YEAR, *drowning in romantic crushes for the young women who fawned over me and Giuliano, has this palace been filled with so much laughter and good will.*

Savonarola's genius and healing hands have given me a new life. All I want is to stay close to home, to spend more time with my children, my faithful Clarice, and the sweetest jewel of all, our infant, Contessina, born like a gift for my new life, the week after my healing.

Mother Lucrezia's circles around her eyes, darkened by nightmares and her worst imaginings, have taken on the peaceful color of peach flesh. The walls of this palace absorb only a constant flow of joy. And with Giuliano and Claudia cooing like lovebirds, the winds of ease and grace are upon us.

Still, our guards surround us day and night. Hearing good cheer and laughter, they too have loosened their regimented postures. Soon we'll dismiss them or enlist them to go after some of our defaulting debtors.

Today I brought little Piero to the Signoria. Six years old, he already shows all the makings of a diplomat. He sat still and serene, his eyes open wide and his attention fully on the speakers. Not once did he whine or beg for some of the sweets in front of him. His buoyant curiosity put all at ease. A river of loyalty flowed from the other men, through me into the rapt gaze of Pierino. This is the way to run a country. Keep the family first and foremost. Others will follow suit. How refreshing to have harmony, loyalty, and domestic values suffuse our once stuffy meeting rooms. The spring air, the new blossoms, and the new, happy, healthy Lorenzo are surely signs our beloved city will continue to flourish.

April 2, 1478

I'm sure the banking situation is going to improve if we can hold on a bit longer. I refuse to think cash is all we bring to this city. We add so much more, and soon, when the debtors repay, we'll resume our solid footing. In the meanwhile, I've arranged with my private accountants to tap into Medici cousins' funds—Piero's inheritance, which he won't need for another few years, and those of some other cousins. Before they find out, we'll put the money back and then some. No need to bother anyone with this. Keeping these things inside the family is only right after all.

Thanks to Savonarola, too, I've renewed my contact with San Marco's, even making a habit of weekly visits to our family cell to contemplate these changes and to share them with the Lord.

When words of anger toward that short, fat, toothless, and balding Pope Sixtus want to slip out of my mouth, I stop myself, proclaim a blessing on all, and stay a few extra moments in prayer in the cell. I understand why Grandfather Cosimo went there in his later years. It's so good to get away from all the pomp and privilege and constant responsibilities, even for a few hours, to quiet my spirit, and connect with my Maker.

April 6, 1478

Two days ago, Sandro's father, Mariano, came running to the palace to warn me. He'd heard the name Giovan Battista da Montesecco whispered by other mercenaries in his tannery. Montesecco, the feared assassin. Mariano said he'd never be able to sleep at night if he didn't protect the family who had given so much to his son. Then he started listing all the gifts we'd given them over the years. On and on he went about the plants and how he now had the same aromas in his humble courtyard as we do in ours. When the guards stopped him at the door, he lied to them about doing some work on my Morello's hooves, and they let him in with a smile.

"I could have been harboring a knife to slice you down, but they let me pass and didn't question my lie," he said. The man was shaking, and I had to calm him.

His concern gave me a great brainstorm. "We'll open our doors to everyone. Show we no longer fear them. This fear has got to stop!" I told him, but he insisted I should be careful. Perhaps I was indelicate when I told him, "That's why you're a tanner and I'm a prince." I thanked him for his concern, and told him that because of his information I was going to hold a Lenten party night. It's scheduled for one week from today. I told him I'd invite the Pazzis and all the rest as a prenuptial celebration for Claudia and Giuliano.

When he said, "What have I done?" I told him he'd helped me so much to show me my guards are useless, that I'll offer love and generosity to all. In the spirit of that openness, I told him, I doubt anyone will attempt anything. I'll demand protection through affection and not hide in defense and fear.

Then I told him about my visit to the priory with little Piero and how God is on our side, as are the people of Florence.

April 20, 1478

A stroke of genius, if I do say so myself! The Lenten party was a grand success! All came and went through the palace offering their congratulations for Giuliano's upcoming marriage. We included even families with whom the Medicis have known friction and animosity. Who would dare an attack in such circumstances! Genius, Mother Lucrezia called me.

We even invited Montesecco. He and I sat side by side in the main salon while daughter Lucrezia recited classic Greek poetry. This big, bad Montesecco watched tears of pride slip down my face. I told him that with art, music, and poetry, there's no need for war, no room for killing. He said he'd be out of work, but I countered, "Exactly the opposite, your duty will be to protect the rights of all, to engage in the inner war of separating art from commerce, freeing the spirit to pursue beauty at all costs!" I know he was impressed. I see nothing to fear here.

Oh, and the Pazzis. I included them. After all, Nannina's married into the Pazzis. I was being a respectful brother-in-law.

April 21, 1478

France is troubling. Their default is hurting, but we've got enough to keep up appearances. My folly over the Volterra alum mines I chalk up to my youth. Even that stain is going to be wiped out. They'll get back on their feet. I've apologized for my orders, which destroyed the mines. But I've sent a committee there to explore other economic options. It will recover. In a hundred years no one will even remember.

I told Mother Lucrezia that by the end of this month, we should be able to withdraw the soldiers, but she said she wasn't ready.

CHAPTER SIXTY

Giuliano Comforts Claudia

"I DREAMED WE WERE at the wedding march," Claudia whispered. She and Giuliano lay in the predawn light that draped everything—the bedclothes, the walls and ceiling, and the face that touched her own, the face of her beloved—in shades of gray. "We had all assembled in the Piazza della Signoria. Nine men were to pass judgment on our union."

"The council can't interfere in the business of relationships."

"But your 'relationship business' is not in the family style. I am not part of the political ladder."

"Nor do I want you to be." Giuliano threw the covers aside and started to wrap Claudia's swollen ankles in cloths that had been boiled in a pomegranate seed mixture—the concoction had become an all-purpose healing remedy after Lorenzo's "cure" by Savonarola.

"Someday," Giuliano said, "historians will look back on our marriage and say we were the first to honor the institution for what it is meant to be, the legalization of love between man and woman and not the merging of two bank accounts by two families."

"Then, my sweet, you're more of an innovator than your brother, Lorenzo."

"He hardly sees it as innovation. He sees it as a weakness he must tolerate."

"You judge him harshly," Claudia said. "Wasn't it he who convinced your mother to agree to our marriage? She's beginning to warm to me. But I'll still keep my distance."

"That's no longer necessary."

"It's safer that way. If she changes her mind, I'll not feel betrayed. She has been nicer."

"Why, my sweet, then are you so restless about the silly dream?"

"It was not silly. It was serious, and they had all voted in my favor, but there was one complication."

"And that was . . . ?"

"The approval would only last for twenty-four hours, and we had to be married within that time, and you were nowhere to be found. Suddenly, in the dream, bells rang louder and louder. The crowd assembled, their voices like the roiling of the sea, and I, perched at the top of a large platform in the center, was shouting out to you. My voice was shouting in my head, but the words never came out of my mouth and the bells and voices drowned me out more and more as I looked for you in every corner of the square. Then I awoke."

"That's why you woke me? To make sure I still wanted you?"

"No, it was to make sure you were still alive so I could breathe again."

"This is common, they say, to dream of lost lovers before a marriage."

"And who has told you that? I've never heard that before."

"The tarot signorina, Stella Cameo. Remember her, the one who read our cards?"

"I remember her well. She only told the good things awaiting us and that made me nervous, but she reassured me in the end."

"She was here last night," Giuliano said.

"Why wasn't I called?"

"Because it was one of the rare moments you were able to sleep. We didn't want to disturb you."

"What did she say?"

"She was here only briefly. My mother had sent for her despite Lorenzo's misgivings."

"What did she see?"

"She dealt the cards three times and three times recalled them without even turning up any of them. 'At least pick one,' Lucrezia had said. 'I prefer not to,' said Stella, then spun a story about how her father was sick and she was much distracted. She had seen the vision of his coffin in the middle of a gondola heading toward the Venetian island of San Michele for burial instead of on the main island as though he was being exiled even in death. When these visions overcome her, she said, she must decline to do a reading. Lucrezia took her at her word."

"She saw something bad. Maybe that was not her father's coffin. Maybe it was the coffin of our child or of me or you."

"Or Lucrezia, or Lorenzo, or Stella's father. Why must you worry yourself so now that all is well? Even in the dream all was well. Approval from all."

"But the bells. So loud I can still hear the clanging in my bones." Claudia whimpered. "Something's not right."

"What's not right is that you have not slept for days. So sleep, but do not dream, my sweet, except of the baby at your breast and all of us around you loving you and him."

"And will they even let me keep the baby to my breast or must I use a wet nurse?"

"If I have anything to say about it, our baby will suckle your breasts as long and hard as he likes. So calm yourself. Rest here in my arms. I'm not going anywhere until I hear your heavy breathing and see a peaceful face that smooths your worried brow."

"I do love you so," she said. "Our life is too good, and so I fear punishment."

"Who's going to punish you?"

"Because I have kept you from—"

"If you don't shut up now and sleep, I'll leave you here to fend for yourself with your swollen ankles. I offer full affection, and you give me whining. You choose," he said, peeling her hands off and rising from the bed.

"No," she said. "You're right and sweet. Don't go. Come back now, I beg you. But first, bring me the gardenia plant. Its perfume calms me."

Giuliano plucked off a blossom and tore the petals one by one, slipping each petal into Claudia's cleavage.

"You must promise me something," she said.

"I kiss each petal to enhance its perfume with my love and devotion to you," he said.

"If you are so devoted, you'll sneak me out of here tomorrow and we'll elope. It will be our secret."

"Why would I do such a thing?" he said, pulling the petals out of her bodice. "Our engagement was announced at the Lenten party. We received raucous applause and trumpets! Plus, we've got the official engagement certificate right under this mattress!"

"Engagements can be broken. You must promise."

"I promise to marry you."

"Tomorrow?"

"Not tomorrow, but I promise I'll think about it."

Claudia pulled his lips onto her own as he wrapped his arms about her and the last few petals fell to the floor.

CHAPTER SIXTY-ONE

Piero Brings Sandro to Manfredo's
April 24 and 25, 1478

WITH A FEW BOLD STROKES of iron oxide wash, followed by light patches of flesh tones, Sandro had captured not only the outline but the three-dimensional form of Piero's sisters. The three girls had danced as one being, absorbed in the joy of movement. He had transformed Renata, Margarita, and Donata, all three of whom he thought might have been more easily cast as the three Fates—the unappeasable sister goddesses who preside over the birth, life, and death of man—into the three Graces, helpers of Venus, mirroring the three stages of love.

Once he had painted enough of the image to know he could go back to it later with confidence, he walked toward Piero's chambers with his next demand. He could smell Piero's wet paper glue in the corridors, and decided to interrupt the doll-making anyway.

"We're at work on the new baby," Poppi said as soon as she saw Sandro. She wore a pincushion around her neck and worked with needle and thread, holding fabric close to her eyes.

Piero concentrated on a small wad of papier-mâché from which he was modeling tiny hands.

"Which baby?" Sandro asked.

"Floriana's, of course," Poppi said. "What others?"

"Claudia and Giuliano's is due a month later. And Lorenzo's Clarice gave birth to little Contessina after the new year."

"Take a look at this one," Poppi said. "She's sublime."

The exquisite doll, a miniature Floriana, had blonde hair, rosy cheeks, and a long nose. A pattern of Stars of David embroidered in golden threads decorated her dress. Sandro cradled the creation, still awaiting its tiny hands, in his palm, then handed it back to Poppi.

Sandro tapped Piero on the shoulder. "You'll take me to her, won't you?"

"I can't leave until tomorrow afternoon after I receive word from Lorenzo about the Easter Mass. I'm expecting a messenger with an invitation for us, including you, to the family chapel and the main chapel for Easter Sunday."

"Tell him I couldn't pull myself away from the painting."

"How can you be here painting and there at the birth at the same time? Make up your mind," Piero said.

"The important things to me are two: that I continue my work here and that I pursue my family life."

"Who is stopping you?" Piero said. "I thought you had renounced your family by living as though your patron is all the family you needed."

"I might want a wife and family of my own."

"And you're willing to risk your life and reputation on it?"

"Maybe yes, maybe no. I'm not abandoning my work, Piero."

"But she's a Jew. If she wouldn't convert, she's surely not going to take up with someone outside of her faith. A painter of Madonnas, no less. Imagine you!"

"She's taken up with me and I with her," Sandro said, "and you, by association, are our ally."

"I did not choose that role."

"It was chosen for you. Call it what you will, we need your help."

"And if I help you to find her, what is that going to do for me?"

"Must there be something of material value to you?"

"Is my helping you going to help or harm the painting? Is my helping you going to raise or lower the interest the Jew is charging me? Is my helping you going to separate me forever from Savonarola's healing hands?" Piero said, all the while modeling the miniature hands for his infant doll, viewing them up close, then examining them at arm's length.

"Your helping me is an act of kindness. For the sake of helping, with no monetary reward, no benefit, save the knowledge that you are stepping outside your role as landowner, nobleman, and big brother, in order to help someone, someone special to me and others, someone who has helped you by being an important part of the picture you have still not seen."

"All right, all right," Piero said, putting down his work, then plunging his hands into a bowl of water to scrub off the glue. As he placed the miniature hands on his workbench to dry, he said, "I'll take you, but only after the messenger from Florence arrives tomorrow."

"Fair enough, or else you can make me a map. I'm leaving tomorrow—with you or without you."

"When Rabbi Manfredo—"

"Now he's a rabbi?"

"Well, he's a wise man. When my friend Manfredo made this deal with me, knowing I was to procure your services, he specifically said he did not want you to come to his place."

"Why?"

"He does not want anyone to know his business."

"I think it's you who doesn't want me to go there."

"We've already discussed this. Lorenzo does not know of Manfredo's part in this financing. And I need to keep it that way."

"Put me in a disguise, if you must. My desire is a simple one: to protect the woman I love. I need to let her know I will sacrifice for her what is necessary."

"As long as that sacrifice does not place me and all I hold, and by association all that you hold, in jeopardy."

"What is this resistance, Piero?"

"Danger. There's an element of danger associated with consorting with Jews, or are you not aware of this?"

"I'm aware they're hunted like animals. I'm aware Bernardino, a most respected Franciscan and friend of the pope, is probably at this moment threatening my sister, Oslavia, for having released one of the catches."

"That's not what I mean," Piero said. "There's something more I haven't told you from the beginning."

"And that is . . . ?"

"A lie bigger than the one of the inheritance." Piero wiped his hands clean and removed his artist smock, which had covered his brocaded shirt. He sat on his bed and strapped the spurs to his boots.

"Are we going to war?" Sandro asked.

"We Medicis are always at war, even when we are dining in our own houses with our blood relatives."

"And the lie?"

"I'll tell you all about it when we leave tomorrow."

PIERO AND SANDRO rode off on their journey in the late afternoon. The plan was for Piero to bring Sandro to Graziella and Manfredo's property by evening and to travel the rest of the way into Florence on his own. Sandro had disguised himself as a shepherd, including rubbing his body with the oil from the sheep's hide so he might smell the part.

"It's time you told me about the great mystery," Sandro said once they were off the villa grounds.

"Eyes are everywhere. Even when you think no one's watching, there are people watching. People with tongues. Long ones."

"Go on," Sandro said.

"Most consider me a fop, an embarrassment to the family. The fact Lorenzo and I have begun to communicate is a break with tradition. My father and his father never spoke."

"How do you account for this?"

Before Piero could answer, a small group of pilgrims in clerical garb approached. As soon as Piero saw this, he motioned to Sandro to drop behind him "in a posture of respect." The small band passed, crossing themselves as they continued on the road.

When Sandro took his place beside him again, Piero said, "If you'd worn the sign of your guild, Saint Luke, they'd speak and tell the wrong people that I have an artist, and your work of art would become an object of curiosity. More investigation might lead to someone observing Graziella giving you money and, worse than that, more clerics talking about this painting of heathen subject matter—with a Jew in the center, no less. Imagine you!"

"The subject matter is of beauty and love. I should have let you see it by now."

"I don't want to see it until it's finished. I'll keep my word, but I have heard things."

"What kinds of things?" asked Sandro.

"There are no virgins with child, no annunciations, no crucifixes in the painting."

"Savonarola has been poisoning you! You gave me permission to paint what I wanted, Piero. This is the best work I've ever done."

"Exactly. I don't want to attract any more attention to it. Or to you."

"Isn't it a bit late to worry about these things?"

"I've heard the pope is cracking down on all the new artwork, insisting artists work alongside clerics and the works be a collaboration of spirit."

"Why are you so concerned all of a sudden?"

"Because, I've heard things."

"What kinds of things?"

"About the plot to take down my cousins, backed by the pope."

"This has been going on for years."

"But something big is in the air."

"And how do you know this?"

"Ficino told me not to bring my sisters into Florence for the Easter service. He predicts fires in the streets."

"And why do you tell me this now, when I'm going in the opposite direction?"

"You've made your choice. If something happens and I don't make it back, you must continue with the work and keep our agreement for my sisters' sakes."

"You imagine disaster where there's only gossip."

"I hope you're right. Once we go into the forest beyond that hill, I'll leave you and continue on to Florence. Trust me, Sandro, it will be too late to enter Manfredo's compound. You'll have to camp the night and go early in the morning. Hopefully I'll be on my way to the Duomo with my cousins by that time. I'll explain your absence as your dedication to your muse, whatever. You can change back into your normal clothes so you don't frighten Floriana."

"I think I'll keep the disguise to the end and play a trick on her to see her face and then unmask myself."

"Be careful. Manfredo hides his guards. Don't approach the property until tomorrow. I beg you."

As soon as Piero, bedecked with his spurs, feathers, and formal wear, trotted off toward Florence, Sandro set up temporary camp. It was a spot in the forest several miles from the point where Piero had told him with the aid of a quickly sketched map that he would "easily" find the entrance to Manfredo's. There he would, at last, reunite with his Floriana.

CHAPTER SIXTY-TWO

The Medici Palace
April 25, 1478

ON THE EVE OF EASTER, strains of music and laughter filled the Medici house. The swelling in Claudia's ankles had subsided. Giuliano walked with confidence through the corridors of the palace, holding his brother Lorenzo's baby Contessina in his arms as he rehearsed the posture of proud father he was about to assume in a few short weeks.

"Fatherhood agrees with you," Lorenzo said as he came upon Giuliano cooing at the baby. "But fatherhood in theory is never the same as fatherhood in practice." Lorenzo tried to take the infant into his own arms, but his brother refused to release her.

"For now, let me enjoy the moment," Giuliano said. "Do you think before the end of the holiday I'll be a father? The day the midwife predicts is almost a month away, but it could happen any moment now."

"From the time the waters break it can be a full day with lots of screaming," Lorenzo said.

Giuliano handed Contessina to her father, Lorenzo, as the baby squealed and squirmed in his arms. "That kind of screaming I can bear," Giuliano said. "I'm actually looking forward to it!"

"And Claudia?"

"She says she's looking forward to it also. To be back in her normal body with the babe at her breast."

"You'll use our wet nurses, of course."

"She wouldn't consider such a thing."

"The two of you are going to change the political structure of this city with the giddiness of your love."

"Is that such a bad thing?"

"I'm not saying bad or good any longer when it comes to your choices. I'm only asking: is he happy or is he miserable? And for sure you are happier in this love than I have ever seen you."

"Even Mother Lucrezia has begun to smile at Claudia," Giuliano said. "And Clarice has taken her under her wing and calls her sister-in-law."

"The entire city of Florence will rejoice for you both. Tomorrow, however, I expect you to be with me at the Easter service."

"If the water breaks tonight I'll not be with you. I will wait until the last moment before I decide if I'll join you or not."

"Our duty lies with the city of Florence."

"Your duty," reminded Giuliano.

"And yours, too, in whatever way you conduct yourself. You have your love, and your city loves you. You are the darling still."

"We are the darlings."

"You more than I. You have only made enemies of traditions where I have made enemies with living, breathing men. Volterra was a disaster I'm still trying to erase."

"Aren't you frightened of those enemies?" Giuliano said.

"I cannot live my life in fear. I'd have no life of the mind or the heart, and you, my baby brother, have taught me much of late about a life of the heart."

"*I* have taught *you*?"

"I've become domesticated in my old age. Bringing the boys to meetings, and watching them play marbles as we decide the fate of nations. The whole air in government has become one large family, and it has only helped humanize us."

"Don't be so confident," Lucrezia said as she glided into the room. She placed her arms around her sons. "On holidays like this with everything green and blossoming, and both my sons in my grasp, I feel all is right with the world and no harm can come to us."

"Then why did you pace all last night? And why are the circles under your eyes growing darker?" Lorenzo asked.

"Because when night descends, my tiny innocent sparrow fears become crows pecking out my heart with terror. I awake exhausted from the trial."

"You should take some herbs to sleep," Giuliano said.

"Worse. Dreams come. I see the heads of those who assassinated the Sforzas, and in my dream last night I saw other heads and blood was everywhere."

CHAPTER SIXTY-THREE

At the Convent and Monastery
April 25, 1478

IS YOUR PUGNACIOUS BROTHER going to join us for the Easter holiday tomorrow, Maria Oslavia?" Gerome asked Oslavia as they shared a meal prepared by Piattini and Dono, who stood in the wings of the great dining area of the monastery.

"Please don't call me Maria Oslavia."

"But you've been given an official name. I am respecting Bernardino's wishes in small ways since I will not be able to respect them in larger ways."

"Don't waste your time on the small ways."

Gerome waved Piattini and Dono out of the room, then looked at Oslavia with great concentration. "You must forgive me for what you saw me doing the other day."

"You must forgive yourself. Through your actions. Through your restraint. I don't choose to think about it, for you fall in my esteem to a hairy ape, and I lose you as a spiritual partner."

"We're not partners. We are friendly opponents."

"We both practice prayer and surrender, and we both seek to save, rather than spoil. Isn't that enough?"

"I fear what Bernardino has said will come to pass, at least for me," Gerome said. "I am certain. The visions of blood in the streets of Florence, of vice and vanity—a plague that grows carbuncles on the soul—are what drive me. I could never be content to stay in a country setting like this one."

"God is everywhere. Don't belittle what is humble, for there resides powerful faith."

"I don't seek those of powerful faith; I seek to awaken powerful faith in the hearts of those who have placed their worship in the wrong places. I'll leave tomorrow for Florence after my Easter sermon."

"So you will stay? I feared you'd leave us tonight to attend the one in Florence tomorrow."

"Florence will be crowded with heretics and fanatics of all persuasions and enough pomp at the cathedral to satisfy several popes. I don't care to be part of that. I will weave my way into the streets later, after all has calmed down."

"And where will you stay?"

"A cell at the church in San Marco has been promised to me by Lorenzo any time I want it."

"Can I confess something to you, Brother Gerome?"

Savonarola lowered his head to signal the affirmative. Oslavia moved her chair closer to his and began.

"My confession, Brother Savonarola, is that I feel no fear. For the first time in my life, I'm at peace. If anything frightens me, it is that this sense of peace might be a veil, a deeper blindness. I trust my heart and soul are with Christ. This internal peace has its own sound so strong and true all I heard of Bernardino's threats were the noises his voice made. It was as though I were witnessing a bleating pig dressed in clerical robes."

At this Gerome burst out laughing, spraying a mouthful of water over the table.

"I hear you, Sister Oslavia, and I take your confession and do not doubt for one moment it is your truth of which you speak. And thank you for the image of the bleating pig, for it softens my own fears, which are many on this matter."

"And how will you manage your fears?" Oslavia asked.

"God has sent me visions, and I am his soldier, his doctor, his rescuer of souls. To this task I'm now bound, blindly perhaps, but nevertheless fully. It has become my heart's desire, my passion. As long as the Almighty chooses to bring air in and out of my lungs and blood to pump inside my heart, then that desire will grow into a fire much greater than the fear of what awaits me. I have only this time, this moment, to act and so I cannot sit by here, while you, on the other hand, have no calling to wander forth."

"Don't tell me of my calling. Perhaps I have one for which I am being prepared, and this calm is part of the preparation."

"It matters not," Gerome said. "We have both been called."

"And mine is to trust this calm and spread it to all I touch without fearing the loss of my station. And if the day of reckoning comes that Bernardino promises, I will have had this time of clear conscience."

DURING THE NIGHT, Oslavia slept peacefully, her heart full with the blessings she had wrought: Bernardino had come and gone, and she was still living and breathing, still abbess of her humble convent. Her brother had come into his own heartfelt decisions and she blessed him and blessed his art, for through it she had found her own voice when she set Floriana free. There was a calm too in the knowledge that no unknown cleric on the other side of the rambling expanse of roses was about to curtail or challenge her newfound independence. How perfect that this would all be happening on the eve of Easter and the resurrection. She prayed for Floriana and blessed her for an easy delivery. She imagined Sandro by the young girl's side, pure in his affections and ready to serve in whatever way was needed. All had changed in Oslavia's world. It was all for the good. Where there once was worry, she would substitute harmony, and if not harmony, then harmonious thoughts.

SAVONAROLA, on the other side of the compound, fell into a dark dream. Throughout the night, visions of torture, pain, and suffering pierced his sleep. He repeatedly awoke with a start, then would calm himself with prayer until the exhaustion overtook him, only to sink yet again into the dark, narrow streets of his dreams. He heard the hooves of horses and the sound of water dripping. In his dreamlike state he saw darkness, walls smeared with blood, and words written in blood. He tried to read the words in his memory upon awakening.

At the earliest hint of day, his view of the peaceful monastery, quiet with a sparkling shimmer of dew, did not relieve him from the haunting image of a bloodstain soaking up his robes and his hands splattered in red. He felt a trembling, a fear rolling in his belly, and an urge to go to Florence to make sure his dreams were only dreams.

Upon rising, he washed his hands, imagining the hands in his dream, and willing that image to cleanse itself, but in the act of imagining it, the pitcher from which he poured the water was filled with blood. How, under this powerful incubus, this terrible omen of violence, was he about to give a sermon on resurrection and hope?

OSLAVIA AWAKENED, still in a state of peace and harmony. When she looked to the horizon from her quarters, she saw the silhouette of two monks mounting their donkeys. Her first impulse was to run outside and question them, for she assumed it was Gerome and one of his companions, but she resigned herself to the unfolding of this new day and all it had to bring her. Whatever it was, she kept in mind her sense of liberation. She was finally free to have her life, and her convent, and her peaceful thoughts in the cradle of her own long-sought serenity.

CHAPTER SIXTY-FOUR

Sandro the Prankster Meets His Match
April 26, 1478, outside of Florence

PIERO'S HASTILY DRAWN MAP had sent Sandro in the wrong direction. Only after several hours of frustration at being unable to find Manfredo's land did he remember Piero's difficulty in reading and writing, and took a harder look at the map. Piero had drawn it backwards, and Sandro had gone right when he should have gone left. It was the middle of the afternoon when he finally reached the entrance to Manfredo's property.

Within seconds of entering the grounds, he found himself knocked off his horse into a pile of dung by a weighted branch that seemed to fall out of a tree. As he raised himself up, a rope tightened around his ankles, and he was suddenly yanked upside down into the air, where he hung helplessly for close to ten minutes.

He heard a rustling in the branches of a tree. Although the dung had softened his fall, its fumes made him dizzy and nauseous as gravity's force caused blood to pound inside his head. He heard more scrambling in the bushes. "Who goes there!" he shouted. Just as he was about to lose consciousness, Sandro saw an older man with robes and sidelocks approaching him with knife in hand.

"What is your business here?" the man asked, keeping a distance from Sandro.

"Are you Graziella's father?"

"I am. How do you know my daughter? Where is your flock?"

"It's a disguise to keep the nature of your relationship with Piero de' Medici a secret. I'm Sandro Botticelli. I know your daughter but never met you. Cut me down before my eyes pop out!"

"Yes, and if you're Maestro Botticelli, then I'm Lorenzo the Magnificent!" Manfredo said.

"No, you have it all wrong. How else would I know your daughter? I am truly Sandro! I'm here to be with Floriana. She's sent for me. Go to my saddlebags and pull out a letter. It's Floriana's plea that I come to her for the birth."

"Why the disguise?" Manfredo asked again as his face broke into a smile. Instantly he released the ropes to lower Sandro to the ground.

Once upright, Sandro said, "Piero did not want to bring any attention to me or you so he insisted on a disguise. I *do* have proper clothes."

As Sandro scraped the dung off and started to remove his costume, Manfredo said, "Don't change a thing! I, too, am an enthusiast of the prank. Let's carry it to its natural conclusion."

"But I might shock Floriana into labor from my stench," Sandro said. "And who or what knocked me to the ground, then strung me upside down?"

"One who guards this property night and day for us. He stays invisible on purpose. He lives over there." Manfredo pointed to a small hut on the edge of the clearing. "The rope from the tree connects to my small villa and that is how I knew someone was caught. All new uninvited visitors get the same welcome."

"You are a man of surprises," Sandro said, extending his hand toward Manfredo in an offer of friendship.

"Let's shake hands once you've cleaned yourself," Manfredo said. "But

I can't resist the chance to watch a surprise, so please tolerate your disguise a bit longer for my enjoyment."

"If you can, Signor Manfredo, then I can too."

"Follow behind me, please, shepherd Sandro. Let's make our way to the bath where your beloved Floriana sits for relief from the heat and the internal contortions of childbirth that is so close. Let me lead the way." He called out, "Graziella, Graziella. Come and help me!"

Graziella approached, then stepped back in fright when she saw her father had a knife raised toward the shepherd.

"A prowler. A foul smelling one."

Sandro brayed like a sheep.

"He seems to have lost his flock and his mind. Too long among animals. He speaks no words but only that bleating and braying," Manfredo said.

Sandro rolled himself on the earth, trying to scrape off the dung.

"Harmless, though a bit stupid. We can use him around here," Manfredo said.

"What are you thinking? Who knows if he can control himself around women?"

Sandro crawled on all fours. He pantomimed a goat mounting its female counterpart.

"Oh my God," she said. "How can you consider such a creature, Father?"

"I have my reasons. I don't appreciate your belittling the beast as though he can't understand our words. I want to see what is under all his filth. A strong pair of arms can be trained to even tend to the new baby."

"You are crazed, Father!"

Sandro made the sound of a baby crying and rolled himself again on the ground.

"Take him to the bath right now and place him in it," Manfredo said.

"Floriana's there."

"She's been bathing long enough!" Manfredo said. "Will you take him, or do I have to do it myself?"

"I will," she said.

"Place this rope around his neck so you can pull him toward the bath. I'll follow to make sure he does you no harm."

Graziella tied a noose, threw it gingerly around Sandro's neck, and gently yanked him along. He contorted himself and limped as though a wounded beast, issuing forth snorts from his nose and vibrating his lips.

"How can such a one as you be riding on a saddle?" Graziella asked, as her sense of reason overtook her annoyance.

"It is I, Sandro, here to see Floriana," he whispered. "It is your father who wants to play a joke on you and Floriana."

Graziella stopped moving. "I don't like your joke," she told her father.

"But I insist we take it to the natural conclusion," Manfredo said laughing, his eyes excited with the twinkle of a small child at play, and with feigned authority he said, "In fact I command it!"

Now that Graziella was enlisted in the prank, she told Sandro to get on all fours and wiggle his rear end to add more color to his performance. "Now snort more," she said as the three approached Floriana.

"What is that? Is it a man or a beast?" Floriana asked as soon as she saw and smelled the new visitor.

Sandro hissed and raised his leg as though to urinate on clothes drying on the ground.

"He's going to wet all over my dress," Floriana said.

"Stop!" shouted Graziella to the shepherd. She took the noose off. "Stop that now. Pick up that gown and bring it to the lady in the bath."

Sandro pulled two leaves from a tree and used them to lift Floriana's dress without touching it. Holding it as far away from himself as he could, he made his way up the stone staircase toward the bath.

Floriana, mesmerized by this gentle yet oafish creature, felt a surge of compassion for his gesture and smiled at him, yet out of modesty kept her naked body below the surface of the water.

"There, there," she said. "How sweet of you to help me."

The two stared at each other for a moment, Floriana recognizing something behind all the filth. And then, at the same moment she recognized Sandro's eyes, she saw a corner of the tiny Star of David sparkling through the mud on his neck.

"My sweet Floriana, I offer you a bit of protection," Sandro said in his natural voice.

"Sandro! What joy!" she said and pulled his filthy smiling face toward her own.

Sandro laughed while Graziella climbed the steps to shield Floriana's modesty as she got out of the bath.

"And all this joking aside, what about my painting?" Manfredo said from the ground below.

"I'm refueling for inspiration, Signor Manfredo," Sandro answered but without taking his eyes off Floriana.

"As well you should," Manfredo said. "Come down from there. I'll take you to a place where you can clean up. Let Floriana and Graziella finish. We'll bring you two back together again soon enough for some food and relaxation after your long trip."

"I'll help her out of the bath," Sandro said to Manfredo, still not turning his head away from Floriana. "Could you and Graziella please give us a moment alone together, and I promise you all I'll clean myself."

As Floriana watched Graziella and Manfredo turn away, the warmth of Sandro's gaze enfolded her. Perhaps it was her embrace of the drawing of his flying *uccello*—as they had named the firm mass that had risen beneath his clothes and pressed against her body during their most intimate moment together at the villa—or maybe it was the sensation they were together alone again at last, but forgoing all modesty, Floriana rose from the water fully naked to Sandro's eyes.

As Sandro took in her beauty, he imagined the opening of clouds and beams of light pouring on her. He knew in the deepest recesses of his artist's wisdom, this moment, this figure, in all her innocent, unadorned nakedness, with her hair dripping about her shoulders, would be the subject of his next painting. As he wrapped the towel around her, being careful to keep any of his filth from touching her, he knew this vision of her had been burned into his soul with such detail he would never forget it.

For Floriana, it was a moment to show him her trust, holding back nothing, to take him, mud and all.

Sandro didn't see Manfredo turn toward them, but when Floriana wrapped the towel even tighter to cover herself, he heard Manfredo's voice saying, "You'll have more than enough opportunity to see her later. Let Graziella attend to her while you come with me to clean yourself."

"You have separate baths?" Sandro asked.

"No. But we have a stream where you can remove all the dirt so we can see you better."

AS SANDRO WASHED HIMSELF in the stream, Floriana and Graziella watched him from behind the bushes. Floriana had forgotten the discomforts of the earlier part of her day. The mood of lightheartedness seemed all around her until she turned toward Graziella, whose face contorted in a grim expression as she watched Sandro.

"Is he not beautiful?" Floriana asked.

Graziella said nothing.

"Uncircumcised dog," Graziella whispered under her breath.

"How dare you say that!"

"He's no Jew."

"I love him. I love his generosity, his protection, his willingness to be a bleating goat man. He's a man of God, for surely he uses the gifts to honor life."

"He's a Christian, Floriana, and has painted his sister as the Madonna with the baby Christ above her head and both of them right next to you! He has worshipped with those who want our people dead."

"Why do you say these things to me now?" Floriana said. "You're cruel! He's no Bandini! He has sat with the great Lorenzo and learned from him about the people of the world. He is not our enemy!"

"I'm telling you the facts. Your child is Jewish because you are. If you take up with him, as wonderful as you think he is, you'll be giving away your Jewishness. You'll never be a part of his world and you'll lose your place in your own. You may as well have converted!"

"How dare you question my faith? You're torturing me!" Floriana pulled away from Graziella, making her way back to the main house. Graziella ran to catch up with her.

"I'm not torturing you. I am preparing you for the reality of what lies ahead in a life with him. If you stay with us, you'll have protection, your faith, a safe home for you and your child."

Floriana stopped walking. She would not look at Graziella. "He's here to protect me."

"He's here because you called him here. Where will he be in five years when he's in some cathedral in Rome painting apostles and you're having his Christian child? Is that child going to be raised as a Jew? Listen to me, Floriana. I love you. We love you as much if not more than he does. Can't you see? We must stick together or we will be swallowed by them." She tried to put her arms around Floriana, but Floriana cringed at Graziella's touch.

"Why do you say these things now that he's here? Why didn't you say them before?"

"There was no need if he never came. I'm not cruel. The world we live in is cruel. Why do you think my father keeps that monkey man in the trees forever guarding us?"

"To keep you safe."

"Because we have lost all before and could easily lose it again. Your connection to Sandro could threaten what protection we have from others."

"I don't want to hear this, not now! Not now!" Floriana said and broke away from Graziella, running into the house toward Manfredo.

As she rushed up the steps a gush of water broke between her legs, and she let out a cry. "Devorah's coming!"

"Sweet Floriana," Manfredo said, as he bolted from his chess table to run to her aid. "I must speak to you about Judaism and babies and, and, and, and—" Floriana writhed with her first contraction.

"We'll speak later. Later," he said. "You're going to have a fine Jewish baby. Stay calm."

"But Sandro. Where is he?"

"He's washing. He's here. We are all here to help you," Manfredo said as Graziella helped him bring Floriana into his private chambers. Once Floriana was on Manfredo's bed, Graziella approached.

"Don't let my words disturb you," Graziella said, reaching for Floriana's brow, but Floriana turned her head away. "I was worried, wanting only the best for you. Do the work you were made to do and welcome this baby into the world. I'm sorry if I confused you. Don't think about that now. Don't worry. Just shush your thoughts and let us help you get ready for your baby's arrival. I'll massage you between contractions and we'll welcome the baby into the world with blessings for all."

Floriana's chest heaved while her face grew red and blotchy. When she saw Sandro approaching, she reached her hand out to him. He sat beside her, taking both her hands in his.

Even though Floriana refused to look at her, Graziella continued to speak lovingly as though her earlier outburst had never happened. "You see! He's here. He'll be here when this is all over. Now let me help you. The men usually stay outside."

"I want to stay here with her," Sandro said.

"Our tradition is otherwise," Graziella said. Sandro squeezed Floriana's hand and looked to Manfredo, who motioned he should step outside beyond the curtain, but Sandro did not move or release Floriana's hands from his own.

"You can help by being nearby, by being there to assure her when the labor is over," Graziella said.

Floriana looked from Sandro to Manfredo and to Graziella, whose hateful words, "uncircumcised dog," still echoed in Floriana's head as she released her grip on his hand.

"I'll be all right," Floriana said. "Manfredo has taken such good care of me so far, we should respect his traditions and allow them to do it their way. You'll be here when I am done?"

"Of course," Sandro said. "I'm here for you no matter how long it takes."

"It may take only a few hours," Graziella said.

"But this is her first," Manfredo said. "It could take twenty or thirty hours. You'll have to be patient. I'll send for the midwife."

"The midwife? Who's the midwife?" asked Floriana, her eyes darting back and forth.

"Breathe more deeply. Calm yourself," Graziella said, and she began to work on Floriana's left hand. Floriana pulled it away, turning toward Sandro. Graziella reached again for Floriana's hand, and this time she did not pull away.

"Can he sing to me from behind the curtain?" Floriana asked Graziella.

"Will you sing to her?"

"I'll do whatever she wants," Sandro said, not taking his eyes from Floriana's. "I'll sing until my voice is gone."

"Hum with me," Floriana said, and she began the soft humming she used to calm herself time and time again. It was the same humming sound Sandro had heard when he came upon her while she was weaving in the cellar room at the villa—the first time he had held her in his arms. As Sandro's voice joined hers, Manfredo led him out of the room beyond the carpet wall. He settled in with his sketchbook, humming and humming through her contractions, which came about every twenty minutes and then suddenly stopped, allowing her to sleep, and giving his voice a rest as darkness fell.

CHAPTER SIXTY-FIVE

Chaos in the Streets of Florence
April 26, 1478, Day

THE OUTSKIRTS OF FLORENCE appeared deserted to Savonarola and Piattini, even though bells rang unceasingly from every direction. As they moved closer toward the center, a scream—half human and half beast—pierced through the cacophony of deafening alarm bells. Running toward it, they encountered a swarm of people, all screaming "*Palle, Palle*"—the word that referred to spheres on the Medici family crest.

Fighting through the crowds into the Piazza della Signoria, they were greeted by more tortured cries from the Bargello, the chief of police's headquarters. Savonarola ran toward the building, while Piattini headed through the square toward the Arno River. As Gerome reached the square of the Bargello, he saw it.

A body in cleric's robes soaked in blood dangled on a rope from the Bargello window. Blood ran from the head, down the shoulders, and dripped from the gnarled and crippled hand Gerome had seen on the young cleric Bagnone, the young priest of the campfire.

Amid the shouts of *Palle, Palle, Palle,* Savonarola saw another body in blood-soaked cleric's robes slide from the same window and slam against the walls as a length of rope jerked it to within a few feet from the outstretched arms of the mob. This body's throat was sliced open and its head was wrapped in a black blindfold.

What Gerome Savonarola had seen in his dream had not been his own robes, but the ones he was witnessing at that moment. He heard more cries from inside and ran from one person to another trying to stitch together fragments among the conflicting and horrible stories to learn what had happened: the Pazzi had struck.

During High Mass at noon, two priests had attempted to kill Lorenzo and Giuliano inside the Duomo. Lorenzo had escaped with a slight wound to his neck. Giuliano had been stabbed to death.

The surviving Medicis had locked themselves in the palace, sending out soldiers to round up as many of the Pazzi faction as they could find. One of the pope's own had been involved, and he might be thrown out the window at any moment.

The bells never ceased. Gerome's skin grew cold as an involuntary shivering overtook him. In all his dreams of blood running through the streets, in all his visions, nothing had equaled the reality of what he saw and heard.

Body parts flew out the window. The shouts of the crowd told him they were scrotums and penises of those priests and some hands of the people still alive inside.

Without thinking of Piattini or the philosophical and religious differences between himself and Lorenzo, Gerome rushed to the Medici Palace. He pounded on the door shouting his name and was ushered inside. He heard moaning and screaming of the mourners. People ran up and down the stairs. Weapons and shields were being dispensed to common citizens as well as servants of the house.

"Do not spare anyone connected to that despicable family," Lorenzo shouted to the others as he ushered Savonarola into his chambers.

Giuliano's body lay on Lorenzo's bed, his clothes in shreds from the multiple knife piercings. Claudia's fingers clutched the hands of her beloved. On the floor next to Giuliano lay another body.

Lorenzo's neck was wrapped in bandages, but he could speak.

"Francesco Nori," he said. "A dear friend who stepped in between the murdering priests. He saved my life with his own."

"The cowards left Giuliano to bleed to death," he told Gerome as he stood by his brother's body. "He did not have a chance."

At this, Claudia let out a deeper sigh.

"You must give the last rites," Lorenzo said.

"I saw others, the archbishop from Pisa, in the house," Gerome said.

"They're under house arrest," Lorenzo said.

"The archbishop of Pisa?"

"They were all together with the blessing of Pope Sixtus. It's a good thing I never went to Rome. I might never have made it back."

Gerome knelt by Giuliano's body.

"I did not bring all of my sacramental equipment. It's with Piattini. We got separated over at the Bargello. Other priests were strung up out the windows."

"They were the ones who attacked me!" Lorenzo said. "Knives as long as anyone else's. I don't know who is with us and who is against us."

"All I hear on the streets is *Palle, Palle, Palle*. The people want only you," Gerome said.

"Because they know we will slice down anyone against us."

"What about all your humanism, your talk of love and beauty, your civilization based on the values of a republic and liberty you so admire?"

"Civilization is skin deep. Blood and instincts fight for survival below it."

"After I perform the last rites," Gerome said, "you must promise me you will bring an end to the bloodshed in the streets."

Lorenzo's rage turned on Savonarola. "Are you bargaining with me? You will give the last rites because I command you to. I'm not making any deals until the people who are behind this are excised like a rotten boil from this city."

Savonarola looked at the red eyes and full belly of Claudia. "My poor child, you've lost the father to your baby, but our Savior will be your Father and the child's Father and you will survive this."

"What do you know!" Claudia hissed at him.

"I know there is only one Father, and it is He to whom we must turn for justice."

"I see no justice, Brother Gerome. I see my beloved, father to my child, husband-to-be—dead and gone, cut down in the blossom of his youth, and all I want to do is to end my own life to join him."

"This is not what God wants. We each have a divine plan leading us, and yours is to survive and care for your child and mine is to pray for the end of blood in the streets of this city," Gerome said, provoking another livid and silencing gaze from Lorenzo. As Savonarola prepared to administer the last rites, Lorenzo locked his chamber doors. With the sound of that lock, Savonarola knew he, too, was under house arrest, and so he began, "Father, forgive them in their revenge for they know not what they do. In the midst of this horrific moment take the soul of this innocent man into your bosom. May his life not have been taken in vain. Send through his sacrifice a call to all to cease bloodshed and hate."

Savonarola could feel Lorenzo closing in on him to cease this extemporizing, so he slipped into Latin and recited the words of the last rites.

As Savonarola rose to his feet he said, "The body must be washed and prepared for burial. He must not go to rest in the garments in which he met his violent end."

Claudia clung to Giuliano's hand and wept, repeating Gerome's words, "*May his life not have been taken in vain.*"

Clarice, who had been let into the room during Gerome's Latin verses, knelt behind Claudia to gently pry her away from the corpse, arms encircling her never-to-be sister-in-law.

"Thank you for giving the last rites to him. Now, please, you must do the same for my fallen companion, Francesco," Lorenzo said.

Savonarola stooped to the floor where the other body lay and said nothing more except the Latin phrases, which he dispensed with quickly.

"He, too, must be washed and prepared with all signs of wounds sewn up."

The servants looked to Lorenzo for affirmation of Gerome's direction, and Lorenzo simply nodded once to indicate agreement.

When both corpses were removed with weeping women trailing behind, Lorenzo turned to Gerome.

"And now, Father Savonarola, I request a prayer to beg for assistance to rid this town of the plague of this bloody revolt and to lead us to every perpetrator."

"I cannot condone more bloodletting. Revenge is not the answer."

A loud knock on the door from one of the in-house guards brought news of another priest outside the palace covered in blood who said he was Lorenzo's friend and the companion of Brother Gerome.

"Piattini," said Gerome. "He may be wounded."

"Bring him here," Lorenzo said.

Lorenzo and Savonarola waited in silence. Any words Gerome might utter would be ones against bloodshed. The wild look in Lorenzo's eyes told him his own life hung in a precarious place.

Someone knocked on the door.

"You open it this time," Lorenzo ordered Gerome.

Piattini's face was splattered in blood and the hem of his robes looked as though he had waded through a stream of blood. When he pulled up the sleeve of his robe he exposed a deep gash above his elbow.

As Gerome gathered Piattini into his arms to lead him into the center of Lorenzo's chambers, he lied, "We're safe here."

"Tell us what you saw," Lorenzo prompted. "Spare no detail."

"When Brother Gerome went off to the Bargello," Piattini said, "I headed toward Piazza della Signoria. I heard screams coming from Palazzo Vecchio and then a body was thrown from the window. His throat had been sliced open and his hands cut off. I approached the victim in an attempt to give the last rites but the crowd came forth with knives and sticks to attack it. They kicked me aside when I told them sinners deserved last rites too. I didn't move fast enough because someone in the crowd sliced into my arm and pulled me further away from the corpse. 'This one will rot in hell,' he said, 'what's left of him.' The crowd attacked him like a piece of fresh-killed meat, cutting him to pieces and placing the body parts onto stakes and spears. They howled with an insane laughter as they began to run through the streets. When

I pulled myself to my feet, another body was thrown down and more of the crowd came forward to mutilate and parade the parts. Intestines were everywhere. Some people vomited at the sight, while others waited for the next body to fall. I headed to the Bargello and there the same. Someone had climbed the wall to cut the rope for a priest. Instead of rescuing his body, they began the same assault. The bells have not stopped and the city is in a frenzy. I came here hoping to find refuge and to find Brother Gerome."

Piattini turned to Lorenzo. "Bless you, Master Lorenzo, for protecting us. My heart is broken for your brother, Giuliano, may his soul rest in peace in heaven."

Lorenzo turned to Savonarola. "Clean his wound and stay here until nightfall. I want you out of the city gates by dawn. Do not say a word about stopping this madness in the streets. I'll allow it until tomorrow when I'll take control of the city again."

"And why," Gerome asked, "would you not do it now?"

"Let the crowd do to the perpetrators what I wish to do, while my heart has been torn out of my chest by the death of my brother. At least the people of the city will do for me against the guilty what I want to be doing. And then I will stop them."

Piattini looked at Gerome with a plea to stop Lorenzo's declaration, and then he fainted.

CHAPTER SIXTY-SIX

As Darkness Descends across Tuscany
April 26, 1478

DURING THE SAME DARK NIGHT that Floriana slept exhausted from her false labor, relieved her love was nearby and the birth of her child so close, bells of alarm traveled through the black sky from the edge of Florence out in all directions. Stories of the assassinations bled off tongues and slipped past the city gates before they slammed shut. As the word spread, so did confusion.

Mercenaries, out of uniform, galloped for their lives. The hooves of their horses resounded not only on the surface of the land but into the fitful and worried sleep of all who heard.

And so, the day of April 26, 1478, ended in a darkness more terrible than anyone had imagined.

Lucrezia tore her clothes, paced, collapsed, then cut her hair off, hoping the ends might bleed and relieve her in some way of the cavern in her chest where her heart had turned to stone. Her Lorenzo, at least, survived, but the anguish over the loss of her Giuliano had grown even harsher by the broken promise of Claudia and Giuliano's sweet love.

Lucrezia blessed the child in Claudia's belly and tried, between her own grief and ranting, to console the woman whom she had so long disliked, but who had found a place in her family, if not her heart. If any semblance of Giuliano's live tissue remained for her, it breathed in the unborn Giulio.

As for Lorenzo, his years of warrior poses and sword brandishing in mock tournaments were now torn asunder with the flesh of his brother. Pomp fell away as he declared the battle of his life. No one would be spared, no suspicion unchecked. He would enlist the whole of Florence to track down the guilty, and he would cut himself off from the pope before the pope could cut him off. And he would bring his favorite artist and friend, Botticelli, to comfort him and paint something to commemorate this awful day. He would stop the mutilation by the crowds and let those bodies—however many there were—smolder and stink, rot and putrefy, under the gaze of all.

CHAPTER SIXTY-SEVEN

Lorenzo's Tears and Piero's Fears
April 26, 1478, Night

ATCHING HIS BROTHER Giuliano's body being sewn back together, Lorenzo's thirst for blood only increased. He had dismissed Savonarola and Piattini, and while the moon still hung in the sky, he watched them leave. They were his one connection to his church, but it was a connection he had severed when he banished them.

No more would poetry, art—all of the things he so treasured—no more would they occupy such a high place in his life and spirit. Now revenge and cleansing and protecting his family were the only things that mattered. If only he had sensed, if only he had not been so fearless and open. Now the weight of his brother's death had fallen on his shoulders. Only he could make things right.

Expelling Savonarola had not been easy. This young and passionate priest had relieved Lorenzo of his crippling gout and had stopped his cousin Piero's lifelong head tremor. Yet agreeing to Savonarola's plea for nonviolence would have been intolerable. Yes, he was choosing blood over forgiveness.

More blood, more punishment, was the only way to protect. He knew that nothing, nothing short of taking his own life and hopefully meeting Giuliano on that other side, could bring Giuliano back to him. There was no choice: *Sweep through the city and finish what the crowd has begun. But do it swiftly and do it well.*

ALL THE DARK AND SUMPTUOUS COLORS and fabrics in their marriage suite, a richness that had comforted Lorenzo for so long, aggravated his rage. Only cold marble, stone, and ice were the surfaces that could comfort him, and so he lay on the marble-tiled floor, a cool sensation on his cheek like a breeze frozen in time.

"Why are you not coming to bed?" Clarice said. She had knelt beside him, gently pulling at his arm with enough force to get him moving and closer to their bed.

"Not there!" he said, recoiling at the memory of Giuliano's corpse having touched it hours earlier.

"Let us go to the chapel," she said. "We'll pray for courage and strength to—"

"Cut down our enemies."

"Then that is what you must pray for, Lorenzo."

"Savonarola says I must forgive and pray for peace."

"We must make peace through war," she said. "How else can we do it?"

The two knelt in front of the crucifix. Surrounded by Gozzoli's fresco of the journey of the Magi, Lorenzo started to wail and writhe, at last allowing his grief to tear into his chest and viscera as deeply as the knives had cut into his brother. Swaying along with his every contortion, Clarice held him fast. When his body stilled and the moans subsided, Clarice spoke. "And this war, my love," she said in a soft voice close to a whisper. "How are you going to finance it? A war against the pope is no easy thing."

"We'll tax the suspicious ones until they leave. It was done to us, and we can do it to others."

"That takes time. My brother says the banks are draining fast."

"We still have 'family' resources," Lorenzo said. "Extended family resources. Piero's inheritance is enormous. We can borrow from it and replace it once we stabilize the banks."

"And he will agree."

"He knows nothing about who keeps a hand on it. He only thinks he does. I, however, have allies who have counted it, and I have ways to tap into it if needed. These are exceptional times, and I can stretch myself to adopt exceptional means. What he doesn't know will not hurt him."

ALONG WITH OTHER DISTANT COUSINS, Piero had been sent into a large hall, the one so often used for joyous occasions, as temporary sleeping quarters. Lorenzo told them they must stay there the next three days or longer until the city calmed down. He told Piero he would send a messenger for Ficino and Sandro, and to tell the girls and Poppi that all were well and to pray for the family, pray for the victors, and pray for the soul of Giuliano's unborn child.

Certain that the search for Sandro would lead to the moneylender's house and the truth about the secret loan he had secured to purchase Villa di Castello, Piero could not sleep in the palace of his mighty cousin. He did not dare to disobey. He did not dare to raise his voice in suggestion when he heard Lorenzo give the orders for Ficino and Sandro to be recalled from Villa di Castello.

He knew when the messenger would return the next morning with Ficino and without Sandro, he would have to invent some excuse—some story. Hopefully, he would awaken with it, clear and concise, but not now. Now he needed to sleep. Try as he might to erase the image from his memory, he still saw the dead Giuliano in front of his eyes, for he had been in the palace when they brought Giuliano's body from the church. When they removed the blankets, Giuliano's intestines had fallen out of the wounds. At that moment Lucrezia had fainted and he himself, Piero, had turned aside to retch. The servants had knelt and pushed the body parts back inside the poor Giuliano. Lorenzo had looked away and then the body was taken into Lorenzo's chambers.

As Piero lay sleepless on the bed, he tried to recall Giuliano's once sweet face, but instead the images of Giuliano's innards spilling onto the floor played in his mind's eye over and over again. Adding to these gruesome scenes, he projected other frightening ones from the future. He saw himself under pain of torture having to reveal Sandro's whereabouts. He could imagine Lorenzo's cruel and cajoling tone forcing him to spit out Manfredo's name. Surely, his head would start to jerk and shake as he spilled out the information like those involuntary intestines, the stink of his own secret around the villa's purchase, the loan, the paintings, and on and on. His mind reeled, catastrophizing until he finally fell into a fitful sleep at dawn.

CHAPTER SIXTY-EIGHT

An Eerie Light Enters the Darkness of Night
April 26, 1478

HE SOUND OF THE FAINT BELLS sewn into Stella's clothing, along with gasps and whispers, awakened Sandro. Floriana, exhausted from her false labor, slept deeply.

"I have roused the whole house," Stella said when she saw Sandro.

"This is the Master Botticelli," Graziella said. "He's come to attend at the birth."

"The father?" Stella asked.

"I only wish it were so," he said. "Call me a protector, one devoted to her and the baby. You're familiar to me. Haven't I seen you before in the house of the Medicis?"

"That house!" Stella said. "That house will never be the same. I knew something dark was heading toward them. There was no way to warn them. I could not see the details, only the darkness."

"What has happened?" Sandro said, his pulse rising.

"Death today to Giuliano."

"What! Who! How! Impossible!"

"Yes, possible. They were in the cathedral this morning for Easter

Mass. Two priests attempted to kill Lorenzo, but he was too quick for them. At the same time, Giuliano was set upon violently by the Pazzis and all fled, leaving him in a pool of blood. I was able to leave the city because I am on the edge of it and your messenger got to me before they closed off the gates. But the bells were ringing far and wide. Did you not hear anything?"

"Nothing," Manfredo said. "We were all occupied with Floriana expecting the child at any moment."

"I cannot stay here," Sandro said. "They were like brothers to me. I must go back into the city to help. No one, only Piero, knows my whereabouts, and my father and mother will be frantic until they know I am safe. I cannot stay here."

"But you've pledged your support to Floriana," Graziella said. "You can't bring back the dead. You must stay with the living and the new."

"You're right," Sandro said, but he was unable to stay still. "Lucrezia was like a mother to me. She must be crazy with grief. And Lorenzo, how is he?"

"I know nothing of their condition, only what I saw and heard in the streets."

"And what was that?"

"People screaming *Palle, Palle, Palle,* and young boys with pieces of human flesh on stakes as though they were running to cook and eat them on some terrible fire."

"And the priests. Who are they?"

"Who *were* they, you mean?" Stella answered. "They were the first to have their throats slit and their bodies hung outside of the Bargello walls until the crowds cut them down and cut them up. That is all I know. You'll be much safer here."

Manfredo and Graziella looked at Sandro.

"A divided heart," Manfredo said, "makes a wound that never heals."

"And how do you suggest I cure such a thing? I'm more than divided now. I'm cut into pieces like the corpses themselves. The pain is more than I can bear."

"Sit and calm yourself," Manfredo said.

"I cannot sit. I cannot think. I cannot wait." His voice had risen and Floriana sleepily came into the room.

She wrapped herself around Sandro. "You can wait. She's coming soon. I know it. I can hear her crying voice in my head already. She's screaming to come out." Floriana smiled but no one returned her smile.

"This is Stella, the midwife who's going to help you," Graziella said.

Floriana stood in front of the young woman who wore bells and spangles like a gypsy. "But I thought midwives were old ladies. This woman is an enchantress. Maybe she can coax my little one to come forth."

"You're not going to need much coaxing. Your belly has dropped, and you're going to be a mother before the next nightfall," Stella said.

"See that, Sandro, you'll not have to wait long at all," Floriana cooed.

"Sweet jewel of my heart," Sandro began, "I cannot wait to see your child, but I cannot wait because others need me more."

"Who needs you more? Your painting? It's just a piece of wood with paint on it?"

"My brother Giuliano has been assassinated," Sandro said.

Graziella draped her arms around Floriana's shoulders. "There is blood in the streets of Florence."

"He's not your brother!"

"And you are not my wife! But does that mean I love you any less?"

Even though he had said those words, and said them with so much passion, in that moment he was drifting away from her with the speed of a falling star. In spite of his words, in spite of the fact he stood there in front of her—a loving gaze still burning through his grief, she knew in her womb bursting with life that she had already lost him. The falling star's lightning path played over and over again behind her watery eyes. She reached out her hand for his and squeezed it tightly, then dropped it, tore her gaze from his face, and said, "Of course you must go to them."

"My other brother, Lorenzo, needs me near him. My other mother, Lucrezia, is surely going to need my comfort. They are my family, not by blood, but by life."

"They may need you less than you think," Stella said. "The crowds are killing for them and you'll not be safe."

"I'll go as the shepherd again and make my way. I cannot sit here. I must go. I'll be back. I promise."

Floriana refused to look at him, then flinched from a strong contraction.

"She's going now. See that," said Stella. "It could be just an hour or—"

"It could be twelve hours or another twenty," Manfredo said.

"If he goes now, he'll never come back!" Floriana said.

"She doesn't know what she's saying," Graziella told Sandro. "She's just upset."

Floriana turned to him and spoke with an almost sarcastic edge. "He has made his choice. The only one he could ever make. Be safe, my sweet protector," she said, then turned her eyes away from him.

"I am not choosing. I refuse to choose. I'm leaving now and I'll be back. I can't be torn in two, for I will be in neither place. My heart is with you always, but today my loyalty must go deeper than my own heart."

"Then you have chosen," Floriana said, holding her belly, and turning to look at him one last time.

"My heart is big enough to contain you and your child and my own family and my sister, Oslavia, and my parents. You are driving a knife into its center with your giving up on us, your insistence I have made my choice. I cannot choose, I will not choose."

"Do not waste time convincing me. I release you fully to your family that needs you. I am sorry for your loss. But go now and stop the pain for both of us!" she said, as the falling star continued to play in her imagination and Graziella's earlier cruel words of condemnation, "uncircumcised dog!" rolled on her tongue involuntarily, though she willed herself not to speak them.

The pain of Floriana's all-too-easy release of him belied an anger he knew must be behind her words—formal words of condolence delivered a blow from which he knew no way to recover, except to flee.

CHAPTER SIXTY-NINE

At Villa di Castello
April 27, 1478, Morning

OPPI FED LORENZO'S MESSENGER as she dictated her response to the palace: all were well, Master Piero could rest assured she would take care of the villa as usual, but Master Botticelli was not present, and she was not sure exactly where he might be. Telling this messenger any of the details would solve nothing, so she said that upon the artist's return she would send him straightway to the Medici Palace.

The gardeners and other helpers whom she had recruited over the winter and spring to help expand the gardens could see something serious was happening. She did not offer explanations when she exchanged her red leggings and red work clothes for a black dress.

Ficino quickly assembled his belongings. When the last crumb was wiped from the messenger's face, the two men left for Florence.

Later that morning, the girls came downstairs in black dresses and veils, already teary-eyed, with the loss of their handsome young cousin, distant though he had been from their lives.

"Will we be sent to the convent now?" Renata asked.

"Hardly. Your cousin Lorenzo has declared war on the pope. Excommunication will be the next step for him and perhaps for all of us."

"Excommunication!" gasped Margarita. "How exciting!"

"Stop!" Poppi said. "Let no one hear you say such a thing."

Ignoring Poppi, Margarita went on, "I always knew cousin Lorenzo was strong enough to start his own church, and now he will."

"Silence!" Poppi said. "This is a time of mourning, not of celebration. In times like these, one never knows who the enemy is. Tongues that wag too long can surely be cut out."

"What an awful thing to say," Donata said.

"You girls know nothing of the violence out in this world. There are instruments of torture, and your cousin Lorenzo is no shy boy. He'll be using them without much control over the next few days. I've heard stories."

"You and your stories. What do you know?" Margarita said.

"More than you want to hear," Poppi said. "I had a brother whose fingers were clipped off like the stems of roses simply because he stole some fruit off the wrong table."

"Why didn't you ever tell us this?" Donata asked.

"Because I came here to your family and tried to forget such acts of brutality."

The three girls huddled together.

"And what about Sandro? What about his portraits of us?" Renata asked.

"All interrupted," Poppi said. "Lorenzo has ordered him back to the palace."

"But he isn't even here."

"Exactly. Your brother is the only person who knows where Sandro is."

"Why didn't he tell Lorenzo that Sandro wasn't here?"

"Stop asking so many questions. Just be prepared. Life is going to be different for some time now and you'll surely be part of a funeral soon."

"God bless the soul of Giuliano," Renata said.

"God bless the soul of Giuliano," echoed Donata, "and the souls of Claudia and the unborn baby. I would kill myself if I were she. Slice open my belly and end it all right there and then!"

"Just the opposite," Poppi said. "She's now elevated to permanent member of the household and that child with Giuliano's blood will keep mother and child safe. Little Giulio will be guarded for the rest of his days."

"I cannot eat anything," Donata said.

"You all must be strong for when we go to the palace. You must make your brother proud."

"What about Sandro?"

"If I know Lorenzo at all," Poppi said, "he'll find him. Be grateful he was not at the scene. Twenty blows to Giuliano's body, they said. No one came to his aid for fear of getting cut down. That's what the messenger said."

"Poor Giuliano."

"Poor Claudia."

"Poor Piero. Pray for your brother. Pray for the city of Florence," Poppi said.

"Amen," the three sisters said in unison.

CHAPTER SEVENTY

Savonarola and Piattini Return to Oslavia's
April 27, 1478, Afternoon

BY THE TIME Savonarola and Piattini had reached Oslavia's compound, the blood on Piattini's robes had dried to a deep reddish-brown stain. Dono studied it with a horrified expression, while Luigi touched the bandage on Piattini's arm.

"It's what you think it is," Gerome said. "And we left rivers of it behind. Giuliano de' Medici is dead. Lorenzo is launching a campaign of terror. He banished us. We were lucky to get out alive."

"Blood all through the streets just as Fra Savonarola has been predicting," Piattini said.

"Do not frighten the boy," Gerome said.

"I'm not a boy. I am a young man, and I have seen plenty of death already, so you don't have to worry about me crying any more about these things. Who else is dead?"

"Mostly those who mounted the attack," Gerome said, "but I saw only a tiny bit and then we came back here."

"I must tell Mother Oslavia," Luigi said as he turned to run toward the convent.

"Stop!" Gerome said. "I will tell her, but first let's get this poor soldier to a bed and change his robes. You, Dono, take him inside and you, Luigi, if you like, you can come with me to Sister Oslavia's compound."

"She is so happy these days," Luigi said. "I hope she does not faint."

"She will not faint," Gerome said, "though *I* might."

"You! You were the one who told us about the blood in the streets, the wildness," Luigi said.

"To dream it, my son, is not the same as to live it. I am afraid this is just the beginning of the end unless God makes his way into their ailing souls. Go, Luigi, and knock on her cell. I'll wait back here. Once she sees my face, she'll know something grave has happened. Go and tell her I'm waiting in the dining hall for her. On second thought, don't tell her to come right away. I'll change these bloody robes. I'll wash first then pray for a moment. Tell her to come for evening prayer."

Luigi stood tall and walked slowly toward the convent, proud that he was going to bring Oslavia to the place where Brother Gerome would tell her the truth. Though he knew his face should not be grave, so as to worry her, he also knew he should not be smiling. Yet he felt a strange kind of joy and excitement bubbling inside him. No fear. He had seen the beautiful and elegant Giuliano in November when Lorenzo had brought the feast of all feasts to the Villa di Castello and he had met the brilliant Ficino. This crisis was finally going to bring the philosopher closer to him. This is all he thought about: reliving moments at the villa and feeling that at last he'd be going there again soon.

Once at Oslavia's door, he straightened his shoulders and his clothing, twitched his mouth into various configurations, wiped a hand across his lips to erase any hint of a smile, then, raising and lowering his eyebrows to prevent worry wrinkles on his forehead, he knocked.

"And what does Master Luigi have in mind for Mother Oslavia?"

"Mother Maria Oslavia," Luigi corrected.

"I can live without the extra name," she said. "You've known me all these years as Mother Oslavia; let's not change it now."

"But Monsignor Bernardino said—"

"Monsignor Bernardino is not God, only one of God's representatives, just as I am, so what I say is what we'll do."

"But . . ."

"Don't worry," she said. "God is in you and in me and all we must do our whole lives is listen to God's voice within and follow it."

"But," Luigi said, so quick to abandon the need of the moment for a philosophical discussion, "if someone kills us with a sword, does that God within escape and leave the body?"

"You are always asking good questions, Luigi. But do tell me why you are looking for me."

"Father Savonarola wishes you to meet him at the next bells in the prayer room."

"And did he say what he wants?" she asked. "Do you know what he wants? Who died?"

"I did not say anyone died. I asked if the God within escapes if a sword makes enough holes in the body for it to leave and for the person to die."

"Who has died?" she said, now shaking him without giving him a chance to cover his words.

"Lorenzo, the Magnificent."

"What!" she said. "Lorenzo?"

"No. I meant to say Lorenzo the Magnificent's brother, Giuliano. But I was not supposed to tell you or upset you. He wants to tell you but he wanted to take off the bloody robes first."

"What bloody robes? What are you talking about? Where is he?"

Luigi began to cry, his voice cracking between boy and man sounds.

"Take me to him this instant!" Oslavia's equanimity vanished, and she yanked Luigi by the arm, dragging him toward the monastery.

"Please, Mother Oslavia. Please calm yourself. I was not supposed to say anything. Now he'll think me a child blabbing."

She stopped. They were halfway to the monastery when she took Luigi by the shoulders. He was gaining in height, and his eyes were almost level with hers. "I am calm," she said. "I do not believe what you are saying. I just could not believe it. My heart sank. What about my brother?"

"I know nothing," he said, now whimpering behind her. "But tell me. What's the answer? Please!"

"What answer? What are you talking about?"

"The God within. Where does it go when the body dies?"

"To heaven," Oslavia said, not wanting to engage Luigi's philosophical inquiries anymore. "The God within travels to the bigger God in heaven and they are both happy to be reunited."

"Did my mother's God within go there? And what about Bandini and Petrarchio?"

"All there. All together. Happy and smiling in heaven. Smiling on us clumsy mortals, who fumble when we walk and talk. Now go, sweet Luigi, leave me in peace here. Go back to your father." She waited for him to turn away before she continued toward the monastery.

"But Brother Gerome will know I told you," Luigi said in one last effort to stop her.

"I'll not tell him. I am calm now. Go and let me handle this by myself."

"But you're early, you're too early."

"He'll be surprised," she said, and then reconsidered. The last thing she wanted to see, given the terrible news, was the hairy, naked Gerome stretching out his lingam to find the strength to go on. She decided, instead, to play along with Luigi's plan. She reached out her hand to him and he came running toward her.

"You're right," she said. "I must respect his wishes. He has gone through much, seeing all that blood. Let us take a walk together and when the hour is done, I'll do as you want."

"Thank you, thank you so much, Mother Oslavia. This way he'll not guess I have disappointed him with my big mouth."

"Keep up," she said, for she had set a wide stride and she walked with force, dragging Luigi into the woods with her. "How are your sisters?"

"They are missing their mother, but the nuns, your other initiates, have been helpful to them. They're talking about becoming nuns themselves as though they want it."

"Some are called and some are drafted," Oslavia said, remembering how she had cried so terribly when she was informed of her fate.

"And about the God inside, Mother Oslavia. What is your God inside called? Have you given it a special name?"

"A special name? I assumed it was the Lord our Jesus Christ, his Christ consciousness in me."

"But would the Christ consciousness in me say the same things to me the Christ consciousness in you says to you?"

"You are incessant, Luigi!"

"I can't stop my mind, Mother Oslavia. I want to be a philosopher like the wise Ficino."

"And what do you know of him?"

"I met him, remember, at the banquet. He answered the question about lying to save a loved one. He said friendship is higher than formal worship, that it's a kind of worship."

"And why were you asking such a question of him?"

"It was when we were calling Floriana Rosanna to confuse the old Bandini. We were deceiving him, were we not?"

"We were, but with a higher purpose. To save one who chose not to adopt our faith. To free her from hating us. Let me have my thoughts in silence, Luigi. Just walk with me tonight without speaking or asking questions for this one evening. Please!"

The boy-man obeyed and kept his swirling questions to himself. And she, the abbess of the convent of what his father had called the order of the *Disgraziati*, breathed deeply and walked into the woods as images of the Florentine carnage flashed through her mind. Rosary beads in hand, she worked them as she walked, returning to prayer as she fought off her imagination and her worries.

CHAPTER SEVENTY-ONE

Sandro's Return to the Medici

BY THE TIME SANDRO GAINED ACCESS to the Medici Palace on Via Cavour, it was the second night after the murder. Banners of mourning hung from every parapet. Giuliano's portrait—the very one Sandro had painted barely one year ago—had been removed from the palace gallery and lay propped at the entrance, surrounded with white gardenias and memorial candles. A mourner's vigil had gathered outside the palace to grieve the loss of their angelic prince Giuliano, cut down in his twenty-third year.

As Sandro mounted the stairs, a chilling scream from the courtyard below stopped him. Torches lit the inner garden, and Sandro peered over the railing to see a young man bound to a torture table. His arms were tied above his head, and his legs were spread apart with the ankles tied down and the feet extending over the edge of the wooden board.

Lorenzo, not his henchmen, but Lorenzo himself, stood with a knife in his hand slicing open the bottoms of the poor unfortunate's feet as Lorenzo's helper applied flames from a torch to melt the fat under the skin. It oozed from the wounds and, like a sticky syrup, dropped and sizzled onto a pot of hot coals at the foot of the torture table.

"Speak!" shouted Lorenzo. "Tell me who else was part of this vicious act."

Again the young man screamed and whimpered that he knew nothing. He swore.

Lorenzo sliced again, this time peeling off the entire layer of skin on one foot.

Sandro watched his friend—this poet, artist, intellectual, humanist, musician—peel flesh as though he had always done so. Il Magnifico brought the same perfect movements and mastery to this most horrific act he had brought to the finest expressions of his artistic nature. Sandro had chosen this madman over Floriana.

A wave of nausea passed through Sandro's belly toward his own feet. A fiery pain pierced the soles so he could not move or take a step except to collapse onto the floor with all his belongings scattering around him.

At that moment Lorenzo looked up, and showed the flesh still hanging on his knife to Sandro. "You see what we have become," he said. "And yet I know this will not bring back my brother."

Sandro turned to run down the steps, out of the palace, and back to Floriana. Surely if he came back to her so soon, she would forgive him. All would not be lost. At the bottom of the stairs, Lorenzo's men apprehended him, holding him in the entryway until Lorenzo, with blood on his hands and on his clothing, faced Sandro.

"Remember the words of Pericles?" Lorenzo asked. "'Just because you do not take an interest in politics doesn't mean politics won't take an interest in you!' There's no escape, Sandro."

Sandro struggled to free himself, to run out, to undo his decision, to return to what he'd left behind.

"You've done what you promised, my friend. You've returned to me in my hour of need."

"That was before I knew you were a madman," Sandro said as he tried to free himself from the guards.

"House arrest!" Lorenzo ordered. "Until he comes to his senses."

"It is you who has lost all his senses! I came to help you mourn, not to watch you kill and maim."

Sandro stood face to face with Lorenzo, frightened and repulsed by the wildness in his friend's eyes. He could see Lorenzo was beyond reasoning, so he said nothing more as he was led into the room where others, including Piero and Ficino, were sequestered.

"THANK GOD YOU'RE HERE," Piero said the moment he saw Sandro being led into the large ballroom. Sandro embraced Piero with a fierceness and affection that brought him immediately back to the scene all those months ago when his disdain for this Medici cousin had hardly allowed him to look directly into his eyes. The young man he clung to at this moment had become his friend.

"Ficino and I were trying to figure out what to say to Lorenzo about where you were," Piero said. Sandro pulled himself away from Piero's embrace and looked at the boy as though he had become a fully matured man.

"How did you find out?" Ficino asked.

"The midwife," Sandro answered.

"Did Floriana have her baby?" Piero said.

"Surely by now. She must have by now."

"Weren't you there?" Piero asked.

"She had just come out of a false labor and was asleep when I heard the news of Giuliano's assassination. I chose to come here to comfort the family instead of waiting for the birth," Sandro said. "I thought my friendship would comfort Lorenzo. But now I know I made the wrong choice."

Piero's and Ficino's attention turned away from Sandro to Lorenzo, who had slipped into the room.

"What choice was that?" Lorenzo asked.

"The choice to leave the woman I love at the hour of her need to come to you. When I heard the news, I—"

"You did the right thing, Sandro," Lorenzo said.

"I did the wrong thing for the right reasons," Sandro said. "I did not think I was coming to help a murderer. I was coming to be with my family."

"Your family? Then why did you come here?" Lorenzo said.

"My Medici family. My Medici brothers," Sandro said.

"You are no Medici, Sandro!" Lorenzo said, his voice assuming that strident nasal tone he often adopted without thinking.

"He meant, I'm sure, to be loyal," Piero said.

"He is loyal to his work. To his art. But he knows nothing of the real world of flesh and blood," Lorenzo said.

"Nor do I care to know the one you inhabit now," Sandro said. "I will not kill for you, so let me go. I must return to the woman I love, to the work I've been hired to do. It must go on even with all this chaos."

"No one is going anywhere!" Lorenzo said as he turned abruptly to exit the room.

"Does he know where you were?" Piero asked.

"He never asked! He doesn't know where *he* is anymore. He simply arrested me."

"Sequestered, you mean, as we are?" Ficino asked.

"No. He said the words 'house arrest!'"

LATER THAT NIGHT, Piero and Sandro hatched a plan. They would leave together when Lorenzo was ready to release the detained guests, and they would head out of the city. Just as they had a few short days ago, they would pass by Manfredo's property, only this time Piero would lead the way onto the property to avoid any unfriendly guards. Sandro would win over Floriana and the baby, insisting that she come with him to live at Villa di Castello. Sandro would resume his work on the painting. With this plan to calm him, Sandro pulled out his sketchbook to plan the last figure in the painting. It would be an image of Giuliano as Mercury reaching for the heavens and immortality as he plucked the fruits of the tree of life.

ONE WEEK LATER, Piero and Sandro were summoned into Lorenzo's private office. Sandro noticed less wildness in Lorenzo's eyes as he told them the citizens of Florence could once again walk freely through the city. He had put a stop to the butchery in the streets, but had ordered bodies of the perpetrators and suspected conspirators be left rotting on the Bargello wall as well as in the Piazza della Signoria. He had condoned continued interrogations inside the Bargello. As a warning to anyone entertaining the slightest murmur of dissent, each day he displayed more dripping corpses out of the Bargello windows.

"And so, *Cugino*," he said, putting his arm around Piero. "You and Ficino are free to return to Villa di Castello. No villains will jump you on your way back."

"We were going to leave together, Lorenzo. I must get back to the painting that is almost finished. I am obliged to," Sandro said.

"What about your woman? Your Jew?" Lorenzo asked.

"She will be with me there at Castello. I'm under contract to finish the work I started, the work you sent me away to do."

"You are only obliged to me and no longer to him," Lorenzo said. "The painting can wait. I need you here. You are still under house arrest."

"Because . . . ?" Sandro asked.

"Because you would run away without it. And because I have an assignment you must complete before you can go back to Piero's."

"What is it?"

"The decomposing corpses," Lorenzo said. "I want them to smolder and stink, rot and putrefy under the gaze of all and I want you, Sandro, to sketch this for the next month. Finally, when you're done with the drawings and the bodies are removed, you will paint those images for all to see, generation after generation, on the Bargello wall."

Lorenzo turned to Piero. "You can go now. I'll let your artist go to the villa after a month's time to retrieve his assistant and his materials after he's done with the sketches and before he starts the mural. But he will be under heavy guard, and he will not be returned to you until he is finished with my project. Is that understood?"

"Understood. Understood," Piero said as he gave one last look at Sandro. Sandro saw a calmness in Piero's face. His head no longer twitched. He saw through the months they had spent together a young man who had been devoted to their pursuit of art and beauty, Piero in his own way an artist with his elaborate dolls. Sandro had been so wrong to belittle him. Now in Sandro's eyes, Piero had become the more manly of the two cousins.

"May I at least walk down the steps with Piero to say goodbye to him?"

Sandro asked, hoping somehow that he might be able to get word to Floriana through Piero.

"You may not," Lorenzo said. "What else could you possibly have to say to him after seven days of confinement together? And you and I are not through with this conversation."

"Wine?" Lorenzo asked as Piero slipped out of the room.

"No, thank you," Sandro said, thinking how drastically his life had changed. The last place he wanted to be now was in this Medici Palace, his former "home." From the perspective of time, experience, and calamity, he could finally see he was and had always been a servant. A servant with privileges, a servant with access to an inner sanctum, but never really part of the family. Piero, with all his eccentricities, had given him respect and, yes, had given him friendship. If he couldn't be with Floriana in the flesh, at least he could be with the Floriana he had created on that board in the villa with the dancing sisters, the yapping dogs, under the care and friendship of Poppi too.

"If I may be so bold as to share my artistic and technical experience, Master Lorenzo, that scene on the Bargello wall will never last. The elements will crack and fade the paint. The moisture from the bricks will blister it."

"You will use all your knowledge to delay that. And if it will not last, then so be it. I want no one to forget what took place here. One year or two or three or five will please me greatly. It will not be wasted. And as you paint it, you, too, will begin to realize what we were up against here and not judge me so harshly."

"I came to help you mourn, to mourn with you, Lorenzo, but seeing you that night as you flayed that poor unfortunate's feet, what could I think but that you in all your refinement and culture and learning had sunk below the level of those who tried to cut you down. That you were not honoring Giuliano."

"Not honoring! It is not about honor. It is about revenge."

"But it can't bring him back. And painting that grotesque scene will surely not bring him back. And besides, it does not honor him. The subject of violence is not a subject of victory."

"And did you not take the subject of violence, a rape, and make art out of it?"

Sandro took the question, tasted it, rolling it around in his head as though it were a sip of a strange wine before agreeing to drink it. "My motivation was to find beauty in the darkness of the deed as a seed to rebirth. Your motivation is hate. An eye for an eye as law."

"What would you have me do?"

"Bury him with dignity. Stop the bloodshed. Let me paint something that honors him, that memorializes him. I've already sketched something I have in mind."

"You sound like the Dominican you sent to cure my gout. I'm walking, thanks to him."

"He has his tricks. He is as much a hypocrite as anyone."

"Hypocrite is not how I would cast him, though cast him out I did for the same nonviolent nonsense he wanted me to use after Giuliano had been slain."

"The more you see enemies everywhere you turn, Lorenzo, the more alone you will be. I am not your enemy. And not your brother as I had fancied myself."

"Then what are you?"

"No longer your friend. Your prisoner. Your servant artist who wants to buy his freedom any way he can."

"Then you will paint exactly what I tell you to paint. It's the only way you'll ever be able to leave here."

CHAPTER SEVENTY-TWO

The Girls Wait and Wait

AS THEY WAITED for the return of their brother, Piero, and their resident painter, Sandro, the three sisters, Renata, Margarita, and Donata, would creep each day into the greenhouse studio, carefully remove the protective covers over the painting, and look at themselves in Sandro's work.

"Look how beautiful he has made us!" Donata said.

"But when, oh when, is he ever going to finish it?" Renata asked.

"He's going to forget about us and the painting and run away with Floriana if he hasn't already!" Margarita said.

"That, my young ladies, he cannot do," Poppi said, as she put the cover back over the painting and shooed them away like hungry mosquitos. "You know Master Botticelli is a man of integrity. He is going to finish what he started."

Eventually, Piero returned with Ficino, but without Sandro and no explanation of his disappearance, which caused the girls to fight among themselves, imagining how he might be with Floriana, yet hoping for his return with her and the baby by his side.

When Piero finally tracked his sisters down in the kitchen, they were astounded at how much weight he had lost—even though he had been gone only one week. He told them that the recurring image of Giuliano's pallid, pierced body had so stripped him of his appetite that his clothes had begun to hang on him.

"Tell us, tell us everything!" his sisters begged him as they pulled at his baggy clothing.

"Later, later," Piero said. "Enough to say, the city is officially now at war with the pope, and Lorenzo is officially excommunicated!"

"We know that already! What about Sandro?" Renata asked.

"Sandro arrived on the second night. He's under house arrest!"

"And what of Floriana's baby?" Donata asked.

"He never saw it," Piero said.

"What! This is impossible," Margarita said.

"They were meant to be together!" Renata said. "Both artists that they are: she with magic fingers at her weaving and her flowers and he with all he does!"

"He could not talk about it without having his eyes fill with tears and a rage at himself for having left her behind as she was about to give birth. He refused to say anything more about it. When I tried to draw him out, he was so dark. He sketched and sketched in his little notebooks. A few days before I was released, he started to talk a bit more. We made a plan. I was supposed to go with him to Graziella's. But at the last moment, Lorenzo said that Sandro had to stay. He said he had an assignment for him that was more important than anything he was working on here at Castello."

"What was more important than us?" Renata said.

"To sketch rotting corpses as they hang out of the window of the Bargello. First he's going to spend a month drawing them in various stages of decomposition, and then he'll come here to get Filippino and his supplies. He'll be under guard. He's going to be stuck there all summer!"

"Filippino left days ago," Poppi said. "He said he was going to try to get into Florence, and if he couldn't get through the gates, he was going to go on to Fiesole and wait."

"Now he'll never finish us!" Donata said.

"When it's all over he will be back and I doubt we will ever have to fight over him again," Piero said. "Lorenzo has treated him badly."

"Will he live with us then? Will he bring Floriana and the baby back to live with us?" Renata asked.

"I have no idea what will happen. I know he will come here and finish the painting. He has promised me this. And he swears another painting—daring and unlike anything we've ever seen before—is bubbling inside him, and he asked if he could stay on longer once he finishes the first one so he can paint that next one too."

"But what about his love? His Floriana? The baby?" Renata said. "We must send for Graziella today."

"Not now," Piero said.

"But she will think the work has stopped," Renata said.

"It has," Margarita and Donata said together.

"Let's be grateful for—" Piero began.

"For what?" Donata said. "A half-finished Botticelli? Never!"

THAT NIGHT, WHEN THE VILLA WAS QUIET, Renata and her two sisters scoured the grounds looking for the homing pigeons. They did not dare to ask Piero or even Poppi for the whereabouts of these messenger birds. They searched first in the greenhouse, expecting the birds might be in some corner of Poppi's perfumery. They found nothing. Back in the villa, they whispered and tiptoed through all the corridors. Finally they climbed to the top floor filled with the stuffy spring air, which hovered beneath the lowest ceiling in the villa. *Who is feeding those birds anyway?* they wanted to know.

As they stood by the small door, at the far end of the longest corridor, they heard what could only be cooing pigeons, but the door was locked!

THE THREE WHEEDLED THE KEY out of Poppi the next morning and stood, charmed, by the remaining pigeons. "How many should we let go?" Renata asked of her sisters.

Each of the three girls held one. All three pigeons had markings they had never seen before—white breasts and mottled feathers, beige heads and necks, and a smattering of black-tipped white feathers on their backs like a cape. All three had red cords on their ankles.

"I can feel its heart beating," Renata said. "Do you think Graziella will come? Will she assume it's Sandro sending them?"

"I say we send all three!" Donata said. "Then she'll know this is important."

"I don't think she'll even come," Margarita said. "She probably already knows Sandro is under house arrest."

"And how would she know?" Donata asked.

"Same way that he found out about Giuliano's murder. From the midwife," Margarita said.

"I want to be a midwife!" Renata announced. "Being at the birth of all this new life, and being free to travel by myself through the land. What a delight that would be!"

"Not for me," Margarita said.

"Why must you always see your future like that?" Donata asked. "All I care about is staying out of a convent."

"Open the hatch!" Renata said. "I'm going to release this one."

"I'm going to let mine go too," Margarita said.

"We can't leave one all alone by himself," Donata said as she released hers. It was the whitest of the three, with dots of gray and black.

CHAPTER SEVENTY-THREE

Sandro Begins the Bargello Commission

NDER THE CONSTANT EYE of palace guards, Sandro was brought by day into the square to sketch the ghoulish scenes. At night he would be returned to his former room. Those four walls had been the springboard from his humble beginnings into the ethers of the Platonic Academy and all things intellectual and philosophical. Now they were his prison. And his crime—his irreversible crime—had been to offer his loyalty into the hands of a brutal warlord.

Each day he tried to send notes to Piero to be given to Floriana, but each day they were returned to his room torn in half.

On the evening of the last day of the sketching phase, Sandro walked into the square accompanied by one of the house guards to do his final drawings. The light was fading, and the crowd had finally dispersed.

All seven Pazzi brothers had been strung on the scaffold in the Piazza della Signoria. With bags tied over their heads, the limp bodies with broken necks hung in the evening air. The only live person Sandro saw was a young child leaning transfixed out a window to take in the ghastly scene.

Once Sandro's sketches were complete, the decomposing corpses would be removed and the Bargello walls washed and readied by Filippino for his mural.

This had earned Sandro two days—always under the accompaniment of several house guards—to put his affairs in order, reclaim his supplies from the Villa di Castello, then return to paint the mural. That would take him well into the summer. If he found no word from Floriana waiting for him at Castello, he feared it would mean she had given up on him. Still, he was resigned to looking for her as soon as he was released and before he resumed work at the Villa di Castello. One concession Lorenzo had agreed to, however, was enough time for Sandro to visit his sister's convent.

On the way to Oslavia's, Sandro had pleaded with the guards to wait for him at Federico's cottage. They could watch his movements from a distance, giving Sandro his first moments of relative privacy outside of his room at the Medici Palace.

AS SOON AS SANDRO was twenty yards away from his guards, Luigi ran to him.

"Master Botticelli! Master Ficino has accepted me into his private school. I'm going to become a philosopher."

"You already are a philosopher," Sandro said. "He may teach you too many ideas that will confuse your native abilities. You must keep your own natural ways no matter how much Greek or Latin you learn."

"Greek and Latin?" Luigi's face fell. "I'm only now, with Mother Oslavia's help, learning to read and write. But I can think."

"You'll soon learn how to write and read several languages along with Greek and Latin, both of which you'll be able to sing like a poet."

"All I want to do is answer the important questions."

"You'll have to learn what the other wise men have said over the centuries."

"Why should I learn what all those wise men have said if people are still killing each other and if people who love each other cannot be together?"

"Your questions, Luigi, make me sad."

"I see only people suffering and losses everywhere. No one has an answer that pleases me."

"So yes, you will be the philosopher who finds answers to make people happy."

"I want to do that, but I want to do it my way."

"We are all trying to find happiness, each in his own way."

"But why does it include so much killing? I can't even talk to Brother Gerome any longer because he forces me into incessant prayer for the people of Florence."

"What he believes is needed."

"And what do *you* believe is needed?"

"More people like you, who ask, and ask, and ask. But asking must leave off and making must take its place."

"Is that why you paint?"

"I paint because I cannot speak any longer. I paint to receive ideas and images beyond me. And you too, Luigi, under the tutelage of Maestro Ficino, will learn to find your own wisdom. I pray you will."

"That he will what?" Oslavia said as she came toward them and threw her arms around Sandro, but he stopped her, motioning at the guards who were watching from Federico's cottage.

"The baby? Have you seen her?" Oslavia asked.

His only answer was to forget the guards and fall into his sister's arms. He could not help himself. He wept for the innocent and probing words of Luigi, questions he could not hope to answer. He wept for the love that ached inside him but had no resting place. He ached for Lorenzo, crazed in his wrath, and for the punctured Giuliano with worms making their way through the thin casing of his flesh. He wept for the interruption of his passion, the painting that had brought him so much joy, but above all he wept for the loss of his beloved Floriana, the loss of her sweetness and the ignorance of her whereabouts, the health of the infant, and the loss of his own self-respect.

Luigi stroked Sandro's hair and made whimpering sounds too. Oslavia came to her knees and spoke to him as she had when they were young so many years before, "Weep, my Sandrolino. Weep and cleanse your heart, for we will plant new seeds in that soil and you will find the strength to carry on."

She motioned for Luigi to leave them in peace. The young boy withdrew his hand from Sandro's head.

"I'll find an answer," he said to Sandro. "Don't cry. I'll help you."

When Luigi was out of earshot and Sandro calmed down, he released his hold on Oslavia and said, "I chose, instead of birth, death and more death. When I heard of the killings I ran from her side to the side of Lorenzo, who, crazed with grief, had frozen his heart to stone with only one redeeming thought, to kill, to maim, to cut away the threat to his family. In leaving Floriana I left my chance for happiness."

"But you owed it to him to go in his time of need. Did she not understand this?"

"She told me if I left her I would never come back! All the messages I tried to send were destroyed. I don't even know if the baby and she are alive! She was just starting her labor, and I left her at that moment! I chose death over life!"

"You're a dreamer, Sandro. She chose her faith above you. She had chosen it when I released her and again she chose it. And what of the other child, the one that Claudia carried?"

"That child entered the world surrounded by black velvet. Flags and curtains of black surround the infant Giulio. Could he be called anything but Giulio? He's colicky and boisterous. His screams pierce the palace walls, and all who try to comfort him run out after a few minutes for his crying never stops except when he is at the breast."

"And does she feed him or is it a wet nurse?"

"She insists only she should do it, and all suspect that is why he cries. Her milk has curdled from the day Giuliano died. It barely flows, but she'll not give him to anyone else's care."

"Lucrezia?"

"Lucrezia is in black. She, only she, is able to calm the tiny infant, whose body writhes in rigid convulsions when he cries. And this, the gift of calming she brings, is the only reprieve to the palace, and while she does, she sneaks the babe to another wet nurse behind Claudia's back. It's a sorry place. A tomb. A morgue. And I have been consigned to stay there until I finish a mural of the decaying corpses that rot on ropes outside the Signoria walls."

"How ghoulish! No wonder you're shaken. Stay with us tonight at least."

"We will stay one night at the villa where I'll gather up my supplies and then the day after tomorrow I begin the job. At least the pay is good."

"It is a high cost for you."

"It is an interruption. He promises Piero will get me back to finish. If I cannot be near the real Floriana, I must at least be close to the one I have created in the painting. To be away so long from both is not to my liking, but I am resigned."

"And have you told her you know who her attacker was?"

"Never! Why put a face on the one who wronged her so? She need never know."

"I disagree."

"She is beyond me right now."

"I doubt it is the end of it. God works in His mysterious ways," Oslavia said. She held his hands and squeezed them.

After a long pause, Sandro said, "If I'm going to reach the villa today I must be off, but first I need to speak to Savonarola. He must know the news from Rome."

"And that is?"

"Pope Sixtus has officially excommunicated not only Lorenzo de' Medici, but this week he's added all the residents of Florence and Tuscany. I must put Savonarola on notice that he may be called upon to serve as spiritual advisor. Lorenzo trusts only him."

"But Lorenzo banished him."

"He did not kill him. That was his fortune. He could not keep a man of God about him when he committed himself to so much bloodshed. I suspect now with the pope's declaration of war not only on the entire Medici family, but all of us in Tuscany, he'll be calling for Savonarola's return."

"And would he return to Lorenzo?" she asked.

"I doubt he would serve such a master, since his greatest vision of destruction and the end of the city is being carried out by Lorenzo. But, then again, Lorenzo was not the first to spill blood."

"I think he's in shock from what he has seen. He left Dono here but his Piattini almost died and recovers slowly. Aligning with Lorenzo would mean declaring oneself against the pope and that, in and of itself, might be the only way he would consent."

"He still does wield influence over Lorenzo, I know," Sandro said.

"Talk to him yourself. So pure he likes to sound. Yet his animal self lies below the skin."

"As it is in all of us," Sandro said. "If not for sex, then for blood, we thirst below the surface of our arts and crafts, our banks and trade and fancy velvets and jewels. A shepherd's rags speak more truth than art."

"Do you no longer value what you do?"

"I value it, but not when it's used for what I am about to do."

"The mural of the corpses?"

"The celebration of victory won with steel instead of diplomacy or love. Violence begets violence, and painting it sickens me," Sandro said.

"Why do it?"

"Did you not see my 'companions'? They are my guards to make sure I follow Lorenzo's orders. I was forced at knifepoint to be loyal, to accept this commission. Loyalty extracted by force is still a form of loyalty. Loyalty to my destiny as an artist. As much as I dreamed myself part of the intellectual academies, as much as I preened and let myself feel haughty, I'll never be more than a tanner's son pretending to be a Medici. Divided loyalties divide absolutely."

"Go now, my brother."

"Pray that one hundred years hence after the rains and icy breezes peel the paint of the Pazzi blood off the walls of the Bargello that no one will remember me for that work, but instead for the love I painted in the country. Pray that love wins over violence. That—"

"I'll pray for your healing, Sandro. That when you return to your chosen work, you'll paint the victory of love over violence with every stroke."

CHAPTER SEVENTY-FOUR

Fear and Faith Collide

BEFORE HE ENTERED the monastery grounds, Sandro stopped to gaze at the expanse of rose hedges that separated the monastery from the convent. The hedge was like an intricate, hand-knit armor, and yet, roses in bud and flower flourished upon it.

Sandro stopped to pluck a rose with one stroke. His fingers touched the velvety softness of the petals as he inhaled their sweet aroma. Plucking was only a momentary pleasure, for he had cut off the life of the blossom and only with a carefully wielded pruning knife might he have been able to go below the blanket of thorns and extricate a stem, tenderly removing it for the longer pleasure of a day or two or three.

Had he tried with Floriana to pluck her away from the source and thorns for her sweet perfume? Had he been so selfish to think he could pluck and not nourish? He tossed the petals into the air, save one that rested on his palm. That one he placed between pages of his sketchbook filled with drawings of her. It was the tiny one he kept in the small purse he always wore.

As he stood in front of the monastery door, Sandro held his hand in mid-air before grasping the knocker. What was it he wanted from this meeting? What was his intention? Did he have a plan, a scheme? None. No agenda except to deliver the message of Lorenzo's excommunication and Sandro's wish that Savonarola might stay on there for the protection of his sister, Oslavia.

The moment Savonarola opened the door, Sandro said, "Take my confession." The priest's eyes seemed without their usual fire. He had lost weight. His beard had flecks of dried food tangled in it, and his appearance carried a shadow of that stuttering, earlier ascetic Sandro had met in the square on his last night in Florence before he had moved to the Villa di Castello.

The bruise he had inflicted on Gerome weeks ago had faded, but dark circles under the priest's eyes suggested a deeper trauma—the horror Gerome must have seen on that day of April twenty-sixth. "You look as though you've seen a ghost," Sandro said.

"I've seen worse. I've seen the future, and I do not know if I have the strength to fight it."

"What about your faith? Your visions?"

"I've seen my visions made real."

"And I too have seen some of them, though not as bloody as you witnessed."

"More will come. It is not the end."

"Lorenzo's revenge is a hunger that has not been satisfied," Sandro said.

"Nor will it ever be unless he is stopped."

"He'll listen to you."

"He'll listen to no one now except the pope."

"It is precisely Pope Sixtus himself to whom he will not listen. The pope, who had initially excommunicated the Medici family, has this week decided to excommunicate the entire state of Tuscany. Sixtus has officially declared war against the Republic of Florence."

"Excommunicated?"

"All citizens. But the city is behind Lorenzo, and he has set up a church just the same. He is going to need you."

"What can I do?"

"You can calm him. Not now. After I finish the mural of the Pazzis."

"What mural?"

"On the Bargello walls. I have been ordered to do so. I do not draw blood but I draw the memory of it. What should I do?"

"Refuse! Say it goes against your Christian soul."

"I've tried every argument, but he has threatened to suspend me from my other works, and I am, in the end, a servant. I'll not bite the hand that feeds me."

"Then you are a coward."

"I am what I am. I am an artist who must survive."

"What about your work in Castello?"

"It has been interrupted."

Savonarola grew silent. He turned away from Sandro and walked into the main sanctuary and sat in the last pew. Sandro followed him inside, sitting next to him.

"Why a confession? Now? And with me, someone you hate, someone you threatened to kill?"

"I do not hate you. I respect you for declaring your sin openly and making it your last."

"Sitting in this church inside the state of Tuscany I am sinning according to the pope. We are all sinning in our excommunicated status."

The two sat for several moments in silence.

"I am not a coward," Sandro said.

"You are fulfilling your destiny as I am fulfilling my own. Christ accepts us both and loves us both and even loves Lorenzo, though not what he is doing. The girl, did she have her baby?"

"Your baby?" asked Sandro. Gerome made no response, so Sandro continued, "I left her in her moment of need."

"Was she alone?"

"She had a midwife and friends about her, but I had pledged protection and I left to serve Lorenzo and return to violence and terror. His thirst for blood is greater than his thirst for art and music."

"This is the kind of duplicity I see when people's vanity pulls them away from their souls. You must stop all of those paintings. Art is meant to elevate the soul, to reconnect us with our Father in heaven, to connect us to our highest selves."

"That *is* what I do!"

"With satyrs and myths from pagan times? I think not."

"I think you do not understand how art can elevate the spirit."

"And what spirit moves your Master Lorenzo, Magnificent Patron of the arts? Is that what your Platonic Academy has got you? From his very mouth came the truth that 'Civilization is skin deep,' Sandro. People are children who need to be led to purity, not given so many choices. The day you stop painting for the pagans and paint for the church, that will be the day you know peace."

"That day is not here for me, nor are you convincing me it should be."

"I am not here to convince. I am here to reflect back to you where you have been, where you are, and where you are headed."

"You are not my mirror. I am God's mirror. And I reflect what God must see. It is my destiny and path. Even though I cringe at what I must do next, I do it because someone must. It is my destiny that it be I to do so. And as for where I am headed, Brother Gerome, it is out of this church and back to the city of blood to reflect to God and others the blight of its darkest hour. In fact, for the first time, I believe there is going to be divinity even in this bloody wall, and you, without meaning to, have given me the inspiration I had lacked to do it."

"I will pray for your soul."

"And I will pray for yours," Sandro said as he stood and slipped out of the chapel.

"FORGIVE HIM, FATHER, for he knows not what he does," whispered Savonarola. And now, to his waking dream of more blood flowing, of images of him as the soldier of God taking over the city of Florence—images that played on a stage behind his closed eyelids and traveled with him nightly—Gerome Savonarola added the image of Sandro Botticelli placing his blasphemous works on the top of an enormous bonfire.

CHAPTER SEVENTY-FIVE

Botticelli's Nightmare

BY THE TIME Sandro returned to Florence, his mood had sunk blacker than a moonless night. Flanked all the way by his four guards, his brief visit with Gerome had played over and over again as he rode back to the city. The choices he had made, his hesitations, his moments of hovering between those choices, decisions he had made even as far back as his childhood, taunted him with remorse and regret. He was and had been a coward. Hesitation had soured his life and his love for Floriana. He crawled under the covers, knowing his next day would be even darker, as he would begin this most despicable of murals.

Within moments he fell asleep only to be battered further as he traveled deeper into a dream where Savonarola's words directed him to burn all his erotic work, especially his collection of Floriana images. In the dream, his sketches of her face shed tears, blurring the ink until her image disappeared. A clanging sound of faraway bells drew closer and closer—the same incessant bells he heard on his way back into Florence on that fateful night when he placed his loyalty into the wrong hands. The bells continued louder and louder until he awakened.

Sandro found himself on his bed in a pool of perspiration. The sound of bells ringing all over the city in his dream turned out to be merely the usual morning church bells. The darkness of his dream had been so convincing he checked his sketchbooks to see if they were whole and safe. He quickly wrapped the notebooks filled with Floriana's image in a silk scarf and placed these sacred objects under his mattress. They should remain uncontaminated by the subject he was about to paint.

As he buckled on his sandals, he heard a faint knocking on his door. It was not the bold summoning he was used to from his guards.

"Sandro," a familiar voice whispered outside his door.

"Lucrezia?"

"Yes, it is I. Open."

Still dressed in black, Lucrezia swept into his room and opened her arms to Sandro, who backed away from her.

"You are still angry," she said.

"I am a prisoner about to serve my sentence."

"Do not judge us so harshly, Sandro."

"I do not judge you, but I'm awake, finally, to my role in your family. I'm grateful for what you gave me, but when this commission is done, I will never set foot in this palace again. Forgive me. Please know I mourn Giuliano's death and the death that has come to your home and this city."

"In time, Sandro, you will see we did what we had to do. And you, too, must do what you have to do," Lucrezia said, then pulled a small package from underneath her flowing shawls.

"This came for you this morning. I passed by earlier, but you did not answer."

"What is this?"

"It's from Stella, the midwife. She says it is from your friend Floriana."

She held it out to him, holding on to it just a moment longer as his hands touched hers. Sandro could see tears in Lucrezia's eyes. The dark circles were even more pronounced and the efforts to mask them long abandoned, but he would not offer her affection or comfort. His only focus was on what she held in her hands.

"Thank you, Signora Lucrezia," he said, as he took the package and turned away from her. He brought Floriana's gift to his nose to breathe in any hint of Floriana it might contain. He stood with his back to Lucrezia, waiting until he heard the door close.

Shaken by this unexpected joy, he sat on his bed. The guards would soon be coming to bring him to the Bargello, where Filippino would be waiting, so he turned toward the package, sewn shut as always. He broke the delicate threads with his teeth. A small scroll of many papers tied with a silk ribbon around them was inside the package as well as another object wrapped yet in more silk fabric.

He opened the leaves of paper and read:

Dear heart of my heart, Sandro,

The child is small with jet black eyes and a sweet smiling face. Manfredo was right. It was long after you left before she made her first cry on such a sad and joyous day. Sad you were not there with me. Sad you were heading from a house of new life to one filled with so much death. And even though I knew you had to go, I was angry with you. Seeing her beauty, the black hairs on her scalp shooting toward the heavens, I said to myself, There must only be room for love in my heart.

I was so distraught when you left. I worried for your safety and as much as I told myself to believe in your promise of return, I knew in my heart I had lost you. Two weeks later, three of the pigeons with the red bands on their ankles lighted on their roost, so Graziella and I thought you were back at work at Villa di Castello. I asked her not to go to you, but she said it was business and she had to.

When she got back she was shocked at the news that you had been placed under house arrest. Piero told her of your melancholy and desire to come to me and how it was the only thing on your mind. Then she told me how you broke Savonarola's nose in one blow because you learned it was he who had soiled me. I pulled it out of her. I remember his face and the shyness of a stuttering priest—like an ugly duckling, awkward and never looking any of the girls in the eye. I would never have imagined him to be the one. But now I see him in Devorah's dark eyes.

When I didn't hear from you, I decided to move to a small settlement on the Po River, outside of Verona, where I will be safe.

I will write to you again when I reach there. Love is in my heart for you. As much as I tried to make it leave, it has not gone away. I dream of you still. I hope you forgive me for my icy words that sent you away. If your memory returns to that terrible hour with remorse and regret as mine has, we must burn those pains with the fire of love. The delight we took in each other's gifts, your wonderful painting of me and all the things I made for you with my hands. I made them with love from the first day I wove the crown of flowers for you.

By the time you get this letter I will be gone from Tuscany and hopefully finding my small place in a new world, which is called Sabbioneta, a tiny town filled with weavers and many Jews. It is far away from the priests who want only to convert us. I will be safe. The town even has its own printing presses to make our Hebrew prayer books. 'Imagine you!' as Piero always said.

Stella, the midwife, was the only one I could trust to get this letter to you unopened. I had thought to send it to Oslavia, but since that monk is often there, I did not dare to send it to her. Stella told me she trusted Lorenzo's mother, Lucrezia, to get this to you and this small gift too.

Hold me in your heart, Sandro. I give you the doll we found together. I have placed a new dress on her, new hair, and woven a tiny blanket for her. Do not see the death that surrounded it, but more the delight and comfort the small child might have known with it. Please keep her with you and keep her as a symbol of endings and new beginnings. Of hope lost and found once again.

I need to grow strong on my own, to find the God of my life within my own two hands, as I weave stories and embrace the mystery of life. It is because of your love and generosity toward me, and Oslavia's compassion, that I am even alive and well enough to consider such a life of freedom. Your small books have inspired me to make my own with drawings of flowers and ladybugs and anything that shows me its beauty. I do not belong in the convent, but also, not in the convent of Graziella's world, and not as your muse without first being a muse to myself.

I will write to you again when I am settled and pray you will come to find me. Maybe someday we will continue that candlelit evening in the cantina at Villa di Castello. I will never forget you and how I felt in your arms and you in mine. You, my sweet Sandro, are my love and protector, forever with me. I carry the mantle of your love about me like the most beautiful weaving that God could create, and I still dream of the day we will be together again. With all my memories of you, I will weave together now my hopes for the future for each of us in our separate worlds and for the day when those worlds will combine. All my love, Floriana

"For the day when those worlds will combine," Sandro whispered, weak from the surprise of her words of love, a love he had feared was lost to him. He sat motionless on his bed, stunned by her gift. He unwrapped the covering which held the small doll, now transformed by the touch of life Floriana had given it. No longer a musty, encrusted companion to the lost soul they had set to rest in the cave, this tiny treasure would be with him always. Just as he tucked the small doll into the pocket of his shirt, another knock shook his door. This time, it was the familiar one, the pounding of his guards.

"I hear you!" Sandro said. "Give me five minutes!" He stared at Floriana's handwriting. "I will write to you again when I am settled and pray you will come to find me."

She has forgiven me. She even asks for my forgiveness! Sandro thought, then scrambled around his room to choose the best place to hide her letter, though he couldn't bear to be apart from it. The possibility of losing it as he climbed the scaffolding, or stripped his clothes off in the heat of the summer sun, was too great. *No hiding place is good enough.* Another loud knock shook his door. "*Basta!*" he said, rolling up her letter and putting it into his traveling bags, safe in the bottom. The knocking that had always irritated him and reinforced his annoyance and anger during the sketching phase of the project had become at that moment a faint sound that could not compete with the music and scenes of reunion playing in his head. *A second chance. She's giving me, giving us, a second chance. And she knows why I couldn't come to her.* He took a deep breath and let out a sigh of great relief as he threw his materials together to meet the guards at his door.

Walking to the Bargello, he composed the letter he would write to her, how he would pour his heart out to her, how he would tell her that he had made the wrong choice. But then, how could he get that letter to her? He would need to be patient. She would write.

That day, Sandro and Filippino worked side by side. In one day they had sketched the entire expanse of the wall in iron oxide lines as the citizens of Florence watched. He determined that from that day forward he would not bring anger to this task. Instead, he would think that each brushstroke brought him closer to the end of the mural and closer to the time he would be set free to join Floriana. In spite of his determination to believe in happy thoughts of his beloved—imagining their reunion and the life he would build with her once he found her—as the weeks passed, the subject of the mural infected him. At one point, while depicting one of the corpses whose hands had been cut off, Sandro felt in his wrists and fingertips an exaggerated vibration and heat as though he were sharing phantom limbs for that victim. Instead of each brushstroke becoming an act of trust that this work would soon take him back to his passion, each brushstroke brought him deeper into a profound melancholy from the poison that had crippled the city, the rage that had taken over Lorenzo's life.

The sadness that settled in his limbs, his bones, and his heart was not a sadness born of fear or those unpredictable waves of melancholy that had plagued him most of his life. This was a grieving for the acts of cruelty and madness that led not only to the flaying of one poor unfortunate's feet but to the torture of the entire human race. As he chronicled the worst in men, in war, in the effects of power and greed, he felt lifted out of his own personal anguish. What began to form beneath his sadness was an ever-present belief in the healing power of love, its ability to transport and transform beyond brutality. Day by day, as he waited for more news from Floriana, that belief took form, not only as a vision, but a fount of determination to paint, not an imitation of life at its worst, but to make art that could elevate life beyond and above its basest drives. Finally he understood that the work he created at the Villa di Castello had been his first true connection to that impulse. That was why he had been so happy creating it and he needed to complete it and create others to follow. This was what he was meant to do, not to be influenced by the dictates of some cleric or nobleman.

Each dawn, before he headed to the Bargello, he worked on sketches for the completion of his unfinished painting at Piero's. The thought of being allowed to finish that work, of seeing Floriana again—somehow—filled him with enormous stamina. After Filippino would leave for the evening, Sandro continued to work, assisted by a massive scaffold of burning candles to illuminate the Bargello wall while he painted.

When the death mural was finally complete, Lorenzo's men released Sandro. The two old friends did not meet or exchange farewells, and that was how Sandro preferred it. On his last day, Lucrezia knocked on his door again with a small package from Floriana. It was a bound volume of her sketches of flowers and plants with a few sentences of commentary. She said that she was moving away from the town with a small family of bookbinders who would be traveling toward Tuscany and that she would come to him at Villa di Castello as soon as she could. He should do his work and wait for her and not try to find her, because she did not know the route they would be taking or how long they might stay in each town.

CHAPTER SEVENTY-SIX

Botticelli's Surprise

BUOYED BY THIS WORD FROM FLORIANA, Sandro set out for Villa di Castello, yearning to finish the painting at last. After he arrived, Piero's younger sisters showered him with their excitement. As the weeks went by, he painted them, seeing them no longer as the sometimes annoying and always bickering young girls, but as the mature and lovely women they were to become. With hands entwined and hair abundant and flowing, they became under the magic of his artistry three similar yet different Graces. The violence of their cousin Giuliano's death had added a compassionate and serious aspect to each one of their faces. Once he painted their solemn yet lyrical dance, he turned his attention to the final figure, Giuliano as Mercury reaching for the golden apple of perfection, the heavens, and eternity. By transforming Giuliano's gruesome slaughter this way, Sandro was righting a wrong. Just as he had turned Floriana's rape into a story of rebirth on the far right end of the painting, so too Giuliano's death would be turned into a message of peace on the other end. A full circle at last complete. The small figure of Cupid disturbed him as it hovered above Oslavia's image. He placed a scarf across the infant's eyes to emphasize the blindness of Love and its fickle partner Fate. Finally, it was finished.

Piero loved the painting, which he named *La Primavera*, for its evocation of springtime, and installed in the dining room of the villa, the same spot he and Sandro had selected all those months earlier.

Unlike the insecure artist who groped for inspiration while belittling his young orphaned patron, Sandro had emerged from his trials a determined and confident man. Having broken ties with Lorenzo, then aligning his loyalty to Piero, Sandro chose to stay on at Villa di Castello voluntarily. Now that his work on *La Primavera* was done, he dared not leave, knowing that Floriana and her child, Devorah, might appear at any moment.

When other commissions called to him, he assigned them to his Florence *bottega* apprentices. Out in the country, he began sketches for a painting—in direct defiance of Savonarola's warnings—with full nudity. Its inspiration came from the moment he saw Floriana emerge from her bath on the day he, in a humble shepherd's disguise, had joined her at Manfredo's. Her image at that moment had continued to burn in his imagination. He would paint Floriana as the *Birth of Venus* without shame. There was no need to cover her, to mask her beauty. She was, and would ever be, his Venus, his goddess of love. His homage to her through the act of painting would sustain him during their separation. But that work was destined to be interrupted.

At the start of 1481, a murmur in the air hinted the pope would soon remove his excommunication edict from all Tuscans. Whether or not this would come to pass, Sandro's studio was first in line for a commission to paint frescoes at the Sistine Chapel in Rome. Intent on bringing his bold, Floriana-inspired work from charcoal to paint, Sandro cared little for the honor that would come with such a papal commission and less for the religious subject matter it would dictate. But the pope insisted that Sandro do the work, not his apprentices. Sandro and Filippino spent eleven months in Rome, finally returning to Villa di Castello in the spring of 1482. And still no word from Floriana.

Exhausted from the demands and limits of the religious frescoes he had created at the Sistine Chapel, and also the latent devotional impulses they had reawakened in him, Sandro was not able to turn back easily to his *Birth of Venus*. How could he move from all that religious imagery to full nudity? He needed a transition.

A memory mixed with joy and agony provided the subject: the day he came to Manfredo's in disguise, half man and half beast to be with Floriana. In the painting, the comical, scruffy, and bleating shepherd contorted into a centaur, the divided self once more. To heal the agony of that day he placed the tortured creature under the power of the goddess of wisdom, Minerva. Perhaps her presence in the painting might heal his divided soul and grant him the peace and confidence he would need to return to the *Birth of Venus*.

In addition to his centaur painting, he finished a design he had begun for Piero just before the trip to Rome. It was an elaborate display case for Piero's dolls, finally out of their secret closet. Every day, Poppi and Piero arranged and rearranged them on the shelves of the new cabinet, which stood in the main room of the villa, the same room Sandro had used as his winter studio.

After Sandro lingered for a few weeks alone over the unhappy centaur in his greenhouse studio, Piero and his sisters convinced him to move his work back into the villa's main room. Although he was subjected to more interruptions there, the longer spring days provided sufficient light, and the company helped keep his growing disappointment with Floriana's absence at bay.

One early afternoon, close to the fourth anniversary of the last time Sandro had seen his muse Floriana—Piero's dogs yelped as they always did to announce someone on the property. Poppi had just rearranged a shelf of dolls, and Piero's hand encircled the effigy of a most pregnant Floriana.

Poppi and Piero looked out the window, then turned to drag Sandro away from his work. They all watched as Renata, Margarita, and Donata ran toward a cart led by one donkey that hobbled along the path. When it stopped, a woman with a small child in her arms climbed down from the cart and was immediately surrounded by the girls.

"Imagine you!" Piero said as he looked at the doll still in his grasp. "We really do make magic here, Master Botticelli!"

Coda

Coda

November 1478

Urged by Queen Isabella of Spain, Pope Sixtus signs the papal bull that sets the Inquisition in motion. The edict moves slowly and silently through the land, culminating in the Inquisition in Spain in 1492 and the first ghetto in Venice in the early sixteenth century.

April 1479

In retaliation for Giuliano's assassination, Lorenzo's men finally are able to kill Cardinal Riario of lmola.

1480

The year that Piero is due to receive his inheritance, Manfredo and Graziella are taxed by Lorenzo, forcing them to give up their lands and flee, leaving Piero's debt to them uncollected. The painting becomes the joint property of Piero and Lorenzo, the newly appointed official guardian of Piero's inheritance—what little had remained of it after Lorenzo confiscated it to finance the eradication of the Pazzi family after Giuliano's assassination.

1481

Twenty-seven years before Michelangelo painted the colossal ceiling of the Sistine Chapel, Sandro and Filippino spend eleven months in Rome painting frescoes on the Sistine Chapel walls.

1482

Lorenzo's mother, Lucrezia Tornabuoni, dies. The pope forgives Lorenzo, officially removing the status of excommunication for him and all of Florence. Piero marries, but within a few months the marriage is annulled. After his roaming ministry, Savonarola and his two companions return to Florence.

1483

To prevent his nephew Giulio from being perceived as a bastard, Lorenzo legally adopts him into his family, leaving Claudia to fend for herself. When she produces the engagement certificate in front of a tribunal, she retains the right to stay in the palace to be close to her son.

1485

Sandro completes perhaps his most famous work, the *Birth of Venus.* The public response to it is one of outrage. It languishes in the dark closets of the villa for decades, then in the warehouses of the Uffizi Gallery for many more years, until it is rediscovered and proclaimed a masterpiece in the mid-nineteenth century. This delayed appreciation of its magnificence comes well after the death of Vasari, who ranked Botticelli as a minor figure in his authoritative study, *The Lives of the Artists.*

1490

Savonarola's first Bonfire of the Vanities, when he mobilizes the city, especially the children, to collect and throw all forms of sinful dress and art onto a huge bonfire set up in the Piazza della Signoria.

1492

Crippled from his losing battle with gout and numerous other ailments, Lorenzo sends for Savonarola to give him the last rites but dies before the priest arrives at the palace. Savonarola takes over the city.

1493

When Sandro sees the effigy of the moneylender Manfredo on the top of yet another bonfire, he flees Florence, determined to reunite once and for all with his love, Floriana, and bring her back to Florence to stay. He assigns his primary protégé, Filippino Lippi, to manage his studio and subsequent commissions.

1498

After being excommunicated, Savonarola and his two companions, Domenico da Pescia (Dono) and Silvestro Maruffi (Piattini), are burned at the stake in full view of the public in the Piazza della Signoria. Later, their charred remains are cut down and paraded through the square.

1513

Giulio de Giuliano de' Medici becomes cardinal and serves until 1523 when he is elected Pope Clement VII. It is only Claudia's engagement certificate to Giuliano and Lorenzo's adoption of Giulio that provides the loophole that allows him to sidestep the requirement that no bastard be installed as pope. He is weak and vacillating, ill-suited to govern the church. His refusal to grant Henry VIII of England an annulment of his marriage to Catherine of Aragon causes Henry to leave the Catholic Church and found the Anglican Church.

Glossary

allora well then

amore love

basta enough, stop

bocce a bowling game played outdoors

bottega workshop

cantina cellar, basement

castello castle

cazzo shit

citronella (olio di citronella) mosquito repellent

coraggio have courage

cugino cousin

cuginone big cousin as in "fat" cousin

disgraziati, disgraziato unfortunate ones, disgraced

donare to give

farfalla literally butterfly, also homosexual

farina the grain and flour from which pasta is made

forza force, courage

il petto breast

-ino diminutive suffix as in Girolamino (young Girolamo)

ladro thief

maestro master, teacher

mikvah Jewish purifying bath for women

padrone di casa head of the household

palma di Cristo a castor plant (thought to resemble the palm of Christ, reflecting its inherent healing power)

pasticciotto fat pastry, an affectionate term Claudia uses

piatto plate, dish

poverino poor one, oh poor soul

profumeria a laboratory/studio for concocting perfume

puttana, buttana whore

puzzi stinks (as in bad smell; conjugated form of "puzzare," the verb for "to stink")

scendi come down, descend

spiccioli pennies, small change, money for the poor

stai calmo relax, stay calm

subito immediately

uccello bird, also erect penis

va bene O.K., very well, I agree with you

zitto shut up, be quiet

Zohar sacred document of the Kabbalists

Acknowledgments

WHEN I CONSIDER HOW LONG it has taken me to publish this story—over twenty years since a mysterious voice spoke to me inside my journals—it's clear that, even before that moment, it was my 1963 trip to Italy at the age of nineteen (the same age Floriana is when she meets Sandro) that planted the novel's first seeds.

Botticelli's Muse began as a free-write session in my living room in 1992. It took a full year for me to discover the voice belonged to a character in a Botticelli painting. A visit to Italy in the summer of 1993, and an unplanned sojourn in hotel Monna Lisa (a building that had lodged the religious heads from Constantinople and Rome for the Council of Florence in 1438), introduced me to the matron of the hotel, Oslavia, who inspired the character of Sandro's sister. I searched the archives of Florence's synagogue/temple library and the Jewish burial grounds, using my rusty Italian to find names and places that might show me a way back in time. As my imagination expanded these historical scraps, a story began to unfold.

THOSE WHO HELPED BIRTH THE FIRST DRAFT . . .

Chris Keane's novel workshop at Emerson helped me flesh out the characters, weaving actual historical events into an ambitious thirty-two chapter outline that spanned 1477 to 1498. Conferences with other faculty members, *Robin Riley Fast* and *James Carroll*, provided further encouragement. After graduate school, I set the project aside to collect its requisite pound of dust.

Then in the summer of 2002, a fellow writer *Anne Gilman* sent me an inspiring essay by Aram Saroyan entitled *The Lake Matters: Notes about Writing and Life*. Following Saroyan's suggestion to write without editing to get the story down, I set aside the outline and resumed work on the manuscript. In fourteen months the book grew from fifty to eight hundred pages. And the time span of the first volume of the story that became *Botticelli's Muse* shrank from twenty years to eighteen months.

THANKS GO TO SO MANY

Leslie Skimmings, childhood friend and fellow writer who dared to read the first raw eight hundred pages.

My brother *Jay Rubin*, who read an earlier draft, encouraged me to keep going with it, and subsequently became one of two content editors.

Michele Sdougas, a student of the Renaissance and owner of a vast library, loaned me books and also read the manuscript in several drafts. After I had formatted it for publication over a year ago, she suggested that I illustrate it. Within a few short weeks, my illustrations began to emerge. They combine the intricacy of a meditative style of abstract drawing, introduced by *Rick Roberts* and *Maria Thomas* of zentangle.com, with realistic forms of people, vegetation, and animals. I generated over one hundred drawings for the book, which I credit to D. Bluestein.

I'm grateful to all of my beta readers, among them *Jeanne Winner*, *Lauren Harris Karp*, *Ronnie Blackman*, *Elaine Dobinson*, *Bobbi Ruggiero-Hickey*, *Barbara Steiner*, and *Claire Daniel*, who gave me honest feedback.

My dear friend *Jonathan Holdowsky*, who sustained me emotionally, through his unceasing encouragement, and financially, extending loans to get me through rough patches.

Friends and family cheered me on from the sidelines even though most never read the book: *David Carter*, *Amy Pechukas*, my sons *Aaron* and *Michael Bluestein*, *Mary Kelley*, *Nancy Raskind*, *Rob Raskind*, *Jill Ginsburg*, *Jan Caserio*, *Judith Dancoff*, *Anna Comolli*, and my daughters-in-law, *Carrie Wilksen* and *Marti Zuniga*.

Local agent *Carolyn Jenks* connected me with a content editor, *Ann Marie Monzione* of RedMoonWriting.com, who guided me through another draft.

Lisa Kleitz of Inner Assets Coaching continues to help me fight off the gremlins of fear, doubt, and insecurity to fashion strategies that harness and feed my desire to keep going.

I am grateful to my mother, *Frances Rubin*, an avid reader. A bold innovator in her own right, she would simply chop off the legs of a table if it was too high. Even though our home library was mostly *Reader's Digest* condensed books, she passed on her love of reading to me.

Bennington College professor *Mr. Ricks* (sorry, his first name escapes me) inspired me with a fascination for history, a subject I hated in high school. Writing historical fiction, I can cast characters into a scene with their contemporaries, even though they might never have met, and add in imaginary siblings, as I have done for Sandro's sister, Oslavia.

I am grateful for my brief reunion with *KT* in my sixties, which enabled me to transfer emotional highs and lows, including the devastation of lost love, to characters in the novel.

To my Italian friends who took me in all those years ago when I was a wandering nineteen-year-old woman, enthralled with Florence, Abruzzi, Perugia, and the Italian language. *Manfredo Nanni, Piero Albissini, Pierluigi Properzi, AnnaMaria Forcucci, Franco Colonna, Paola Carli, Patrizia Cameo,* and my private Italian tutor, *Laura Belli.* Once back in the States, and still in my twenties, I worked as a bilingual secretary at Boston's Italian Trade Commission, where I met *Adriana Campo* and *Luigi Mian,* who kept the language fresh in my heart.

In the final stages of finding a home for *Botticelli's Muse,* I want to thank my London connections: *Scott Pack,* editor at Unbound and Abandoned Bookshop; cover designer *Jo Walker*; editor *Katherine H. Stephen,* and *Bridgeman Art Library* for the use of the image of Flora from Botticelli's painting *La Primavera.*

I am grateful to *Kirsty Walker* of Hobblebush Design in Brookline, New Hampshire, for her work on the print edition, and *Brad* of Vellum Software, who helped me convert the manuscript into an e-book. In addition, I am grateful to my proofreaders *Eric Howard* and *Lauren Ruiz,* and to *Julie Levesque* for her excellent work on my author website dorahblume.com.

Thanks to *Michael Berg* of the Kabbalah Centre for introducing me to the old fable of the dark angels, the light angels, and the gray angels that he retells in his book *The Way: Using the Wisdom of Kabbalah for Spiritual Transformation and Fulfillment,* and that I retell in *Botticelli's Muse.*

Staying in Touch . . .

THANK YOU FOR TRAVELING BACK WITH ME to the world of Sandro Botticelli and his muse Floriana. I hope you enjoyed the journey.

If you loved the book and have a minute to spare, I would appreciate a short review on the page or site where you bought the book. Your help in spreading the word makes a huge difference in helping new readers find stories like *Botticelli's Muse* and fueling the continuation of the trilogy.

Thank you!

Dorah Blume
www.dorahblume.com
Twitter: @walkinghead2009
www.juiceboxartists.com

Address all written correspondence to:
Juiceboxartists Press, P.O. Box 230553, Boston, MA 02123

About the Author

PHOTO BY CLAIRE BRUECKNER

AN ITALOPHILE since the age of nineteen when she studied painting at the Academy of Fine Arts in Florence, Italy, Dorah Blume has published short fiction and nonfiction in newspapers, magazines, and literary journals. Considering herself a late bloomer, she expanded her artistic reach from the visual to the written word in her forties with an MFA in creative writing from Emerson, and has navigated between the two ever since. As a certified Amherst Writers & Artists (AWA) facilitator, Dorah has led writing workshops for adults in Greater Boston as well as Tuscany.

CPSIA information can be obtained
at www.ICGtesting.com
Printed in the USA
LVHW04s1625180618
580994LV00005B/535/P

9 780998 131603